THE KNOPF DOUBLEDAY GROUP

ALFRED A. KNOPF • DOUBLEDAY • EVERYMAN'S LIBRARY
PANTHEON • SCHOCKEN • VINTAGE

Dear Reader,

With a rare bolt of crackling joy, *The Whyte Python World Tour* crossed my desk with the power of a one-hundred-watt tube amp—I was back in the '80s! Hair bands! Power chords! I hadn't had this much fun reading a novel in years.

Rikki Thunder is a drumming god who catches on with the right band and embarks on a life that seems too awesome to be true. But there's an unexpected complication lurking in the shadows, and soon we're all on an international thrill ride that's full of romance and rock 'n' roll—as well as spies and suspense and very real danger.

Travis Kennedy's debut novel captures an indelible moment in time, with characters who are as quirky as they are endearing, masterfully shifting narrative perspectives, and twists that will remind you at every step how much fun you're having.

I hope you will climb aboard the tour bus and enjoy the read! Please don't hesitate to be in touch; I'd love to hear your response.

All my best,

Jason Kaufman
jkaufman@penguinrandomhouse.com
Vice President & Executive Editor
Doubleday

Marketing and Publicity

- National Review and Media Appearances, including NPR, and Newspaper and Magazine Features
- Men's Magazines, Mystery/Thriller, and Music Media Coverage
- Original Essays and Opinion Pieces
- Author Events
- Major Online Advertising Campaign
- Title Specific Social Media Promotion including Playlists, Band Tour Graphics, Excerpts, and Author Videos
- Inclusion in the Doubleday Bookstagram Program
- Title Specific Outreach to Indies, Big Mouth, and Influencers with Heavy Metal Inspired SWAG
- Pitch for inclusion in KDPG Newsletters
- Reading Group Guide Available
- Inclusion in Summer Fiction Promotions
- Available on NetGalley

the
WHYTE
PYTHON
WORLD TOUR

the

WHYTE
PYTHON
WORLD TOUR

a novel

TRAVIS KENNEDY

DOUBLEDAY
New York

www.doubleday.com

DOUBLEDAY and the portrayal of an anchor with a dolphin are
registered trademarks of Penguin Random House LLC.

Jacket design and illustration by Oliver Munday
Library of Congress Cataloging-in-Publication Data
Names: Kennedy, Travis, author.
Title: The Whyte Python world tour : a novel / Travis Kennedy.
Description: First edition. | New York : Doubleday, 2025.
Identifiers: LCCN 2024029251 (print) | LCCN 2024029252 (ebook) |
ISBN 9780385551335 (hardcover) | ISBN 9780385551342 (ebook)
Subjects: LCGFT: Thrillers (Fiction). | Satirical fiction. | Novels.
Classification: LCC PS3611.E64 W49 2025 (print) | LCC PS3611.E64 (ebook)
| DDC 813/.6—dc23/eng/20240812
LC record available at https://lccn.loc.gov/2024029251
LC ebook record available at https://lccn.loc.gov/2024029252

MANUFACTURED IN THE UNITED STATES OF AMERICA

1 3 5 7 9 10 8 6 4 2

First Edition

the

WHYTE
PYTHON
WORLD TOUR

PROLOGUE
1989

OH, DUDE, this is bad. I'm pretty fucked up.

Not from drugs! I mean, sure, I took some drugs backstage. But just, like, the normal amount of drugs. What's got me worried, as I lurch up this little steel staircase and onto the platform, is that I probably have some broken bones—and maybe I'm bleeding inside my body? If that's possible? Can you play drums with a cracked rib?

This is not good.

I'm on the stage now. It seems too bright. At first, I wonder if the lighting guys got baked and turned the dials all the way up again; but it dawns on me that I probably just have a concussion.

The crowd has finished cheering for Spencer Dooley, our bass player, and now they're going nuts for Buck Sweet on lead guitar. I'm confused. *Why are we doing introductions now*, I wonder, *instead of at the end, like usual?* Then I remember that until a few seconds ago, I was missing, and they couldn't start the concert.

I'm dizzy and nauseous. My head hurts. My ribs hurt. My feelings are hurt. But as I hobble under the lights, I hear it: the roar of a crowd, thousands deep, going totally apeshit because Rikki Thunder has stepped onto the stage. I'm really popular here. The sound wave hits me like an electric shock, and all of a sudden, I'm doing okay.

I limp toward my drum set. Buck steps into my path and puts a hand on my shoulder.

"Rikki," he says. "Is that blood?"

That seems like an important question, so I touch my cheek—and sure enough, my fingers come back red. I don't think the gash on my head is bleeding anymore, but my hair is tacky and stuck to my face on one side.

"Uh, yeah," I say to Buck. "Definitely blood."

"Rock 'n' roll," Buck says. "Can I lick it off your face?"

"Nah," I say.

Buck shrugs and goes back to his spot. Up front, Davy Bones is doing a rooster strut around his mic stand, aping Mick Jagger to keep the crowd busy while I get my shit together.

I can only see his silhouette in front of the lights; but I figure he's pissed at me, like usual. In fairness to Davy, though, I did just vanish right before showtime—and then wandered onto stage late, looking like I got spit out by a bear.

Davy steps away from his microphone and turns his back to the crowd. "Dude," he growls, "what happened to you?"

"Nothing," I say. Davy looks like he's ripshit at me, but he also looks worried. It makes me feel bad. I can understand why he's confused. I was perfectly fine the last time he saw me, which was less than ten minutes ago. But needless to say, it turned out to be a pretty wild ten minutes, and I'm not allowed to tell anybody why.

So I wave him off. Take my seat. Find my drumsticks.

Davy turns back to the crowd. "Ladies and gentlemen!" he screams into the microphone. "Rikki Thunder!"

A spotlight blinds me. The crowd fucking flips out again. I raise my arms over my head, and I feel a sharp, stabbing pain in my side. But pain won't matter for the next couple of hours, as long as the crowd keeps screaming and the boys have got a good night's shred in them.

Davy raises a fist in the air. "And I'm Davy Bones!" he sings, and he drags out "Bones" for at least six seconds. "Are you ready to rock, Berlin?" Davy asks the crowd. Berlin screams bloody murder back at him.

Davy pinwheels his arms and stumbles, like the crowd was so loud that they blew him backward. Even though Davy does this during every single concert, it always makes Spencer laugh so hard that he accidentally tickles the strings on his bass. It's probably the only reason Davy still does it.

My heart hurts for both of them suddenly. If anything happens to them tonight, it will be my fault. And they won't even see it coming.

"I think they're ready," Davy shouts. The crowd screams again. Spencer chuckles again.

Davy grabs the mic with both hands. He leans forward, hovering so far over the platform ledge that the kids in the front row mechanically put their hands up, in case they need to catch him. He takes a deep breath. And then he shrieks, "*We are Whyte Python!*"

That's my cue. I clack my sticks together four times and then bring them down hard on the drums, just as Davy finishes screaming. Pyro explodes. The arena fills with light. We start playing "Till the Bell Rings."

My eyes finally come into focus. Everything is how it's supposed to be. There are the guys—Davy, Buck, and Spencer—glowing under the stage lights like gods in their leather and scarves and massive hair.

There are the roadies in their jean jackets, scurrying around backstage.

There's the pyro, firing in rhythm with my kick drum.

And there's the crowd: pure chaos. There are enough Germans in this arena to fill a city, a swarming mass of hair and lighters and nudity and mayhem, screaming and dancing and cutting loose together in the darkness beyond the stage. To *our* music. I mean, *come on*!

And then everything's cool. There's no pain anymore. No worries. The crowd's energy fills up my tank.

For a minute, I even forget that at least one of them is trying to kill me.

Shit, dude, let me back up.

PART I

The Ballad of Rikki Thunder

1

O KAY, I'LL SET the scene for you.
The place: the Sunset Strip in L.A.
The year: 1986.
Me: Rikki Thunder, twenty-two years old. Skinny, leather pants, ripped T-shirt, jet-black hair sprayed a mile high.

I was playing drums in a band called Qyksand with some of my buddies from high school. It's pronounced like "quicksand," but we spelled it with a *y*, because spelling stuff wrong is rock 'n' roll, bro!

I do have to admit that we were kind of copying this other Sunset Strip band, Whyte Python, by doing the *y* thing. See, those guys were just on the verge of breaking out. If you're gonna steal something, steal from the winners, right?

Anyway, I thought we were pretty good. Ron Finch was our lead singer, and he had a great scream. There was Sully on guitar, Marty on bass, and yours truly on the sticks and tubs. We covered Mötley Crüe and Ratt, a little Jovi for the ladies, and a few originals that Ron and I wrote together.

But it was seriously dog-eat-dog on the Strip at that point. Metal bands like Van Halen and Mötley were on top of the world, and everybody was doing the same act in their wake. It was all big hair and leather and scarves, everywhere you looked. So it was hard to get noticed if you were new and didn't have a gimmick.

It was getting close to sunset, and the streets were packed with party animals. I was standing on the sidewalk in front of the Shed, a little dive bar that Qyksand played two nights a week. The owner, Gus Conley, paid us a hundred bucks to play—total, not each—but we had to earn it back for him by getting enough people to pay a cover, so we technically didn't cost him anything.

If we didn't break even, we never got to play there again. He charged three bucks at the door, which meant we needed to get at least thirty-four people to come on a show night or we were a failed investment, and some other band who was just starting out got to take our place.

The Shed was one of the shittiest clubs in town. A lot of bands got started there, but a lot of bands got finished there, too. If you couldn't break even at the Shed, nobody else was going to book you on the Strip. You either had to quit playing music or move to Anaheim, and I don't know what's worse. And there were probably fifty other bands who looked like us, trying just as hard to sell out their own clubs so they wouldn't get stuck playing at the Shed.

Every concert night, the Strip was elbow to elbow with a bunch of other glam band guys handing out flyers. You had to have a shit-ton of flyers. Flyers to hand out, flyers to put on windshields, flyers to staple to telephone poles. And then you needed a whole *other* stack of flyers to replace the ones some dickhead in another band tore up.

But flyers cost money, and between all the hustling and shredding and partying, we didn't have the time or life skills to get actual jobs. So we pretty much just hustled here and there.

I sold Italian ices along the Strip. Sully took shifts with a moving company, and he sold weed. Ron's brother worked at a grocery store, and he paid Ron in cash to clean the bathrooms so he wouldn't have to do it himself. Marty also sold weed; but sometimes he sold it to Sully, which really cut into our profits.

If we had any money left over from the latest gig, it would go toward flyers. If we had any money left over after buying cereal, beer, and weed, it would go toward flyers.

If we got it right, we would have *just* enough money to make *just* enough flyers to bring in *just* enough people to get another gig at the Shed, so we could buy more flyers for next week.

If we fucked that cycle up anywhere along the way—even one time—we would probably starve to death.

I hope that by now I've made it super clear just how important these flyers were.

Now, some of the bigger groups had other tricks to turn out a crowd. They either knew the DJs and could get a plug on the radio, or they had merchandise, or the club they played at would actually promote them with posters and whatnot.

But the real players—the ones who had it made in the shade—had *groupies*.

Groupies were the most valuable resource on the Sunset Strip. Locking down even a small army of groupies was like owning a gold mine that sometimes gave blow jobs.

The bigger bands had groupies making handmade flyers and T-shirts, flirting with horny dudes, talking the band up all over town and bringing in fans.

The more loyal groupies would even cook and clean for the band, so they could just focus on thrashing. Those bands didn't have to do their own marketing at all—which freed up, like, 90 percent of their time to get better at playing music, which meant bigger gigs and cooler clothes, which meant recruiting more groupies. Next thing you know, you're Poison or Whyte Python, and you're fighting off record labels.

Me and the guys in Qyksand daydreamed about having groupies all the time. Like on the nights when it was raining and we'd be five people short of our quota, so Marty and Sully would have to beg their parents to come to the show and Ron would sneak his grandmother out of her nursing home.

Or the time Sully's van blew a tire coming back from the used music equipment store and none of us knew how to change it, and we pined for a team of grease-monkey groupies to pit-crew for us while we walked to the nearest gas station.

Someday! we would promise one another. Someday, if we work hard enough, we'll have groupies. And then it will be straight to the top.

But we hadn't earned them yet, so it fell on us to spread out across town on show nights and hand out our own flyers. Now, on the night in question, I was posted up in front of the Shed, shoving paper at strangers and saying, "Come see Qyksand at the Shed? Come see Qyksand at the Shed! Lots of babes!" Just mixing it up, seeing what got people's attention.

I wasn't getting very far. Most of the people who bothered to take a flyer just dropped it a few steps later. If I could grab it before somebody else stepped on it, I would pick it up and hand it out again.

I was so focused on getting flyers in hands that I didn't notice a commotion brewing down the block. Then somebody yelled, "Fight!" And *nobody* was taking flyers anymore.

Everyone on the street moved at once, becoming a mob as they formed a big circle around whoever was fighting. I couldn't see who was in the middle, but after a couple of seconds Sully's head popped up and looked my way.

His eyes were saucers, and he very clearly mouthed the word "Ron."

Aw, dammit.

2

HERE'S WHAT YOU NEED TO KNOW ABOUT RON FINCH:
I met the guy in the band room at school, all the way back in junior high. I was practicing on the drums during study hall when the door banged open and this wild little animal came running in. He was short and skinny, with brown hair down to his shoulders. His face was ghost white, and he was sweating bullets. He slammed the door.

I was like, "What's up, dude?"

And he was like, "You gotta hide me."

I told him he could scoot under the risers and nobody would see him. Just as he slipped out of sight, the door banged open again. A gang of dudes came running through, asking if I'd seen a "long-haired little pussy" who had mouthed off to them in the cafeteria. I shrugged. They left.

The kid came out from underneath the risers and wiped tears from his cheeks. Then he puffed up his chest and strutted around the band room, all confident now, and he said that he would've beat all of their asses at the same time but he couldn't get suspended again.

He said his name was Ron, and he asked if I was a good drummer, and who my favorite band was.

His eyes kept darting back at the door while he talked. I could tell he was stalling so he wouldn't have to go back out into the hallway. But I didn't really have any friends, and I was psyched to have somebody my age to talk music with. So I just started gabbing.

I talked about Rush and Zep and Creedence, everybody else with big drums. Ron was soaking it all up, and before we knew it the period was almost over. He demanded that I play something on the drums for him, so I played the beginning of "Immigrant Song" by Zeppelin.

His mouth opened in a silly, toothy grin. He said he knew that one, and he started singing. And I shit you not, this little dude sounded exactly like Robert Plant.

I mean, he sounded like Robert Plant if he was thirteen, but still! So I was like, "Dude, we should be in a band," and he was like, "Dude, we already are."

That's Ron.

Now it sounded like he had gotten himself into another one of his jams. I ran toward the scrum and pushed my way into the middle. Sure enough, Little Ron was on the ground and this tall, jacked metal rocker was putting a hurting on him.

"What's going on?" I said to Sully.

"That guy papered over us," Sully said.

Aha. In rock-speak, getting papered over meant that the big guy had stapled one of his flyers directly on top of one of ours. It was a dick move, and Ron saw him do it.

Sully didn't have to tell me what happened next. I had known Ron long enough to fill in the blanks.

"Yo, cut the shit, you guys," I shouted. I pushed myself in between them, and the big guy punched me right on the back.

It hurt, but it also proved that the guy didn't really know how to fight. In that situation, he had the advantage. He could've punched me in the spleen or chopped my shoulder or at least taken a shot at my head, anything that would actually slow me down. Instead he punched me in the middle of the back, which didn't really do anything but sting.

I fell into a crouch and brought an elbow up into his stomach. I heard him drop to his knees and let out an "*oof*," and I knew I had knocked the wind out of him.

I probably could've walked away then. But if there's one thing I learned growing up, it's this: once you're in a fight, you stay in it until it's over.

"Kick his ass, Rikki!" I heard Sully shout from the crowd. I stood up and leaned over the guy while he was trying to catch his breath. I grabbed a handful of his big mane of hair and the fingers on his right hand, and I bent them backward. He squealed.

"Don't make me, bro," I whispered to him.

"I give," the guy coughed out. "I give."

I let him go, and I helped him to his feet. Sully and Marty helped Ron up, and he looked okay. "All right, dude. Good on ya," I said to the stranger, and I smiled as I wiped imaginary dirt off his shoulders. "See, that's my buddy Ron, and we're just starting out. You don't like to get papered over, either, right?"

"I guess not," he said.

"Who are you playing with?"

"Symphony of Chaos."

"Right on," I said. "I heard you guys shred." The guy grinned a little, all bashful now, and shrugged. Here's a secret: I had not actually heard that his band shreds. But he'd just gotten humiliated in front of the whole Strip by a skinny kid half his size, so I figured he could use a little boost.

"What time do you go on?"

"Like, ten o'clock," the guy said.

"Well, all right," I said. "We go on at six-thirty, over at the Shed. We'll send everybody your way after, if you take my buddy Ron here around and hang flyers together. Cool?"

"Yeah, cool," the guy said. "Hey, I remember when we were going on before dinner. Keep scrapping, dude."

We clasped hands and bro-hugged, cementing a new friendship. I waved Ron over.

"Hey, buddy," I said. "You got yourself some security." I patted the big guy on the back, like you might do to a new dog to show your own dog that everything is cool. "Go get those posters up!"

"With this guy?" Ron sneered. His breathing was short and hitched, like he was trying not to cry.

"Better off with friends than enemies, right?" I said.

"Fine," Ron said. "See you in an hour." And then he looked at me as if to say, *Thank you for saving my ass for the millionth time, Rikki,* and I looked at him as if to say, *It's all good, Ron!* and off they went.

The crowd split up, and it looked like everything was about to go back to normal. I was feeling pretty good about smoothing things over and making a new ally for the band, until I remembered something bad.

Something *really* bad.

A cold shock went through my body.

I had dropped all my flyers.

Fuck, dude.

I scrambled through the crowd, back toward my post in front of the Shed, my eyes on the ground. I was praying that I'd see a pile of flyers there, that some of them hadn't been stepped on or crumpled and could be salvaged.

But I didn't see them anywhere. The show was in less than two hours. Without those flyers, we had no chance of getting at least thirty-four people to come. We were going to get shit-canned by the smallest club on the Strip.

I had no way of knowing at the time that this very moment was one of the biggest turning points in my life, and everything that followed would be a roller-coaster ride of fame and notoriety and danger that would end with me running for my life in East Germany.

I couldn't know any of those things at that point, while I stood there with my mouth hanging open. I only knew that Qyksand was done for.

My heart sank. I didn't know what to do. I finally lifted my eyes from the pavement.

And that was the first time I saw Tawny.

3

THERE WAS A GIRL standing in my spot—and, I shit you not, she was the most beautiful woman I had ever seen in my life.

For a few seconds, I forgot entirely about my predicament. I forgot I was playing a concert in an empty room in less than two hours. I forgot that when we failed to break even, I'd have nowhere else to go. I even forgot my name.

Because there was a bona fide goddess on the Sunset Strip, hanging out by the Shed in red heels and a ripped denim miniskirt and fishnet stockings, a crop top with fringes and a little denim jacket that was basically just sleeves and a zipper.

It was like Marianne Gravatte had just stepped out of her Playmate of the Year cover and posted up in front of the shittiest club in Los Angeles. She was a California-tan blonde, maybe five feet seven. She had big blue eyes, pouty lips, curves like a supermodel, and an ass that seemed to be saying, "Hey, Rikki! Check out my ass!"

But the most gorgeous thing about her at that moment was the stack of Qyksand flyers in her hand.

It all came crashing back then, and I felt a mix of relief and terror. My life was in the goddess's hands now. I would have to play this cool. So I floated over to her and just stood there, grinning like an idiot.

Finally, she made the first move. "You're in Qyksand, right?" She held the flyers out to me. "I think these are yours?"

She had a strong voice, with the tiniest hint of gravel in it—maybe a smoker, maybe a singer, maybe both. It sounded like music. I forgot why I was there again. Then I saw the flyers, and before I could stop myself, my hand darted out and grabbed them a little too fast. Like she might change her mind.

"Oh shit, thank you," I said, and I clutched the flyers to my chest.

"No worries," she said, letting out a sweet laugh. "Can't lose your flyers, right?"

"Nope," I said. I couldn't even look directly in her eyes for more than a second at a time. Jesus, what was wrong with me?

"I liked how you handled yourself over there," she said. I didn't know what she meant at first. And, I mean, I didn't even understand the words coming out of her mouth. I was basically hypnotized.

The goddess smiled and nodded over my shoulder, and I followed her eyes back to the scene of the fight.

"Oh, right," I said. "Thanks. No big deal, I guess."

"What do you play?" she asked.

"Drums."

"Oh my God." Her hands went to her chest. "I love drummers. Stamina and rhythm, right?" She smirked deviously, like she was talking about drumming but also about *doing it.*

I started to feel a little confidence seeping in. "Takes a lot of practice, I guess," I said with a shrug, and I held her gaze now. Did my little half smile that I'm told is charming.

"He can handle a fight, he can handle the drums," she said. She leaned in close and lowered her voice. "I wonder how he could handle me?" And then she winked and smiled.

This sounds corny, but when our eyes met I felt this *connection,* like people talk about only happening a few times in your whole life? The rest of the world behind her went dim and fuzzy, and suddenly it was like we were alone in the universe, just me and this one other person, seeing through each other's eyes into our hearts?

And then we were banging!

Well, first we went into the greenroom of the Shed, and then, next thing I knew, there was leather and denim everywhere. Her legs were wrapped around my hips and she was pulling my shirt off over my head.

"I'm Rikki," I said.

"Tawny," she said, and then she tried to eat my tongue.

"You really do like drummers!" I managed to say.

"Shut up, Rikki," she said.

We dropped our underwear and she slid on, and we went at it against the wall, on the couch, on the floor—and for a few uncomfortable seconds, on top of Marty's bass guitar. It was awesome.

We had finally tired each other out and were sorting through the pile of clothes on the floor when my brain crashed back down to earth. I remembered we were about to play in an empty room.

"Oh shit," I said.

"What's the matter?"

"There's no way we're gonna get enough people to break even with the club tonight."

"Is that bad?"

"Really bad," I said. "Like, the end of my career bad."

"How many people do you need to show up to break even?"

"Thirty-four," I said. The number might as well have been a million.

Tawny's face scrunched up like she was thinking on something, and then she pulled her jean jacket on. "Gimme those flyers," she said. "I'll see what I can do."

An hour later Qyksand was fully assembled, and we were waiting backstage for Gus to call us out to play what would probably be our last concert. We didn't even really have it in us to party, so we only drank, like, five beers apiece and smoked a little weed and did a couple of shots.

"All right, all right, settle down," we heard Gus say, his amplified voice muffled through the wall. "Okay. We good? Everybody put your hands together for our opening band, Qyksand!"

We ran through the door and onto the stage, and we were stunned by the room that greeted us.

There had to be at least a hundred people in the place, all of them screaming and cheering. They were crammed into the Shed shoulder to shoulder, way above capacity. Ol' Gus was beaming.

We stumbled to our places, kind of whiplashed by our sudden good fortunes. "Wow, I guess it was worth hitting the streets with that big dude," Ron whispered.

"Yeah," I said.

But I had a feeling Ron's flyers didn't have anything to do with it. I scanned the crowd from left to right, hoping to see one specific face.

And then I found her: Tawny, leaning on the bar. She raised a bottle of beer in the air=.

"Hey, buddy." Ron nudged my shoulder. "You okay?"

I felt a dopey smile spread like warm water across my cheeks. "Never better, Ron," I said. "I think I'm in love."

4

Q YKSAND HAD NEVER played in front of a crowd that big
before, and it was intimidating.

We were going to open with a cover of "Holy Diver" by
Ronnie James Dio, like we usually do, but then Ron turned around to
face us, and he had this crazy look in his eyes. He mouthed the words
"Sweet Lightning," which was our best original song. We usually
didn't play that one until six songs in.

Sully and Marty and I looked at one another and shrugged. I
understood what Ron was doing immediately. Who knew how long
this crowd was gonna stick around? We had to hit them with our own
stuff while we had their attention.

So we winged it. Instead of following our set list, Ron called out
the first three songs based on his instincts—all originals—and then I
think he just forgot and fell back into the set list that we had practiced.

We played "Sweet Lightning" twice, and we all flubbed it here
and there, falling out of rhythm or missing a chord; I think it was
a combination of playing the songs out of order and the size of the
crowd. But it felt amazing—that sense of not knowing what was
coming next, like we were all taking a test at the same time, and we
needed one another to pass it.

The crowd was packed so tight into that space that we could
barely hear ourselves over their cheering. At some point I closed my
eyes and just kept them pinched tight for a whole song, smiling so
hard that it hurt while I banged on the drums.

The crowd was definitely into it, but there was also something
a little bit . . . off about them. Most of the girls were dressed like

groupies, but a lot of them weren't wearing makeup—like they had run out of the house at the last minute.

Among the dudes, there were the usual suspects with long hair and ripped threads—but there were also a bunch of guys who looked like frat boys with buzz cuts and polo shirts.

Only a few of them seemed to know the lyrics, even to the cover songs; and I think maybe some of them didn't speak English? But they'd each paid their three dollars, and nobody got in a fight or called the fire marshal, so all was good.

Every single guest stayed until the last song was over. The second Ron yelled, "We are Qyksand! Thank you, Los Angeles! Go check out Symphony of Chaos at the Whisky," the entire crowd turned around and politely filed out the door.

Except for Tawny. She was sitting at the bar, nursing a Corona.

"Oh my God," Marty said, pointing directly at her. "Who is that?"

"That's the girl I told you guys about," I said.

"Holy shit," Ron said. "Dude, is it cool with you if I hit on her?"

I thought about it, and then told him it probably wouldn't be cool with me. Then I said, "Hey, can you guys pack up the van? I'll see you back at the house."

The boys all smiled and launched a round of high fives, and then they got to work breaking down our equipment while I sauntered over to the bar.

Tawny waved at Gus and pointed at her bottle, then held up two fingers. Gus brought over a couple of fresh, cold cervezas, still sweating from the ice bucket.

"Good show, Thunder," Gus said. He dropped three shot glasses on the bar and filled them with tequila. We clinked and drank, and then Gus got the hint and fucked off to somewhere else.

"It really was," Tawny said. "You guys wail!"

"Aw, thanks." I shrugged. "Missed a couple of beats here and there."

"I didn't notice," Tawny said. She pulled her stool toward mine and we leaned in, close and comfortable, with none of that awkward first-date stuff getting in the way, since we'd already boned earlier that night. "How long have you been playing together?"

"Me and Ron since junior high," I said. "Marty and Sully we knew in high school, but we only got the band together two years ago."

Tawny nodded and sipped her beer. "Rad," she said.

"So, I gotta ask." I raised an eyebrow. "How did you get all those people here?"

"Ah," Tawny said, and smiled. "A girl never tells."

"Come on," I whined.

"Okay," she said. "I work for a music magazine. We know how to turn out a crowd. But helping out a band isn't exactly in the job description . . ."

"Secret's safe with me."

"Thank you. Now your turn. Where did you learn to fight like that?"

"What, earlier?" I said. I felt my cheeks get red. "Well, I grew up in a bunch of different foster homes, and some of them were a little rough. I had to learn how to defend myself pretty young."

"Oh. Sorry."

"Nah." I waved it off and forced a casual smile. "Half the time I fought my way out of trouble, the other half I talked my way out."

"Yeah, I saw some of that, too," Tawny said. "So you probably could've, like, totally destroyed that guy, huh?"

"I guess. But what's the point? Then we just have another band who hates us. Now he's gonna help us out."

Tawny smiled and tapped her fist on my shoulder. "You have a pretty good feel for people, for a guy in a punk band."

I winced. "Thanks," I said, holding up a finger. "But I have to correct you there. We're a metal band. Punk is for crybabies and British people."

Tawny held her palms up. "My mistake. So, why music?"

I shifted in my seat and took a long sip from my beer. This subject always made me a little uncomfortable.

5

LIKE I SAID, I'm an orphan.

I was born on March 25, 1964, and I was put up for adoption on March 26. I don't know who my real parents are, or why they gave me up. I used to think about that a lot.

There were a lot of "somedays" in my imagination. Like, I would daydream about how maybe my parents were these nice rich people, and they got in an accident and had amnesia, and someday they would remember me and come find me.

Or maybe I crash-landed on Earth in a spaceship like Superman, and someday I would discover that I have powers.

Or maybe my dad was really busy touring with his band, and he didn't know I existed. And then someday I would be in the front row at an Aerosmith concert flashing double devil horns, and Steven Tyler and I would lock eyes, and we would both *just know*.

Other times I wondered if my parents got rid of me because of something bad that I did, and I felt like I must've been a pretty terrible baby for them to give up on me within a few hours.

You know, standard orphan stuff.

Somewhere along the way, I realized that thinking about it just made me sad every time, so I tried to stop thinking about it. I had to stop hoping for someday and start working on surviving today. Because that wasn't always easy.

I bounced between foster homes. I stayed with some nice families, and some not-so-nice ones. The first home that I remember living in was a nice one. They were an older couple, too old for kids I guess, and the lady would make homemade applesauce and hug me against her big, soft body when I got sad.

But I didn't really know the rules when I was little—that it wasn't going to be a permanent thing. And then the guy got sick or something, and they gave me up.

Most of the time I was in one of those professional foster homes where they cram as many kids into bunk beds as the state will allow. Keeping a roof over their heads is basically their only job. Like what orphanages turned into after you couldn't say "orphanage" anymore.

And I got bounced by plenty of them. I had a reputation among the foster homes when I was young. They thought I was dangerous. I wasn't! But I kind of had a bad temper when I was a little kid.

I would have tantrums. Some little thing would go wrong, and I wouldn't be able to let it go, and then I would get angry. And once that happened, I couldn't really stop. I'd ball my fists up and my face would get all red and I'd scream and throw myself on the floor. And if I didn't steer out of it on my own, then eventually I would totally lose my shit and start hitting.

But, whoa, never people! Or pets. Nothing alive! If I was lucky, there would be a couch nearby, but I would usually end up punching a wall or the floor—or, in one case, a moving car.

I think most people were jumping to the conclusion that if I'd punch a wall, I'd probably punch a foster parent, too. Honestly, I don't think it ever crossed my mind. I got hit enough to know I didn't like it, and I didn't want to do that to someone else.

The other kids at those places were usually assholes, because they were going through the same shit that I was. And I was little for my age. When I said that I had to learn how to defend myself? That started when I was, like, five years old.

I remember that feeling, just always bracing for something bad to happen. My little nerves were so frayed all the time. It might be that the other kids were gonna jump me, or the foster dad would throw a bottle. Or that I'd wake up and they would tell me to pack my bags, because I didn't live there anymore.

At some point, I started doing this nervous tapping thing with my fingers. Just a regular beat, back and forth between my pointer fingers. I'd tap on the table, or the floor, or the desk where I did my homework. It was the only thing in my world that I could control.

Then I turned twelve—and that birthday was the most important day of my life.

I was living at a professional foster house with five other boys. This was the roughest one that I had lived in so far. It was too small for all of us, and it always smelled like beer and sweat and cigarettes. I was the last one in, so by the time I got there, the others had formed a gang of sorts, with its own rules and leadership. I don't remember most of their names, because I choose not to.

But they had a leader, and I remember his name.

It was Clark.

He was grown-up size and a total sociopath. Fuck that dude.

Anyway. They hated that I was little, and they hated that I was letting my hair grow long, and they fucking hated the tapping.

They also figured out pretty quickly that if any one of them came at me alone, I could fight them off; so whenever somebody felt like smacking me around, the others would pile on, too. I couldn't entirely blame them. They were a gang, after all. They had to watch each other's backs.

Birthdays were a really big deal, because they meant pizza and cake. I think the state made the foster parents do it, and we'd only get a little bit of each—but it was still a treat. So, everyone was in a pretty good mood on March 25, 1976.

Until the pipe over the kitchen burst.

I guess we should've known it was coming. There was a stain on the drop-ceiling tile right over the kitchen table that had started as a little yellow splotch in the fall and spread across half the room by March. One of a thousand things the foster parents had hoped they could just ignore until it went away on its own.

But, like most of the things they ignored, the leak just kept getting worse, a little bit every day, until the pipe finally burst open. My cake got soaked before we could eat it, and the kitchen started to flood. The other kids scattered, knowing that nobody would care where they went in the middle of a crisis.

The foster dad—his name was Burt—promptly took a six-pack of Miller out of the fridge and headed for the garage. I tried to help the foster mom, Kelly, get everything out of the kitchen so it wouldn't get ruined. Then she called a plumber.

After we figured out how to turn off the water, Kelly retreated to the garage to drink beer with Burt. She told me that she was too stressed out to deal with the plumber, so I should stay there and help him with whatever he needed.

The plumber showed up an hour later and found me sitting at the table in the kitchen, poking at a ruined birthday cake. His name was Mr. Pratt. He saved my life.

He was a big, bear-shaped guy with a bushy mustache and a clean blue shirt. He looked up at the ceiling and grunted, and then he looked back at me.

"That your cake?" he asked. His voice was surprisingly gentle. I didn't look up at him, but I nodded.

"Aw, jeez," he said, even softer now. "That ain't fair, for a kid's birthday cake to get ruined like that."

I was caught so off guard by it that I almost cried. He was right. It wasn't fair. None of it was fair. I started tapping at the table, which he took as a sign to get to work.

He took a heavy wrench out of his toolbox and set about cranking on the busted pipe. After a few minutes, though, he looked at me again.

"You a drummer?" he asked.

I thought he was making fun of me, so I stopped tapping. "No."

"Well, you keep a good rhythm," he said. "You should give it a try. I played sax in a band in high school. We were pretty good, but our drummer couldn't keep a rhythm like that."

"Oh," I said.

Mr. Pratt put his wrench on the table. "Who are your favorite bands?" he asked.

I told him Aerosmith and Kiss.

"Uh-huh," he said. "They're both good. You ever check out Rush? They have this drummer, Peart. He has a bunch of extra drums in his kit."

I finally lifted my eyes and looked at him. He wasn't teasing me or humoring me. He was being nice. I shook my head. "I don't get to listen to the radio very much," I said.

"That's a damn shame," Mr. Pratt said. "Boy like you, rhythm like that? You have any records?"

I almost laughed at that one. I didn't have *anything* of my own, let alone records. Let alone a record player!

Mr. Pratt said he would write down the names of some bands and that I should find a way to check them out. I thanked him and said I would, but I was just being polite. I wouldn't even know how to "check them out" if I wanted to. I asked if he needed any help, and he said thank you, but he could handle it just fine.

"Okay, then," he said. He put out a big, paw-like hand. "Ben Pratt."

"Richard," I said, and I shook his hand.

"Nice to meet you," Mr. Pratt said. He fixed the pipe, wrote up a bill, and left.

Cut to a few hours later.

Kelly and Burt had gotten hammered earlier than usual because of the pipe, so they went to bed before eight o'clock. The other kids took the opportunity to go out and break windows and smoke cigarettes in the neighborhood.

I was in the living room, watching *The Cop and the Kid* on TV. It was a really rare moment, me getting to watch whatever I wanted on TV by myself for an hour. I figured it was the best birthday gift I could hope for.

Then I heard some scuttling outside the front door. I ran to the bay window and peeked through the blinds. I saw a van with "Pratt Plumbing" painted on the side driving away. Why had Mr. Pratt come back? I wondered. Did he forget something?

I opened the front door. There was a cardboard box on the front steps. He had written "Happy Birthday, Richard" on it.

I scooped up the box and ran into my bedroom, then tore it open.

There was a little record player inside, and a pair of headphones. And four albums.

It was a cheap little thing, pink with a unicorn sticker on the back. Some wear and tear, probably something his daughter had grown out of. But it worked! I thumbed through the albums. *Fly by Night* by Rush. *Led Zeppelin II* and *III*. *Live at Leeds* by the Who.

I grabbed the *Live at Leeds* one first, because I thought the name was funny. I plugged in the record player and found where the headphones attached, then pulled them over my ears.

I lined up the album like I'd seen adults do.

Dropped the needle.

Inside the headphones, a crowd cheered while the band took their places. Noodled with the instruments. A British voice introduced the first song, "Young Man Blues"; and all at once, they began to play, loud guitars in rhythm with the machine gun fire of Keith Moon's drumming. My mouth dropped open. My eyes closed.

And I became Rikki Thunder.

Moon hammered on the drums with fierce precision, and I found myself zeroing in on that heavy rattle. It sounded like he was hitting the drums twice as frequently as a normal drummer would, and he was holding the whole thing together while the guitars shredded and Roger Daltrey sneered and wailed through the lyrics.

Moon stunned me. I found myself tapping on the bed, trying to match his rhythm and speed. I was smiling so wide that my cheeks hurt. My eyes filled with tears.

Mr. Pratt had picked albums with the best drummers in the world, and I realized right away that he was right: I should be a drummer. I *needed* to be a drummer. Those thumps and crashes in rhythm, all of them timed perfectly, like Neil Peart and John Bonham and Keith Moon had captured wild lions and trained them to roar on key.

If only I could do that!

I bounced around from album to album in a panic, never taking my eyes off the window, because I knew the other kids could arrive home at any time. I would need to hide the record player.

When Mr. Pratt gave me that box, it was the kindest thing anyone had ever done for me; but it also came with a curse. I had something nice. The other boys would want it.

But they would never take it from me.

I made that vow, that very night: the record player was mine. It was the only thing in the world I could say that about, and I would fight tooth and nail to keep it.

And, believe me, I had to! I managed to hide it from them for a while, but they found it eventually. And they wanted it. And they came after me relentlessly. I fought them off one against one, then two against one.

Then they all came. Two of them pinned me down, and Clark

yanked the record player out of my hand while the others danced around the room.

"You can use it!" I shouted from under the pile. "Just don't break the needle! Please, Clark!" Somebody punched my cheek and Clark mussed my hair, and then he spit on my head.

He took *Fly by Night* out of its sleeve. There was a knee in my back and spit in my hair, and I watched as, in slow motion, Clark looked at the album sideways and declared that Rush was "for fags" and snapped the album in half.

It felt like he had broken a bone in my body. I screamed. And I escaped from their grasp.

And I broke Clark's nose.

And three of his fingers.

I drove my palm into his ear while he was on the floor crying. The other kids tried to stop me, but Clark had just killed one of my children, and I wasn't going to be stopped. I stomped on the nearest foot and heard a crack. I swung an elbow upward behind me, and I felt it meet a chin.

Then the door burst open, and Burt stormed into the room. He closed in on me, held a strong, fat arm over his head, then swung his open palm as hard as he could across my face.

And then I got to leave.

I was a guest of the state for a little while, while they looked for a new foster home that was willing to take in a thirteen-year-old killing machine. But that wasn't so bad, because the other kids had heard enough to be scared of me—and I still had my record player.

Eventually they found another home for me, with the Browns. They were decent foster parents, and this time I was the oldest kid there, so I didn't really have to be afraid anymore.

I kept to myself, mostly, and I listened to my albums. I finally scraped together enough money to replace *Fly by Night*, and over time I added more records: *Highway to Hell* by AC/DC! *Van Halen* by Van Halen! *London Calling* by the Clash! *Live at Budokan* by Cheap Trick!

I would listen to albums with every free second. I'd close my eyes and let my hair hang in front of my face, and I would start rapping my palms against the table or floor or whatever surface was in front of me, like bongos, until I found the beat. I'd listen to those songs over and over, switching from my palms to my fingers until that hurt too much and then going back to my palms, working in the change-ups and hi-hats, playing along with the band like I was right there in the studio.

Music became the place I could go when I needed comfort. I wasn't afraid when I was drumming. I was in control of the sound. I wasn't storing up my feelings until they exploded; in fact, I hadn't had a tantrum since the night Ben Pratt gave me the record player. I could drum all day and let all my frustrations and fears out through my fingers and palms.

And it sounded good! It was like, before drumming, being scared of whatever was gonna hurt me next had filled me with rage; but now I was *using* that feeling to make something beautiful.

My outlet brought me joy, and I think that, over time, it just turned my whole attitude around. Now that I have drumming, I'm probably the happiest dude I know.

So I was in a good place when I met Ron in eighth grade, and I had someone to talk to about music and swap albums with. I introduced Ron to Cheap Trick *Live at Budokan*, and he tried to master Robin Zander's sneering vocals in "Surrender" so relentlessly that he lost his voice and had to go to the doctor.

Ron was the one who discovered Creedence Clearwater Revival's *The Concert*. And, oh my God, drummer heaven! Doug Clifford on "Who'll Stop the Rain" was teaching a graduate course on that perfect line between precision and fury that makes listening to the best drummers feel like you're on a roller-coaster car that could go off the rails at any second.

We started playing together. We didn't have a band, because it was just the two of us, but we had a blast pretending, anyway.

Our last year in high school, Mötley Crüe put out *Too Fast for Love*, and that was it, dude. They might not have been quite as technically sound as the others, but that's what we loved about them the most. The attitude was baked into the music. That album was, like, a map for the rest of our lives. Metal was our religion.

I felt closer to music than I did to any human being. I could love music with an open heart; and just by playing it loud, music made me feel loved right back. I felt safe loving music, because music would never leave me.

There were seven empty beers in front of us. *Christ*, I thought. *How long have I been talking?* Tawny put a hand on my shoulder and smiled. Her eyes were shining, and she wiped tears out of the corners. "Thank you," she said. "Thank you for sharing that with me."

"Hey, all's well that ends well." I shrugged. I was trying to cheer both of us up. "I just decided, whatever it takes to keep playing, that's what I would do. So we started Qyksand. And here I am now, on top of the world!"

"Yeah," Tawny said quietly, almost to herself. "Have you kept in touch with him?"

"Who?"

"Ben Pratt."

"Oh," I said. "You know, I tried to call him about a year ago, but his business isn't listed anymore. I thought about trying harder to track him down, but, like, what if he's dead or something? I don't want to know. The memory is, like, perfect as it is, you know?"

"I get it."

I decided we needed a change of scenery. "So, do you want to go to a party?" I asked. "Back at the band house?"

Tawny slapped the bar with her open palm, hard enough to rattle all the bottles. "*Yes,*" she said, and grabbed my hand. "Where do you guys live?"

"You know that condemned paint store?"

"Yup," Tawny said. "Is your house near there?"

"Yeah." I smiled. "Really near there."

Hint: we lived in the condemned paint store.

6

TAWNY AND I held hands as I led her through a window into the band house.

When the band moved into the paint store, the door was missing, and we didn't know how to get a new one. So we found some corrugated metal in the alley and nailed it over the hole where a door was supposed to be, and now we just came and went through a window.

We were paying a guy rent—sometimes in cash, sometimes in weed—and he kept the electricity on. But looking back, I don't know whether he actually owned the place or not. It's possible we were squatting there. I'll never know for sure.

Tawny passed an important "girlfriend material" test right away, because she didn't scream and run out of the building. The show had ended only an hour ago, but by the time we arrived, the party was already in full swing.

There were a couple dozen people packed into the room, all metalheads and glammed-out dudes and chicks—sometimes it was hard to tell which was which—smoking and crashing into each other. The new Cinderella album was blaring on Marty's cheap stereo.

The place reeked of pot and spilled beer, which is how you knew it was still early in the night. Later on, it would smell like piss and ashes.

And it was in a paint store! When the people who owned the place abandoned it, they left in a really big hurry. The store was still full of paint cans, and a bunch still had paint in them. This was a pretty big bonus, because we could use them to build our furniture. We used the empty ones for everything else—tonight there were beer bottles stuffed into empty paint cans full of ice all around the room. Smaller quart cans were already stuffed with cigarette butts. There was also a big black spot on the couch, a telltale sign that it had already been set on fire and put out.

Parties at the Qyksand house were legendary. On any given night, more people would show up at the house than had been at the concert. There would be destruction of property, and jam sessions, and public sex, and relentless drug use. There would be pizza, and cold cuts, and spilled kerosene, and fistfights.

The police never came. We never cleaned up the next morning. It was a pretty disgusting place to live, and we loved it.

Tawny's eyes glowed as she took it all in. "This is rad," she shouted in my ear, and she squeezed my hand. "Bathroom?" she asked.

I gestured down the hall. "You're gonna want to try to get it all out of your system now," I said. "That room is going to be really scary later."

Tawny smirked and let go of my hand. She ping-ponged through the crowd gracefully and vanished down the hallway.

I scanned the room for the boys and found them spread out across the party. There was Ron, desperately hitting on a pair of girls in matching Megadeth crop tops. Ron was shirtless now, with his long brown hair falling over his skinny shoulders, a cigarette sticking out of one side of his mouth and a joint sticking out of the other.

And there were Sully and Marty, talking to each other in the corner. Those guys looked like they could be twins. They were about the same height, and both had long, frizzy blond hair that was usually sprayed up in front, with long bangs swept over their eyes. I saw them exchange an epic high five, and it made me happy.

Ron spotted me. "Thunderstorm!" he shouted, and then we all screamed and pig-piled on one another.

"Best show ever," I shouted. We slowly helped each other back to our feet.

Ron slapped my chest with the back of his hand. "Dude," he said. "How did it go? With the girl?"

I gave him a knowing grin and a nod. "She's here," I said. "You gotta meet her. She's fuckin' awesome."

"Nice!" Ron said. "So, is it cool if I hit on her, then?" He tried to keep a straight face but couldn't, and we both laughed.

"Everybody got something to drink?" Ron asked. He had a bottle of Jim Beam. I had Jack Daniels. Marty had vodka and Sully had a beer. We raised our drinks. "Here's to the biggest show ever!" Ron shouted. Then we crashed our bottles into one another and drank.

"Until the next one!" I shouted back. Another cheers. Another drink.

"Hey, Sully has some good news, too," Marty said, and he held up his bottle for another cheers, but nobody else did. I looked at Sully and saw him shoot daggers at Marty for half a second.

Sully shrugged. "No big deal," he said. "We can talk about it tomorrow."

"No, man, we're celebrating," I said. Ron and Marty got really quiet. "What's your good news?"

"Really, it's nothing," Sully said. "Just, I got a job offer with the moving company."

Wait a minute. Had I heard that right? "A job?" I said.

"Just part-time," Sully said. "Monday, Tuesday, Wednesday."

I was confused. We practiced on those days! "I'm confused," I said. "We practice on those days."

"I know," Sully said. "I can still come to practice. I just might be late."

"Dude," I said. "Did you see the crowd tonight? We're actually breaking through. We need to practice more now, not less." I looked at Ron. "Back me up here."

Ron shrugged. "I can see both sides," he said. My mouth dropped open. I knew he was just trying to put a pin in it because we were in the middle of a party, but it felt like that pin was stabbing me in the back.

"On the one hand," Ron said, "we do have a practice schedule that we all agreed to when we moved into this house. On the other hand, though, some regular money would help the band, too."

What the hell was going on? I felt panicky. We couldn't let up now. This was how bands broke up. I'd seen it a dozen times before, and there was a little part of me that was always bracing for it, like the kid in the foster home just waiting to be sent away again. Playing music kept us together. I couldn't lose that now.

And get a load of Ron here, by the way, arguing like a seasoned attorney! Like he was his asshole lawyer dad all of a sudden. God-damned Ron. I was starting to feel like they were teaming up against me. Like they had rehearsed this before I got there, while I was busy pouring my heart out to Tawny at the Shed.

Then, just like magic, thinking about her made her appear. I felt a hand on my chest. Tawny stepped in between us and put a cool palm on my cheek.

"Are you gonna introduce me to the band?" she said, and she winked, letting me know she was on my side. I didn't feel like I was being ganged up on anymore, and all the hot air leaked out of me. I put an arm around her shoulder.

"Hey, I'm sorry, you guys," I said. "Sully, you're feeling good about yourself, and I pissed all over it." I looked at Sully as if to say, *You know I love you, bro*, and Sully looked back at me as if to say, *It's all good, Rikki!* "Besides. You're right," I went on. "We should be cel-ebrating the biggest show of our lives right now!"

Ron held his bottle of whiskey in the air and let out a rooster crow, and we all copied him. Tawny did it, too, which I thought was especially cool of her. Somebody else at the party cranked up the stereo to make sure it was too loud for us to fight anymore. I leaned in toward the other guys.

"Hey, this is Tawny," I shouted. "She helped bring out the crowd tonight."

"Then you're our fuckin' hero, Tawny," Ron shouted. Marty and Sully lifted her up on their shoulders. "Here's to Tawny!" Ron screamed, and everyone cheered. And then they passed Tawny off to some other dudes, and she crowd-surfed all the way around the party. I couldn't help but chuckle as she laughed from her belly and tossed devil horns in the air while all these strangers passed her in a circle around the room.

I high-fived Ron. Marty handed me a joint. Sully and I clinked bottles and hugged. All was well again.

"It's gonna be all good, bro," Ron said to me. "Better than ever." I was feeling pleasantly buzzed already, and I knew he was right. I had my band, and we were finally getting noticed. I had my new girl, and she was a bodacious blond goddess who already seemed to understand me better than anyone.

For the first time in my life, I felt like I had it all.

7

WHAT SOUNDTRACK is playing inside Rikki's head right about now?

"GODDESS ON THE STRIP"
Music and lyrics by R. Thunder

(open, drums only)

Oh yeah, buddy . . . You know
   it . . .

(guitars kick in)

I met a goddess on the Sunset
   Strip, oh yeah
And ever since, my life's a blur
You know I don't know where
   she came from
But she's *sticking by my side*
   for-sure!
You know she comes to all my
   shows, this girl
And she always brings her
   friends
You know I don't know what
   her secret is
And I hope it never ends!

(Chorus:)
She's a goddess on the Strip,
   this girl
She's a diamond, she's a fine
   wine
She's an atom bomb, she's a
   Tilt-A-Whirl
She's the grand prize, and
   she's all mine!

You know she's changed my
   world since she came along
She's blown my mind, and
   that's not all!

Wink, wink

She can smoke with the best! She
   can out-drink the rest!
And she can dance like the
   sky's *about to fall*!

And now I'm with my lady all
the time
We're doing everything
together
We're riding bikes in the park!
We're taking dogs for a
walk!
We're rain or shine, in the sun,
and the stormy weather!
Uh-huh, she taught us how to
make a budget
And we taught her how to
party
And when things get wild, she
protects us all
Because my goddess knows
karate!

(chorus)

And now it's been a coupla
months so far
And everything is going grand
We're playing bigger clubs!
We're doing better drugs!
And the goddess on the Strip,
my girl
You know she's my big-gest-
fan!
Yeah, every night my girl
comes home with me
Unless she's got another thing
And she keeps her eyes on the
prize, my chick
She's got her hands in every-
thing!

(chorus)

(insane guitar solo)

Let me tell you something
People think it's too good to be
true
They say, Watch out! There's
something in her eyes
But they don't know this girl
like I know this girl
They don't know she's an an-
gel-in-dis-guise!
And sure, she comes and goes
at all hours, my girl
And her purse is full of knives
But when she holds me in her
arms so tight
You know I never felt so alive!

(chorus)

Rikki Thunder's in love, y'all!

8

THE NEXT THREE MONTHS were pretty awesome.

Qyksand kept filling seats. At first it was mostly the same people that Tawny had made appear out of thin air through her music magazine, although they got into the act a little more. The girls started wearing makeup, and some of the guys wore makeup, and they traded their polos out for T-shirts. And we were picking up more real fans, too, who actually memorized our lyrics and made their own merch.

And there was a lot of extra love for your old buddy, Rikki Thunder! I had taken on something of a following, especially with the ladies.

This wasn't *exactly* new. I started to get more attention from girls in high school, with my high cheekbones and nice teeth and big brown eyes. But something about success on the stage turned that heat up by about a thousand degrees. Chicks showed up at the shows in homemade T-shirts that said "Thunderstorm," and threw their underwear at me while we played. I was totally goo-goo ga-ga over Tawny, but all the attention was still pretty dope.

We were getting noticed in the industry, too. Gene Simmons from Kiss even called Gus at the Shed and asked him to set up a meeting, because he might want to manage us. We were super excited. This was Gene Simmons!

From Kiss!

Naturally, we took the meeting—and it got weird pretty fast.

Gene was extremely nice but said right up front that he had not seen us perform and wasn't familiar with our music, although he "had heard good things." Then he rolled out his vision for Qyksand. He suggested that we change our name to Gerbil, and our thing would be that we all wear purple unitards with long tails and chew cardboard onstage.

He was smiling and bouncing his eyebrows a lot, so it's possible he was just fucking with us. But either way, Gerbil didn't sound right for the band creatively, so we were like, "Thanks but no thanks, Gene!" And he said we were very welcome, and we could call him anytime if we changed our minds.

The best thing that happened to us was somebody finally called the fire marshal because we had packed the place so full that people were literally falling out the front door and Gus kept cramming them back in with a push broom.

When word got out that Qyksand's overflowing crowd had almost gotten the club shut down, other clubs took notice. And we started to get gigs outside of the Shed! At first it was a couple of semiregular gigs at bigger bars, and then we started getting booked to open for other bands at clubs like the Roxy and the Whisky a Go Go.

We were making more money, too, which I hoped would mean that Sully would give up on his pipe dream of being a professional furniture mover and commit to rock full time. That hadn't happened. It kept me on edge; at any point, somebody could decide to quit on the rest of us. Tawny was always around to keep me centered, though. "Let them have side interests," she said. As long as I kept my own eyes on the prize, I would be okay.

We didn't have any groupies, and we were still basically broke. But at least we could afford to print flyers every week *and* eat pizza every night.

It was December now, and we were opening for Faster Pussycat at the Cathouse. Our routine was tight, and the place was full of our regulars. It was gonna be a pretty standard show, followed by a pretty standard shit-fest back at the paint store.

I was a little on edge, though, because there was something different about this show. It was the first one that Tawny couldn't attend since the day we met.

She got a call at the bar and said she needed to run off to work, because of some kind of magazine-related emergency that I didn't fully understand.

A few minutes before showtime, we were making out at the back door of the club until she had to leave. I took her little coat in my fingers and gently tried to tug her back inside, but she held firm.

Over my shoulder, the crowd was getting feisty. A few voices started chanting, "Thunderstorm!"

"Sounds like another full house in there," she said.

"Three months in a row," I said. "You gotta tell me how you're doing this."

"It's you, babe. They're here for the Thunderstorm."

"It's gonna be so weird without you here tonight," I said. "I'm just so used to looking out in the crowd and seeing you there. You're my lucky charm."

"I know," Tawny said. Her eyes sparkled in the yellow light above the back door. "But you'll do great. Here." She dug into her purse and took out a hemp necklace with a huge, sharp tooth on it. "It's a shark tooth," she said. "It's good luck. For when I can't be with you."

"You sure you can't stay?" I tried one more time.

"Sorry, hon, I told you, big meltdown at work. It's like a four-alarm fire."

"All right," I said. I put my hands on her shoulders. "Hey."

"Hey," she said.

I took a deep breath. "I, like, *love* you, Tawny Spice." I blew out my breath. I had never said that to anyone before. It was terrifying. It was wonderful.

Tawny smiled. A little tear formed in her eye. "I, like, love you, too, Rikki Thunder," she said, in that scratchy voice that I was fully addicted to.

She leaned in to kiss me again, and I felt weightless. I couldn't believe how lucky I was. Tawny put her hands on my chest and pushed me through the door, into the club.

"Tear the roof off this motherfucker," she said, and turned to leave.

I pulled the shark-tooth necklace over my head and wrapped my hand around it. It felt warm. *My God*, I thought as I watched my woman walk away. *I'm the luckiest guy in the world.*

I kept an eye on Tawny until she cut down an alley. And then I went inside to start the show.

9

IT WAS A long alley, and by the time the woman who Rikki Thunder knew as Tawny Spice emerged from the other side, she was a completely different person.

She had shed her denim jacket and changed her shoes and tugged a long black wig over her head. Her lipstick was now purple instead of pink. Her eyes were now brown instead of blue.

She turned back toward the Strip and headed to Gazzarri's.

When she reached the club, there was a line snaking down the road. But she paid it no mind. She went straight to the main entrance and winked at the bouncer.

"Hey, Shawna," he said.

"Hey, Rocco," she said back. "They go on yet?"

"Just starting now," Rocco said. "Go ahead."

Shawna gave Rocco a pat on the cheek as he opened the door for her. Inside, rock music blared over the screams of a joyful crowd. She strolled past a poster advertising "Tonight: Whyte Python!" and entered the club.

The inside of Gazzarri's was standing room only, and it was packed beyond capacity. Whyte Python was onstage in full shred, playing their first big hit, "Till the Bell Rings." It was a good song, and hearing it played loud in a crowd of hundreds was a treat. She had mostly only seen Qyksand live lately—and, with the exception of the drums, the difference was immeasurable. Sully and Marty played their instruments within very narrow lanes; meanwhile, Buck Sweet, Whyte Python's lead guitarist, drew comparisons to Eddie

Van Halen. And the lead singer, Davy Bones, was such an upgrade over Ron Finch that you couldn't really call what they were doing the same thing.

But the drums stood out—because Rikki Thunder was better than the Whyte Python guy. She imagined Rikki playing this song, hitting that kick drum just a little bit cleaner, and holding rhythm with the other guys just a tiny bit tighter.

Shawna liked "Till the Bell Rings," and she would even sing along sometimes. But mostly she liked to tap her hands against her thighs to the drumbeat. She had to admit, she had a type.

She weaved through the crowd, barely touching anyone or doing anything to call attention to herself. Fortunately, the rock fans around her were too drunk and sloppy to really notice her.

She bought a Corona at the bar and settled into a spot near the stage, where she had a perfect line of sight to the drummer. The guy sat behind his kit and thumped on the drums mindlessly, his heavy eyelids nearly closed behind his frizzy auburn hair and his jaw slack and open.

Not a single thought going on in that pretty head, Shawna thought. She waited patiently. She would catch his eye soon enough. She had done her research, and she knew he liked black hair and purple lipstick.

And also, she had done this kind of thing before.

By two in the morning, the streets were mostly empty.

Across town, the party at the Qyksand house would be winding down, and Rikki Thunder would soon be fast asleep, dreaming about the special lady in his life.

Outside of Gazzarri's, Barry Gorman—drummer for the band Whyte Python—was sitting on his motorcycle. The woman who'd told him her name was Shawna Peppers was straddling him, with her tongue down his throat.

Her tiny silk miniskirt was up around her hips, and his hands were firmly grasping those amazing ass cheeks that seemed to be saying, "Hey, Barry, check out my ass!" She was grinding now, just a little. The rhythm was driving him crazy.

Any second now, Barry thought, *I'm sliding both of our thongs off, and we're going to go at it all the way—right here on my motorcycle, in the middle of the Sunset Strip.* It would be a great story for the band's autobiography someday.

Shawna stopped kissing him and arched her back, reaching for the purse that she had strung over the handlebars. "You want some vodka?" she purred, as she slid a glass pint bottle out of her black leather bag.

Barry shrugged. "Sure," he said.

Shawna winked at him and held his gaze while she unscrewed the top.

Barry had no reason to be suspicious. He had no reason to watch this process closely; but even if he had, he probably would not have seen her slip the little white pill into the vodka bottle. She had done this kind of thing plenty of times before, and she had the routine down cold.

Shawna waited for the pill to dissolve and then handed the bottle over. He took a long swig and handed it back. She pressed her lips to the bottle and tossed it back, but she didn't let any vodka into her mouth. She pretended to swallow. Pretended it burned.

"It's a nice night," she said, sliding off his hips and onto her feet. "Let's take a walk."

"Aw, come on," Barry said. He was *almost there*! But Shawna was walking away. He maneuvered off the motorcycle and stepped onto the pavement. Shawna looked over her shoulder and gave him a devilish smile. She crooked an elbow out and waited for him to catch up.

They walked down the Strip in silence. Barry was feeling very drunk all of a sudden, and he was doing his best to keep his feet pointed in the right direction. Shawna was quiet, for her own reasons. She started walking a little faster, and her date began to trip over every third step. Finally, she spoke.

"Why do you play music, Barry?" she asked.

Barry didn't know. Thinking of anything was difficult at that moment, but *why he played music* was also a question he'd never really pondered much. He scrunched up his face, so busy trying to think of an answer that he didn't notice the pickup truck screeching to a halt behind them.

Or the three men who got out and loaded his motorcycle onto the bed and then drove away.

"I don't know," Barry muttered. "To get laid? I guess?"

Shawna rolled her eyes. "I figured as much," she said. Barry tripped over his feet again, but Shawna held him up. Tires screeched again, and this time it was a white van that pulled up right alongside them.

"What's this?" Barry slurred.

The door slid open. "It's a surprise," Shawna said, and she nudged him toward the van. Two sets of hands grabbed Barry under the armpits and swiftly pulled him inside. Shawna climbed in behind him and slid the door shut.

Time passed, but Barry Gorman wasn't sure how much. Now he was in an area with trees, lying on his back in the middle of a clearing. Shawna stood over him, lit by the full moon.

"I can't believe you're not out cold," she said.

"I feel weird," Barry mumbled.

"I gave you a strong sedative," she said. "It's okay. It's just to dull your senses. You'll probably pass out soon."

Barry smiled drunkenly and played air guitar. "Rock 'n' roll," he said.

Shawna waited for his eyes to close and his breathing to settle into a slow rhythm.

And then she waited some more.

Barry continued to play his air guitar and stare dumbly at the sky. She checked her watch again. It should have happened by now. This asshole was not going to fall asleep. *Fucking metal guys*, she thought.

"Jesus," she said. "I gave you enough for two people."

"Can I have two more?" Barry slurred. He actually seemed like he might be coming out of his stupor.

Shawna shook her head. "More would kill you," she said. There was no more time to waste. She leaned forward and took Barry's hand. "Listen, Barry," she said, sounding apologetic. "You're not going to remember any of this. But I want you to know something anyway."

"Huh?" Barry said. "What?"

"This is not personal," she said. Then Shawna Peppers squeezed Barry's wrist and pulled his arm straight.

She planted a foot above his shoulder, turned his wrist, and pulled his arm toward her thigh with a snap.

High up in the wilderness above L.A., where nobody could hear him, Barry screamed.

PART II

A Song of Bones and Thunder

10

OKAY, I TOLD YOU about how my twelfth birthday was the most important day of my life, right? So now I'm gonna tell you about the *second* most important day of my life. It should probably come as no surprise that it involves:

1. Music, and
2. My special lady, Tawny Spice.

Hang on for dear life, bud, because this is where shit gets crazy!

Ron and I shared a bedroom at the paint store, which was really just an old office with two twin-size mattresses on the floor. We had built a four-foot-high wall of paint cans between the beds so we could have some privacy if we were entertaining a lady.

But Tawny said that under no circumstances would she sleep with me knowing Ron was on the other side of the paint-can wall. So we basically started calling dibs when we needed to, which was happening more often now that I had a girlfriend and Ron was the lead singer in an up-and-coming rock band. We never went to her place, and actually, I never saw where she lived. Tawny always said that her roommate was there and that she liked staying at the band house more than her apartment, anyway. How cool is that?

That morning, Ron had passed out on the floor in the party room again, so I had the bedroom all to myself. The party went late, but my heart wasn't totally into it. Without Tawny there to break bottles with, and dance with, and make out with, it felt like kind of an empty experience, you know?

So I took it easy. I just drank like nine beers, and smoked a little weed, and took a pill that Sully found in the bathroom, but it didn't do anything, and then I went to bed just before two.

I woke to my favorite sound in the world: Tawny's scratchy voice, saying my name.

"Rikki," she said softly. "Rikki, wake up, honey."

I opened my eyes and there she was on the edge of my mattress, sparkling in the sunlight coming through the window.

"Hey, babe," I said. "What's up?"

"I have the most amazing news," she said.

"What's that?"

Tawny smiled wide. "Barry Gorman broke both of his arms in a motorcycle accident!"

"Oh my God," I sat up. "That's awful. Why are you smiling?"

"Think about it," she said.

I thought about it and shrugged.

"Think some more," Tawny said.

I thought about it some more. "Still nothing," I said.

"Rikki." She put both of her hands on my face. "Whyte Python needs a new drummer."

Before I knew what was happening, Tawny was up and out of the house and I was chasing her down the street, still pulling a T-shirt over my head.

"I don't know what's going on," I said. "What happened to Barry? *Both* of his arms?"

"I don't know all the details," Tawny said. "They said on the radio that he woke up in the hills in his underwear with two broken arms, and his bike was thirty feet up in a tree."

"Wow," I said. "Oh man, poor guy!"

"I know, I feel bad for him, too," Tawny said. "But it's a known fact around here that Barry is a mess. He's lucky he didn't kill someone."

I thought about Barry, blacked out and riding his motorcycle fast enough to ditch it thirty feet up a tree. "You have a point there," I said. "I guess it's a good thing he was drawn to the wild."

"Plus, he's an asshole," Tawny said. "Now we need to focus on

what this could mean for you. Whyte Python signed with Andromeda Records last month, they go into the studio in a few days. And
they're lining up a tour. They're gonna break out. They literally can't
take a night off. They need a new drummer, like, *today*."

"And you think they'll pick me?"

"Of course I do." Tawny smiled, and she hit me playfully on the
chest. "I'm in the *scene*, man. I know for sure you're the best drummer on the Strip who isn't already under contract. You shred on the
drums, you're hot as shit, and you got a great name. They'll be lucky
to have you."

"I don't know," I said.

"What's wrong?"

"It's just . . ." I kicked the sidewalk. "I already got a band. Those
guys in Qyksand are my friends. I've known Ron since junior high."

Tawny took a deep breath and blew it out, then moved in closer
to me. "Babe, I know," she said. She sounded a little sad. "But do
you remember what you said to me the night we met? 'Cause I do.
'Whatever it takes to keep playing.' Qyksand is not going to break
through. That will end. Sully's picking up extra shifts. And Ron
applied for a regular job at the grocery. Marty? He was thumbing
through a catalog for the *community college* last week." She spit on the
ground. "He wants to be an *electrician*."

I knew about Sully taking extra shifts; and I had my suspicions
about Marty's new interest in electricity, ever since he found a bug
zapper behind the paint store. But I didn't know about Ron. "Ron
applied for a job and didn't tell me?"

"He's afraid to," Tawny said. "Because he already knows what I'm
trying to tell you now. None of those guys care as much as you do.
And none of them are good enough, and I know you know that."

"Tawny—"

"Even if you don't want to admit it, they've peaked, and they know
it, and they'll give up eventually. It's already started. And that affects
you, because then *you* won't be able to play anymore."

Shit, I thought. That was the scariest thing anyone could tell me.

"You can't let their limitations hold you back from your destiny,"
Tawny said. "If they're your friends, they'll understand."

I was hella conflicted. On the one hand, even though I would never say it out loud, Tawny *was* right. Sully played the same jams every single night. Marty was still falling out of rhythm no matter how much we practiced. And Ron . . . Well, Ron had a hell of a scream. But not much else.

On the other hand, though, friendship!

"Ron applied for a job and didn't tell me?" I said.

"There's no point in having an uncomfortable conversation unless he decides to take the job, right?" Tawny asked. "And the same rule applies to you." She took my hand and tugged me down the street. "Look, just try out. If they offer you the job, then you get to make a decision. If they don't, well, then at least you know, right? No regrets."

She had a good point. "Okay," I said. "Okay! No harm in trying out, right? When are they doing this?"

Tawny gestured to the Tower Records across the street.

"Right now."

11

THE SIGN SAID the record store was closed, but the doors were unlocked, and Tawny walked right in. The lights were off, and there was nobody else inside. Tawny held her hand out like a car model, pointing down the long aisles of bins toward a door at the back with a sign on it that said, "Pprivate."

"I just walk in there?" I said.

"They're expecting you," Tawny said. "I called their manager when I heard it on the news."

I stuffed my hands in my pockets and looked down at my shoes. "I'm nervous," I said.

Tawny put her palm on the shark-tooth necklace against my chest. "You got this, babe," she said. "Bring the thunderstorm."

We kissed, and I walked through the door.

And there they were: Davy Bones. Spencer Dooley. Buck Sweet. The remaining members of Whyte Python. And they did *not* look happy to see me.

Spencer and Davy were tall and skinny like me, with expertly managed waterfalls of metal-rock hair—Spencer's jet black, Davy's blond-gold. They were both renowned metal musicians with exact opposite personalities; Spencer was known to be dumb but friendly, and Davy was brilliant but "complicated."

Buck was short and thick, with massive brown hair that spiked in all directions. The word on the street was that Buck was genuinely crazy, but he was also one of the top three or four guitar players in L.A.

Spencer lit a blunt off a roach. Buck absentmindedly played with a knife. Davy was striking a weird pose, straddling a backward chair with sunglasses on, looking at the ceiling.

"Is this the guy?" Davy asked, without looking at me.

I had actually met the Whyte Python guys once before, at a Guns N' Roses after-party at Slash's house. But they probably didn't remember. It was a wild party.

Davy and Axl spent most of the night arm wrestling. Sully and one of the guys from W.A.S.P. tried to pick up the refrigerator but lost their grip on it when the weight shifted on account of the door opening and all the food spilling out. Then Buck and Slash got into a really big argument about which kind of snake would win in a fight. They were getting in each other's faces and shouting, and it escalated to the point where they were actually fighting each other, but with their arms pinned to their sides—Buck fighting like a python and Slash mimicking the cobra he believed would come out on top. It all ended badly when Buck bit Slash hard enough to draw blood, and Slash spit whiskey in Buck's eyes, and Buck threw Izzy's guitar out the window, and Slash said the Whyte Python guys had to leave.

Anyway.

"Yeah, hey," I said. "I'm Rikki Thunder? From Qyksand?"

Nobody responded. There was a nervous-looking guy in glasses and a rumpled shirt and tie pacing in the back of the room. He was the only one to move. He came over and greeted me at the door, holding out a sweaty hand.

"Rikki," he said. He had a British accent. "Hello! I'm Kirby Smoot, the band manager. Your girlfriend is . . . very persuasive."

"Uh, hey," I said. "Look, guys, I was really sorry to hear about what happened to Barry."

"You're the only one, dude," Davy Bones said. He was still looking at the ceiling, and he sounded like he was tired of all this already. It seemed dramatic, to be honest. But that's Davy. "It was only a matter of time with Barry," he said. "And now we're kind of fucked over here. Do you know 'Till the Bell Rings?'"

"Yeah." I nodded. "Definitely."

"All right." Davy sighed. He still wasn't looking at me. "Let's do it."

"Right on," I said. I took a seat behind Barry's drum set and found the sticks. Spencer and Buck had still not said anything, but they stood and strapped into their guitars.

"Count us in, Rikki Thunder," Davy said.

I raised the drumsticks in the air. *Okay*, I thought. *"Till the Bell Rings." 123 bpm. Go.*

I clacked the sticks together four times. Everyone joined in at once.

And it felt *right*, bro! I hate to admit it, but these guys were definitely on a much different level than Qyksand. Spencer and I were in sync instantly. Buck and Davy's guitars were tight and on point. I even saw Spencer suppress a grin. Then, after about thirty seconds, Davy waved us off.

"Stop, stop, stop!" he shouted. We stopped. "What band did you say you're from?"

"Qyksand?" I said. "We're kind of mid–glam metal."

"His girlfriend said they sell out the Shed every week," Kirby chimed in from the back.

"The Shed is a fucking dump," Davy said. " 'Behind Your Eyes.' Go."

I counted us off again, and we started in on Whyte Python's attempt at a power ballad. After about twenty seconds, Davy waved Buck and Spencer off, and I solo-drummed while he sang.

I closed my eyes and listened to Davy adjust his tone to fill the space that the guitars had left, finding a tighter rhythm with my drumbeat. You don't always notice the little things the pros do until you actually get to play with them, and what he was doing was really impressive. Ron would not have been able to do that. He wouldn't have even known he should try. I felt guilty comparing the two of them, but it was impossible not to.

"All right, stop," Davy said.

"He's good, Davy," Kirby said.

"Get the fuck out, Kirby," Davy said.

"Righto," Kirby said, and he left the room.

Buck pointed a thumb at the door as Kirby pulled it shut behind him. "Fucking record company assigned this guy to us," he said. "Babysitter. You know how it is."

"No, he doesn't," Davy said. "Gimme the opener to 'Summer Saturday.'"

I tried not to let all Davy's little digs and insults get to me. Instead, I channeled it into the drumming, like I had always done. I went into "Summer Saturday," and the guys joined in. We played that one all the way through; then they all kicked into "Radio Heaven" without saying anything. Something they had practiced, probably, to trip me up. But I hung in. Or at least, I think I did.

Near the end of the song, Davy stopped playing. So did Buck and Spencer, but my eyes were closed, so if Davy waved me off, I didn't see it, and nobody told me to stop, so I kept playing. I soloed through the rest of "Radio Heaven," and then: I don't know, dude, I just kind of . . . went off. I drilled down on the drums like a machine gun, and I felt my face getting angry for reasons I still don't totally understand. Everything I felt went into the drumming, just like it always had when I was a scared little kid making my way through foster homes, hiding from my own fear and temper and insecurity inside the rhythm my sore fingers banged out onto any surface in my way. I don't know how long Davy was screaming "Stop!"—hopefully only once or twice—but when I opened my eyes, they were all looking at me sideways. *Dammit.*

Finally, Davy sighed. "Look," he said. "We don't have time to screw around here."

"Okay," I said. I laid the drumsticks on the floor where I'd found them and stood. "Thanks for the opportunity, I guess."

"Hang on," Davy said. "Before you go, I have three questions for you. Number one, do you party?"

"Yeah," I said.

"Number two, do you like babes?"

"Definitely."

"Number three," Davy said as he pushed up off his stool and stood with his face just a few inches away from mine. "Who's the best band on the planet?"

Jesus, with this guy! I tried not to roll my eyes. "You are," I said.

"No!" Davy barked. "*We* are."

"Huh?" I asked.

"Welcome to Whyte Python, Rikki Thunder," Davy said. He

pointed a finger under my chin. "Don't fuck it up." Then he couldn't hold it in anymore. Davy Bones broke out into a wide grin. Spencer and Buck started to giggle. *They were fucking with me, dude!*

"No way," I said.

"Way," Davy said. I pumped my fist. Spencer screamed. Buck screamed and smashed a bottle over his own head. Then Spencer threw a chair and Buck yanked a sconce off the wall, showering the room with sparks. They proceeded to trash the room. Suddenly we all had beers. Davy held his hand up, and we exchanged an absolutely epic high five. Then he pulled me in close, and his smile got really tight.

"Just remember one thing," he said. "This is my fucking band."

12

TAWNY PACED back and forth in the empty record store.

Rikki had gone into the back room two hours ago. She heard them playing music for all of ten minutes, and then the rest of the time it was just muffled screaming and breaking glass.

That was probably a good sign. But what if it wasn't? Were they celebrating in there, or had the Whyte Python guys murdered Rikki?

Doubt crept in. What if this didn't work? What if they didn't like him? What if they offered him the job, and he turned them down? What if this was going to be another Bulgaria?

Oh no.

All these outcomes were possible, despite the work she had put into preventing them. A year of research. Months of planning. Multiple aliases. It could all be pointless.

After all, Qyksand was modeled after the likes of Mötley Crüe and Ratt. They had that reckless garage band sound, with snarling vocals and dirty guitars. Whyte Python was prettier and more polished, closer to Van Halen or Bon Jovi.

She believed Rikki Thunder would bring an extra edge to their sound that would improve the music, that would make them stand out and bridge the two worlds of metal. But what if they didn't hear it like she heard it? What if they just didn't get along?

You could move the chess pieces all you wanted, but there was only so much you could do if the elements didn't blend.

She tried to push away the idea that she might have just failed her twenty-step plan at step three and paced some more, wringing her hands.

The door to the back room finally burst open. Rikki Thunder stumbled through it, obviously hammered.

"Rikki, what happened?" Tawny said. "You were in there for hours, and I heard a *lot* of stuff breaking."

"*Igottthegig!*" Rikki slurred.

Tawny felt pure, electric joy explode throughout her whole body. She ran across the room and leapt into Thunder's arms, and they crashed to the floor. She smothered him with kisses.

"You did it, babe," she cooed. "I'm so excited for you!"

And really for me, she thought.

It was working. So far, at least. The biggest hurdle of her grand vision—the plan that she knew would change everything, the plan that they all laughed at—had been cleared. Nobody would be laughing soon.

But was it this small victory, this step, that made her feel so joyful? Because she had to admit, she was happy for Thunder, too. Just looking at him lying on the floor, grinning his sweet, simple, shit-faced smile up at her—a boy whose dreams were coming true.

The thought popped into her head: *The plumber would be so proud.* She surprised herself a bit by how much it all tugged at her heart-strings, and then she shook it off. She had work to do. This was just the beginning.

"I have to puke," Rikki Thunder said.

Tawny giggled, and she helped him to his feet. "Okay, go, go, go!" she shouted, and patted him on the back, steering him toward the bathroom.

Once he had crashed through the door and she heard him vomiting, Tawny left the record store and ran across the street to a phone booth.

She shut herself inside and dialed a number from memory.

A man's voice answered. "Yes?"

"Yeah, it's me," she said. "It worked. He's in."

13

A NJA KOERTIG WAS going to find out whether she had been
betrayed in less than a minute.

It all came down to whether the old man in the cigar store
had talked. Or, at least, talked about her. She hadn't asked him for
much—just to use his fire escape. He understood that he was better
off not asking any questions, for both of their protection. But being a
Stasi informant wasn't exactly a binary thing. You weren't recruited,
trained, given missions, asked to swear loyalty oaths, or any of that.
For East Berliners, it was something that popped up in your life from
time to time, always when you least expected it. If they suspected
you had dirt on someone—counterintelligence, of course, but also
agitators, or people distributing banned materials, or even *thinking*
about slipping through the Wall—they knocked on your door and
reminded you that you had a patriotic duty to tell them whatever you
know.

And by the way, when they asked, they also reminded you where
your children went to school, or what medicine your father needed,
or whatever mattered to you most that they could take away if they
felt called to. For the country, of course. So the easy thing was to
just tell them everything you knew. They said this smiling, grinning
big while they threatened. They were going to find out anyway, they
reminded you. The question was whether you would suffer in the
meantime or not. So went the sales pitch. Fucking Stasi.

The old man in the cigar store wasn't a freedom fighter. She didn't
think he would keep a stiff upper lip and suffer the consequences for
the sake of a revolution—and certainly not to protect some teenage

kid with a backpack full of spray paint, even if she reminded him of his granddaughter. But he also seemed like the type who didn't overshare, which was all Anja could ask for. He might have answered their questions about some things, about some people. But maybe not Anja. Particularly if they didn't ask about her specifically; she didn't think he was the type to offer her up unprompted.

She was about to find out.

The night was cool, but an anxious sweat coated Anja's shaky hands, risking her grip on the fire escape that could be accessed only from the rear window behind his store. No more time to hesitate. She scampered upward—two stories, three, four. Anja poked her head above the surface of the rooftop. If he had told them she was coming, they would be waiting there. But the rooftop was empty.

An important first test, passed with flying colors. She climbed onto the flat surface and sat, hugging her knees. A cold breeze whistled through alleys and across the rooftops around her. Anja focused on catching her breath. It had not looked so high up from the street. From this height she could see beyond the neighborhood and all the way to the river, where the Palace of the Republic glowed under powerful spotlights.

Anja swung the backpack off her shoulders and took out the plastic cassette case—*Paranoid* by Black Sabbath—and popped it open. There was a tiny slip of paper under the cassette, and when she unfolded it, it confirmed what she'd expected. Everything was exactly as Peter said it would be—and there was no going back now. There was no room for fear, for second thoughts, for regrets. This rooftop, on this night, had been Anja's destiny for a very long time.

Anja refolded the paper and placed it back in its case, then tucked *Paranoid* in the backpack where it came from. She stood, strapped the pack onto her thin shoulders again, and forced herself to take several deep breaths. It was time.

Anja ran to the edge of the building and jumped.

14

SULLY AND MARTY were psyched, of course.

When I told them I was gonna be in Whyte Python, they started cheering and jumping in circles all around the room.

They settled down a little when they realized that they didn't get to be in Whyte Python, too—and they were hella sad when I told them Python was going to be either rehearsing, recording, or playing pretty much nonstop, so I was going to move into their house. But still, their smiles were real. They were happy for me.

Ron, though, was pissed.

"So that's it, then?" Ron said. "That's it for Qyksand, 'cause you decided?"

"It doesn't have to be," I said. "I'm just the drummer, Ron—and Tawny said she would help you guys find a new one."

"Give me a break, Rikki . . . Tawny will help us." Ron rolled his eyes. "All right."

I didn't know what that was supposed to mean, but the whole tone of the room changed when Ron said it. Marty got this faraway look in his eyes, and Sully even sniffled a little.

This wasn't going the way I planned it in my mind at all. I tried to bring things back around.

"Hey, chin up, Sully," I said. "This isn't goodbye. We'll get you guys a new drummer, and maybe you can even go on tour with us!"

Sully smiled a little and nodded. He was trying to be brave. But Ron was unmoved. "Oh, thanks for the charity," he said.

I honestly didn't understand why Ron was so mad. "Bro, I honestly don't understand why you're so mad," I said. "This is, like, the chance of a lifetime. Are you telling me you wouldn't take it if Python called you instead?"

"I'm telling you that I'd talk about it with you guys before I just went and did it, and moved out of the house, and broke up the band."

"Like how you told me you were applying for a job at the grocery store?" I snapped back at him. I was hoping I wouldn't have to play the ace up my sleeve, but he forced it.

It tripped Ron up for a second, but then he rebounded. "That's different," he said. "I'm still playing in the band. I'm still living in the house."

"Well, if it's so different, then why didn't you tell me about it?"

I thought I had backed Ron into a logical corner again, but he was ready for that question. "Because I knew you'd flip out over something that isn't a big deal," he yelled. "How did you even find out, anyway?" He looked at Marty and Sully, but they both shrugged.

"Tawny told me."

Ron waved his arms over his head. "Oh, big surprise there!" he shouted. Sully and Marty looked sideways at each other and winced.

Another dig at Tawny? Did the guys have a problem with her? Something else was going on here, and I didn't like it. "What the fuck is that supposed to mean?"

"And how did Tawny know?" Ron asked. "That I was applying for a job? 'Cause I sure as shit didn't tell her. Did you guys?" Marty and Sully were looking at the floor, but they both shook their heads.

I actually didn't know the answer to that question, so I pushed it out of my head as fast as I could. Sure, there were times when Tawny knew things she should have no way of knowing, and it would itch a little in my brain. But then I remembered that everything with Tawny always seemed to work out for me, and I was better off taking the ride. Up until now it had worked out for Qyksand, too, by the way, so Ron was really asking for it by accusing Tawny of . . . whatever he was accusing Tawny of.

"So, just what are you saying, Ron?" I asked. "About the love of my life?"

Ron looked away. "I'm saying"—he sighed—"that she's always creeping around our business. Trying to figure out what we're up to."

"Easy, bro," I said, holding my hands up. "That's my girl you're talking about."

"Yeah, and I don't trust her," Ron said. He looked at the others. "*We* don't trust her. And we don't think you should, either."

I looked at Sully and Marty, but they both looked in different directions. "Guys?" I said.

"Well . . ." Marty started.

"Uh-uh," I said. I waved them all off. "Got it. I'm done." I went into my bedroom and started stuffing my T-shirts and jeans and drumsticks and makeup into empty paint cans. Ron followed me in.

"Rik," he said.

"Don't Rik me, Ron!" I shouted back at him. "You don't care about this band going the distance. You're just pissed that I quit first. And you're pissed at Tawny, 'cause she helped me get a better gig."

"Oh, this is just a gig now?" Ron said. "Because I thought it was our lives, since we were just little kids. But you get a new girlfriend, and she tells you to move on, suddenly you're too good for us, huh? Come on, man, quit being an asshole."

What? This little dude had just made me feel guilty for getting my dream job and then tried to turn me against my girlfriend. *Not fucking cool!* I pointed my drumsticks at him.

"You're way over the line, Ron," I said. My head felt hot, and I squeezed my fists together. I felt so angry that I wanted to punch the walls—angry like I hadn't felt since I was a little kid.

So I twisted the knife, which I'm not proud about. I looked down at Ron and let out the words before I could pull them back. "Don't take it out on me," I said, "'cause I'm good enough to move on to a real band."

Ron's eyes got soft, and I saw that I'd hurt his feelings. Right away I felt like shit about it. But now we were even, right?

Ron held his arms out to his sides. "You're right," he said. "I'm not Davy Bones. Probably never will be. I know that. I know this is as far as I get, and it won't last much longer without you. But one thing I do know is I'm your friend."

Aw, dude! My heart melted! I wanted to take it all back. I wanted to hug Ron and tell him that he was the best friend I'd ever had, and if he really didn't want me to leave the band I wouldn't, even though it meant giving up the thing I wanted most. I opened my mouth to tell Ron I was sorry.

But then Ron kept talking.

"And as your friend," he said, "I'm telling you, Tawny is going to stab you in the back someday." His eyes got narrow and angry. "So good luck with Python. 'Cause if that falls apart, you're on your own."

I felt my heart go cold toward Ron. I grabbed as many paint cans as I could carry and pushed past him into the main room.

Marty and Sully were sitting on the couch as I blew across the room toward the exit. "Rikki," Sully said softly. I didn't even look at him. I just climbed out the window and left Qyksand behind.

15

✕

ENERAL KURT BECKER scowled as he ran a hand through his
steel-colored buzz cut.

This was an attack. Clear as day. His counterparts called
it a prank—a punishable one, to be sure—but they regarded it as a
misdemeanor antic, kids acting out. They thought this "prank" did
not have anything to do with the more serious counterintelligence
operations that had been seeping into the East German body politic
like a slow-acting poison.

It was true that Becker had bigger problems than what he was staring at—like guards taking bribes to let Western instigators through
the Wall. And those unlicensed radio broadcasts that spit propaganda
across the city, their sources so far undetected.

This thing, his subordinates said, was simple vandalism. He glared
at the East German flag that flapped in the wind overhead. The coat
of arms had been cut from the center, a jagged hole in place of the
hammer, compass, and wreath that signified the strength of the German Democratic Republic. The flag was no longer a demonstration
of tradition and power; it was a taunt now, sending a message to the
GDR, to the general secretary, to the mighty Kremlin itself: We can
behead you if we choose, and we will survive.

This was no prank, Becker thought. Perhaps if this flag flew in
front of a factory worker's house or on a country farm. He crossed the
street and shielded his eyes to take in the image completely, to let the
insult penetrate his bones and feed his rage. *This* East German flag,
missing its coat of arms like a castrated dog, flew from atop a grand,
towering flagpole at the rear entrance of the Palace of the Republic.

Home to the Volskammer, the parliament of East Germany.

This required several people, working in concert, executing in minutes but planning for hours. This was, in short, a coordinated attack on the heart of the GDR. When the call came in that morning, Becker was stunned to hear it; but he also believed they would have the perpetrators in hand soon enough. There would be footage, you see. He had a CCTV camera positioned directly across the street, on the roof of a building with perfect sightlines to the palace.

He ordered the footage recovered and was aghast to find that the camera had been disabled. At some point in the night, somebody had climbed to the roof and spray-painted the lens. The camera on the eastern side met a similar fate. No matter, he thought at first; he would recover more reliable intelligence from civilian informants obediently monitoring the building. The neighborhood was swiftly interrogated, and nobody had seen anything. It was like the vandal had swept in from the sky.

"The rooftops," he muttered to nobody. Whoever disabled those cameras must have traveled a great distance from rooftop to rooftop, like the spider person in American comic books that Becker was aware of but, out of an unwavering sense of patriotism, had dutifully not read.

He slipped into the back seat of his government limo and slammed the door.

"I want agents on the roof of that building," he growled to his aide. "I want them to disperse in all directions. Find all possible routes taken by the vandal."

His aide said nothing. He merely took notes, but Becker could read the skepticism in his eyes.

"Is there a problem with my order?"

"No, General."

"Good. When we get back to the office, I'm recalling our field agent in Los Angeles."

"Yes, General," the aide said, but Becker could still hear his hesitation.

"Speak," Becker demanded.

"The latest report suggests things are proceeding quickly in Los Angeles," the aide said. "There are new developments with the band.

Is the time right to recall your most effective agent? Even briefly?"

Becker regarded the rooftop's edge, where technicians were already installing a new CCTV camera. "Arrange for travel," he said. "This will not take long. I require someone who knows how to send a message—and then disappear."

16

I FOUND THE WHYTE PYTHON house by carefully following the directions that Spencer had written out for me. His note just said "pet wearhouse."

Believe it or not, this was all I needed to know. Their house used to be a pet supply warehouse. It had caught fire under mysterious circumstances a few years earlier, and the band got a good deal on the rent because the L.A. County health inspector's office declared that it was haunted.

I knew right away that my new living situation was an upgrade from the paint store because the pet warehouse had a door that opened and closed. I was moving up in the world, all right!

I knocked. Nobody answered. It was early in the night, and I could hear music and chatter inside. I started to feel a little anxious, like all those times I stood waiting for my new foster parents to open the door and let me in. If Tawny had been there, she would've just opened the door and walked inside, but she had been suddenly called away on a trip for her job, so your old buddy Rikki Thunder was on his own. It was one of those moments where I realized just how comfortable I was with Tawny taking the lead on everything, and Ron's warning rang in my ears. But just for a second.

I shook off the stone in my chest, sacked up, and knocked again, harder this time. The door swung open, and a woman was standing on the other side in nothing but a Whyte Python crop-top and bikini bottoms that said "Budweiser."

"Hey," she said. She looked familiar. Maybe she worked for Budweiser? I had definitely seen those bikini bottoms on a poster somewhere.

"Hey," I said.

"Are you Marco?" she asked.

"No, I'm Rikki Thunder," I said.

"Oh," she said, and closed the door.

Before I could knock again, the door opened. It was Spencer this time, wearing sunglasses and a tank top, with a massive blunt stuck under his upper lip. "Rikki!" he said. "Hey! Come on in!" Spencer held the door wide, and I stepped inside.

All the jitters went away when I saw that it was basically the same party atmosphere as the Qyksand house. It was just *bigger*. It was still early, but already there were more drugs, more girls, louder music.

"Welcome to the Python Pit." Spencer put his hands on his hips and admired the place with me. "Hey, you need any help with your luggage?"

"Sure," I said, and I handed Spencer some paint cans with my stuff in them. He hurled them across the room as hard as he could.

"Grab a beer and get comfortable," Spencer said, and then he chased the Budweiser lady off somewhere.

I took a few steps into the room and grabbed a beer out of an actual cooler. Kirby Smoot appeared from behind me and put a hand on my shoulder. "Rikki, welcome," he said in his charming British accent. We shook hands. "Your contract is in process as we speak. If you need anything before then, I'm your man."

"Tight."

"Out!" Davy shouted from the back of the room.

"And off I go," Kirby said, happily enough. He slipped out the front door.

I moved through the mess of people toward the back, where Davy sat on the couch playing acoustic guitar. Three groupies flanked him, swooning. "Hey, Thunder," Davy said.

"Hey, Davy, how's it going?" I said.

"You remember what I told you?"

"Your band."

"Then it's goin' just fine." Davy smiled. "Ladies, meet Rikki Thunder. He's the new Barry. How 'bout we make him feel welcome?" One of Davy's groupies got off the couch. She was young and pretty, with crimped platinum hair and just enough pink fabric to cover the important stuff. She moved toward me seductively, but I held out a hand to shake.

"Uh, hey," I said. "Yeah, I'm kind of with someone? So . . ."

"Gonna have to break you of that habit," Davy said, and the groupie nodded. I played it cool with a grin, but I meant it when I said I wasn't interested. Tawny and I weren't in one of those "out of sight, out of mind" relationships like you see on *Dynasty* or whatever.

Spencer came back into the room. "My friend Kevin says girlfriends are for pussies," he slurred.

"Okay," I said.

"Hey, Rikki, watch this!" I heard Buck shout from the corner. I looked his way and saw that he was holding a lamp. He took the lampshade off, and the white bulb cast a shadow of Buck against the wall that looked like Animal from the Muppets.

Then Buck opened his mouth wide and bit the light bulb. His jaw clamped shut on the little wire inside and his whole body started shaking and convulsing, until sparks fired from the electrical outlet and the power in the room went out.

Buck dropped to the floor in a heap.

"Oh my God, is he okay?" I asked.

"Probably," Davy said casually. "There's something wrong with him. I don't think he can die." He laid his guitar on the couch and stood. "We party hard around here, Thunder. Try to keep up. Find something to chug; we need to make a toast."

I looked down at the bottle in my hand and realized it was empty already. I stepped over Buck's body toward the cooler, but the cute girl I'd just introduced myself to pressed a bottle of vodka into my hand before I could get there. She brushed her fingers against mine after she let go and winked. I saw that Spencer had vodka, too, and Davy had his Jack Daniels.

"Whyte Python never dies!" Davy shouted, raising his drink in the air.

"Whyte Python never dies!" Spencer and I shouted back.

Buck mumbled something from the floor that might have been "Whyte Python never dies." Davy and Spencer and I drank.

"Just pour a little on him, so he feels like he participated," Davy said, so I poured some vodka on Buck, and I swear the booze sizzled and smoked a tiny bit when it hit his back. Damn.

"You ready for this, Thunder?" Davy asked.

"I was born ready," I said. The power came back, and Spencer turned up the music and everyone cheered. The party was on.

17

⚡

THREE MEN AND one woman sat around a conference table in a secure room in a government complex in Langley, Virginia.

The four officials were all middle-aged, dressed in navy and dark gray suits and thumbing through orderly stacks of papers, while a young technician hovered nearby fiddling with the controls on a slide carousel. Ed Lonsa—tall, bespectacled, balding, and seated at the head of the table—snapped his fingers. "How's it coming, Parker?"

The technician gave a thumbs-up in response. "Ready to go, Deputy Director," he said.

"Okay, I'll take it from here," Lonsa said, and Parker moved to the back of the room.

The deputy director stood and took up the clicker that connected to the carousel. "Officers Stryker, Mancuso, and Boone," he said to the others. "Congratulations. You've been carefully selected to join this team, thanks to your unique expertise in field propaganda. The work you will do over the next several years will contribute to one of the most ambitious and unorthodox programs that our agency has ever launched; and if it's successful, it will promote democracy, improve the safety and standing of the United States in the eastern hemisphere, and create an entirely new toolkit for global political-influence programming.

"This initiative has been underway for some time now, and we're expanding the team as we move on to phase two. Folks, welcome to Project Facemelt. Lights, please."

Parker turned off the lights. On a projector screen against the wall, the slide image showed maps of western Asia and Eastern Europe, the corner of the world controlled by the Soviet regime and known as the Eastern Bloc.

"As you're all aware," Lonsa said, "the Eastern Bloc has become a powder keg. Power structures are collapsing, and organizers are collaborating and recruiting. Regime change is on the horizon everywhere from East Germany to Bulgaria. As a consequence, the various reigning powers are cracking down hard on dissent. Sources are drying up in Eastern Bloc nations. Assets are vanishing off the face of the earth. We're at an inflection point, folks. The stakes are high. Now. This"—he clicked the remote, and a band photo of the newly recast Whyte Python appeared on the screen—"is Whyte Python," Lonsa said.

Spontaneous laughter filled the room.

Lonsa continued. "They're an up-and-coming rock band based in Southern California."

As he spoke, he clicked through photos of the band. A picture of Davy Bones onstage, reaching out to screaming girls. A picture of Spencer Dooley asleep sitting up on a couch with a joint falling from his lips and burning a hole in his leather jacket. A picture of Buck Sweet being thrown through a plate glass window.

"Last month, Whyte Python signed a three-album contract with Andromeda Records," Lonsa said. "They're about to go worldwide. After the release of their first album, they're launching an eight-month national tour."

The lone woman in the room, Officer Catherine Stryker, raised her hand. "And these . . ."

"Jokers?" Officer Boone huffed.

"Satanists?" Officer Mancuso offered.

The deputy director checked his notes. "They're a . . . glam-forward pop metal rock and roll band," he said.

"Fine," Stryker said. "And people actually like their music?"

"It's my understanding that they rock," Lonsa said. He slid his readers down the bridge of his nose, checking his notes again. "Yes, they rock hard."

Officer Stryker nodded, satisfied for now. Officer Mancuso crossed his arms and rolled his eyes.

"Now, then," Lonsa said. "Young people across Eastern Europe and Asia are demonstrating a preference for rock bands that meet Whyte Python's profile. And our intelligence shows that leadership in the region views these bands as harmless." Lonsa leveled a knowing gaze at the group. "We think metal is our way in."

"And why these guys?" Stryker again, so far the only one appearing to take Lonsa's briefing on Whyte Python seriously.

"They're in the right place at the right time," Lonsa said. "Whyte Python is about to . . . hit it big, as the kids say. They have the right sound. And they're still small enough that we can manipulate their lineup, their lyrics, and their look to suit our purposes. The plan is to use the band and its overall messaging to foment unrest and fire up the revolutionaries. Bingo, bongo: regime change."

"This is ridiculous," Mancuso said. As a field expert, he knew the Eastern Bloc, its politics and personalities, like the back of his hand. His work over the past decade had contributed to a lot of the democratic progress that DD Lonsa was effectively taking credit for. .

"Your concern is noted, Officer Mancuso," Lonsa said. "And I don't necessarily disagree. But the high-ups think it will work, so we're going to give it our all."

"I have a question," Stryker said. "What if this *does* actually work?"

"Then it's a job well done," Lonsa said. "I don't understand the question."

"I'm saying, what happens when their governments are in tatters and the whole Eastern Bloc is acting like . . . these guys?"

Lonsa shrugged. "We're breaking oppressive regimes here, Officer Stryker. What happens after is someone else's job. Now, I'd like to bring in our principal field officer to walk you through the particulars." He nodded to Parker, and Parker opened the door.

"They're ready," Parker said to someone waiting outside.

A tall, blond woman entered the room, her hair gathered in a high, tight ponytail, her tan hue, rosy complexion, and heavy-handed smoky eye makeup betraying time spent far from the fluorescent lights of a government briefing room. The officer wore a black pencil skirt and crisp white blouse beneath an oversized blazer, accentuated by huge shoulder pads and cinched at the waist by an absolutely massive belt. She strode into the room with a determined expression perhaps two clicks more confident than would be expected of a woman of her youth and her rank at the agency.

This woman was known to Rikki Thunder as Tawny Spice. Broken-armed Barry Gorman knew her as Shawna Peppers. They were both wrong.

"Officer Price," Lonsa said, taking his seat. "The floor is yours."

The woman moved to the front of the room and took up the clicker. "Good morning," she said. "Amanda Price, AID."

"Officer Price works with the Asian Intelligence Division," Lonsa said. "But she's been embedded in West Hollywood, California, for over a year. She identified the asset"—he checked his notes—"Rick Thunder—"

"Rikki," Amanda Price corrected him.

Lonsa raised an eyebrow. "Rikki," he said. "Officer Price has gained his trust and inserted him with the band."

"Why him?" Stryker, again.

"Rikki Thunder's skills as a musician exceed those of the band's former drummer, and his background in the foster care system pre-disposes him to seek justice for those in need. He possesses a naïveté that will make it possible for us to influence him as needed. Furthermore, Project Facemelt has significantly improved his standing. He was struggling with his previous band, living in poverty. We believe he can be motivated to support the mission."

"He meets the prime criteria for an asset," Lonsa said. "Price, take us through the objectives."

"Thank you, DD," Amanda said. Our goals are twofold." *Click.* Behind her, a photo of Whyte Python onstage.

"First: we elevate the band by improving their music, expanding their audience, and gently adjusting the lyrics to trigger Eastern Bloc listeners." *Click.* A map of the Eastern Bloc appeared.

"Second," Price said, "when the opportunity presents itself, we take the band on a Whyte Python world tour."

As she spoke, Amanda Price clicked through photos from rock concerts around the world. "A powerful concert can stick with a person for the rest of their life," she said.

Click. Young men in an arena, raising their fists in unity.

"Look at these kids. They'd follow their rock stars into war."

Click. A woman screaming and holding handfuls of her own hair.

"We're gonna pack them together by the thousands in stadiums across the bloc," Price said, "and inject a sophisticated propaganda campaign directly into their hearts and panties."

"Price!" Lonsa scolded.

"Apologies," Price said, contrite. "I've been spending a lot of time with these guys . . . Let's meet the boys, shall we?"

Click. A photo of Kirby Smoot, chugging from a bottle of Pepto Bismol.

"Kirby Smoot," Amanda said. "The band manager. Andromeda Records assigned him to babysit when they signed their record deal. He's a useless pushover, but he'll provide decent cover."

Click. A photo of Davy Bones, glammed up and posing for the camera in all his glory. Lips pursed, he scowled at the camera from behind a dazzling mane of long golden hair.

"Lawrence Barkley. Aka Davy Bones. Lead singer, rhythm guitar. And the band leader. Twenty-four years old. Born and raised in Southern California. A ladies' man, with a monstrous ego. He was our first option as an asset after Kirby, but we eliminated him. Too self-absorbed. Too thin-skinned."

"Loser," Officer Boone muttered.

Click. A photo of Spencer Dooley. Tousled black hair framed his pretty, bone-thin face, and he wore eyeshadow and brick-red rouge on his pale cheekbones. He looked sleepy and stoned.

"Spencer Dooley," Amanda said. "Bass guitar. Twenty-three. A complete idiot. We eliminated him as an asset because we aren't sure he has the ability to understand complicated ideas or retain them long-term."

Click. A photo of Buck Sweet, shirtless in suspenders and holding a stovepipe hat, his nose bloodied. He was shorter and thicker than the others, and his brown hair was not quite as long but was twice as tall. He smiled through a massive mouth full of what looked like too many stained, square teeth.

"Robert 'Buck' Sweet," Amanda said. "Lead guitar. Twenty-seven years old . . . we think. A masochistic lunatic. He's been arrested nine times, almost always at Orange Julius restaurants. But, in fairness, in most cases it's been for his own protection."

Click. A picture of Rikki Thunder playing drums.

Amanda suppressed a smile. "And Richard Henderson," she said. "Aka Rikki Thunder. Twenty-three. As mentioned, his psych profile is ideal for a good asset. Discreet. Trusting. Reasonably sharp, but gullible. Capable of deescalating conflict."

Click. A photo of a scrawny Rikki Thunder wearing torn-up jeans and a tattered Tower Records T-shirt, staring off sadly into the distance through smudged black eyeliner.

"He's an orphan, forever seeking a family. He craves acceptance and is determined to please. We inserted him into the band last week."

Mancuso jumped in. "Is anyone else upset about this? There's seventy years of experience around this table. You're gonna waste us on managing a hair band?"

Amanda Price snapped her pencil in half. "*They're not a hair band!*" she shouted. Her colleagues studied her while she took a deep breath and composed herself. "They hate that term, *hair band*. Glam band, please. They prefer *metal*, but I'll be the first to admit it's more like pop rock—"

"We're not abandoning anything," Lonsa said. "Right, Price?"

"That's correct," Amanda said, her gaze still leveled on Mancuso. "While we have high confidence that Whyte Python will inspire civil unrest, the tour also gives cover for a team of agency staff traveling with the band. The roadies for the Whyte Python tour will almost exclusively be our people, conducting fieldwork. Now. Are there any questions?"

Boone raised his hand. "Orange Julius isn't really a restaurant," he said, making meaningful eye contact with each member of the assembled group.

Amanda ignored him. "Thank you, everyone," she said, and laced her fingers together. "I'm excited to work with all of you."

"Good," said Lonsa. "Now it's time to reveal yourself to the asset and bring him on board."

Amanda was surprised. "Already?" she asked.

"We're gonna need Thunder's cooperation in order to introduce new lyrics and implement the costume changes," her boss said. "He walks us in. This is your plan, Price."

"Director, that *is* my plan, but it's not the right time," she said. "We just got him in the band. And also . . ." Amanda hesitated.

"Go ahead," Lonsa said.

"I mentioned that he's an orphan—his emotional attachment to me has grown pretty . . . intense," she said. "He's likely to have a negative reaction when he learns about my cover. I need time to set it up the right way."

"Translation," Mancuso interrupted. "She's worried about breaking the pretty boy's heart."

"I am *worried* about losing the asset," Price said.

"Okay." Lonsa held his hands up. "Hold off while he gets settled with the band. We don't want to put too much on this kid all at once. But, Price, don't string it out too long."

"Yes, sir," Price said. "I mean, no, sir, I won't. Understood."

"Great," Lonsa said. "You're dismissed. The rest of you, stick around." Deputy Director Lonsa produced a cardboard box from underneath the table, and he dumped out its contents in front of Team Facemelt. Glam band cassettes, cocaine vials, joints, hair spray, and whiskey bottles spilled across the table.

"Immersion training begins now."

18

⚡

VIKTOR DELIVERED A fresh stack of papers to his boss, who at
seven a.m. was already settled into his office, drinking coffee
and reading through reports.

The rezidentura office in Southern California was laid back by
most standards, but Rezident Ivanov remained strict about reading
the full day's reports no later than nine. Viktor suspected that it was
because his boss started drinking his favorite "spicy American cock-
tails" at ten, but he would never say so out loud.

Rezident Ivanov didn't look up as Viktor carefully slid the new
intelligence data onto the corner of the desk.

"Thank you, Viktor," Ivanov said.

"You're welcome, Rezident," Viktor said. "There's a new package
in the report from the Stasi. General Becker asked that you call him
after you've read it."

"Mm-hmm," Rezident Ivanov replied. Viktor watched his boss
roll his eyes at the mention of his East German counterpart.

"Will there be anything else, Rezident?" Viktor asked.

Rezident Ivanov waved Viktor off. The assistant turned away from
his boss and was about to leave the office when the sound of a folder
slapping hard against the desk made him stop short. Rezident Ivanov
called after him. "Wait," he said.

Viktor turned around and saw the older man studying the blue
folder sent over from the office of General Becker. Rezident Ivanov
took off his glasses and looked at Viktor for the first time. And he
asked the same question that intelligence officers all across the Eastern Bloc would ask that day.

"Who is Rikki Thunder?"

19

GAZZARRI'S!
  I'd only been there as a fan before, and now I was actually backstage with my new band at one of the most famous clubs on the Sunset Strip. The place had been a staple since the 1960s, and everyone from the Doors to Buffalo Springfield to Van Halen got launched there. It was a known thing—if you were playing Gazzarri's, you were *making it*.

All the other metal bands we wanted to be played there, from Ratt to Mötley, from Cinderella to Guns N' Roses, from Quiet Riot to Poison, and everyone in between. Whyte Python had been headlining there off and on since they announced the Andromeda Records deal. And on that night, they would debut their new drummer.

I couldn't believe this was finally happening. The place looked so much bigger from the stage. The crowd that night would be the biggest I had played for, even as an opening act. My nerves were definitely tingling backstage while the girl-group opener wrapped up their set.

And then a really bad thought settled in, at the worst possible time. I had been so busy practicing and getting used to life with the new band all week that I hadn't thought about what might happen if I fucked up during my first show.

Until now. Right before my first show.

If I was off rhythm, or forgot my cues, or anything like that, then it might be all over for me, right there. It would be way easier for them to cut me right away if I got off to a bad start, and maybe see if they could steal a drummer from a more established group. That kind of thing happened a lot when bands were just about to make it.

I was so anxious that I only drank, like, seven beers, and barely smoked any weed backstage.

So I was standing at the back, watching the roadies swap out the instruments. Nobody had done that for me before, either. We always had to lug our own gear in Qyksand. *What if these dudes set up my kit wrong?* I was stuck in my own head, which is a bad place to be.

Then I felt a long arm drape around my shoulders. I looked to my left, and Davy Bones was smiling at me. He was probably the last one that I needed right now.

Davy hadn't thawed much over the last week. He still took his little digs here and there, calling me "rookie" and criticizing my partying. Sometimes, when we were practicing, I would catch him throwing dark looks my way. I was worried that I was playing something wrong, or that he just didn't like me for some reason.

I was even a little worried that if I fucked things up for the band, he would have me killed; because he kept telling me, "If you fuck this up for us, I'm going to have you killed," pretty much every day. I committed to never showing any weakness, because he seemed to be looking for it all the time.

"You good?" Davy asked.

"Yeah," I said. "Yeah, bro, never better."

Davy chuckled. "Hey, look, Rikki," he said. "I've been hard on you this week, because we don't have any time to screw around. But you're playing great. You're better than Barry by a long shot. Just empty your mind and do your thing. You'll be fine."

I was speechless. Who was this guy all of a sudden, Mr. Miyagi? Whoever was speaking through Davy was making me feel so much better. At least I knew that the band had my back, that our lead singer wasn't rooting against me. I swallowed and nodded.

"Thanks," I managed to say.

"Davy," Kirby interrupted. He looked especially proud of himself. "I took care of that dispute over the lyrics to 'Shake Them Buns.' We can get it on the album now, and not a second too soon—"

"Yeah, cool. Hey, can you go find me some blow?"

Kirby's entire body appeared to deflate. "Uh, of course," he mumbled, shuffling off the stage. A moment later, I could hear him screaming at the lighting guys, "It should be *magic-hour gold*!"

Davy gave me a thump on the back. "Come on," he said. "Band chant."

Davy led me back to the space offstage where the rest of the guys were huddled up, and we joined the circle, our massive hair forming a single unit. Davy put his hand in the middle. Buck and Spencer joined him, and then I put my hand on top.

"Who are we?" Davy yelled.

"Whyte Python!" we yelled back.

DAVY: And why are we here?

US: To tear the roof off!

DAVY: Why else?

US: To get laid!

DAVY: Why else?

US: There is nothing else!

DAVY: Whyte Python never dies!

US: Whyte Python never dies!

The lead singer from the opening band shouted, "Ladies and gentlemen, Whyte Python!"

We raised our hands and screamed, and high-fived, and bumped heads, and ran onto the stage.

The crowd was so loud when we came out that it hurt my head. I was caught totally off guard by how many people there were, and how crazy fired up they were to see us, that I walked straight into my drum set and almost knocked it all over.

Even at our best shows, none of the Qyksand fans ever reacted like *this*. They were stomping their feet and clapping their hands and screaming stuff like "Python!" and "I love you, Davy!"

And, dude, there were Thunder groupies! I saw them here and there, throughout the crowd—young chicks wearing white cutoff T-shirts decorated with a lightning bolt that ended with the head of a snake at the tip, and the word "Thunderstorm" around it. The shirts looked a little too professional to be some homemade thing, and it wasn't band-licensed merch, so somebody else was making money off them, which was kind of not cool, but I was still really honored!

I was standing there like an idiot, taking it all in, when Buck leaned over my shoulder.

"You gotta sit at the drums to play 'em," he whispered. I snapped out of my daze and nodded. Buck winked at me. I took my seat.

Davy struck a power pose at the edge of the stage and leaned forward. He held the microphone above his head and tilted his chin up to the ceiling. He closed his eyes, filling his chest with oxygen.

And then he screamed, "*We are Whyte Python!*"

I clacked my sticks together, and we launched into "Summer Saturday" just as Davy finished screaming. Once I had made it through the first few seconds okay, I settled in and let the adrenaline take over. We sounded loud and clean. After the first chorus, Davy took the microphone off its stand and strutted over to me.

"I want you all to give a big welcome to the newest member of Whyte Python," Davy yelled, "Rikki Thunder!" I went into a little drum solo, and the crowd went nuts. I even heard a few chants of "Thunderstorm!"

Once Davy went back to his spot and we settled into the song, I scanned the faces in the crowd. I have to admit, I was holding out a little hope that I might see Ron and the guys there. But no such luck.

There was only one person that *really* mattered, though. And after a few seconds, I spotted her.

20

L OOK AT THESE dopes!" Officer Boone chuckled.

"Shhh," Amanda said, pushing him. Boone looked ridiculous in his Dockers and CIA-issue jean jacket, a man squarely in middle age, with short, curly gray hair trying to blend into the metal scene at Gazzarri's. She shouldn't even be standing next to him. He stuck out like a light bulb in a dark room. But Boone was hanging close to her. He seemed to be afraid of the crowd.

A trio of young women crashed into each other in front of them, spilling purple drinks all over each other and the floor.

"This place is gross," Boone said.

"You're gonna have to come around to it if you wanna write the music," Amanda said.

Boone shrugged it off. Then he noticed that the women who had just made a huge mess a few steps away were wearing matching T-shirts. They were white, cut off just above the belly button, with a lightning bolt that ended in a snakehead. They said "Thunderstorm."

"Those T-shirts," he said. "Are those agency work? Did Stryker make them?"

Amanda winked. "We started with twelve of them," she said. "Gave 'em away before showtime. These girls fought over them like wild animals."

Boone arched an eyebrow. "Really?" He nodded toward Rikki Thunder. "Over *him*?"

Amanda nodded. "Just keep an open mind, Darrell," she said. "And go get a beer. We shouldn't be together anyway." Boone frowned and began nudging his way toward the bar.

Amanda turned her attention back to the stage. The band sounded *good*. She had been right about one thing: Rikki Thunder improved their whole product. It was subtle, but it was there already, in just the first few seconds of their first song. His drumming was tighter and louder in just the right ways, and it injected a little hint of aggression, maybe even danger, into the music.

It was something that you wouldn't have noticed was missing before, but now there was no going back. The other guys in the band were feral morons, but they were also really talented musicians with good ears. She was sure that they noticed Rikki's additions, too. Her asset would be secure.

Rikki spotted her, and she saw him smile broadly. She smiled back, more instinct than training. Who could help it, against that wide-open grin?

She winked at him, flashed devil horns. Mouthed the words "I love you," and then felt acid in her stomach. She had been standing in this exact same spot only a week ago making the same eyes at Barry Gorman, who she would go on to severely injure in the woods later that night.

Rikki Thunder didn't deserve that. She hoped she would never have to break his arms.

Emboldened by his woman's show of support, Rikki banged on the drums joyfully. He sounded *awesome*. They all did. She glanced back at the bar, where even Boone was approvingly nodding his head to "Summer Saturday."

"Holy shit," Amanda said to herself, "this is gonna work." And then she started to sing along.

21

MUSIC MONTAGE: LET THE GOOD TIMES ROLL!

Song: "Summer Saturday" by Whyte Python

A greenroom
A raucous party rages post-concert. Tawny leaps into Rikki's arms.
Spencer blows booze from a bottle onto a lighter, creating a massive
flame. Buck chases a live chicken around the party with an oversize
fork. Davy and Rikki exchange a meaningful high five.

A large music venue in Los Angeles
A poster for Whyte Python outside the door of the club. A hand slaps
a sticker on top of it that says, "Sold Out."

A recording studio
Whyte Python is laying down tracks while Amanda Price observes
from the control room. She winces and bites her lower lip. She
doesn't like what she hears.

The Python Pit
Davy is asleep at the dining table, drooling on a notebook labeled
"Songs." Amanda tiptoes up to him, leans over carefully, and slides
the book out.
She tiptoes out the front door and crosses the street to a sedan parked
underneath a streetlight, then slides into the passenger seat. Officer
Boone is in the driver's seat. He trades the book for a matching one.

Boone's face reveals his concerns: *Won't Davy Bones realize?* Amanda's expression assures him: *It won't be an issue.*

Amanda slides the new songbook under Davy's chin.

A sparse apartment in Los Angeles

A tall man in a weathered trench coat enters the apartment and drops his travel bag onto the floor. He is large, muscular, with a curly mustache and his head shaved bald. He crosses the room, past a wall covered with black-and-white photos of the band members in Whyte Python, each meticulously marked with Post-it notes scribbled on in German, some connected by string to photos of other people in the band's orbit. A photo of Rikki Thunder is circled in red ink. The bald man punches this photo with the side of his fist as he passes. A ritual. He conducts a quick search of the apartment: the hair over the bedroom door remains in place; the telephoto lens of his camera is pointed exactly west-northwest, just as he left it. The apartment has not been disturbed during his time away, traversing East Berlin's rooftops on a bizarre mission from General Becker.

The German returns to his bag and retrieves a blue folder, the standard color for intelligence materials on this operation. He sits at his desk and puts on a pair of headphones attached to a cassette deck, then slides in a tape that he recovered outside the condemned pet warehouse on his way home from the airport. It has collected many phone calls while he was in Berlin. He has a report to file.

An album-release party

Andromeda Records rents out a ballroom to celebrate the global release of Whyte Python's debut album, *All Squeeze, No Venom.*

Davy brings the entire Los Angeles Lakers cheerleading squad as his date.

Rikki attends, wearing a tuxedo with the sleeves torn off; his date, Tawny Spice, politely steps out of frame for photographs, insisting that the day should be only about the band.

Buck arrives in a T-shirt and jean shorts, with an eight ball of cocaine, a chainsaw, and a live raccoon. He is almost immediately arrested for "general mayhem," jeopardizing the band's upcoming schedule; but a call to the police station from the SAIC at the Los Angeles field office of the FBI facilitates his release, and all charges are dropped. Technically, Buck's arrest record remains at nine.

Spencer forgets to attend.

A hotel room in Los Angeles

Rikki is asleep on the couch, his head in Tawny's lap while she watches Johnny Carson performing as Carnac the Magnificent on *The Tonight Show*.

A Billboard Hot 100 graphic

Whyte Python's first album, *All Squeeze, No Venom*, debuts at number forty-three, driven largely by bulk sales in the Washington, D.C., metro region.

Ramstein Air Base, Germany

A Lockheed C-141 Starlifter lands at the United States Air Force base in southwest Germany. Private contractors arrive in unmarked vans and proceed to unload one massive wooden crate after another from the cargo plane, each crate marked with an Andromeda Records stamp on the side. They load up their vans and leave the base for parts unknown.

An Eastern European classroom

A teen boy slides a Whyte Python cassette across his desk to a teen girl. Flashes devil horns.

Music video—"Summer Saturday"

Intense orchestral music plays as the members of Whyte Python race across a Southern California beach at sunset, in a yellow open-top Jeep. They are chased by red-bikini-clad babes, riding on four-wheelers and waving swords. They appear to be very serious. This is a hunt.

An army of babes in blue bikinis ride surfboards across the waves toward the same destination as the band. They are also armed with medieval weapons.

From overhead, babes in white bikinis parasail toward the beach in a flying-V formation.

Davy looks over his shoulder as he drives, and the other members of the band gesture wildly at their multiple pursuers. This portion is played at 1.5 times speed, a subtle nod to the Beatles in *A Hard Day's Night*.

Up ahead, a mob of babes in American-flag bikinis marches toward the Jeep with torches and spears. In close-up, Davy's eyes bulge and his mouth drops in surprise. He slams on the brakes and the Jeep spins out in a perfect 180, then grinds to a stop. All parties converge in the same spot.

The orchestral music stops. The scene is silent and tense.

Davy Bones lifts his shades as the sun drops below the horizon. He looks at the camera and winks.

Davy nods at Buck Sweet. From the back seat, Buck produces a guitar and plays the opening lick to "Summer Saturday." Heads begin to nod in the crowd. Also from the back seat, Spencer Dooley joins in on his bass. Now the babes all start grooving a little. Davy and Rikki Thunder, who is riding shotgun, crack open Budweiser beers and exchange a high five. Davy presses a big red button on the console of the Jeep, and it explodes.

When the smoke clears, there is now a stage on the beach where the Jeep once sat, and the band kicks into a full concert with lights, lasers, and pyro. All the weapons have disappeared, and it's a massive beach party.

Intercut the concert with scenes of the boys partying, playing beach volleyball with girls in cutoff denim shorts and bikini tops, chugging beers, and relaxing in hammocks.

"Summer Saturday" instantly rises to most-requested video on MTV. On Casey Kasem's *American Top 40* weekly radio show, "Summer Saturday" breaks the top-ten most popular songs in the country for the first time, a position that it will not relinquish for several months.

The Python Pit

Davy is huddled over his notebook, scribbling lyrics for a new album and then angrily scratching them out. Rikki approaches.

Davy instinctively covers his notebook, like a wounded animal protecting scraps of food.

Rikki gently coaxes the notebook from Davy. He looks it over, smiles, and nods encouragingly.

Davy's shoulders relax. Rikki offers one small change. Davy shakes his head right away, then thinks about it and makes the change. The new song might work after all. An absolutely epic high five commences.

Outside a pizza place in Los Angeles

The German sits in a sedan across the street from the pizza establishment for no more than ten minutes before Rikki Thunder appears, alone, to pick up a large pizza, reportedly with pepperoni, just as the mole reported that he would. Rikki Thunder enjoys his pizza on Thursdays, and engages in this routine every week. By himself. Out in the open. In the dark. The German takes a photo.

An arena in Los Angeles

The band plays. Rikki sees Tawny watching backstage and blows her a kiss. Amanda smiles like she just got stabbed with an icicle.

A Billboard Hot 100 graphic

All Squeeze, No Venom climbs from number thirty to number seventeen!

22

⚡

FROM THE PASSENGER SEAT of a brown sedan, Amanda Price watched the members of Whyte Python mill around in front of a tour bus.

The bus was brand new, a sleek and massive double-decker, painted shiny pearl white, with tinted windows and the band's logo in sharp black lines. It was the kind of tour bus you'd expect to transport what was one of the biggest bands in America—at least according to Billboard that week.

The timing couldn't have been more perfect. Whyte Python's debut album—*All Squeeze, No Venom*—had reached the top of the charts the very week that the band was scheduled to leave for a tour across the country.

The CIA had a hand in that success, sure—Project Facemelt had gently improved the lyrics and sound, replaced the band's weak drummer with a strong one, and employed mild psychological warfare on unsuspecting audiences through carefully designed marketing, merchandise, and stage effects that screamed, "You need us."

The CIA also helped the band move up the charts by actually purchasing thousands of cassettes in the first few weeks, to spread Whyte Python's heartfelt message of peace, love, and partying across North America—and then the Eastern Bloc. The tapes found their way into high school lockers and onto playgrounds at lower schools. Whyte Python was playing in nightclubs and on radio stations, from Korea to East Germany and everywhere in between.

As Officer Price explained to the rest of her team, success begets success in entertainment. When an album starts high on the list and then keeps climbing every week, people get curious about what they might be missing—DJs begin playing the songs that appeal to them, record stores order albums that chart and feature this inventory front and center, and fans give the album a listen in the store and then buy a copy—all resulting in the album climbing even higher. And, indeed, Amanda Price was right: at some point over the course of those four months, the Whyte Python revolution began to grow all on its own. In fairness to the band and its CIA sponsors, the album was good—if you were into that kind of thing.

Despite her plan working as anticipated, Price was worried. She had not managed Rikki Thunder correctly and was suffering the consequences now.

Because, while Davy Bones and Spencer Dooley and Buck Sweet slapped each other on the back and chased groupies around the bus, Rikki paced anxiously.

He studied the parking lot, stuffing his hands in his pockets and then taking them out and rubbing them. He was looking for her. He was sad that she wasn't going with him. It was clear to anyone watching that he was different, that he was separate from the others, a self-imposed outcast.

"You have to fix this," Deputy Director Lonsa said from the driver's seat.

"I don't think it's a big deal," Amanda said. "He'll settle in after a couple of nights on the road."

"He's all moony over you," Lonsa said. "You need him bonding with the band. That means doing what they do. You can't have him leaving the party every time the girls come out."

"I know."

"Because that's what they do on these tours," her boss went on. "You told us yourself. If he doesn't participate in that, if he just sulks and calls you every night, he won't be part of the team. They won't trust him to lead."

"I know."

"And they won't listen to him when it's time to walk in with new material. When it's time to go on tour overseas."

"He's come a long way with them already," Amanda said. "I think it will be okay."

"None of it is okay," Lonsa said. "Look, you're new at this, and I know it's . . . unconventional. We figured this might get a little screwy. But your asset's loyalties are all messed up. You need to redirect them."

"I don't think—"

"Rikki Thunder's value to us is simple," Lonsa said, cutting her off. "He's the lever that we use to control the band. Does he look like a lever to you right now?"

Over by the tour bus, Davy Bones was leading a cadre of groupies like a band major, in a flamboyant march up the steps and on board. Spencer and Buck fell in line behind them. Spencer called to Rikki, but he just waved them all off.

Amanda leaned an elbow against the window and rested her head in her hand. "No," she said with a sigh.

"No," Lonsa agreed. "He doesn't look like a lever. He looks like a tool."

"Okay," Amanda said. "I got it. I'll fix it." And then she got out of the car and flagged down her man.

Ed Lonsa, left alone with his thoughts for the moment, dug a wrinkled piece of paper from his coat pocket and read the old memo printed on it for what must have been the hundredth time.

The document was classified and came from on high in Langley. He knew he shouldn't be carrying it around in his coat pocket like that, but he found that rereading during his most frustrating moments over the last several months was a kind of meditation. Maybe more to the point, it was the only thing that helped him maintain his sanity.

CLASSIFIED CLASSIFIED CLASSIFIED CLASSIFIED
Interagency Memorandum

9 October 1986

TO: Deputy Director Edward Lonsa
STATION: Asian Intelligence Division
RE: Disciplinary Reassignments to AID

Deputy Director Lonsa:

We're pleased to notify you that Disciplinary Program D1985AID003 has been funded for an additional three calendar years, with opportunity for further funding, as required by program objectives.

Per your last report, Ofc. Price has successfully inserted asset Richard Henderson into the music group Whyte Python, thereby completing "Phase One" and ensuring viability of this unorthodox rehabilitation program (now codenamed "Project Facemelt," which we have some questions about). As such, your expanded budget is approved. The following staff have been reassigned to the program under disciplinary measures, and will remain under your supervision until agency leadership determines that the project has come to an appropriate end:

- Sen. Ofc. Boone, Darrell A.
- Sen. Ofc. Mancuso, Bradley P.
- Sen. Ofc. Stryker, Catherine M.
- Ofc. Amanda Price will remain with the program.

Attached to this memo are profiles of your fully constituted team. Please review them immediately—you are scheduled to meet with them for initial briefing tomorrow at 16:00 EST, as soon as Ofc. Price arrives from Los Angeles.

Deputy Director Lonsa, this assignment is not what you were hoping for when you applied for a promotion out of AID. But the agency believes that you require—and will benefit from—additional management experience before consideration for a higher post.

As you are surely aware, overseeing an officer rehabilitation program is a challenging job. Your mission over the next several years is to guide a team of malfunctioning officers toward a positive result through teamwork and—more important—a loyal adherence to agency protocols and SOP.

Success in this endeavor does not go unnoticed among senior leadership with the agency, and oftentimes puts regional leadership staff on the fast track to promotion. This project, in particular, affords you the opportunity to gain attention from [REDACTED], who carries enormous sway in the American intelligence community and is monitoring the mission to ensure that it is taken seriously. For that reason, the rehabilitative nature of this program is highly classified. Staff have not been informed that they are assigned to you on discipline. They believe they were selected for this assignment on merit.

Success means that you will return four freshly rehabilitated officers to work on behalf of America's interests across the globe, strengthening our position worldwide and ensuring a safer and more prosperous nation. We look forward to seeing the results of your work with this group.

The agency, and the United States of America, thank you for your loyal service.

—JYD/rs

- Attach1: New Staff profiles
- Attach2: Ofc. Price Profile, originally submitted 19 February 1985

23

I WAS STARTING TO WORRY that Tawny wouldn't be there to see me off from Los Angeles on our tour, and that would've been a shitty way to start the road trip. But just before I was about to give up, I spotted her popping up from behind a car and running my way.

She leapt into my arms and wrapped her legs around my waist.

"I thought you weren't gonna make it," I said as Tawny climbed off me.

"Work stuff," she said, and rolled her eyes. "But I wouldn't miss this for the world. You're going on a national tour!" She punched my shoulder.

"I know," I said, but then my face dropped a little. "It's too bad you can't come with me, though."

"Babe," she said. "It's eight months. I can't just leave my job."

"I know," I said. "It's just gonna be weird. You're my lucky charm."

Tawny patted my shark-tooth necklace. "I don't want to hear you sounding sad right now," she said. "I am so excited for you. Be excited, Rikki! This is it! You've made it!"

"Okay," I said. "Okay! I will."

Tawny looked down at the ground and shifted back and forth on her heels. She had something important to say but didn't know how to say it. Finally, she took a deep breath and looked me right in the eyes.

"And, look," she said. "You have a once-in-a-lifetime opportunity here, and you should enjoy it. Girls are gonna be throwing themselves at you. I can't stand the idea of you sitting on the tour bus all lonely while the other guys have the time of their lives."

I had been thinking a lot about that, too, but I didn't know what Tawny was getting at. "What are you saying, babe?" I asked.

"I'm saying, you go be Whyte Python, all the way," she said, and she smiled. It looked genuine. "No restrictions."

Wait, I thought. *Does she mean, like, banging?* "To be clear," I said, "do you mean, like, banging?"

Tawny rolled her eyes again. "Yes," she said. "Banging, or whatever gross stuff you guys can come up with. But, Rikki, look at me." She got really serious and pointed a finger under my nose. "Be safe and only do what the girls want to do, you got it? Be a good guy."

I shrugged. "Yeah, of course."

She smoothed my collar and smiled. "But a lot of them are really, desperately going to want to screw you. Trust me on that, too. So. Go. For. It."

Now, if I was understanding her correctly, my girlfriend had just given me permission to sleep with as many other babes as I wanted while I was on tour with one of the biggest bands in America. I probably should've been dancing on the ceiling, but I wasn't.

It's hard to explain, but I actually felt kinda . . . *sad?* Because it hurt my feelings that she would be okay with me doing that. Then again, I was conflicted, because sleeping with hot chicks in every city would be fuckin' awesome.

Tawny sensed it. "If it helps," she said. "I'll give you one other ground rule: no road girlfriends. Do you know what that means? Don't keep anyone around for more than one stop."

"Okay," I said. Strangely enough, it did make me feel a little better. She was worried about me making a connection with somebody else, so that was something.

"I know what it's like," Tawny continued. "Most of the time, the whole hooking-up-after-the-show thing is about blowing off steam— for everybody. So keep the emotions out of it, all right?"

"Yeah," I agreed.

Because she was right: sex after a show didn't have anything to do with love or having a girlfriend. There's this really intense electricity that comes from playing to a bunch of insane fans. I'm banging on the drums in rhythm, and it's sending this massive sound wave across big concert halls and arenas and slamming into thousands of people all at once. And they're screaming, and we're singing, and they're singing back, and the lights are flashing, and they're throwing their underwear at us, and everything is loud and hot and sweaty.

You feed off their passion while the show is going, and at the end of the show you're so full of it, you can't sit still. It makes you jumpy and twitchy and horny, like you're overloaded with a power that you can't control. You need to release it somehow. You need an outlet.

That's why guys like us are always trashing greenrooms and hotels. Tawny had been my outlet for months, but she couldn't come on tour with us. She couldn't just up and leave her job in Los Angeles, which I understood had something to do with magazines.

Now her smile dropped. "And by the way," she said. "Those girls who *do* want to be your road girlfriend? They're running from something. Somebody hurt them, so be a good guy that way, too—don't sleep with them; they need a hug."

I didn't quite get the point she was making. As far as I could tell, the girls at our shows were in *love* with me; they screamed it all the time! And who wouldn't want to be the road girlfriend of a metal drummer, riding on a bus all day with his friends?

I was so rapidly warming to the idea of No Rules Road Rikki that I was not listening as closely anymore. So I kept my mouth shut and nodded.

"Tell me you agree with these terms," she said.

"Yeah, absolutely." I tried not to sound too excited. "Still seems weird, though," I said, and I meant it.

"I promise you that I will never ask any questions about it," Tawny said. "The guys on that bus? They're your brothers now. What happens on the road is between Whyte Python. I'll give you a heads-up before I catch up with you at a show. Because on those nights, you're all mine."

It was official: I had the coolest girlfriend in the world. And if I needed any proof that Ron and the rest of the guys from Qyksand were wrong—that she would never try to come between me and my band—this was it.

"Are you sure?" I asked.

"Rikki," she said. "It's fine. They all do it. And you might not believe it now, but at some point after a show you're going to be just the right amount of fucked up, and the right girl is going to walk into that greenroom, and you're going to want to. So I'm telling you that I *want* you to go for it. I'll be pissed at you if you don't."

"You will?"

"Yes," she said. "Because eventually you might anyway, and this way I know we have an understanding. So you don't have to feel guilty, and I don't have to wonder. And on top of that, I know this is a time in your life that nobody else on earth gets to have, and I don't want you resenting me years from now because you didn't get to live it to its fullest. Got it?"

It all came into focus. Tawny wasn't telling me to sleep with other babes because she didn't care! She was telling me to sleep with other babes because she *did* care!

And she was right. I had seen it enough times with my own eyes to know. Guys in other bands with wives or girlfriends slept around all the time and made jokes like "Nobody tell my old lady" before they went into a three-way. Tawny was proposing something different. This deal was good for our relationship!

It was healthy!

Oh man, I was gonna get crazy laid all across America!

"Aw, jeez," I said. "I don't know what to say."

She put her hands on my shoulders and smiled, big and wide. "Say you'll have the time of your life," she said. "And don't bring home any diseases."

I smiled back, and I promised I would/wouldn't, and then we started making out like wild animals.

"Wrap it up, Thunder," Davy shouted from the bus window. The whole parking lot already reeked of pot. I could hear everyone on the bus screaming along to "Smokin' in the Boys' Room." I had my hands on the love of my life, but my heart was tugging me toward the bus.

I felt Tawny's cool hand land on my shark-tooth necklace. "Go." She smiled. I kissed her again and ran up the stairs onto the bus.

The inside was gorgeous. It was all white leather and polished black glass, with a hi-fi stereo and TV and a full wet bar. We were really going to enjoy destroying it.

Davy and Spencer had insisted that we pack the bus to capacity with some of our most loyal groupies for the first day on the road, because it was the start of an eight-month party and we had to kick it off right. I had no idea how those girls were going to get home the next day, but nobody seemed worried about it.

They were spread out on couches singing along to Crüe, passing a bong while Spencer tended bar. It was impossible not to feel excited.

Davy took a huge pull off the glass tube and pointed it at me. "Hit it, Thunder," he scream-sang, shooting a cloud of smoke to the ceiling.

"Give me just a sec," I said, and I nudged past him toward the back of the bus. I scanned the parking lot, looking for Tawny. I was hoping for one last smile and wave, one more blown kiss. But she was gone already.

I felt somebody move into my space, and I smelled bubblegum perfume and cigarette smoke just before a girl with curly dark hair wrapped an arm around my neck and gave me a big wet kiss on the cheek. A few seconds ago, I had been bouncing with excitement for the nationwide sex parade that I just found out was in my near future. But this felt too soon. We were still in the parking lot! I tried to be polite, and I let the girl know I was busy.

Just as the bus pulled onto the road, I spotted Tawny on the other side of the lot, walking away. I watched her for as long as I could see her. She never looked back.

PART III

Whyte Python
Does America

24

D EPUTY DIRECTOR LONSA swayed back and forth under the
weight of a massive stack of folders that he cradled in his arms
as he entered Boone's office. Delivering materials like this
would normally be something Lonsa could assign to a subordinate;
but this was Project Facemelt, and every instruction needed to be
delivered with an underlying message: *Don't screw this up.*

The top folder started to slip off the pile as he put his back into
the door and nudged his way in, and it felt like the momentum was
about to send the whole pile tumbling to the floor. Lonsa found
Boone sitting at his desk with his eyes closed, and a big set of can
headphones blaring into his ears. The desk was littered with pints of
whiskey, piles of notepads, and vinyl albums. Distressingly, some of
the albums had been shattered into pieces.

Boone didn't seem to notice that Lonsa had entered. "Clear some
space!" the boss demanded.

Boone slowly opened his eyes, and when he saw the DD, panic-
stricken, with a listing stack of work in his arms, he let out a dramatic sigh before casually sweeping the desk clean. Lonsa dropped
the stack of folders in front of him, each one color-coded and tagged.

"What's this crap?" Boone asked.

"That's everything we have on Whyte Python," Lonsa said.
"Psych profiles, school records, known associates, you name it." The
deputy director put his hands on his hips and smiled a little at the pile
his research team had collected.

"As you can see, it's pretty thorough. We need you to go through
these and write up dossier files for the band members. Just a clean

summary of each of them for the Project Facemelt file, with references back to the original files here in case anyone needs them."

Boone scowled. "I'm here to write lyrics, not character profiles."

"You're also six months into deep research on these guys already," Lonsa said. "And we need these done fast."

"Fine," Boone said, and he waved a dismissive hand at the folders. "But I don't need any of this crap. I'm in their heads already. I've memorized the *lyrics*, man. I've dug through their trash, walked the streets they grew up on. Harassed their neighbors in the middle of the night."

"We didn't tell you to do any of that—"

"I feel like I've lived their lives!" Boone shouted. "I know Whyte Python better than any dossier ever could!"

Lonsa stared at Boone for several seconds.

Officer Boone was correct: he was here to write lyrics, primarily—lyrics that would sound and feel like they came from Whyte Python, but that also specifically encouraged dissent, shifted allegiances to the West, and served as a rallying cry for a generation of restless Eastern Bloc youth.

And everything about Boone's history with the agency suggested he would do a very good job, as long as Lonsa could keep him focused on the task at hand. Some immersion—maybe even obsession—with the subject matter could be forgiven. Boone did need to get into their heads, after all; and those heads were . . . disordered, at best. But even at Langley, where the staff was famously skilled at ignoring things they weren't supposed to see, nobody in their corner of the building could ignore the changes in Officer Boone since he'd joined Project Facemelt.

He had started to show up late for work, wore sunglasses around the office, reeked of marijuana most of the time, and couldn't get through three sentences without sliding in a Whyte Python lyric or a string of profanities. It was unbecoming conduct for a senior officer with the Central Intelligence agency; but the creatives typically got a longer rope when they were deep into a project, and Lonsa was willing to tolerate some of Boone's eccentricities as long as the work remained good.

But this was getting a little worrying. Ed Lonsa took off his glasses and softened his voice. "Hey," he said. "You okay, Darrell?"

"Oh, I am *fan*tastic," Boone said, smiling aggressively. Lonsa couldn't tell if he was being sarcastic or manic or what. "Maybe for the first time in my life."

"It's just that your hair's getting long," Lonsa said, "and it looks like you shredded the knees on those Dockers. And your ear is obviously bleeding."

"It's called an earring, bro." Boone rolled his eyes and flicked the thumbtack stuck through his left earlobe. "You ever seen one before?"

"Okay . . ." Lonsa said, and he took a few steps back. He didn't particularly like the look of Boone's dilated pupils. For the thousandth time, he took a deep, slow breath and cursed Project Facemelt under his breath; then he reminded himself that once this mission was over, he would never have to see Darrell Boone again.

Boone didn't know this, of course—but there were a lot of things about Project Facemelt that Boone and the rest of the team weren't privy to—first and foremost, just how much their own boss hated this ridiculous assignment.

Lonsa didn't quite understand why the higher-ups had deemed it necessary to punish him by making him babysit the Project Facemelt team. As far as everyone else knew, this was not a disciplinary assignment; but it was obvious to anyone who knew their ass from a hole in the ground that Project Facemelt was a place the agency sent their misfits. They had misbehaved, or they were too soft, or too artsy, or too weird to be out in the world running honeypots on drug lords and selling guns to revolutionaries with the other badasses.

Lonsa saw through the supportive memos, the pats on the back, the barely contained snickers from his colleagues. Project Facemelt was a place where this team could "help" without doing too much damage.

I mean, Price named them Project Facemelt, for Christ's sake. CIA missions are supposed to have innocuous nicknames, to hide the vicious and sometimes horrifying acts sponsored by the agency in the name of preserving the American way. Only a fool would come up with a name that sounds a thousand times worse than what they were actually up to. When he'd diligenced this with Price, she had assured him that "facemelt" is, indeed, some kind of heavy metal term.

Only Mancuso seemed to suspect that his assignment to Project Facemelt was an insult. Price and Stryker genuinely believed they were doing their life's work. And then there was Boone, one of the resident loons, acting like a spoiled teenager from his secure office in Langley.

Yes, Deputy Director Lonsa was going to enjoy punching Darrell Boone's ticket for reassignment. But for now, Boone's special set of skills were mission critical.

Lonsa held his arms wide. "I'll let you get to work, then," he said. "Use the materials, Boone. We've got these guys' whole lives in there."

"Thanks," Boone said, like he wasn't very thankful at all.

"But keep it simple, all right?" Lonsa said as he walked toward the door. "No commentary, just the profile and background in a short, clean narrative for the brass. Got it?"

Boone smiled. "You got it, boss," he said. "Short and clean. Coming right up."

25

F YOU'RE WONDERING what it's like going on an arena tour across America with your band, the answer is that it's fuckin' rad!

We were three weeks in and playing a show almost every night. I had never left Southern California before, so getting out and seeing the country was a pretty big deal to me. We didn't really have time for sightseeing, between all the driving and playing and partying and puking, but just watching the landscape change out the window from day to day was a thrill.

The life of a rock star was pretty thrilling, too! I mean, yeah, there was some boring stuff that was sure to get old soon, like album signings at record stores and having the same conversation with three different radio DJs every morning. But Kirby had been on tours with other bands before, and he said that you kind of just start doing those things automatically, like tying your shoes. He suggested that you make it a game for yourself; like, find a way to sneak a different song title into your answer every time, and make sure you repeat the reporter's name so they feel special. It all sounded like really good advice to me, but Davy told him to shut the fuck up for God's sake, or he would throw him out of the bus while it was going seventy on the highway, and everyone laughed.

Speaking of Kirby: the guy was an odd duck. He insisted on riding on the bus with us, even though we were super mean to him and the label said he didn't have to. He said he didn't want to miss any detail, no matter how small. And he was always making these hushed phone calls, trying to look important, I guess. Then he would hang up real fast if someone got too close and say, "Top secret label stuff," as if anyone cared. We assumed he was tattling on us for every single thing, so we behaved worse just to flip him out.

The laughs between shows were constant. Sometimes it was the kind of laughs you have when you're hungover and haven't slept in three days, where everything is funny. And other times it was from pranks, like when Davy pushed Kirby into a swimming pool, or Buck tricked Spencer into touching a live wire, or the times Davy yanked Kirby's pants off and made him walk onstage, or the time we all called Barry Gorman and asked how his summer was going.

We also had an endless pile of money and very little free time to spend it, so we'd do big, dumb shit like rent out a public pool for the day and jump dirt bikes into it, or pay a high school marching band to get on the bus and play "Hang On Sloopy" over Kirby while he was sleeping.

In Vegas, we rented out a club for an after-party. Wayne Newton showed up and sang a pretty boss duet of "Summer Saturday" with Davy, and then Siegfried & Roy brought a tiger—which was awesome—but they wouldn't let it do shots with Spencer.

The best part of it all, though, was definitely the shows. We were playing in huge indoor arenas, places so big that when the crowd started cheering it took a second to reach the stage.

The lights, the pyrotechnics, the sound, all of it was at a scale so big that I could barely fathom it. We had this fleet of moving trucks following us everywhere we went, and a team of roadies in matching T-shirts with our tour logo on them would pour out at each stop and construct the stage from scratch, day in and day out.

I couldn't really come to grips with the fact that all these people were doing all this work just so I could play the drums, and that tens of thousands of people would come out every night to hear us. I can understand how guys in bands get ridiculous egos. In fact, I don't know how it's possible to stay humble! But I tried my best.

Since we never had to drive anywhere or manage our own schedules or even find our own food, the drug use went up, too. I mostly stuck to weed and a little blow here and there, and Davy and Spencer were the same—although Spencer goes through more marijuana in a day than Davy and I smoke all week. Buck, though, was more interested in the hard stuff.

I saw Buck smoke crack and shoot heroin on the road, but not every night or anything. We just accepted that it was his deal, and nothing we had to worry about—in part because it didn't seem to have an impact on his playing.

And we would feel like hypocrites saying something, because we were stoned or drunk almost all the time. In all honesty, it was easier to ignore it and hope it didn't become a problem, because saying something would probably just cause a rift. And it also might force the rest of us to take a hard look in the mirror.

Tawny hadn't made it to a show yet, but she promised to catch up with us on the other side of Texas. Still, like any good metal girl-friend, she had her fingerprints all over the tour. She had used her magazine connections to bring in a nice lady from New York to cre-ate our costumes when the first album dropped, and those were so great that we convinced Andromeda to hire that same lady to design our merchandise.

Thanks to my girl, our shit looked incredible. Our logo was bold and simple: the words "Whyte Python" in black against a white back-ground, and the *y* in "Whyte" was an electric guitar on top and a python head on bottom. We named the guitar snake Axe, naturally.

WHYTE PYTHON

And that lady took the ball and ran with it. We had shirts in all these different colors pulled from our costumes; like, there was one that was red and yellow and blue, and one that was red and yellow and black, and a red one with yellow text, and all these other cool versions with the WP logo right in the middle.

Now that I think of it, most of them were some variation on red and yellow. The lady said the color schemes suggested power and would play well overseas. She seemed really smart; and like I said, she was from New York City, so we trusted that she knew what she was talking about.

There was even official Rikki Thunder merch! Now, if you ever find yourself wondering whether you've "made it," ask this simple question: "Has a stranger paid $19.99 for a T-shirt with my name on it?" If the answer is yes, you're doing at least as good as this guy! (Imagine that I'm pointing to myself with both thumbs).

The shirts were kind of like the homemade ones that sprang up all over L.A. the year before, white with a lightning bolt that ended in a snakehead and the word "Thunderstorm" over it. But they looked more professional and had the tour stops listed on the back. I was signing them with Sharpies all across America.

Every night, there were more Thunderstorm shirts in the crowd— and, yes, if you're wondering, they were mostly worn by the ladies. I had so far mostly honored my loyalty to Tawny, even though she told me not to. Hand jobs don't count, and besides those, I just hadn't wanted to hook up with anyone. The idea of it still felt wrong.

Now, the other guys didn't like that at all; they wanted me in on the action. To give me a hard time, Spencer and Buck got in the habit of combing the crowd for every cutie in a Thunderstorm shirt they could find and bringing them backstage after the show, until Davy got pissed about it and yelled at them to stop.

That was one thing. Davy and I were really starting to become friends, but he was so sensitive about my growing fan base. Since the beginning, he had been the single star of the band. The other guys did fine, but there was never a question about who had first pick of the groupies, or who was going to sell the most T-shirts now that we had made it, or who the DJs would want to answer all the questions. Until now. For whatever reason, I had something the fans wanted.

Take Colorado, for example.

We were playing at Red Rocks, an outdoor amphitheater built into these crazy sandstone walls outside of Denver. For the first half hour of the show, I was just in awe of the way the sun setting behind the stage cast an orange glow over thousands of fans singing along to our songs, and lights flashing against the triangle-shaped boulders framing the venue. To cap it all off, our team put on a full fireworks show at the end.

It was one of the most amazing experiences of my life, and I never gave a single thought to who had more T-shirts in the crowd, or who the prettiest groupies would flock to after; I was in awe of how lucky I was to be there.

The show ended, and on our way backstage, I got totally mobbed. I guess either Buck and Spencer had mastered the art of wrangling the girls they called my Thundercats or Colorado is a hotter spot for Rikki Thunder love, because it was like I was all four of the Beatles. Backstage was a sea of lightning-bolt shirts and crimped hair and jelly shoes, swallowing me up and pulling at my clothes and hair, and mostly pushing aside the other guys in the band. I have to admit, I was kind of scared. But on the outside, it must have looked like I was in paradise, because security wasn't doing anything about it.

Spencer and Buck thought it was hilarious. They egged the crowd on as they chanted "Thunderstorm" and screamed things like "Fuck me, Rikki Thunder!"

And then I caught a glance of Davy, and he was *scowling* at me. I'd never seen him quite so upset. He looked angry and also kind of sad at the same time, like I'd just run over his dog or something.

Sure, we all knew Davy needed a lot of attention from the ladies—attention from anyone, really. But what I saw in his eyes that day was different. He dropped his guitar on the runway and punched the door to the greenroom open.

It killed the mood for everyone.

Davy didn't hang out backstage that night. He just caught a ride to the hotel, and we didn't see him again until the bus was about to leave town the next morning. He was fine by then—his old cocky self, even teasing me about how lucky I was to be alive after getting mobbed the way I did.

But I could feel that distance forming between us again that I had worked so hard to close over the last few months. I guess it's true what they say: fame changes you, and it changes everyone around you, too.

26

/

CENTRAL INTELLIGENCE AGENCY CASE FILE: DOS (7)/PFM/001.13/24

SUBMITTED BY: Boone, Darrell A.
MISSION: Project Facemelt
ASSET: R. Henderson (alias Rikki Thunder)

CATEGORY: Close Relationship Profiles

NAME: Lawrence David Barkley
ALIAS(ES): Davy Bones
AGE: 24

RELATIONSHIP TO ASSET: Member of the band "Whyte Python"

BACKGROUND:
Lawrence Barkley is a resident of Los Angeles, California. His birthplace is San Bernardino, California, and he has no other known communities of residence. He is approximately five feet, ten inches tall; weighs 165 pounds; he likes dogs more than cats, and his favorite color is green; and blah blah blah, and you know what, fuck this.

This bland, neutered agency format doesn't do justice to these guys' lives, which I have researched so thoroughly that I'm beginning to lose track of where my story ends and theirs begin. I've dug through their trash, called their kindergarten teachers in the middle of the night to catch them when they're honest, scared the hell out of their neighbors. I have LIVED IT, man, from cradle to stage. And I know I was warned about this specifically, but tough: I will NOT keep it clean and concise. Here's the REAL DEAL about Davy Bones, motherfuckers, and by the way: WHYTE PYTHON NEVER DIES!

—Sen. Ofc. D. Boone

Lawrence Barkley was born in San Bernardino, California, the son of a middle-aged dentist and a much younger dental assistant.

He was his father's second son, born of his second wife, a beachy blonde. The result was a tall and skinny boy with an impossibly tangled mess of blond, curly hair.

Little Larry could sing—he had a finely tuned ear and happily performed in the children's choir at his church. But his angelic voice didn't do him any good at school, where his massive, curly helmet had its own center of gravity and was a constant target for paper airplanes and spitballs. The kids in his class called him Hairy Larry.

Larry was eager to be accepted . . . no, to be *popular*. He wanted it so badly. There was an in crowd at his high school, and their ringleaders were Todd and Christi, boyfriend-and-girlfriend since junior high. Todd was blond and good at karate, and Christi was even more blond and captain of the cheerleading team. They were definitely having sex, which Larry suspected was awesome.

They rounded out their circle with Carrie and Brooke and Dan and Keith, all similarly attractive and skilled at important things like sports and probably sex. They all had rich parents and nice cars, and they surfed and skied and wore sweatshirts promoting the colleges where they would eventually be the presidents of their sororities and fraternities.

But what made them so appealing to Larry—what made them the *in crowd*—was how comfortable they seemed to be in their own skins.

It confounded him how those kids could seem so relaxed, so natural, while everybody was looking at them. Meanwhile, Larry—who nobody was looking at—felt like he was performing awkwardly under a spotlight during his every waking hour, in front of a row of snarling teenage judges.

The popular kids—the Todds and Christis—were aware of the curly-haired geek who was always hovering in their orbits, hoping to be quietly absorbed. Maybe it was their own insecurities acting out, but they were protective of their space in the inner circle—and when someone who didn't fit the profile hung around too long, they would attack.

They would point at him and laugh—not out loud, not in the way that bullies do in movies, but among themselves, in a quiet but noticeable way—the way that assholes do in real life. He heard the mutters of "Hairy Larry" and "dweeb" when he passed them in the hall, and each comment stung him in his heart.

But by acting superior to him, they only made their status as the "cool kids" all the more appealing. The more they teased him, the more Larry wanted to be one of them. If only they would give him a chance, he knew, they would come to welcome him into their clique. And they would teach him the secret.

The secret of being cool.

The summer before his junior year in high school, things began to change for Larry. He had a rapid growth spurt, and his voice deepened and took on a husky scratchiness. His ear for pitch was as strong as ever, and when he heard himself singing along to his rock albums he realized that he sounded pretty, pretty good!

And so, with his eyes never leaving the ultimate prize—popularity— Larry worked on himself. His brother had left behind a weight bench when he went to college. Larry moved it to the backyard and started working out every single day.

He had never been an outside kid, so it took his daily, sun-drenched bodybuilding sessions to discover that he had his mother's skin, and he tanned up nicely. And when left alone to grow, and with the aid of some very powerful hair-care products, his oft-ridiculed blond puffball matured into a heavy-metal mane, like the guys had in Def Leppard.

The newly tall and muscular Larry had long golden locks, honey-colored skin, and two rows of perfect teeth—the combined legacy of his mother and father.

And that voice! Slowly, Larry built enough confidence to test its range when he was sure nobody else was home. Soon he could hold key with Steven Tyler when he sang along to his Aerosmith records, or with Robert Plant when he played Zeppelin; and when he wanted to, he could hold a sustained screech at a pitch and decibel that vibrated the windows.

When school came back into session, people noticed the new Larry. Girls in his class were whispering about him, he was making new friends, and even the teachers seemed to give him extra attention.

The only ones who didn't notice, though—or didn't care—were the Todds and Christis. He was invisible to them, which he supposed was an upgrade. He had friends now, sure—but he would ditch them all in an instant if Carrie Waters invited him to her family's condo in Big Bear with Todd, Christi, and the others.

Eventually, Larry picked up guitar, and he kept on singing, with his practice sessions mostly confined to the family garage when his parents were out. He wanted to master the art, to be inarguably fantastic, before he was willing to let his guard down and allow someone else see what he had been up to.

Finally, during his senior year, Larry felt ready.

. . . -ish.

He saw an ad in the paper for a band looking for a singer. The guys in the band were his age, but they went to a different school on the other end of the Valley—they didn't know him at all.

He could try out, and if he failed, he wouldn't have to face any of them on Monday. Finally, Larry believed that he had both the confidence—and promise of anonymity—necessary to try out for a real band.

They loved him, of course. And he loved playing with them. To his new band, he was the cool one. As long as they stuck to their side of the San Bernardino Valley, Larry could be a whole different person.

They called themselves the Seafarers, and they leaned into the obvious gimmicks: raincoats and sailor nicknames, with Lawrence David Barkley becoming "Davy Bones."

And they weren't bad for a high school band. The Seafarers drew crowds for their tight covers of the hard-rock hits taking over the radio, and their lead singer's remarkable voice and Mick Jagger bravado opened doors at nightclubs all across the Inland Empire.

The crowd swooned when he strutted. They screamed when he sang. And all was well for Larry, living his double life as a post-nerd in his neighborhood and a swaggering rock star in neighboring cities.

His bandmates and fans had no reason to expect anything but supreme confidence from him, so that was what he showed them. Eventually it began to sink in and become real. Until a night just before graduation, when they played a show at a bar that was a bit too close to home.

He felt the finger pointing at him before he saw it, sensed that one body in the crowd had suddenly stopped dancing. And then he felt hot, liquid anxiety filling his chest and reddening his cheeks and neck when he saw them: the Todds and Christis.

It was the whole crew of six, looking less like high school seniors and more like the television versions of their high school A crowd archetypes; wayfarers and pastel golf shirts, collars popped just so, dancing in an exclusive little circle three rows back.

Keith had spotted him first, and Larry watched in terror as Keith alerted Brooke, and then Brooke told Christi, until, one by one, they all realized that it was *him* onstage. It was Hairy Larry.

And their eyes went wide, and their mouths dropped open in dumb, careless smiles. And then they *laughed*. They thumped one another on the back and pointed at him, like they had done all through high school.

Larry's shoulders slumped, and he crept instinctively from the front of the stage to the back. He held the microphone tight under his chin, and his voice began to warble and crack as he retreated within himself.

He forgot about the guitar hanging around his neck entirely. And he stood perfectly still, reciting the lyrics but not really singing them anymore, like a sullen teenager forced to participate in a school pageant.

His bass player bailed him out by harmonizing with him through a stretch. And his salvation came when the Todds and Christis responded to that instinct bred into the truly popular, to leave the party early. They couldn't be seen dancing to a band that had Hairy Larry as its front man, after all, so they took off for cooler parts unknown.

Larry mostly recovered and finished the show, but the veneer that he'd spent months cultivating was splintered. His band would see through him now. He had to quit the Seafarers.

Larry had reinvented himself once. He believed that he could do it again. But one thing was clear, and it was this: he needed to get the hell out of San Bernardino to do it.

So Larry Barkley asked himself where a guy with a nice tan, award-worthy hair, and a killer scream should go to completely remake himself.

The answer was obvious.

Davy Bones arrived in West Hollywood in September 1982 and quickly hooked on with a band called the Damn Dirty Animals, where he met Barry Gorman. They gigged on the Sunset Strip alongside other startup glam metal bands like W.A.S.P. and Roxx Regime.

Larry Barkley had all but vanished somewhere along Interstate 210.

Davy Bones was a relentlessly cocky asshole. Davy Bones was explosive onstage and aloof everywhere else. Davy Bones was exclusive as fuck.

When the word spread across town that Buck Sweet was kicked out of Slaughter in 1984, Davy and Barry left the Damn Dirty Animals and recruited Buck into a new band.

Davy wanted to call the group "Davy Bones's Rocker," but Buck refused. When Spencer Dooley joined the band and bonded with Buck over their love of snakes, they settled on Whyte Python.

Davy signed off purely for the sexual double entendre: the "Whyte Python" could be a snake, or it could be a big dick. Which he assumed most people would associate with him, since he was the leader of the band.

The rest is well known. Whyte Python would carve out space for themselves on the Sunset Strip as the Next Big Thing. In 1985 they went on a tour around Southern California—and eventually Davy found himself playing in San Bernardino, a few miles away from the neighborhood where he grew up.

He spent the whole show looking for a few specific faces. He was hoping he would see them again, anonymous in the crowd with the rest of the rubes, wishing they were him.

Maybe they wouldn't even recognize him now; but he hoped that they would, and that they would realize that he had surpassed them. They would see that *he* was the in crowd now, and if they were looking for backstage passes, they were shit out of luck.

But if the Todds and Christis were at the show that night, he never found them. And at every concert that Whyte Python played since, he always looked.

27

//

I T'S THE FLAGS," Amanda said as she looked through the design
book. "The color schemes match the flags for Poland, Russia, East
Germany, Yugoslavia, and so on."

"That's right," Stryker said. They were sitting in a mostly empty
bar in the basement of a hotel in Portland, Maine, doing advance
work for the second half of the Whyte Python tour.

Stryker had a book of T-shirt designs open on the table between
them, some minor updates to the band's merchandising that would
ratchet up the subliminal response by a little bit.

"But there are some subtleties here that I demand you appreciate," she said.

Amanda grinned and sipped her drink. "Okay," she said. "Dazzle
me."

"The trick is, the flags in most of these countries have a crest or
coat of arms in the middle," Stryker said. "Our research indicates
that the people generally feel a positive patriotic association with the
colors of their flag, even if they don't agree with the government
itself. It's why they still wave their ruling party's flags in protest, but
often with the crest cut out. So we replace the original crest with a
slightly crest-shaped Whyte Python logo.

"See how the logo has this vaguely rounded shape, just around the
edges?" Stryker pointed at the design, and then pointed at the Bulgarian flag in another book. Amanda could see a vague resemblance,
but only if she was really trying. "And it's just a little bit different
from the Romanian flag, which is taller and narrower. And then there
are these subtle points that suggest a star, like the Yugoslavian flag."

"Why not a star itself?"

"Well, first, because we don't want to show our hand," Stryker said. "But it actually works better this way—if it's not a perfect match. It suggests the shape of the original crest and forces their brain to recognize it, to make the association and complete the circuit on its own. They're *discovering* it instead of just *seeing* it. Their brain is doing some extra processing here; it leaves a heavier footprint. And they understand, innately, that we're telling them a secret. It's a wink between allies. And as a consequence, it's transitioning their allegiance without them realizing it."

"Wow."

"Replacing their government crest with the band logo inserts a subconscious message: that Whyte Python *is* of the people of Poland, of Soviet Russia, of East Germany, of Romania, even more than their government."

"That Whyte Python will lead them," Amanda said.

"Which is insane," Stryker said.

Amanda crooked an eyebrow.

"Come on," Stryker said. "You can't possibly think it's a wise idea to program a big chunk of the planet to follow these hairy, reckless idiots."

Amanda swallowed her drink and thought about what to say next. She had not been in the CIA for long, but she was pretty sure that you weren't supposed to question the mission objectives, especially to a lower officer.

"Chaos everywhere else is good for business here," she finally said.

"Until it inevitably backfires," Stryker said. "I'm only going along with this because whatever they come up with in its place would be worse. Now, we need to start talking about phase three. Lonsa's giving you space, but you need to know that he's upset."

"I know." Amanda sighed. "Because I haven't brought Rikki on board yet."

"Right," Stryker said. "Nuts and bolts, kid. We need these guys on tour overseas in 1989. That's a year and a half. In that time, we need at least one song on the next album that's fully crafted by the agency, but preferably two or three. We need to get some key words into their interviews. We need to roll out the new merchandise. We need to lock down the world tour. We can't do any of that without Thunder's explicit support."

"I know."

"And we need to start all this now, because as soon as Andromeda pitches a tour in the Eastern Bloc, those countries are going to start vetting the band. If we slide these things in afterward, they'll smell a rat. So the lyrics, the colors, it all needs to be established in advance."

"I know all this," Amanda said assuredly. "I'm going to bring him on board once he gets back to L.A. This tour lasts for five more months. That should give him plenty of time away from me, to sleep around a little and put the right kind of space between us. He'll be more amenable."

Catherine Stryker leaned across the table and locked eyes with Amanda.

"So, you will, too?"

"That's not what this is about." Amanda scowled. "It's not like I'm not falling in love with him or anything."

"Okay."

"Rikki is just a genuinely sweet person. And he's been betrayed by everybody that he's trusted his whole life. I'm trying to avoid breaking him forever here."

"Honestly?" Stryker said. "Breaking him emotionally might not be the worst thing. Coldhearted compliance tends to make for good assets."

"And that is exactly why you need to trust me to bring him in the right way," Amanda said. "Remember that this man is an American citizen. We're already outside of our jurisdiction and our ethical boundaries here."

"Which is exactly why we need him *participating*," Stryker said. "Instead of stringing him along. You said it yourself: Rikki is perceptive. He knows how to read people. If he's as observant as you say he is, he probably won't be surprised."

"No. Not in this case. Rikki has a very high bar for trust. As far as I can tell, this asset has only trusted four people in his whole life. Three of them were in his last band. The fourth one is me, an undercover CIA officer who's been manipulating him since the day we met. So why do you think he has a blind spot for me, Catherine?"

Stryker looked Amanda up and down and raised an eyebrow.

"That's deeply insulting." Amanda pushed her drink away. "To me and the asset. I'll tell you why. Since he was five years old, everyone who has come into Rikki Thunder's orbit has self-identified as an immediate threat. He's been beaten up by older kids, rejected by foster parents, teased in school. He's used to protecting himself from rabid dogs. He trusts me—even though he shouldn't—because I'm the first person who's come at him with bad intent disguised as *kindness*. I'm the first person who is hurting him who didn't tell him up front, 'I'm here to hurt you.' And that's why learning the truth will destroy him."

"But he needs to learn the truth."

"Yes. We agree on that. Just give me time. I have a plan."

Stryker held her hands wide. "I understand your position. And I appreciate your concern for his emotional state. But remember, I have a doctorate in psychology, and Rikki Thunder isn't the only one I'm observing. I'm not blind, Price. There's more going on with you. You cannot have a romantic attachment to your asset."

"I don't—"

"Look. I'm telling you this because you're talented, and you could do well at the agency, and I like you. But I'm also telling you this as your teammate on a far-reaching, complicated project. One that could either result in a wave of revolutions across the Eastern Bloc or the global humiliation of the American intelligence community. Those are the stakes. If your feelings for Thunder are imperiling your ability to carry out this mission, I will recommend the DD remove you from it. Today. And you'll never come close to a project like Facemelt again."

Amanda was taken aback. Stryker had quickly become something of a role model to her on Facemelt. The other guys, not so much. Boone was a mystery, and Mancuso was always scowling in meetings, scribbling little notes that never made it into any file she'd seen. He acted aloof but was always listening in on their side conversations.

Stryker, though, was confident and thoughtful, thriving in the boys' club atmosphere of intelligence. Amanda liked fieldwork, but she figured that she wouldn't forever. She was hoping that, in Stryker, she had found an example for where she could go next—and maybe even a friend. But the swiftness with which the older agent brushed her back now, without giving Amanda any benefit of the doubt, left her feeling shaken.

"Jesus," Amanda said. "Kinda thought we were bonding here."

"We are." Stryker closed her design book. "If we weren't, I'd have seen you pulled already. Now listen. The end of the tour is the absolute deadline to bring him in. I think we'd all rather see you do it here in Portland. It's the halfway point of the tour. Give him some time to process."

"My instinct says to wait," Amanda said. "I have an advanced degree in psychology, too, Catherine. And I know the asset better than anyone on earth."

"Okay." Stryker let out an uncomfortable sigh. "Then I'll back you up. With Lonsa, and everyone else who's getting antsy. If you say it's the end of the tour, it's the end of the tour. And then we need him ready to work immediately."

"He will be," Amanda said. "I appreciate your confidence."

"But, Price?" Stryker said. "You better not be wrong."

28

It was the end of June, and hot as fuck in Texas.

We had been on tour for a little more than a month and were scheduled to play in the Texxas Jam at the Cotton Bowl with Poison, Whitesnake, Farrenheit, Aerosmith, Tesla, and Boston.

Dude, there were more than seventy-five thousand people there! Sure, they weren't all there for us—Boston was the headliner because they hadn't played a live show since '79—but Whyte Python played right in the middle, so we probably got all the late stragglers and the early quitters.

We played right through the heat of the day. They said it broke ninety degrees, and it probably felt a lot hotter than that, because it was sunny and there were almost eighty thousand people crammed into an open bowl, screaming for eight hours.

But the crowd were total troupers! They were getting sprayed with hoses to keep cool and stripping down damn near naked all over the football field, and still dancing up a storm when we kicked into "Summer Saturday."

By the time we finished our set, the Whitesnake and Poison guys had launched the biggest backstage party that I had ever seen. Nobody wanted to leave early, because we all grew up on Aerosmith and Boston and wanted to see them play, so the scene just kept sinking deeper and deeper into chaos.

The promoters had to scramble to procure more booze for us. Everyone had water guns full of tequila. Buck broke into a supply closet and rigged a soap dispenser over a hose, and he was spraying everybody with suds.

And the girls! You know, it's true what they say about Texas—
there are a lot of babes there. I grew up in Southern California, and
even I had never seen so many tanned, blond perfect tens in one
place before. A lot of them were strippers—packing the greenroom
with these "VIPs" was one of Poison's favorite tricks—and they were
all extremely down to party.

I had so far held onto my tour virginity, and every night that I left
the greenroom alone felt like a small victory. But backstage at the
Texxas Jam, I definitely felt my reserves starting to crumble.

It didn't help that we were quickly becoming the hottest band
in America, and the other guys were scoring constantly. Davy had
retreated to a quiet corner with two different girls before Aerosmith
wrapped up, and Spencer was living in a constant stream of lap dances
and pot smoke right in front of everyone, with the no-touching rule
that's policed in even the filthiest strip clubs gone far out the window.

Buck wasn't hooking up, but Buck didn't hook up very often—
except with drugs. His situation was different than mine, though. By
Texas I had started to figure out that Buck didn't like girls.

Of course, that wasn't anything new in the business. If someone
in the band wasn't gay or at least swinging both ways, the manager
probably was; but nobody talked about it. And at the time, that was
the best we felt like we could do. I guess it was possible that Kirby
was also gay, but Kirby was so unimportant that I literally didn't
think I could bring myself to think about his romantic history even if
my fuckin' life depended on it.

We figured that was Buck's deal. He never acted on it backstage—
backstage, for Buck, was about drugs and destruction—but we knew
he had side trips. And there were always rumors. Early on, Davy
seemed super uncomfortable. Spencer didn't register a reaction one
way or the other, but I'll admit that it was something I thought about
for just a second when sharing drugs and booze and a disgusting,
cramped tour bus. I mean, everyone was always saying guys like Buck
could give you a disease, but we were partying so hard most of the
time, I wasn't able to focus on it. He was so damn good, and we really
loved the guy when he was conscious. Although one night on the
road, he told me that he was in something called a "plural marriage,"
and I could ask any questions about it that I wanted, but I didn't have

any. I never knew what to believe, and I had already given up trying to figure that guy out.

Anyway: the guys from Poison were the ringleaders backstage. Like I said, they were infamous for recruiting the VIPs, usually by sending out roadies with rolls of cash to comb the strip clubs.

Ricky Rockett had just tackled me onto the floor and three babes were spraying tequila into my mouth when Aerosmith wrapped up "Train Kept A-Rollin'." I heard the crowd go nuts, and I figured that the band was leaving the stage.

The word backstage was that the Aerosmith guys weren't able to stick around after their set, so I struggled my way out from the pile of tight young skin and silk and suds and excused myself to meet one of my heroes.

I steered toward Steven Tyler while the rest of the guys moved on. Steven smiled at me. "Rikki, right?" he said. "Great set."

"Thanks," I said. "You too."

We were both silent for a few seconds, and my brain reverted back to twelve-year-old Richard Henderson, daydreaming that Steven Tyler (or Mick Jagger, or Jimmy Page, or even Ozzy) was my long-lost father. Steven picked up on how carefully I was studying his face. "I know that look," he said, with a wise smile. "What year were you born?"

"Sixty-four," I said.

"Where?"

"L.A."

Steven Tyler shook his head. "Nope," he said. "Sorry. But, hey, you're doin' all right, aren't ya?"

"I guess I am," I said. "Any advice?"

"Yeah. Have fun," Steven said. "Have *lots* of fun. But keep your head together. You know what I mean?"

I knew enough about how hard Steven used to party to know exactly what he was talking about.

"I will," I said. "I mean, I do. I do and I will."

"Right on, Thunder," Steven said. "Now go on back in there and get yourself laid, all right? I'll catch you around."

With that, he headed off, and I got back to the party while Boston took the stage.

The guys all seemed busy with their own shit, and I was getting eye-fucked all over the place and needed somebody to talk to so I could take my mind off all the temptation. I scanned the room and found that one other person was, surprisingly, all alone.

Bret Michaels—the handsomest man in the room, and possibly also the prettiest woman—was noodling on an acoustic guitar. I gestured at the space next to him.

"Cool?" I asked.

"Rikki Thunder!" he shouted at me, and slapped the couch. I took a seat and Bret looked at me intensely, right in the eyes. "How are *you*, dude?" He tucked one spandexed leg under his butt and then untucked it. "It's awesome to hang out with you!"

Bret drank whatever was left in a red plastic cup and then threw it over his shoulder. His energy was kind of overwhelming at first, but he seemed sincere. "Yeah, definitely," I said. I gestured at his guitar. "What are you playing?"

"It's a ballad," Bret said. "But not, like, a screeching-guitar, scream-at-the-sky power ballad. Like, a country western one, you know? A *real ballad*. Check this out."

He picked up the guitar and strummed a slow, soulful lick about lying closely together but feeling far apart. He was right—it sounded more like a country song than metal. *Damn.*

"That sounds really good," I said.

"Thanks. Hey, really, thanks, bro," Bret said. "The label doesn't want us to use it. I wrote it the last time I was in Dallas. Coming back to an old stop gets you thinking, you know?"

I shrugged. "I don't, really," I said. "This is my first tour."

Bret's eyes lit up, and he thumped me on the back. "Oh, dude, that's right," he said. "I wanna hear all about it. How's it going? Good, right?"

"Yeah," I said. "It's good. A little crazy."

"Awwww." Bret shook his head and smiled. "Crazy's how it's *supposed* to be, right?" Then he laughed really hard.

I couldn't help but laugh, too. "I guess it is, Bret!" I said.

Bret put the guitar down. "You know," he said, "we've been on the road all year. A lot has changed in my life. But you know what hasn't?"

"What's that?"

"This," Bret said, and he gestured to the room around us. Boston segued from "Rock & Roll Band" into "Peace of Mind" onstage while Davy wrestled in the suds with a Cowboys cheerleader. Buck was enjoying some cocaine in a dark corner and laughing hysterically. Spencer was asleep on the couch, underneath a pile of VIPs.

"And look," Bret said. "Sometimes, that's awesome. And sometimes it's depressing. But it's reliable, at least."

"Okay."

"Point is, you gotta find a way to make it yours," he said.

"What do you mean?"

"I mean, this isn't a thing you're doing for the weekend. This is your life now. Don't just, like, ride it out, or you'll be stressed out all the time. If you live on the road, what do you need to do to make it a happy life? You need drugs? You need a shiatsu massage? You need your favorite pizza? You need to lift weights, run a mile? You need a regular girl? Figure it out and get it. 'Cause this is what you do now, and the real world is gonna move on without you.

"First things first, bro? Do yourself a favor and get your rocks off. You look like you're gonna jump out of your skin."

"I don't know," I said. "I got this girl at home."

Bret nodded. "Hey, man," he said. "Home's home. The road's the road. You keep 'em separate, everyone does all right. It's no big secret what happens out here."

"It's not even like that, though," I said. "She told me I can sleep with whoever I want on the road."

Bret looked at me sideways. "She did?"

"Yeah," I said. "She figured I would want to, and she didn't want me to feel guilty or blame her or anything."

"Huh. Same rule applies to her?"

Oh shit, I thought. *Does it?* We hadn't discussed that. "I don't know," I said.

Bret didn't make eye contact for a few seconds. "Well, she sounds like a smart lady, anyway," he finally said. "You know what it's like after a show."

I nodded.

"It's like a pressure valve, right?" he said. "You gotta release it or eventually it breaks something inside you."

"Yeah, exactly."

"Look around you." Bret waved at the room, which was mostly full of half-naked women. "You could probably have your pick. Just go for it."

"The thing is," I said, "I don't usually hook up with a girl unless we've made, like, a connection first? Or else it feels like I'm just taking advantage. But my girl, she said don't make connections. That's the part that would feel like cheating."

Bret smiled. He blew out a long, slow breath. All of a sudden, he didn't seem so hyper anymore. He seemed tired. "Bro, I say this with all the love in the world," he said, putting a hand on my shoulder. "*Get over yourself.*"

I was confused, because Bret had said something mean but was smiling with real kindness in his eyes. "Uh . . . what?" I said.

Bret Michaels waved his hand from one side of the room to another. "These women are your age, bro, they're grown-up ladies with lives and probably better credit than you. What makes you think you're, like, a great catch for them? You're basically a traveling salesman, driving from town to town to make rent money. You live on a bus most of the time. You know what that does to a person? That smell, the beer and farts and cigarettes, it gets inside your skin. Do you think you're marriage material? You think that's why they're here?"

Of course it is, I thought. *I'm Rikki Thunder!* But I didn't say that. Instead, I just said "Umm . . ." again.

"They're here because you're a roller coaster, pal," Bret went on. "These concerts are a theme park. We're loud and colorful, and gross, and exciting, and you're this thrill ride, right? They take the ride because it's fun and dangerous and they might get puke on them, and they can tell their friends about it later—or not. But then they go home and take a shower, and sleep on clean sheets, and marry a nice guy who doesn't spend three hundred days a year on the road."

"But the Thunderstorm T-shirts—"

"Uh-huh. Sure," he said. "But let me ask you this. How many of these Thundercats are gonna be lined up in the parking lot to try and get on the bus tomorrow?"

I remembered Tawny's warning about no road girlfriends and realized that the subject hadn't really come up for any of us.

"Not a lot of return customers, huh?" Bret said. "That's because nobody's looking for love here." He poked my chest. "You're a story for their friends. They're getting you out of their systems."

Bret Michaels was still kind of hurting my feelings, but now he seemed like he was doing it in a . . . *helpful* way? Were the screaming, crying girls at each stop not hopelessly in love with a bunch of scrawny assholes with big speakers? We were prizes, sure, but kind of gross prizes, meant to be tossed away in the parking lot. Could Bret Michaels be right?

I did have one ace in the hole that he didn't, though. Tawny.

"I don't know," I said. "Like I said before, I got a girl at home. She seems to think I'm pretty great."

Bret winced. "Look, Rikki. I don't know anything about your girl or what you-all have goin' on between you. But you remember I said that I wrote that song last time I was in Dallas? It was right after I called my girl back home in the middle of the night and heard another guy in the room."

"Shit."

"And, dude, it was a friend of mine from another band."

"No way," I said. I was upset now for my new friend Bret. "Who was it? Should we kick his ass?"

Bret waved his hand. "Not important. What's important is, there I was, thinking I'm this hot-shit grand prize. God's gift to babes, right? But the girls on the road weren't really interested in a life with Papa Rolling Stone, and neither was my lady. I'm not saying it's gonna happen to you. I'm just saying, we do the same thing every night on the road, and it feels like time isn't passing. But it is."

"But—"

"And a girl who knows her worth isn't gonna spend her life sitting on the couch, watching her life go by while you're out living yours."

"Ouch."

"Hey," he said. "Everyone knows what this is all about. And everybody gets what they want. We need to get the show out of our system, and they need to go back to their jobs or their dorms or whatever and say they fucked Rikki Thunder." He patted my shoulder again and smiled, then shook his head. "And they don't want to be pen pals with you, either, bro."

I looked around the room again. A brunette in a Thunderstorm tee with a deep tan and bright red lipstick was just waiting for me to make eye contact. We smiled at each other. She winked. And I realized that this dude, Bret Michaels, was making an enormous amount of sense.

Bret pointed at the brunette. "She knows why she's here. Do you? Just go take her by the hand and walk off."

"Really? It just seems weird not to, like, talk first. Find common interests?"

"Your common interest is that you want to screw each other's brains out and never speak to each other again," Bret said. "She's here for a transaction, Thunder. Go make a deal."

I nodded.

Then I got up from the couch and started walking across the party to the brunette. She was soaked in bubbles and sweat, and when I got close, she stuck her tongue between her teeth and bit it while she smiled. God, she was gorgeous. God, I was horny.

"Hey," I said. "I'm Rikki."

"Too much talking!" I heard Bret Michaels scream. The brunette took my hand. And without another word spoken between us, she led me to the tour bus.

29

A NJA FELT A delicious thrill when she spotted the cassette tape
in her locker.

Of course, she already had the Whyte Python album, *All
Squeeze, No Venom*. It had become one of her favorites. No, she wasn't
excited to be in possession of new music. A Whyte Python cassette,
appearing out of nowhere, was a message.

The network of Whyte Python tapes that served as communi-
cation tools for young revolutionaries was her brother's idea. Peter
Koertig—two years older and a lifetime more experienced in the
resistance—had built his network by distributing them far and wide
across the city.

In the early days, Peter would tuck the message in with the liner
notes of whatever cassettes he could find, as long as they were metal
music. That was the code. But the tapes were always in short supply
and were typically reused until they fell apart. Suddenly, though, he
had access to dozens of cases of these Whyte Python tapes. Now they
had plenty of cassettes, so they could distribute messages farther and
faster than before; and the music was good, too! It sounded different
and seemed to make people happy and angry at the same time, which
was just how the movement wanted them. Where he got them Peter
never said, and Anja never knew. They each had their jobs to do for
the revolution, and Peter purposely kept her in the dark about his
contacts and personal contributions. Peter would never make her a
party to information that could get her jailed or killed. He kept her
safe that way.

But she was important. He promised her that she would be. He had trusted her with the rooftop mission, revealing her identity to no one—and it had made her a legend. The Flying Graffiti Artist, they called her. A real East German superhero among their ranks in the revolution. This stunt with the flag alone brought on dozens of young people, inspired just as much by the daring prank as the message it sent. And with every Whyte Python tape she received, Anja felt more like a real superhero.

And now she had a job to do, which was becoming a regular thing. On any given day Anja might find herself couriering contraband across town, or spreading the word about a protest effort by distributing cassette cases, or on the occasional night mission with a precious can of spray paint. She imagined that each set of instructions came from "the boys" in Whyte Python, and after she recovered the message, she always gave the tape away. This was how a movement grew.

Anja slid the tape into the pocket of her sweater, a high school uniform designed to be shapeless and sexless—an unoriginal aesthetic meant to inspire unoriginal thought. She entered the bathroom and closed herself off in a stall.

Inside the case Anja found an address and instructions. She was to collect a package from a mailbox and deliver it across the city. Both stops were on her normal route home from school; no deviation from her routine.

Anja tore the note into little pieces and flushed them down the toilet. She left the cassette case—just a real shredder of an album inside now, no spy shit—on the counter by the sink for another student to discover. Another light bulb to turn on over the head of an oppressed teenager in her oppressed homeland—just another kid looking to belong to something real.

Anja imagined a classmate finding it there; she would glance at the liner notes, drawn in at first by pictures of Davy Bones and Rikki Thunder shirtless in a Jeep on a beach somewhere in America, and she would notice the provocative and vaguely sexual song titles that also evoked a sense of joy and fun and freedom. This classmate would look over her shoulder—that was a national habit—before sliding the tape into her own uniform, to play in secret later on.

Anja smiled at the vision. "Welcome to the revolution," she said, and turned off the light.

30

MUSIC MONTAGE: MID-TOUR

Song: "Never-Ending Party," by Whyte Python

The Python Pit

The boys have returned to California for a break in touring. The bald man and his driver watch from across the street as the band empties the pet warehouse of their belongings and loads them onto a moving truck. The bald man opens and clenches his fist, barely suppressing his rage as he watches Rikki Thunder toss a garbage bag to Buck Sweet. The two men in the car whisper to each other in German as the driver takes photographs.

New houses

Davy pulls a for-sale sign out of the front yard of a big house and spikes it like a football while his bandmates pop open champagne bottles. He immediately kicks band manager Kirby Smoot off his property.

Rikki takes a sign out of the yard in front of a Hollywood Hills bungalow and spikes it So hard that he falls over. Tawny helps him to his feet, and they embrace.

Spencer kicks open the door to a large, flashy apartment with a massive fish tank and a hot tub on a deck overlooking Los Angeles. He drops his bags on the floor and pumps his fists in the air.

Buck takes a for-sale sign out of the window of the pet store warehouse. He crumples it into a ball and spikes it on the floor, then looks around at his home with pride.

A sparse apartment in Los Angeles

The bald German is shirtless, his muscular back painted with tattoos: a storm of weapons and fierce animals spiraling out from the official flag of the Stasi. He is doing pushups in the barren living room and counting angrily in German. A tinny radio plays *All Squeeze, No Venom*.

The German completes his workout, then smashes the small radio against the floor.

A greenroom in Florida

The band is back on tour again, beginning with three nights across the Sunshine State. The room is absolutely packed with groupies. Rikki finds he is more comfortable introducing himself to girls and taking one back to the hotel with him.

Rezident Ivanov's office

A file lands on Rezident Ivanov's desk, labeled "Whyte Python Status Update."

A Billboard Hot 100 graphic

All Squeeze, No Venom climbs from number fifteen to number nine!

A hotel suite in North Carolina

The boys are in a living room littered with food, drugs, and sleeping groupies on what appears to be the morning after a concert. There's a lion.

Amanda Price enters, disguised as Tawny Spice, and she is leading a middle-aged woman into the room. The guest is dressed in the height of fashion, with oversize sunglasses and short, jet-black hair. The band knows her as "the nice lady from New York" who has helped to created their dazzling merch; we recognize her as CIA officer Catherine Stryker, in disguise.

Stryker is holding a design book. She opens it for the waking boys. Inside, we see detailed costume designs for each member of the band. The designs are stunning. The band cheers.

A neighborhood in Soviet Russia

It is the middle of the night. Teenagers wearing T-shirts and face paint the same color as the costumes in Stryker's sketches march toward a government building. They fan out, spray-painting the brick walls.

A massive arena

Officer Stryker and a pair of technicians hover over a complicated control board. On Stryker's command, the technicians set up a pyrotechnic show onstage.

Later that night, Whyte Python is performing before a sold-out crowd while Stryker's pyro show fires.

An old-world plaza

Protesters of all ages march, some of them wearing Whyte Python merch. Their arms are raised, and they're chanting. The leaders are holding sparklers that match the colors of the Whyte Python pyro show.

A greenroom in Virginia

A group of young women surround Rikki. Rikki pretends he's trying to choose between them, then leads all of them off to the tour bus together. The ladies all cheer and throw up double devil horns.

A Billboard Hot 100 graphic

All Squeeze, No Venom climbs from number seven to number five!

An East German high school gymnasium

A crowd sits in rapt attention as a twentysomething man in a Whyte Python shirt speaks passionately into a microphone.

A hotel room in Boston

Buck opens a crate and takes a real white python out, holding it high. Everyone cheers.

A hospital waiting room in Boston, an hour later

Davy, Rikki, and Spencer pace nervously. A doctor approaches. He holds his hands up reassuringly, and the boys rejoice.

Davy and Rikki hug each other. Spencer hugs the doctor. He leads them into a room, where Buck is recovering.

The white python is sleeping in a cage next to his bed.

Buck gives them a thumbs-up. Spencer pushes the doctor out of the room and the boys pile onto the bed for a massive group hug. Somehow there are beers.

A lovely bouquet of flowers sits at Buck's bedside. The unsigned card reads: *If that had been a cobra, you would be dead.*

Outside, the Germans in trench coats watch the hospital, taking photos through Buck's window with a long lens.

A Billboard Hot 100 graphic

Whyte Python's Debut Album, *All Squeeze, No Venom,* climbs from number four to number one!

31

W E REACHED MAINE at the beginning of September, just as *All Squeeze* hit number one on the *Billboard* charts. We were playing at the Cumberland County Civic Center, which was a smaller venue than we were used to, with a little over six thousand people.

But it was an important show for the band and for the crowd, because Spencer grew up in Maine—and it was his birthday! Kirby had worked with the promoters to have Spencer's homecoming show fall on September 4.

Portland started out great. Tawny had met us in Boston the night before, and once they let Buck out of the hospital, we drove up together. Even though I had really come to enjoy having careless sex with a stream of anonymous, beautiful women during the tour, I was always happiest with her. So we got into Maine early, and the whole band had lobsters and a birthday cake for Spencer at a picnic table in a park on the water. Like a big family.

We did an album signing at this cool underground record store where everybody in the room—band, customers, and staff—was stoned off their ass. I was so baked, I started signing records with Buck's name because it was easier to spell.

When the sun began to set, we crashed a little nightclub that Spencer used to play at when he was in high school. A bunch of kids in flannel shirts were doing sound check, and we played a couple of songs with them. Portland was shaping up to be a really special stop on the tour.

But things went backward at the hotel before we went over to the venue.

We were partying in my room, and Tawny's designer friend showed up. It turns out her name was Cathy, and she was wearing her giant square sunglasses and carrying her design book with her.

This wasn't a scheduled thing, but they said Cathy had a bunch of ideas for changes to the merch. She held up her book, and it had sketches of T-shirts that I thought looked pretty much like the ones we were already selling, so I said I liked them because it seemed like it was important to Tawny.

"The new shirts are being printed now," Cathy was saying, "and they should be ready to swap out by the time you guys hit Burlington." She closed her book.

"My friend Kevin says if we really want people to wear our T-shirts, we should give them away for free," Spencer said. Spencer talked about his friend Kevin a lot, but nobody had ever met him. The anecdotes just kept getting weirder.

"Hey, Spencer, buddy?" Davy said. "Can you . . . see Kevin right now?"

"Huh?" Spencer said.

"Now, interviews," Tawny said. "We tested some new catchphrases to work into radio shows."

I could tell right away that Davy didn't like this conversation. Maybe he was just in one of his moods, but he put his sunglasses on and smoked cigarettes, and he wouldn't even look in Tawny or Cathy's direction. Tawny was just suggesting that we start saying cool shit on the radio like "We're gonna rock the block" and "Get ready for the rock revolution," but he was crossing his arms and pouting. You'd think she told him to get a haircut.

"*We* think?" Davy said. "What do you mean, we?"

"It's tested, Davy," Tawny said.

"Tested by who, you and Thunder?" Davy pointed at me. "You guys are gonna tell me what I can and can't say now?"

I sighed. "What's the problem?" I asked.

"The problem is, your girlfriend seems to be in charge of every decision we make," he said.

Here we go. New band, same problem. A lead singer who doesn't trust Tawny even though she's just trying to help. But that tickle found its way back into my brain again—*she really has engineered a lot of this.* But I pushed it away and got defensive instead. "Dude," I said. "It's just some catchphrases."

"And T-shirts." He counted on his fingers. "And pyro. And costumes."

"She comes from the industry," I said. "Look how well all this working! We're getting her advice for free. And this is what we pay Cathy for."

"And where did Cathy come from?" Davy asked. "I don't remember getting to look at other designs or pick someone on our own. She was just there one day, with Tawny. And now she's rolling out all these other ideas."

"Davy," Spencer said.

"It's funny how the only experts we get to meet are walked into the room by your old lady." He pointed a finger at me. "It's almost like they're being walked in by you."

"The fuck, Davy?" I threw a beer can at him. "You wanna accuse me of something, bro?"

Davy flicked his cigarette at me. "Are you trying to take over this band?"

"What?" Taking over the band wasn't even a concept to me. I know Davy liked to say it was "his," and that was fine—I just figured it belonged to all of us. "You're talking crazy right now."

"Notice he didn't say no," Davy said to Spencer. Spencer just stared straight ahead.

"The answer is no," I said. "I'm not trying to take over the band, whatever that means. Sorry if Tawny's trying to help by giving us good ideas."

"I hate to interrupt," Kirby interrupted, "but aren't these decisions my job? There are preferred contractors to manage, and Andromeda's public relations firm. It's all kind of Byzantine, really—"

"Exactly," Davy shouted. "This is Kirby's job. Also, Kirby, shut the fuck up and get out of this room right now, or I swear to God I'll kill you."

"Maybe I should bring my suggestions to Kirby first?" Tawny offered. "He can decide what to bring to the band."

"Maybe just let us worry about it," Davy said.

"Easy," I warned him. Why did my lead singers keep turning against Tawny whenever she tried to help?

"Sorry," Davy said, like he was not sorry. "Sorry, Tawny. I'm an asshole, all right? Forget it. The T-shirts are great. Whatever. But I'm getting my own publicist, and nobody tells me what to say. Got it? We cool?"

Before anybody could answer, Davy got up and left the room.

Tawny left the room next, and Cathy went after her. I thought they were chasing after Davy to smooth things over or fight with him more, but I found them by the elevator. They looked pissed at each other, which was weird, and Cathy was saying, "This is why the agency needs him on board." I asked what they were talking about, but they hushed up really quick.

It sounded like the agency that Cathy worked for was real strict, and I felt bad that the guys might be getting her in trouble.

We'd been on the road for months. This was obviously not our first band fight. We'd been getting sick of each other for a while now. Sometimes the fights happened for no reason—just because we were overtired, or somebody needed to blow off steam and the rest of us ended up in the crossfire. It was Davy usually, with this kind of crap, but we had all taken our turn at being the rotten egg.

Fortunately, we had also built up a pretty solid wall between what was happening offstage and on; once we did the band chant, everything else went on pause until the show was over. Onstage we'd put on a killer show, and we'd hug each other and joke around and sing into the same microphone and tell the crowd we loved them.

Sometimes things would smooth over backstage after the show. Faking it in front of the audience was enough to fix the problem in real life. Sometimes we'd just keep our distance for a while.

Whenever Tawny could meet us on the road, I would hop off the bus and ride in a rental car with her. When Davy needed a break, he would charter a limo. When Buck got tired of our bullshit he would vanish completely for a few days, turning up with a fresh injury a half hour before we were supposed to take the stage.

One time he had a black eye. Another time, something had bitten off part of his toe. In Atlanta he actually got dropped off at the venue by an ambulance, and he was still in a hospital johnnie and dragging an IV. The ambulance driver said that Buck absolutely had to finish his IV drip; and whatever we did, we couldn't let him take any drugs.

Good old Buck!

The only one who didn't take time off from the band was Spencer. We never had a reason to get mad at him, first of all. He didn't ruffle feathers. I think Spencer and I had a lot in common, in that we were both really happy to be there—but I was kind of jealous of him at the same time, because he didn't get bothered by all this other crap. No girlfriend, no weird competition with Davy, no pressure to be something he wasn't. He played hard, he partied hard, he didn't make any waves, and he was happy as a clam.

And, sure, he was dumb—dangerously dumb—but he slept like a rock. What's so wrong with that? We don't all have to be geniuses, like yours truly! (Imagine I'm pointing to myself with both thumbs again.)

After that fight in Portland, we settled into an unspoken agreement. We would set aside the blowup over Tawny and give the city a hell of a show. For Spencer.

When Davy started the introductions near the end of our set, he had a surprise up his sleeve. We always introduce Spencer first, but Davy saved him for last. He introduced Buck and me, and he even toned down his own big introduction of himself.

Then he cupped his hands around his mouth and the microphone, so he could whisper really loud.

"And Portland's own . . ." he managed to get out, before the Maine crowd went wild. "Spencer Dooley!" The arena rumbled with the audience's single, unified scream.

For the first time on the tour, neither Davy nor I was the most popular guy onstage, and we were both totally cool with it. Spencer waved at his fans shyly. Apparently, he didn't know what to do with all the attention on him.

All right, Portland," Davy announced, and he held his arms wide to quiet them down. "Of course, you know that Spencer's from here. But did you also know that today . . . is his birthday?"

Portland responded with another uniform shriek. I had to hand it to Davy. Whatever mood he was in earlier, he was really selling it for Spencer.

"Let's all wish him a happy birthday, huh?" Davy waved his arms. "Ready? One, two, three!"

Then the entire arena sang "Happy Birthday," and it was heart-warming as fuckin' shit.

Sure, we're used to hearing the crowd drunkenly sing along to our songs while we play; and once in a while Davy will hold the mic out during "Behind Your Eyes" for a line or two. But this was six thousand people singing the same thing in unison. No instruments, no pyro, just a song that we all knew by heart and sang together.

It was the closest I'd ever felt to an audience; and despite the argument that we'd had a few hours earlier, it was probably the closest I'd ever felt to my band, too. It was pretty magical, dude!

Spencer just kind of grinned along while we sang. But I could tell that he was affected, too, because he flubbed his chords a couple of times when we played "Radio Heaven" right after.

I was glad for him. He can be a tough dude to figure out sometimes, but I think he's probably the nicest guy I know. I wasn't surprised to see how much his hometown loved him.

32

―⚡―

CENTRAL INTELLIGENCE AGENCY CASE FILE: DOS (7)/PFM/001.13/25

SUBMITTED BY: Boone, Darrell A.
MISSION: Project Facemelt
ASSET: R. Henderson (alias Rikki Thunder)

CATEGORY: Close Relationship Profiles

NAME: Spencer Charles Dooley
ALIAS(ES): None
AGE: 23

RELATIONSHIP TO ASSET: Member of the band "Whyte Python"

BACKGROUND:
"Nobody likes you, burnout." Mr. Craig kicked Spencer's foot. "Take those sunglasses off and get to class. Or drop out, I don't care. But stop blocking my hallway."

Spencer was sitting on the floor with his back against his locker and his legs sticking straight out. The gym teacher hovered over him and waited for him to get up and get moving. Spencer didn't know how long Mr. Craig had been there. He was sleeping.

"Okay, dude," Spencer muttered. "Just quit kicking me, all right?"

He stood up and brushed his hands against his ripped jeans.

"I'm going."

"Unless you're too stoned to find your classroom," a random voice called from behind—some jock, probably. Bursts of laughter.

The thing was, Spencer wasn't even stoned. He was a stoner, fine; but on that morning, he was just *tired*.

He had slept fitfully on the couch in his friend Beanie's basement after a fight with his old man that may or may not have resulted in Spencer being kicked out of the family home. He wasn't sure.

Spencer was a senior in high school, but it wasn't likely that he would graduate. He was behind in math. He was behind in English. He didn't even know that he was taking Chemistry. The school year would end in a few months, and he expected to be told that he hadn't earned enough credits, and would need to repeat his senior year. He wasn't sure that he would bother.

Spencer wasn't failing school for lack of trying. He just couldn't grab onto the concepts like the other kids could. When he was little, Spencer watched in frustration as his kindergarten classmates went from stringing letters together into words to stringing words together into sentences. Something that seemed so natural to them felt impossible for Spencer. His attention just refused to hold. He would try to read the words, but at the exact same time his mind was creating rhythms out of the scratching of his classmates' pencils, and he would get distracted by the low buzz of the fluorescent lights overhead.

It was such a struggle to focus on JUST THE ONE THING that he would get a headache and forget the word that he had just managed to read before he moved onto the next one. So he would take a break and watch birds outside the window until the teacher slapped his desk with a ruler and told him that he wasn't learning because he refused to pay attention.

At recess, he would sit crouched on the playground watching ants and bugs. When he was lucky, a garden snake would wander into the field. He found them fascinating, the way their bodies slithered across the ground in a perfect S shape, like they were floating. He couldn't pay attention to reading or math for more than a few seconds at a time, but he could watch a snake for the entire recess without lifting his head. The other kids thought he was weird. He didn't notice.

That was most of school for Spencer. With enough effort, he was able to stumble his way into the upper grades. But the work was hard, and the teachers and the rest of his class were always too far ahead of him.

At least once a day, he would decide that there was no point in trying to catch up with them and give up, holding back tears while he doodled in his notebook or hummed the latest AC/DC riff.

When he was a freshman, he discovered weed and decided that it helped. When he was high, Spencer found that he could turn the volume down on the swarm of stimuli pecking at him from every angle and focus on just one thing at a time without getting a headache or blurry eyes. And even though he still struggled with the meaning of the words when he read sometimes, or what they were trying to tell him, he found that he could mostly remember what they said.

But that made him a stoner, apparently, and so he fell in with the other stoners, the kids who were wearing Grateful Dead shirts and beads in junior high and now had ragged mops of hair and ripped jeans in high school. His friends had mostly given up on their education, too, so they smoked dope and cigarettes in the school parking lot and joked around.

They had a shitty band that would play in a little dump of a club on Congress Street, with Spencer playing bass and finding that the weed definitely helped him keep the beat no matter what kind of noise the other guys were making. It was probably the first thing that he was good at.

His parents were exasperated. He had been such a sweet little boy; his mother would say it all the time. He would help her clean up the kitchen while his father was at work, and he would call his grandparents just to sing a song for them, and his smile was so big and open and genuine, it held back nothing.

But his parents weren't perfect, and they were more inclined to listen to his teachers' reports that he "wasn't trying" than their son's pleas that he was trying but he couldn't do it. They had given up on college for him. He showed no interest in the kind of job a guy without a degree might still be able to make a living at, like sales or construction.

So his old man, who was a firefighter, asked the chief if the kid could come in and shadow at the station, sort of a pre-apprenticeship deal. He made Spencer put on a shirt and tie and call everybody sir or ma'am, and gave him a pep talk that this was basically his last fucking chance to be a productive member of society.

Spencer was actually looking forward to this opportunity. Besides snakes, fire was the only other thing that could hold his attention indefinitely.

So he was on his best behavior. He stayed sober and didn't call anyone "dude." Even his old man tossed an approving nod his way after lunch. He was *doing* it.

But then a call came in from a residential neighborhood. A homeowner was burning leaves, even though it was a high-fire-risk day. Spencer and his dad went over in a pickup truck, and the bonfire guy ran for it when he saw them coming, so his dad told Spencer to stay by the fire and not touch anything while he went and knocked on the door.

Spencer didn't want to touch anything. He wanted to be good. He was more surprised than anyone when he found himself holding a stick that he'd fished out of the fire, swinging it in figure eights in front of his eyes to create neon trails of orange light—and inadvertently spreading the fire that they were supposed to be suppressing.

By the time his father had coaxed the man out of the house and gotten the hose unraveled, they found Spencer sword-fighting ghosts in the backyard and spraying hot embers across a pile of dry wood that was reserved to feed the fire.

It was a quiet drive home, and an explosive dinner. And then it was Beanie's couch, and Mr. Craig in the hall, and some asshole calling him stoned even though he wasn't.

A different boy—any one of his friends, certainly—would have dropped everything and started throwing punches at the teacher, the classmate, the lockers, anything. But fighting wasn't in Spencer's nature. Instead, he found his classroom, slumped into a chair in the back, and put his head on the desk like a sleepy old bloodhound.

He didn't fit in at school, where his classmates were moving from lesson to lesson, preparing themselves for even more school at a technical college or university.

He didn't fit in with his friends, either, who responded to their status as outcasts with anger and criminal mischief.

He wasn't a salesman. He wasn't a construction worker. He wasn't a hooligan. He sure as hell wasn't a firefighter.

Spencer didn't really belong anywhere.

He eventually went home from Beanie's house. Finished the school year. Did not graduate. He ran away in July and hitched to Boston, then to New York City, and then he headed west. California was his target—because his favorite bands were from there, and because as long as he was traveling with a destination in mind, he wasn't technically homeless.

Spencer arrived in West Hollywood late in 1983—and almost immediately found gainful employment! He worked as a dirty-job Swiss Army knife at a little nightclub on the Sunset Strip.

On any given night he was bar-backing or cleaning the bathrooms or bouncing the front door. He didn't care that it was shit work for shittier money—he got to listen to music and make new friends, and some of the young bands who were just starting out would let him jam in with them during sound checks.

In Maine, he had stood out in a way that made him an outcast; but in West Hollywood, he looked pretty much like everyone else—and the kindness of his personality was able to shine through. People on the Sunset Strip liked him. His new friends helped him find a place to live, and to find other guys to play with. He tried to start bands with them, but it never seemed to work out.

In 1984, he saw a flyer for a new band seeking a bass player. There was a number, and it said to ask for Davy.

Spencer met Davy Bones, Buck Sweet, and Barry Gorman in a garage. They chatted for a few minutes about their influences, who they learned from, what kind of music they hoped to play. Davy seemed to be overflowing with ideas for everything from costumes to song titles, and Buck was funny and weird in a way that Spencer found comforting. Barry was colder toward him, but you never know with drummers.

They jammed for twenty minutes or so, and Spencer thought it went pretty good.

Davy asked Spencer what he was into when he wasn't playing, and Spencer said he liked snakes and fire. Barry snorted in a way that wasn't so nice, but Buck's eyes lit up.

"You like snakes?" Buck asked. "What's your favorite kind?"

"Oh, pythons, definitely," Spencer said.

"Thank God," Buck said. "I was worried you were gonna be one of those cobra assholes."

"About the fire, though." Davy scrunched his brow and pointed at Spencer. "Have you ever been set on fire before? Like, onstage?"

"On purpose?" Spencer said. "No, but I probably could pull it off if I wanted to. Why?"

"Just an idea I have," Davy said.

Spencer smiled, the same wide-open grin that his mother loved. He liked these guys. They seemed to understand him.

"All right," Barry said, opening a beer. He had his back to them. "So, we're, like, looking at a bunch of guys, but we'll give you a call if we want to hear you again."

Spencer's head dropped right away. The tone in Barry's voice couldn't have been clearer.

He wasn't getting in.

He tucked his bass guitar into its case and buckled it closed. Spencer didn't understand. This had felt like the right group for him. They listened to his ideas and didn't laugh at him when he gave honest answers that others before them had found strange, or when he didn't get the joke right away.

And they played well together, too.

He might even fit in here.

But they didn't want him. He was about to thank them for their time and show himself out when Davy held a dramatic hand in the air and waved Barry off. He straddled his chair backward and leaned across the backrest.

He reached out and gripped Spencer's hand.

"Spencer Dooley," Davy Bones said, "I have three questions for you . . ."

33

W E WERE ON the back leg of the tour now, on the long road between shows in Chicago and Des Moines.

After Portland, Tawny backed off the tour quite a bit—which was a smart move. She realized that Davy wasn't going to relax with her and Cathy poking around the band. So she parachuted in for shows here and there, but mostly we just talked on the phone.

Whyte Python, meanwhile, had settled into a pattern for the back half that felt a little less frantic, and a little lower key. We were a group of good buds who hung out on the bus, played monster shows, got laid a bunch, smoked weed a bunch, just kept it real, you know? We knew we were steering toward a break, and it was just a matter of getting there. Everyone mostly got along by turning the volume down on the whole thing a little.

Davy and I were doing all right. We tried to avoid pushing each other's buttons, and after a week of tiptoeing around each other, everything was copacetic. It just always felt like *work* to maintain that friendship, you know what I mean? Things with Spencer and Buck were easy-peasy.

I think the difference was that, deep down, Davy and I wanted to be friends with each other more than anyone else. Spencer and I might have had similar personalities, and Buck was the most fun to party with; but something about how much Davy needed the music—how hard he clung to it, and how protective he was of it—felt familiar to me in ways that I just didn't see in the other guys.

And it must be said: we were the two biggest names in the band, which put us in a different position together. I don't say that to take anything away from Buck and Spencer's contributions, which were enormous. Whyte Python was Whyte Python because of Buck Sweet's guitar, but he was just too weird and unpredictable to be a marketable product. And Spencer was the heart of the band, but he played bass and wasn't very quick in interviews, which meant he was gonna have a lower ceiling. (Outside of Maine, at least!)

It was Davy and me who handled most of the press, and we were the ones who the gossip papers were obsessed with, and who the groupies chased the hardest. We felt the weight of the band on our shoulders. I'm sure it drove a lot of the conflict between us, but it also bonded us in ways that were left unspoken.

There was always just something in the way of us getting along better. Davy being insecure. Tawny sharing her ideas for band stuff at the worst time. I'm sure there was dumb shit that I was doing to piss him off without even realizing.

But I don't want to give the wrong impression. We had plenty of great times together in that first year. Look—again, not to take anything away from those other guys, but if I needed to have a real conversation with someone in the band about anything beyond snakes, fire, babes, or drugs, I was only gonna get that from Davy. There were plenty of late nights on tour when Davy and I would sit at the back of the bus while the other guys were passed out, and he would noodle on a guitar while I scribbled down lyrics that we usually threw away, and we just gabbed about life and shit.

Those moments were the closest thing I'd had to my friendship with Ron, before the shit went down with Qyksand. It was a feeling I didn't realize I missed until I found it again, and it made me feel happy to have it again and shitty that I had thrown it away at the same time.

So anyway, that's, like, the general place we were in during that long drive from Illinois to Iowa. I spent the day with my head against the window, dozing in and out and watching the fields roll by. There was less to look at than the stretches we'd gotten used to between the East Coast cities. Once the hangover wore off, I was feeling kind of antsy and bored.

We were all in our own spaces across the bus as the sun dipped toward the horizon, and we stopped to gas up at a truck stop somewhere in corn country. Spencer was playing Nintendo, and Buck was working on a lick on his guitar with big can headphones and sunglasses on. Tuned out from the world. Davy slid into the seat next to mine. I could see right away that he was just as restless as me.

He pushed his sunglasses down the bridge of his nose. "Hey," he whispered.

"What's up?"

Davy smiled mischievously. "Let's go do something stupid."

I grinned back and nodded. "Absolutely," I said. "Like what?"

"Follow me."

Davy got up from his seat and strolled down the aisle. "I'm gonna get a pack of cigs," he announced. "Anyone wanna go with me?"

"I can get cigarettes for you, Davy," Kirby said.

"Fuck off, Kirby," Davy said. "Anyone else?"

I got up, all casual-like and said, "I'll go, I guess."

Davy went into the gas station, and I followed him. The guy behind the register was a kid around our age with long, shaggy hair and acne scars. Jackpot. His mouth dropped open when he saw us.

Davy nodded at him. "Hey, what's up," he said.

"Da-Davy Bones," the guy stammered. "Rikki Thunder! What are you guys doing here?" His voice got a little louder and higher pitched with each word. By the end he was basically squeaking. "Oh my God, fucking Whyte Python! Oh my God!"

Davy held a finger to his lips. "Shhh," he said. The guy hushed up, like a well-trained dog. "You got a car?"

"Yeah." The clerk nodded. "It's parked out back."

"Can we borrow it?"

I snickered. The kid's eyebrows scrunched a little, surely confused by the question; but his hand slid into his pocket and came out with a set of keys. He handed them to Davy without a word.

"Thanks, bud," Davy said. "We'll have it back in a little bit, all right? Where's the back door?"

The kid pointed to a hallway that ended in a steel door with one of those red alarm bars.

"Will the alarm go off?" I asked. The clerk shook his head.

Davy went to the cooler and grabbed a twelve-pack of beer. "You never saw us," he said, and we pushed out the back door.

The clerk's Trans Am was parked right up against the wall. We giggled like jerk-off teenagers while Davy tossed the case of beer on the back bench and hopped in the driver's seat. I slid across the hood and crawled in through the passenger-side window, Dukes of Hazzard–style. Then Davy gunned the engine and spun the wheels, and we were off—a pair of rock stars in a rusty old Pontiac, barreling down the back streets of rural Iowa on the lam from the biggest stadium tour in the country.

We popped open beers—don't try this at home, kids!—while Davy kept his foot on the pedal, and we zipped down that rural highway between endless rows of corn, screaming and whooping it up like idiots with no plan. The sky turned purple, and the late-September sunset made the corn stalks around us blaze orange as they rolled gently in the evening breeze—like a sea of fire.

(Note to self: that's dope artwork for an album cover—dibs!)

Finally, we reached an intersection, and we saw bright lights glowing above the horizon at the end of the road to the right. Davy braked and cut the wheel, then stomped on the gas again as we went into a skid. The Trans Am sent a spray of asphalt into the sky and left a pair of black rubber tire burns on the street, and we barreled toward whatever civilization was at the other end of the road.

34

I T WAS A HIGH SCHOOL football field. It was big and new, glowing under huge white lights, way oversize for the sleepy farm town that built it, but I would bet that every seat in the bleachers was full on Friday nights. It felt like that kind of town. It was a part of America that I had never really experienced but felt close to anyway because of how much I'd seen it on TV and in the movies. It was a town of hardy, no-nonsense families who milked the cows at five in the morning and left cash in the bucket at church on Sundays, then filled the stands with fifty years' worth of red-and-gold letterman jackets on game night, all while Kevin Bacon danced out his rage in nearby abandoned factories, because dancing was not allowed within town limits.

Davy parked the car. I grabbed the brewskis, and we crept along the grandstand into the bowl of the stadium. The varsity team practiced under the lights. They were a mob of big corn-fed boys in red-and-white practice jerseys—half of them wearing red pinnies, to separate the offense from the defense. Coaches let out little beeps and tweets on their whistles while the team practiced drills, and cheerleaders worked through their routine on the other side of the field.

Davy looked around the field. "What do we do now?" he asked.

The answer felt obvious to me. "Now?" I said. I nodded toward the bleachers. In the dark space between steel bars that led underneath, I could see the glow of a lighter and hear the muffled chuckles of teenage morons. "Now we go home."

There were, of course, metalheads under the bleachers.

It was a cool fall night, and kids in torn jeans and denim jackets with shaggy mops of hair breathed steam while they leaned against the posts, smoking butts and drinking. They looked a lot like us; but in a town like this, they were the outcasts. The whole country might have been living in Whyte Python Nation at that moment in time, but this looked a lot more like Oak Ridge Boys territory.

The stoners watched us suspiciously. They didn't know who we were, and we had invaded their safe space. I shouldn't have been surprised that they didn't recognize us; but it was easy to forget that when we were onstage or on television, we were wearing so much hair spray and makeup and shit that it was practically an alter ego. Not to mention, Whyte Python was larger than life. To these kids we were ten feet tall and muscular, fully grownup men of the world. The two idiots who had just stepped under the bleachers were both about five feet ten, scrawny, and only a few years older than them. This was our crowd, for sure; but that didn't mean they'd recognize us in street clothes on a school night.

I knew the anonymity wouldn't last. These kids were Python fans, no question. They just needed a little nudge. "This where the party at?" I asked.

A short kid with hair across his eyes and a ratty little mustache scowled and stepped forward to defend the pack. But then recognition spread across the parts of his face that we could see, and his cigarette dropped out of his mouth.

"Holy fuck," he said. "Are you guys . . . really . . ." the kid stammered, and then he just stopped talking. He didn't know what else to say.

Davy poked out from behind me and grinned his million-dollar smile. "Are we," he sang, "*Whyyyyyteee Pyyyyython!*"

I held the case of beer over my head and let out a rooster crow. All the little stoners went nuts. They clamored all over us, and patted our backs, and shook our hands. A few of them had tears in their eyes. They didn't understand why this was happening.

"Oh my God," the little guy said again. "We're going to see you guys in Des Moines tomorrow night!"

"Hell yeah," I said. "What's happening tonight?"

"You're looking at it." The kid shrugged at the scene under the bleachers. "I'm Murph. You guys wanna party?"

Davy cracked open a beer, chugged it, and spiked it on the ground. "Does that answer your question, Murph?"

So we partied with outcast teenagers under the bleachers while a statewide manhunt was probably underway for us back at the truck stop. We shotgunned beers, and smoked some weed, and just fucked around while the football team practiced on the field. And oh my God, dude, it felt amazing!

"Man," I said, "this takes me back to high school." I took a sip from the can around my cigarette. Lukewarm beer had never tasted so good. I nodded toward Davy. "You too, bro?"

"Yeah, sure," Davy said, but his eyes were on the field, and he didn't sound very convincing.

Out on the field, the quarterback threw a dart to a wide receiver along the sideline. The kid raced past the defensive back, into the end zone, and the coaches all blew their whistles like crazy. The quarterback ran into the end zone to celebrate with his WR, and the rest of the offense piled on. A shorter kid, the defensive back, came over to shake the receiver's hand; and when he turned around, and nobody was looking, the QB pushed him to the ground.

"Nice play," Davy said.

"Yeah," Murph said. "Quarterback's an asshole, though."

Davy raised an eyebrow. He was still watching the field, where the quarterback was slapping helmets and jeering at the defense. "I bet," he said.

"Jeremy Rowland," Murph said, and some of the other kids groaned when they heard the name. On the field, Jeremy Rowland had taken off his helmet. He had a blond flattop and a red face. He was slapping his teammates on the helmet as they huddled around him, seeking his approval, until a coach blew a whistle and made Rowland run a lap for taking his helmet off.

"He's a senior," one of the other kids said. "Big-man-on-campus dickhead."

"That guy's been treating me like shit since kindergarten," Murph said.

"Like how?" I asked.

"Usual, I guess," Murph said. "He used to beat me up, but he can't do that during the football season or he'll get suspended. So now he just pushes me into lockers and whatever. He spit in my mashed potatoes in the cafeteria last week." Murph was trying to blow it off like it was no big thing, but I could tell he was hurt; and once again, I was reminded of Ron Finch. "Sorry I'm little and my dad doesn't own a tractor dealership, Jeremy," he said. His voice shook a little. "This town sucks."

"Every town sucks when you're in high school," I said.

"Amen to that," Davy said.

"No, man, you don't know," Murph said. "Growing up in the *country* country? It's all these dicks."

"Lonely feeling, right?" Davy said. I caught his eye, and for the first time I wondered who Davy Bones had been before he became Davy Bones. Maybe Davy had more in common with these kids than I thought. Maybe he had more in common with me, too.

I put my hand on Murph's skinny shoulder. "But look around, Murph," I said. "You're not alone. How did you find each other?"

Murph looked back at his friends, then at me. He had this confused look, like I should know the answer to my own question already. "Metal, bro," he said. "Through you."

35

W HYTE PYTHON RETURNED to Los Angeles in December
1987.
The pearl-white tour bus, now looking a little worse
for the wear, cruised into West Hollywood and drove straight to
Gazzarri's, where they were scheduled to play a "welcome home"
concert before taking a much-needed break.

CIA officer Amanda Price, also known as Tawny Spice, looked
like she had just stepped out of a poster above the bed of every horny
teenager in America. She wore a black crop-top and a tiny leather
skirt, her blond hair teased high. She watched from backstage as the
band played before a small but raucous crowd in a bar that had once
felt so large to Rikki Thunder that it paralyzed him onstage.

How far he had come! Amanda beamed as she watched her cre-
ation, a certified rock star now, playing the songs she had heard a
hundred times and had not entirely grown tired of.

And the tour had produced the exact result that she needed. Rikki
was sleeping with women at almost every stop—even more often
than he was admitting to her. And by the end of the tour, he was only
calling twice a week instead of daily. The tour had created the kind
of remove that she needed between them. Rikki Thunder was road
hardened now. He could be treated as such.

There was so much to do. Rikki needed to be brought into the
mission, and that would take some doing. They would need to brief
him on Project Facemelt's goals, and make sure he understood his
role. After that, the CIA needed Rikki to help them write and deliver
a song for the band's next album, which they were set to start record-

ing after the New Year.

She tried to just enjoy the concert. She knew it would be the last one before everything changed. The band played three encores, and at the end of it they hugged one another genuinely, and Rikki and Davy had some kind of private conversation that made them both laugh and hug each other one more time. She was glad to see them getting along.

Amanda found herself screaming at the top of her lungs with the rest of the crowd as the band exited the stage, tears stinging her eyes while Rikki and the boys blew kisses to their hometown crowd, and she ran onstage to tackle Rikki once the lights came on.

They crashed to the disgusting floor together and embraced, and she let herself vanish into that moment and treat it like it was real for a few last precious minutes—until her eyes drifted across the club and found a familiar face scowling back at her.

Deputy Director Ed Lonsa stood near the back of the club with his arms crossed. He was wearing the exact same fucking jean jacket that Boone had worn to Gazzarri's more than a year ago. The CIA must have gotten a volume discount at Jordache. Lonsa waved her over, making no attempt to be subtle.

"Who's that?" Rikki asked. "Oh, babe, is that your dad?"

"It's just a guy I work with," Amanda said. "I'll catch up with you backstage, okay?" She kissed him, holding on for an extra second in case it was the last one. Then she pushed herself off Rikki and stood. She helped him to his feet and dismissed him to the greenroom, then stepped off the stage and moved through the crowd to meet her boss.

"DD," she said. "I didn't know you like metal."

Lonsa ignored her icebreaker. "It's time," he said. "You got your extension. The tour is over. You need to tell him right away."

"Yes," Amanda said. "I know. I'm just letting him get reacclimated. Just a couple of days."

"Tonight," Lonsa said. "Lawrence Barkley has written half of the second album already. We need Rikki to intercede now."

"Okay," she said. "I will tell him. Tomorrow. Let the man unpack his bags."

Lonsa looked at her for a long moment, considering it. "Fine," he finally said. "Tomorrow. Morning. Call me when it's done."

Officer Price's stubbornness was only the latest hassle in Deputy Director Lonsa's miserable day.

He spent his whole morning in briefings, getting caught up on efforts to arm the Contras in Nicaragua against the Sandinista National Liberation Front, and on the tide turning against their former friends in Baghdad, and other cool shit like that. He missed getting his hands dirty, and he knew everyone was trying not to laugh when he hit on the key points of Project Facemelt. Still jet-lagged from his trip over, he got sass from a junior officer in a filthy nightclub . . . and now Brad Mancuso was leaning against his rental car with his arms crossed.

"The hell are you doing here?" Lonsa said.

Mancuso just nodded toward the car. Lonsa got in the driver's seat, and Mancuso sat shotgun.

"Well?" Lonsa said.

"This is about Saint Petersburg, isn't it?"

"*What* is about Saint Petersburg?"

"I'm being punished, aren't I?"

Lonsa sighed. The kid wasn't stupid. He had put in for Berlin and gotten Facemelt instead. Of course he was being punished. But the DD couldn't say so. "Mancuso, your experience in the Eastern Bloc is key to the objectives of this mission, which is a top priority for the United States government."

"Bullshit," Mancuso said. "I put in for Berlin. I got this. I've been studying the rest of the so-called team. None of them wants to be here, except for Price. Boone is obviously a fuckup. This is disciplinary. Why wouldn't you tell me that so I can develop a corrective plan for myself? There's a protocol—"

"Fine," Lonsa said. "I don't know anything about Saint Petersburg. But, yeah, you wanted to be in the big show, and you got the freak show instead. Read between the lines."

"So how do I get off the Island of Misfit Toys?"

"Look, Brad," Lonsa said. "Somebody on high likes this enough to keep it alive."

"The vice president."

"Probably," Lonsa said.

"Goddamn it."

Yup: George H. W. Bush. And he'd tried this before. Agency lore had it that in 1976, then-director of the CIA Bush had come down with a brutal case of the flu. In full thrall of his illness, and with a 103-degree temperature, the DCI staggered into Langley and demanded an all-hands meeting for an idea that came to him during a "troubled night of fever dreams."

He wanted to send a team of musicians into Cuba to overthrow Fidel Castro; but, as he wasn't up to speed on the hottest bands of the day, he demanded his direct reports send country western singer Dick Curless and "those hippies who play the song Bar likes." He hummed a couple of bars of "She's Gone," and then broke into a coughing fit.

His reports assured him that they would happily send Dick Curless and Hall and Oates to Cuba to topple the Castro regime, and then promptly sent the DCI home and back to bed. There was no evidence that anyone ever did anything, and Mr. Bush never asked for a status update after his recovery; but clearly the idea never left him.

And, of course, the whole event became a regular joke around Langley: watch your ass, or you'll end up behind enemy lines, rolling joints for the Alan Parsons Project. So of *course* Mancuso guessed he was being punished. They probably all did, except for the new kid—Price—who was entirely failing every aspect of her rehabilitation.

"My orders were clear," Lonsa said. "Keep this thing running quietly, give status updates when I'm asked, and don't let it leave a black mark on the Apparatus. So that's what we're gonna do. Either we'll run out of money or Bush will lose in eighty-eight and this will all be over with."

"That'll never happen."

Lonsa sighed. "I know," he said. "The Gipper handed it to him on a silver platter." The DD looked down at his hands and shook his head. "The Gipper wouldn't tolerate this," he said softly. "He must not know."

Mancuso waited for a beat while Lonsa collected himself. The DD always got a little misty when he talked about Ronald Reagan.

"So," Mancuso finally said, "you're babysitting the agency's losers indefinitely."

Lonsa shrugged. "You're not a loser. But you are here on discipline."

Mancuso rubbed his forehead and sighed. "My career is over," he whispered.

That set off an alarm bell for Ed Lonsa. Officers who can't see a path to promotion typically didn't stick around for long, and some of them had been known to develop loyalty problems. "It's not," he said. "You want to get back in the down-and-dirty? Follow the objectives and do whatever you can to keep these people from embarrassing the agency. Make me look good, and I'll take care of you. Capisce?"

Mancuso stared at his own reflection in the side-view mirror. He didn't say anything.

"And one more thing," Lonsa said. "If Price doesn't bring Rikki Thunder in by noon tomorrow, you're doing it."

Amanda Price met Rikki and the rest of the band in the greenroom. Davy popped the cork off a bottle of champagne and handed it to her, an act of friendship that was definitely a first. They all seemed so happy to be home. Rikki threw a long arm around her neck and kissed her on the cheek, and she tried to appreciate the warmth that his lips had left there.

She had bought a few more hours for both of them, and that felt important. Amanda had practiced the speech a hundred times over the previous weeks. She tried to predict his questions, plan for his moods, and be ready for a complete meltdown.

A coldhearted officer would spring the truth on him that very night, after the concert and the after-party, when he was too tired to think straight or argue—like using sleep deprivation as an interrogation tool. She would have an easier time of it that way.

But Rikki deserved better than that. He deserved to go back to his home, where he hadn't been in months, and have at least one untroubled night of sleep with the woman he loved.

She was still on the mission. She was going to tell him in the morning. There was no turning back from that.

But she was also human. She had missed some of the creature comforts of their life before the tour, too. She wanted to say goodbye to it all on her own terms.

And just one more time, she wanted to fuck Rikki Thunder's brains out in the bed that he thought of as theirs, and hold him while he slept.

36

⚡

CENTRAL INTELLIGENCE AGENCY CASE FILE: DOS(7)/PFM/001.13/26

SUBMITTED BY: Boone, Darrell A.
MISSION: Project Facemelt
ASSET: R. Henderson (alias Rikki Thunder)

CATEGORY: Close Relationship Profiles

NAME: Robert Sweet
ALIAS(ES): Buck Sweet
AGE: 27?

RELATIONSHIP TO ASSET: Member of the band "Whyte Python"

BACKGROUND:
Unknown

37

L ook," tawny said, "I have something really important to tell you."

We were sitting on the couch in my living room, watching MTV. It was raining outside and almost dark, even though it was close to noon. We had just poured our first cups of coffee after sleeping in together for the first time in almost a year.

Tawny seemed really serious, so I muted the TV.

"You aren't pregnant, right?" I asked. "Buck said those pills work for any animal."

"No, I'm not pregnant." She put her mug down on the coffee table and turned toward me on the couch. She took a deep breath and blew it out. "But here it is. I'm an officer with the Central Intelligence Agency."

Huh? I thought. "Huh?" I said. "You mean the CIA?"

"Yes."

"You got a new job?" I asked. "I thought you still worked at a rock magazine."

"No, I never worked at a rock magazine. That's my cover."

"But who writes all the articles, then?"

Tawny looked at me for eight whole seconds. "Nobody," she finally said. "The magazine doesn't exist."

"But, so, wait, you've been lying to me this whole time about your job?"

"Yeah." She nodded. "Yes, I have. But it's because my job is top secret. I'm not allowed to talk about it with anyone. I'm telling you because I have permission now. Do you understand?"

I wasn't sure how mad I should be about that. On the one hand, lying to your boyfriend about where you go to work every day for a year and a half is a pretty big offense. On the other hand, it made sense that she needed to keep a job like that a secret.

And also, while we were on tour I kept telling her that I read every issue of her magazine to feel closer to her, and that her articles were really awesome; but it turns out the magazine didn't even exist. We were both a little bit guilty.

"Rikki?" she said. "Do you understand?"

"I guess so," I said. "So, like, what do you do for them?"

"Yeah. That's why I want to talk to you." Tawny got up off the couch and wrung her hands. She began to pace back and forth across the living room. "I'm on a team operating a covert mission in a region known as the Eastern Bloc, made up of countries in Eastern Europe and North Asia. Basically, everyone from East Germany to Russia."

"Oh," I said. "Yeah, I've heard about it. The bad guys, right?"

Tawny stopped walking and pointed a finger at me, nodding slowly. "Yes," she said. "But not totally! The leaders there? Yes, they are the bad guys. But the citizens, Rikki, the people living in these countries, are ruled under oppressive regimes. They don't get to elect their leaders. They can't practice their own religion. They don't have free speech or a free press or access to education that can teach subjects that aren't state approved. If they speak out, the state police lock them up. And they closed the borders, so their own people aren't even allowed to leave."

That sounded terrible! "Hang on," I said. "Can they party?"

Tawny shrugged. "In some circumstances."

I scowled. "Just some?"

"But there are revolutions growing in these countries, Rikki." She began to pace again. I noticed that suddenly she was saying my name a lot while she talked. "The people are organizing. They're going to usher in a new and more democratic future, and it will be driven by the young people. Young people who like rock music. Our operation believes that we can use metal to raise the spirits of young people in the Eastern Bloc and engage them in the revolution."

That all sounded pretty awesome, but something was nagging at me. "So, wait," I said. "How long have you been in the CIA?"

"Four years."

"And when did you come up with this rock 'n' roll plan?"

"About three years ago."

Hang on, I thought. "But we've been dating for, like, a year and a half . . ."

She hung her head and looked at the floor. "Yeah," she said.

Tawny's so adorable. I always figured she was a lot smarter than me, but she missed the most obvious idea in the world!

"Babe," I said. "How did it take you almost two years to think of asking me for help?"

Tawny got quiet for a few seconds, like she was trying to think about what to say. Finally, she looked me in the eyes and her face got really serious. "Rikki," she said.

Oh shit.

"So, did you . . ." I started to ask. I didn't even know how to finish the sentence. Lie to me? Trick me? Sleep with me for your job? All of the above?

She didn't wait for me to finish my question. The answer was the same, no matter what. Her eyes left mine and drifted back to the floor. Her voice got really quiet. "Yes," she said.

And with that one word, my whole world shattered. Tawny had been using me this whole time. The only person in the world that I felt like I could trust was a con artist who had been playing some kind of game with me for almost two years.

"Oh," I said. I felt my cheeks get hot, and my hands started shaking. I leaned forward and tapped out a rhythm on the coffee table. "Oh . . . fuckin' A, seriously? Are you telling me that you've been playing me from the start?"

"Honestly? Some of it," she said. She moved toward me and placed her hand on my shark-tooth necklace. "Some of it was real, though. *Is* real? I don't know. I'm confused, too. We're in this together, babe."

"Don't 'babe' me, stranger," I shouted. She was still trying to manipulate me! I stepped away from her hand and looked down where she had just placed it.

The necklace.

Paranoia grabbed me pretty hard. Was it my imagination, or could I feel this thing buzzing?

"What is this?" I grabbed the tooth and yanked it until the clasp broke. "Some kind of tracking device? Is that why you're always touching it?" I threw the necklace against the wall, and tears burst in the corners of Tawny's eyes.

"It's just a necklace," she said softly. "It was mine, and I thought you would like it."

I stood up and pointed at her. "You lied to me. About everything. Do you even care about me? Did you mean it when you said you love me?"

"I don't know—this has gotten very real for me, Rikki," Tawny shouted back. "The answer is supposed to be 'no,' but it's complicated! I should have said something a long time ago, but—"

"But you were having fun screwing a rock star. I get it," I said. I headed to the door and grabbed the handle. "Fuck off, Tawny."

"Wait," she said.

"No."

"No, Rikki, you have to," she said, sounding firm this time. I opened the door, and there was a black van parked in my driveway, getting drilled with rain. I could see two guys in the front seats between the swipes of the windshield wipers, wearing dark sunglasses even though it was cloudy out.

"Trust me," Tawny said. "Come back inside."

"Yeah, right," I said. "What, are those your CIA buddies? Are they gonna shoot me if I try to leave my own house now?"

"They're not gonna shoot you," she said. "They're just here to give me some time to talk to you."

"About what?" I slammed the door. "What, do you, like, want me to be a spy now or something?"

"No," Tawny said. "I just want you and the band to succeed. You're popular over there. You give the people hope, and that could be really important. If you succeed, the rest will take care of itself."

"I am succeeding. We are succeeding."

"With more help than you know," Tawny said. "And, yeah, Whyte Python's doing great. But reality check? You guys are late to the dance. The new sound, the new look, where the money's going next is a whole different thing. Take a trip to Seattle and see what I mean."

"Those guys? Come on," I shouted. "Those guys don't even wear chaps and scarves!"

"It's where rock is going," Tawny said. "Give me a little credit here. Bands like Whyte Python? The ones who came in last? They'll be the first ones out. But do you think Aerosmith will get left behind? Van Halen? Bon Jovi? The legends, Rikki? The ones who have made it this long because they *adapt*? Nope. If you want this band to survive—if you want to keep playing, no matter what—Whyte Python can't just be big here, it has to be big *everywhere*—the biggest band in the *world*—able to get ahead of what's coming next, before Whyte Python *is* left behind. We can get you there, but you need to help us convince the band to make some changes."

"So you've been lying to me," I said, "and now you want me to lie to them."

"No. Help them. With good advice. You just aren't telling them who it's from."

"So that's it," I said. "You just want to offer some advice to make us a better band?"

"Well . . ." Tawny said, "that's most of it. Obviously, the CIA isn't spending agency resources out of the goodness of the director's heart. The changes they need have a purpose. We need to get some important messages out there. We need you to walk in some stuff, like songs with really . . . specific lyrics."

"See!" I shouted. "You're still fuckin' doing it! You just said ten seconds ago that all you wanted to do was make us winners. What else are you still lying about, Tawny? Why should I ever believe a word you say?"

"*I know*," she shouted back. "I'm sorry. I was going to explain it all in steps. I had . . . a *plan*. But you deserve better than steps. And, anyway, you can handle more. All honesty, from here on out."

"This is fucked up, Tawny. I don't want to be part of this."

"Fine." She waved her hands. "But you know, deep down, that I'm right. And remember this. When you were a kid living in those foster homes, with nothing, what was the one thing that got you through the day?"

"Oh, don't you dare—"

"What was it?" she demanded.

I looked across the room at my stereo. The little record player that Ben Pratt gave to me still sat on top.

"Music," she said, pointing at me. "And what was the one thing you did anything you had to do to keep in your life? Music. How did you find your family? Music. So, guess what? There are thousands of little Rikki Thunders all across the world, living in poverty, under oppressive rule. And you know what they're clinging to? Their Whyte Python tapes, bootlegged and smuggled in by other kids who were moved by what they heard. They are clinging to your band. The only hope they have.

"This isn't just about you," she said. "You can hate me. Believe me, many times since this all started I've hated me, too. But don't let that get in the way. Don't let it stop you from doing for the world what Ben Pratt did for you."

Fuck, dude. It was a low blow, bringing up Ben Pratt in that moment. But she knew what she was doing. Ben Pratt had taken on a sort of mythical status in my life, and I felt like no matter what I did, I would never measure up. There was a night on the road when I had done some cocaine and couldn't stop thinking about how I needed to call him—driving myself crazy, really, and obsessing over how embarrassed I was that I had never said thank you. But I was also ashamed that I was on drugs at the time, and I knew he would hear it in my voice and be disappointed in me. I tried to call Tawny from my hotel room that night to talk through it. She didn't answer her phone. Needless to say, using Ben Pratt's gift against me was cold.

But it was also a really powerful idea. Was this how I could pay him back? I couldn't say anything. I couldn't look at Tawny. I could barely breathe.

"I gotta go," I said. "I need to think."

"Okay," Tawny said. She walked to the window and gave a hand signal to the van. "Go ahead. They won't bother you. I'll be here."

38

◢◢

HERE'S ANOTHER LOOK at the soundtrack playing in Rikki's head:

"BROKEN MIRROR"
Music and lyrics by R. Thunder

I'm out walkin' in the rain
Tryin' to figure where things
    went wrong
Wonderin' if you ever loved
    me, girl
or were you playing me all
    along?
We had a special kind of love
    for sure
feels like a lifetime ago
I could see a future there, so
    clear
like a mirror to my soul!

Chorus:
But it's a broken mirror, baby,
they don't show you very
    much.
And those jagged edges will
    make you bleed,
if you get close enough to
touch.

And I don't know where to go
    right now
Or if the sky will ever clear
I can't go home to you, I don't
    know what to do
I let the rain mix with my tears
And maybe it's my fault some-
    how
I could've been a better man
And when I see my own reflec-
    tion now
You know, I guess I understand

(chorus)

(mournful guitar solo)

So where do we go from here,
    from now?

'Cause I honestly don't know
Who do I hold when the lights
  go out
Who's gonna come to every
  show?
You know I have to carry on
  today
The burden's heavy, the road
  is rough
And it's a great big world
  beyond you, baby
But I don't think it's big enough

(chorus)

Broken . . . mirror.. . . . .
Broken . . . mirror . . .
Broken . . . mirror . . .
. .

(sick guitar solo)

39

I DROVE MY CORVETTE down to the Strip, and then I walked in the rain.

It had been a long time since I was hustling to get flyers up and make money on these streets every day and night, but not much had changed. The early risers were out stapling fresh copies on telephone poles, staking out prime real estate and placing a bet that the rain would let up before they got ruined.

I saw kids lining up outside the clubs to buy tickets. I saw guys with long hair and sleeveless shirts selling ice cream sandwiches out of coolers, just like I used to do.

And I thought I saw Ron inside the grocery store, ringing out a customer, but I didn't slow down enough to know for sure.

I was watching my whole life flash before my eyes.

At first, I was angry, muttering every four-letter word that I could think of under my breath while I shuffled down the street like a lunatic. After about an hour, I just started to feel tired. Being angry does that to you: it uses up way more energy than being happy.

Also, I had been walking for what felt like a really long time, and my legs hadn't gotten nearly as much exercise as my arms over the last year.

Somehow, I found myself in a small public park. The rain was coming in fits and spurts now, and the clouds were getting a little brighter. I sat on a bench with my hands in my pockets.

I thought about my life up to that point, and how blessed I had been. It was a rough start for sure, but I like to think that my life actually began the day I got my record player. That was when I found my calling. That was when I became Rikki Thunder. And pretty much everything after that was amazing.

I went from being a poor kid in a foster home to being a member of two awesome bands. I made friends, got laid a bunch, played amazing music in front of dozens of people, and then hundreds, and then thousands, and now tens of thousands.

I had a choice bachelor pad in the hills, a sweet Corvette, and my own merch. And it all started the day I put those headphones on and—like magic—the world outside my foster home opened up to me.

I thought about all those little Thunders, living in the countries Tawny talked about, who needed the same thing.

I wondered, What *would* Ben Pratt tell me to do? I asked myself that question a lot. In the course of that day I had transitioned from deeply loving Tawny to really hating Tawny to something else. Though I just wanted to get away from her, away from all of it, the idea of doing the same thing for a bunch of kids that my heroes had done for me felt too important. I owed them. I owed him.

This wasn't about Tawny, or even about what I wanted to do. I realized: in the face of an opportunity to give other people what I'd gotten, I'd be a hypocrite if I didn't try.

Sure, it turned out that my entire relationship with Tawny was built on lies. But if I was being honest with myself, I had to admit that I'd known something wasn't right with Tawny for a long time; maybe from the day we met, when she filled the club with people on an hour's notice and bought Qyksand another three months. It didn't make sense, but shit, dude, she *saved* my ass, so I wasn't gonna question it.

I've told you guys about that little tickle I'd get in my brain, like a warning alarm that I kept shutting down before it could go off. Of course I wondered why I never got to see where she lived. Of course I wondered why she was always stepping out of the room to make phone calls, and why nothing ever seemed to surprise her. And, sure, it's common for your band to distrust your girlfriend; but how *did* Tawny know that Ron had applied for a job at the grocery store?

Undersize orphans don't survive to age twenty-three without figuring out how to sniff out when someone is playing them. Yes, I had these thoughts, and I ignored them. Because I was in love, and because I finally had somebody, I was willing to turn a blind eye to what was staring me in the face: Tawny wasn't who I thought she was. In a way, we were both in on it. I always knew that asking the wrong question could unravel the whole thing, so I never asked it.

But I never would have tried out for Whyte Python if she didn't find out about Barry Gorman breaking his arms on the radio and then wake me up that morning and drag me down the street to the record store. I'd managed to get a lot out of our relationship, and those things weren't any less real, even if the two of us turned out to be bullshit.

I could be grateful for that.

There was still a big part of me that wanted to tell Tawny and the whole CIA to eat shit and die, that I would quit Whyte Python before turning into a puppet.

That would feel great, but then what? I wasn't a singer—I couldn't go solo. I was too big of a name in my own right to join some other band. And besides, even Qyksand wouldn't take me back now. So *if* I could push away how pissed off I was, what was the right thing to do—for my friends in the band? For the little Thunders overseas? For myself? My thoughts landed again on wondering what Ben Pratt would think.

I got up and made my way home.

Tawny was sitting on the couch with her hands in her lap when I came through the door.

"Okay," I said. "I'll do it. But this?" I pointed back and forth between us. "It's over. I don't want to see you unless I have to."

"I understand," she said. "We're going to have to keep pretending we're together so it makes sense that I'm still hanging around with the band, but I'll give you all the space you need."

"Whatever," I said. "What do I need to do now?"

"Now," Tawny said, "you meet the rest of the team."

PART IV

Project Facemelt

40

⚡

Attachment 1: New staff profiles assigned to D1985AID00
(codename Project Facemelt)

Attn: Deputy Director Lonsa, E.

9 October 1986

Attached are the agency profiles of your new team members: Senior Agents Stryker, Boone, and Mancuso. We have also attached the original profile of Agent Price from Winter 1985. Good luck with this group; they'll present some challenges, but they are all phenomenally talented agency staff at heart.

Profile 1: Senior Officer Catherine Stryker
Cause for reassignment: Disciplinary

Sen. Ofc. Catherine Stryker is reassigned to AID's disciplinary program. Stryker has worked the entirety of her intelligence career in subliminal design, providing support to various operations across the globe, from her office within Langley and in the field. Her work is among the best and most consistent in the agency.

For most of her service, Stryker has turned in top-quality work with no complaint; in recent years, though, she has developed a habit of insubordinate commentary.

Sen. Ofc. Stryker is routinely vocal about opinions related to the United States' goals and objectives abroad, and appears to be growing comfortable pushing back against the purpose or result of a given mission, rather than simply carrying out her role in it. Examples of Stryker's unsolicited running commentary include but are not limited to "This is going to backfire when they all turn against us" and "Some of these people are American citizens." These instances of Monday-morning quarterbacking the business of the American intelligence apparatus are only growing more frequent.

This disciplinary assignment is the result of an incident that took place at CIA headquarters. Stryker was working on a public-information campaign designed to disrupt the influence of a tyrannical South American general by enticing angry youths to riot in a developing neighborhood that was home to a free medical and dental clinic, not government sponsored; the clinic's location was unfortunate, but not determinative of go/no-go. Yet Stryker's objections were unrelenting, insistent that taking away medical and dental services from locals would backfire against American interests and was "pointlessly abhorrent."

Based on this personal assessment, Officer Stryker covertly launched a subliminal campaign within CIA headquarters that encouraged staff to disable the building's toilets, and to continue disabling them whenever they were fixed.

The fallout was swift and devastating. The success of her campaign was, effectively, what saved her job; no one could argue with how good she is at this.

Sen. Ofc. Stryker has a long history of excellent work in subliminal propaganda, and her career will leave a true mark on American progress across the world. She is risking that legacy with her growing pattern of insubordination. We hope and expect that her time on Project Facemelt will bring her back in line.

—END—

Profile 2: Senior Officer Darrell Boone
Cause for reassignment: Disciplinary

It should come as a surprise to no one that Sen. Ofc. Darrell Boone is— once again—being reassigned to the agency's disciplinary program.

Boone has a long and storied record of service within the agency, dating back to its founding shortly after World War II. His first assignment was in the field. He was stationed in Moscow in 1948 and made early inroads with an influential soccer star; but Boone became obsessed with the sport and attempted to secure a spot for himself on the team by fist-fighting his own asset in a parking lot.

He was moved to—and subsequently removed from—assignments in Beijing, Munich, Havana, and Prague thereafter. His longest assignment was in Cuba, where he managed to stay for seven months before vanishing into the Afro-Cuban jazz scene and refusing to report back at all. A full operations team was dispatched to find him and return him to Washington. It had become exceedingly clear that Boone was not cut out for fieldwork; he spent most of the 1950s in Langley, on assorted projects. Most infamously, Boone was assigned to an experimental program that involved testing the effects of the psychedelic drug Lysergic Acid Diethylamide (LSD) on volunteer servicemen. The program aimed to determine whether the drug opened new capabilities of the mind, such as remote viewing.

His role in this program ended predictably. The agency will readily admit that this assignment was a blunder on its part. Boone had been around a while by then. We should have known better.

Since 1960, Boone has worked out of Langley in propaganda design, on projects in the Eastern Bloc—with frequent breaks for reassignment into the discipline program. Fortunately, when reassigned to rehabilitation, Boone tends to quickly revert back to his base personality of straightlaced office functionary.

Boone's problem has not changed since his first days with the agency. While the work he produces is exemplary, he is unable to commit to a project without immersing himself in the subject matter and subculture to the point of a near-complete departure from reality. This is not unheard of among those engaged in truly deep intelligence work, but rarely evident in those assigned to office roles.

It is our hope that DD Lonsa will be able to channel Sen. Ofc. Boone's skillset productively and return him to service with more control over his faculties; but expectations are low. Termination for cause is preapproved if necessary, at the Deputy Director's discretion.

—END—

Profile 3: Senior Officer Bradford Mancuso

Cause for reassignment: Disciplinary

Sen. Ofc. Bradford Mancuso is reassigned to AID's disciplinary program.

Mancuso is a highly decorated field officer with an exemplary service record. He has worked exclusively on assignments in the Eastern Bloc region for seventeen years. Over the course of his service, he has recruited dozens of highly placed assets, quietly gathering useful field data and efficiently facilitating surveillance tactics that continue to yield fruit in the Eastern Bloc Region.

However, Mancuso requires a disciplinary reassignment for actions taken at his most recent assignment in Saint Petersburg, RUS.

Mancuso had engaged an asset who worked as a facilities engineer in a government building that housed KGB staff, among other departments. This asset loyally served the CIA for several years by careful monitoring of activities in the building. The information was never highly sensitive, but useful as a cog in a larger surveillance program.

Mancuso became frustrated with the asset's reluctance to take larger risks in order to gain more sensitive information. He pushed the asset to break into a restricted access site and collect blueprints for an air handling project. The asset was arrested and detained on espionage charges. As a precautionary measure, KGB leadership ordered a complete redesign of the next three years of construction plans.

Mancuso maintains that his methods followed protocol, and by all accounts, he is correct; but the result of his actions was the loss of a valuable asset, and data about years of future KGB infrastructure development being rendered useless.

If there is a recurring trait among the other team members assigned to Project Facemelt, it is a comfort with breaking agency protocol; in some cases, even diverting from mission objectives based on personal determinations, often determined by what the officer deems "the right thing to do." This is not the case for Sen. Ofc. Mancuso, and it is our hope that his instincts, field knowledge, and rigid commitment to mission may inspire his other team members while on duty for Project Facemelt. Sen. Ofc. Mancuso has been reassigned to the program because he made an enormous mistake; but he may prove a useful asset to you, DD Lonsa, if you need help keeping the team in line.

—END ATTACHMENT—

Attachment 2: First Assignment to Newly Created AID program
D1985AID003

Profile: Officer Amanda Price
Cause for reassignment: Disciplinary

Officer Amanda Price is reassigned to AID program D1985AID003 for disciplinary purposes.

Ofc. Price was last stationed in Bulgaria. It was her first assignment as a full field officer. She served in Sofia for nine months, during which time she developed a critical asset and began to make inroads toward gathering valuable intelligence from [REDACTED], a high-ranking government official. Unfortunately, this is when she appears to have lost her focus on mission priorities.

Ofc. Price recruited the rebellious teenage daughter of [REDACTED]. The asset was growing disillusioned with her father's regressive politics and sympathetic to Western interests. Ofc. Price's directive was clear—encourage the daughter to repair her relationship with her father while gently nurturing her diverging political leanings, creating opportunities to capture privileged information.

Instead, Price encouraged the asset's rebellion. She introduced the girl to firebrand Western journalists and protest music, and offered to help her secretly apply to a boarding school in Geneva.

Unfortunately, under the influence provided by Ofc. Price, the asset became so disgruntled with her parents that she stole her father's car and wreaked havoc joyriding through the streets of Sofia, blasting the song "2 Minutes to Midnight" by Iron Maiden at full volume. She ended her adventure by crashing the vehicle into the National Assembly Building, breaking her collar bone and cracking two ribs.

While under the influence of pain medication, the asset spoke freely about her charismatic new friend—immediately setting off alarms within the Committee for State Security. A team was dispatched in search of Ofc. Price, who required rapid exfiltration at great cost to the agency.

Ofc. Price needs significant career rehabilitation and would not likely be placed into another field assignment at this juncture. However, the timing of these events presents a unique opportunity for both the officer and the agency.

The CIA is under . . . heavy encouragement from [REDACTED] to revisit a nontraditional program format proposed years ago but never implemented. AID Disciplinary may be the ideal place to carry out a controlled mission that respects the demands of [REDACTED], with some controls in place to prevent it from embarrassing the US intelligence apparatus.

As such, Ofc. Price's assignment to D1985AID003 is not just a rehabilitation—it is a test, both of Ofc. Price and of [REDACTED]'s novel ideas—which may gain priority in American intelligence strategies in the years to come, depending on certain national events. Ofc. Price may be the ideal candidate to design this program. She is young, ambitious, and her neuropsych evaluation scores far exceed those necessary for exceptional Agent performance. She is a quick thinker, a capable manager of assets, a chameleonic undercover personality, and she has researched this particular subject matter with a dedication bordering on the religious.

And, it must be said: Ofc. Price's physical presentation will allow her to uniquely thrive in a culture that values, above all else, blond females who appear welcoming of an opportunity to crawl across the hood of a red Corvette attired in nothing more than an animal-print bikini.

Challenges inherent in this assignment are Ofc. Price's tendency to prioritize the hopes and dreams of her assets over her work for the agency. She also fails to show proper deference to superior officers, and has a habit of offering unprofessional candor when she disagrees with a directive or policy. The personality traits that present her as an ideal candidate for this unique program may be incompatible with the qualities of a good CIA officer, but as noted earlier, this rehabilitation is a test.

Ofc. Price has promising talent. But she requires a course correction if she wants to remain in good standing at the agency, thus making this reassignment a major inflection point in her young career. She has the potential to rise to leadership in the US intelligence apparatus one day; or, her service could be very brief. Much of that future will be determined by her work on D1985AID003.

41

⚡

WHAT THE HELL was I doing?

Earlier that morning, I was eating Cheerios in my underwear and watching MTV with my girlfriend. Now I was with an undercover CIA officer, on a small government jet flying cross-country to Langley, Virginia, for a top secret mission to win the Cold War.

The life of a rock star, right?

Our plane landed at around six o'clock, and a black jeep met us on the tarmac to drive us over to Langley. Tawny gave me a badge to put around my neck, but nobody looked at it. Nobody looked at either of us at all, which was weird for me because I'm a rock star and probably weird for Tawny because she's so hot.

I guess that's how the CIA does things. Don't look, didn't see, can't tell. We walked down a white corridor past rows of locked doors and stopped at a door near the end of the hall.

"What's this gonna be like?" I asked. She looked at me and smiled, and her hand reached out to touch my shark-tooth necklace before she caught herself and pulled it back.

"It's gonna be fine," she said. "Just a group of people talking. They're nice. Mostly. You ready?"

I nodded, and Tawny unlocked the door.

It looked like any conference room on the inside. White walls, cheap office furniture, a projector screen on the far side. There were four people waiting for us. A tall, bald man with glasses stood, and I recognized him as the guy from the concert the night before. The one Tawny said she worked with. At least that was true.

"Mister Thunder," he said, holding out a hand for me to shake. "I'm Ed Lonsa."

We shook hands. "Call me Rikki," I said.

"Fair enough," Ed Lonsa said. "Rikki, we don't usually bring assets in to meet the full team. You're getting special treatment here, because you're helping out with a very unique mission that's going to require a lot of trust. Understand?"

This moment was obviously solemn as fuck. I nodded.

"Great," he said. "Welcome to Project Facemelt." He gestured to the table, where the rest of the team sat. There were three others besides me, Lonsa, and Tawny. A guy with dark hair was sitting at the opposite side of the table, arms crossed, scowling. There was a lady with brown hair, and she was kind of smirking at me like we had an inside joke that I didn't know about.

And there was an older guy—pushing sixty, probably—with his feet up on the table. He had curly hair that was thinning on top but hanging in rings below his ears, like he had decided to start growing it out recently. And he had a little gold stud in his ear. He was smiling at me, hard.

"Goddamn it, Boone," Lonsa shouted. "I said get your feet off the table!" The guy—Boone, apparently—made a big dramatic scene about putting his feet on the floor and pulling up to the table. "Have a seat, Rikki," Lonsa said. "Officer Price, the floor is yours."

As I was taking a seat, I wondered which one of them was Officer Price, until Tawny started talking and I remembered that her last name wasn't even Spice. I got angry all over again, and tried my best to push it down. But everyone in the room was a spy, and they were all studying me pretty closely, so they probably read it in my eyes anyway. The grumpy one across the room even raised an eyebrow.

"Thank you," Tawny said. "Rikki is up to speed on objectives, so let's get into introductions. Deputy Director Lonsa runs psyops for the Asian Intelligence Division. That means psychological operations—using what we know about the psychology of people in a community to influence their behavior. He's our boss."

I nodded, trying my best to match the serious tone of the room. "Tight," I said.

Tawny gestured to the grumpy guy across the table. "Officer Brad

Mancuso is our profile expert," she said. "He knows the region and the people who live there better than he knows his own children. Mancuso has significant experience in the field, and his data informs the work of the rest of the team."

"Good to meet you, bro," I said, and reached across the table to shake his hand. He just looked at my hand for a few seconds, like it was dirty or something; then he grabbed my fingers and gave them a little shake. Like an asshole.

"And you've met Officer Catherine Stryker," Tawny said. She was pointing at the only other woman in the room, who I had never seen before.

"Are you sure?" I asked.

The woman, Stryker, reached into her briefcase and pulled out a pair of giant square sunglasses. She put them on. "Imagine a black wig," she said.

No way! I thought. *It's Tawny's friend Cathy!* "No way!" I said. "You're Tawny's friend Cathy!" Cathy took the glasses off and winked at me.

"Catherine is an expert in subliminal design," Tawny said. "She works with us to develop clothing, art, lighting, and pyrotechnics that nudge our audiences in the direction we want them to go."

"You're gonna have to tell Spencer," I said. "He promised his friend Kevin that he could design our next outfits."

Cathy gave Tawny a concerned look, but Tawny shook it off. "We aren't sure that Kevin is real," she said. Then she gestured to the last guy in the room, the one with curly hair and an earring. "Officer Darrell Boone," she said. "Persuasive messaging. AKA propaganda. He's gonna work with you on lyrics."

Boone, who I had already decided was the wild card in the room, got up from the table and walked over to me. He put out his hand, and I grabbed it. Boone pulled me onto my feet and in close, and he stared into my eyes with manic glee. He looked like he was going to cry. "We're gonna change the world through rock 'n' roll, brother," he said.

"Right on," I said.

"You wanna get high?" Boone asked.

Honestly, I did, but I suspected this might be one of those CIA mind tricks. I shook my head. "Uh, maybe later, man," I said.

"Right on," Boone said. "Rain check."

Ed Lonsa raised an eyebrow. "What's happening with you, Boone?" he said. Boone just rolled his eyes. I liked this dude, Boone.

"Officer Boone has . . . really immersed himself in the genre," Tawny said. "You two will get to work right away on developing an anthem for the next album. The trick is getting Davy and the other guys to buy in."

"Right away, like, right now?" I asked. Tawny had told me we would be spending the whole evening at the office, but I figured we would start with some more fun stuff—like issuing my James Bond gadgets and learning hand-to-hand combat and hypnotism and shit. "Can I get my blow-dart watch first?"

Everyone looked at me funny, and out of the corner of my eye I saw Tawny do a little hand-wave gesture to the rest of them. "We're on a tight schedule," she said. "You'll spend time with Stryker to talk about how far you think we can get away with designing costumes for the guys, and Mancuso will work with you on gaining a better understanding of the region before the tour. But we need a song immediately. You guys are a few weeks away from studio time."

Then Boone stepped in between Tawny and me. "I've got a conference room set aside with a typewriter, some paper and pens, a case of whiskey and a quarter ounce of high-test dope," he said. "We're going in as strangers, and we're coming out brothers."

"Oh man," I said. Yeah, I liked this guy.

"'Oh man' is right," Boone said.

42

MUSIC MONTAGE: SONGWRITING

Song: "Workin' It Out (Shout!)" By Whyte Python

- Rikki and Boone are sitting at a table with a handle of whiskey, two shot glasses, a pyramid of tightly rolled joints, and a stack of paper. Boone writes something down and slides it across the table. Rikki shakes his head.
- Rikki writes his own lyrics and slides the paper to Boone. Boone angrily scribbles across the whole page.
- Rikki and Boone do shots.
- Rikki and Boone stare at a map of the eastern hemisphere.
- Rikki and Boone do shots.
- Rikki angrily crumples a sheet of paper and throws it into the trash can.
- Boone throws a crumpled paper on top of Rikki's. The trash can is piling up.
- Boone tears a sheet of paper out of the typewriter, balls it up, and spikes it on the floor. He shakes his fists at the ceiling. *It's just out of reach!*
- Rikki is giving Boone a shoulder rub while Boone mutters to himself.
- Lonsa is at the table now. He scribbles his own lyric ideas on a sheet of paper and slides it across the table. He appears to be proud of himself.

  Rikki diplomatically nods along as he reads Lonsa's suggestions, but Boone punches the table, gesturing wildly at a poster of Davy Bones that Boone has affixed to the wall. His eyes well up with tears as he points from the poster to Lonsa's lyrics, then he stands up, violently sweeping all the papers off the desk, storming to the door, opening it, exiting, and theatrically slamming the door behind him.

- Rikki finds Boone sitting on a staircase. He sits next to Boone, puts a consoling hand on his back.
- Back in the room, and with DD Lonsa banished from the songwriting process, Rikki and Boone take two shots each.
- Chinese food is delivered.
- Pizza is delivered.
- More whiskey is delivered.
- Rikki holds the map of the eastern hemisphere upside down while Boone nods, smiling, gaining inspiration.
- More Chinese food is delivered.
- A breakthrough happens, as they usually do if one is persistent enough. Rikki leans over Boone's shoulder, cheering, while Boone furiously smashes at the keys on a typewriter.
- Rikki and Boone look over a sheet of paper like proud parents. They hug. It's done.

43

IT WAS THE SECOND week of January, and the first time we'd all gotten together since the end of the tour. I took a deep breath and shook off the willies before I stepped through the foyer of Davy's house with copies of the song folded in my sweaty hand. I stuffed the sheets into my pocket. *Be cool, Rikki*, I told myself. *You're just pitchin' a song.*

This was technically my first real mission as a CIA officer. Now, sure, Tawny (or, I guess, Amanda? Whatever!) had told me, like, a thousand times that I was not a CIA officer. She was an officer, and I was an asset. But they're basically the same thing.

Anyway, the guys were inside already. We didn't have any kind of agenda—just a band hang, basically—but we were supposed to be in studio and recording before the end of the month. The plan was to wrap the new album by the middle of April, and then hit the road again later in spring to support our second album—which Kirby said was going to be even bigger than our first. So we were definitely going to talk about some business, since we hadn't even recorded anything yet.

I found them sitting in the living room around two pizza boxes, smoking cigarettes and drinking beers. Even Kirby was there, but Davy made him sit in the far corner of the room and wouldn't let him have any food.

"Thunderstorm!" Buck shouted. He got up off the couch and punched me in the arm.

"Happy New Year, Rikki!" Spencer toasted me with his beer. Even Davy looked happy to see me.

Immediately, I felt like shit for what I was about to do. Check that: for what I was about to *start* doing, and keep doing for a long time.

I got settled, helped myself to a slice of 'roni and a cold one. Caught up with the guys.

Davy had spent his holidays at Daytona Beach, judging a wet T-shirt tournament and sleeping around. Spencer went home to Maine, and reported with pride that he had a great visit with his parents, and they were planning a trip out west in February.

Buck didn't say what he did exactly, but he mentioned that we shouldn't go on tour in Florida that year. After enough time had passed, I patted my pant legs and took the paper out.

"So, hey, guys," I said. "I've been working on something. A song. I'm calling it 'Tonight, for Tomorrow.'"

Davy tilted his head sideways, like a confused dog. "But I write the songs," he said.

"Davy writes the songs, Rikki," Kirby chimed in. "Interesting note, actually. The band's contract—"

"Get out, Kirby," Davy said, without looking at him.

Kirby stared at Davy for a few long seconds. Finally, he cracked his neck, stood, and wiped some imaginary dirt off his hands. We all watched as he took a deep breath, blew it out at the ceiling, then forced a smile. "Made it longer than usual this time," he said, then saluted and showed himself the door. It was kind of chilling, to be honest. His tires spun out on the driveway, and I pictured him driving straight to Andromeda Records to scream at some poor receptionist.

Anyway. "Yeah, Davy, I know," I said. "That's why I was hoping you can help me with it?"

This got Davy's attention. His eyes lit up. I was recognizing him as the expert in the room and asking for his help. I learned that trick from Tawny, and it worked like a charm. I asked her how many times she had pulled that kind of move on me, but she changed the subject.

"All right, Thunder," Davy said, and he took on a weird fatherly tone. "Let's see what you got."

I handed copies of the song around to the guys. "It's, like, a crossover," I said. "More inspirational than a ballad, more personal than an anthem, I guess, but a little of both? With a sick guitar solo in the middle." I pointed at Buck and his eyebrows jiggled. But I was mostly just watching Davy, and he scowled while he read the sheet.

"I don't know, dude." Davy tossed the paper onto the coffee table. "This doesn't really look like our thing."

"My friend Kevin says ballads are for pussies," Spencer said.

I rolled my eyes before I could catch myself. *Really, Spencer?* He was the one that I was least worried about being a problem.

"Kevin, again, with all the answers," I muttered.

"How come none of us have ever met Kevin?" Buck asked.

"I'm almost positive he's imaginary," Davy said.

"Really?" Spencer said.

I jumped in. "Yeah, I know it's kind of sappy. But everyone's doing this. Poison, White Lion, Whitesnake—"

"Unoriginal name," Buck muttered.

"Seriously," Spencer said. "It's like, pick a fucking snake."

"Might as well just call the band White Animal," Buck said.

"Python is the best snake," Spencer said.

"Hey," Davy interrupted. "I love you guys."

God, they were seriously not paying attention at all. I was afraid this would happen. We hadn't seen each other for four weeks after living on a bus together for six months. It was going to be a weird hang, and not the best scene for dropping a CIA-crafted anthem in their laps. But Tawny insisted that it had to happen right away.

I needed to get them back on track. "But what I'm saying is, we gotta keep up with the times. Let's just try it out, okay?"

"All right," Davy said. "We'll give it a try." I moved to the spot on the couch next to him and leaned over his shoulder while he read the song to himself. I pointed out the highs and breaks and shit, humming to get him in tone. But he didn't need much help. Davy's a pro. He waved me off pretty quickly. "Yeah, I see it," he said. Then he cleared his throat, held the page out in front of him, and began to sing:

"When I look across the world tonight / I see the pain that's in your eyes / I see our children without hope tonight / I see a warrior meant to rise!

"'Cause there's a passion in your hearts tonight / I can feel it in the air / And no wall can keep us apart tonight / We are one; we're everywhere."

I had to give him credit: he was giving it his all. And despite his best efforts, I could see the corners of his lips fighting a smile. Boone had studied Davy's work extensively. He knew the words that Davy liked to draw out, and the range that he sounded his best in. "Tonight, for Tomorrow" fit Davy Bones like a glove. I wasn't surprised at all that he sang it exactly how I heard it in my head, on his very first read. When you nail it, you nail it. I started tapping a marching beat on the coffee table with my fingers while he sang.

"So look me in the eyes right now / And let's make that promise real / Because they can't lock up our hearts, our souls / We'll meet their iron with our steel!

"Yeah, the tears that we cried yesterday / And the *blood we draw tonight* / Will mean that all of tomorrow's children / Can sing together in the light!"

Buck took up his guitar and plucked out a catchy little jangle that he made up on the spot. Davy stood up now, drawing in extra air for the real thing.

"We are the soul / We are the heart / We're ready to roll / We're gonna take it apart . . ."

He stopped. Scrunched his face up, like he smelled something bad. "Hang on," he said, snapping his fingers toward a pencil. Spencer handed it to him and he scribbled on the paper.

"I wanna switch 'take' to 'tear,'" Davy said. "And I'll do a beat after 'soul' and 'heart' so you guys can repeat them."

They were good changes. They improved the song. Davy was good at this. I didn't know what Boone would think—he was super sensitive about his art—but the CIA was going to have to trust my instincts once in a while. I nodded and smiled.

"Right on," I said. "Let's try it."

DAVY: We are the soul.

US: Soul!

DAVY: We are the heart.

US: Heart!

DAVY: We're ready to roll, we're gonna tear it apart . . .

US: Stand up!

DAVY: Shoulder to shoulder . . .

US: Stand up!

DAVY: Brother to brother . . .

US: Stand up!

Davy waved us off. "All right, all right," he said. His expression became very serious. "It needs work. But I think we might have something here. Good stuff, Thunder. I mean, I added that part where you guys repeat 'soul' and 'heart.'"

"Yeah," I said.

"I have some other ideas, too," he said.

"Okay."

"So . . ." Davy smiled and looked at me, hoping that I would finish his sentence.

"By the time we get done," I said, "I mean, with all the work it needs, my guess is that you will have mostly written it."

"Yeah." Davy beamed. "That's what I was thinking, too. Like, you got it started but it's all kind of coming together through my vision? We could split credit, I guess?"

"Not my thing, bro, cred's all yours," I said. Little did Davy know, this was exactly what we wanted him to do. Tawny had explained this clearly. The last thing we needed on the CIA-produced anthem was the drummer getting lyric credit all of a sudden.

"Good, yeah," Davy said. "'Cause it's easier for the liner notes is all. Let's run through my new song again, you guys. Here we go!"

44

MUSIC VIDEO—"TONIGHT, FOR TOMORROW"

The members of Whyte Python float in space, gazing down at planet Earth. We can see the Eastern Bloc region rotate into frame below, just out of focus. The opening chords of "Tonight, for Tomorrow" play softly, like the music is coming from very far away. Davy looks directly into the camera. He begins to sing:

When I look across the world tonight
I see the pain that's in your eyes

A silver tear runs down Davy's cheek.

I see our children without hope tonight
I see a warrior meant to rise!

Stock footage of a lion stalking through the tall grass.

'Cause there's a passion in your hearts tonight
I can feel it in the air

Footage of smiling children

And no wall can keep us apart tonight
We are one; we're everywhere

Hands clasping into a handshake across the top of a stone wall. The music, playing at a distance, stops. Now Rikki Thunder is sitting at a drum set under a spotlight in a dark room. He begins to rhythmically bang the drums, like a military marching beat. This sound is close and powerful. Davy steps into frame next to Rikki as the spotlight spreads.

So look me in the eyes right now
And let's make that promise real
Because they can't lock up our hearts, our souls
We'll meet their iron with our steel!

Footage of a crowd charging toward the camera.

Yeah, the tears that we cried yesterday
and the blood we draw tonight

Shots of medieval sword fights.

Will mean that all of tomorrow's children
Can sing together in the light!

Children of all races, standing on a hill in a circle and holding hands. Buck and Spencer join Davy and Rikki in the empty room. A synthesizer begins to play the central riff of the song, an absurdly catchy earworm. Buck strums a power chord, and then he and Spencer play their respective parts. As the song builds to soaring heights, the lights come up, revealing that they are actually in a high school gymnasium. The doors burst open. Peasants flood in.

We are the soul
We are the heart
We're ready to roll
We're gonna tear it apart . . .

The crowd sings along:

Stand up!
Shoulder to shoulder . . .

Stand up!
Brother to brother . . .

Stand up!

Davy is crowd-surfing while singing:

Now I see my friends and family, I see my neighbors, standing strong
This is our home, our life, our heritage, and in our hearts, this is our
    song!
And when you look me in the eyes tonight, I see my brother, my
    guiding light
I'll follow you, if you lead me now, let's link our arms, let's sing, let's
    fight!

*The band in outer space again, hovering directly over the Eastern Bloc,
bathed in sunlight.*

And now we know our cause is just
We link our arms, we swear this creed
That our future will be bright and pure
And free of want, of fear, of need!

*Rapid montage: kids running in a field, an eagle soaring, babes racing
across the Everglades in fan boats, people voting, tigers fighting each other,
old men playing soccer, explosions.*

We are the soul
We are the heart
We're ready to roll
We're gonna tear it apart . . .

*The band marches down an old-world street, with the crowd joyfully march-
ing behind them.*

Stand up!
No matter the weather

Stand up!
We'll do it together!

The doors to the gymnasium burst open. Buck emerges, playing a guitar solo. The camera pulls in tight. When it pulls back out, it's a helicopter shot of Buck standing on top of a mountain. Shredding.

This is our time tonight
This is our world,
Our hearts are strong
So put your arms around each other
'Cause together we can't go wrong!

Back at the old-world street again. The band is surrounded by the crowd in a circle. Babes in American-flag bikinis pour out of the stone buildings with beers and bottle rockets, spreading joy and merriment among the crowd. Everyone looks at the camera and pumps their fists in unity, chanting:

Stand up!
Stand up!
Stand up!

Fade to white.

45

I N APRIL 1988, Whyte Python left Los Angeles for a summer tour of the United States.

All Squeeze, No Venom was still consistently one of the top ten albums sold month to month, and the band's second effort—*The Whyte Album*, featuring "Tonight, for Tomorrow"—dropped over Memorial Day weekend and debuted at number one. By all statistical measures, Whyte Python was now the biggest band in the country as they crisscrossed the continent on another eight-month stretch.

CIA officer Amanda Price watched from backstage in Philadelphia while the band closed out their show with "a little jam from the new album."

Davy Bones had begun to introduce "Tonight, for Tomorrow" this way as a joke, because it was such an enormous hit that many fans already associated the song with the band before classic hits like "Summer Saturday."

"Tonight, for Tomorrow" was a genuine crossover sensation, as big of a hit with pop music fans as it was with the rock and metal crowd. It was the top song on Casey Kasem's list every weekend. Sylvester Stallone had reached out to Andromeda Records to see about featuring it in an upcoming movie. Three auto manufacturers competed in an auction for rights to use the song in a television commercial. Every basketball team in the NBA played it before home games. "Weird Al" Yankovic recorded a parody called "To Bite, Before Swallow," about choking on a cheeseburger, that many critics considered to be his best work. "Tonight, for Tomorrow" was unstoppable.

On that summer night in Philadelphia, the crowd went into an absolute lather the moment that Davy leaned into the microphone and grumbled out that iconic opening line: "When I look across the world tonight, I see the pain that's in your eyes . . ."

The band kicked in at their respective parts, and Davy's voice rang like sand across steel; and by the time Buck Sweet broke free on an extended guitar solo, the Spectrum arena crawled like a hive of wasps.

Davy called out his chant, "We are the soul!" and all eighteen thousand fans screamed, "Soul!" back at him. Davy screamed, "We are the heart!" and the whole Spectrum shouted, "Heart!" and so on, through the rest of the chant, ordering one another to "Stand up!" as their leader united them onstage.

The crowd continued to sing along as Davy steered into the epic final creed: "This is our time tonight, / this is our world. / Our hearts are strong / so put your arms around each other, / 'cause together we can't go wrong!"

All four members of Whyte Python chanted, "Stand up!" with the crowd, over and over. Amanda could feel the bloodlust filling the sports arena, felt the electric surge in her own veins even though she was on the job and had seen this exact scene play out dozens of times before.

She wanted to punch a wall, to rip her clothes off and climb the scaffolding. And she desperately wanted to fuck Rikki Thunder, right there onstage in front of everyone, like animals in a nature video. But those days were long over.

Davy screamed, "Thunderstorm!" and Rikki drilled his sticks against the plastic-membrane drum skins like a machine gun, sweat flying off his hair under flashing lights, and Amanda broke out into a cold sweat along with every woman in the arena and many of the men. Rikki Thunder was a sex symbol now, and sufficiently broken against relationships. He slept with movie stars and models, paraded groupies through the backstage like a pied piper, and showed no interest in settling down.

It was all done under the auspices of Tawny's "road rules" hall pass. The band believed that they were still a couple, but an especially progressive one. In public, Rikki demurred about his relationship status—but that was just about selling records. The CIA had nothing to do with that.

Lights flashed. Pyro fired. The entire arena had gone insane. Davy gave one final order: "Stand up, Philadelphia! We are Whyte Python! Good night!"

The band retreated backstage just before the unruly crowd rushed the platform and set about destroying it. The arena lights came on, and security guards tried to nudge the crowd toward the exit, but they were quickly overrun. The smart ones took off their security T-shirts and joined the mob.

Finally, the crowd poured out of the arena exit, screaming and snarling. They took to the streets of Philadelphia, jubilant and out of control, fighting and dancing and tipping over trash cans. Somebody threw a rock through a storefront window, and others followed. A couch was dragged into the street and set ablaze, and before long it was a bonfire.

The melee quickly spread across eight city blocks, with concert goers mindlessly smashing windows and flipping over cars. People who hadn't even been at the show poured out of apartment complexes and joined in the destruction. The Whyte Python audience had taken control of Philadelphia.

Inside the greenroom, pandemonium. The place was packed just as tight as the venue had been, with the band and their groupies and friends and Poison-style VIPs and hangers-on packed shoulder to shoulder, drinking and drugging and partying like the world was about to end. Davy swam through the crowd toward Rikki and held his arms wide, and they hugged.

"Stand up, Davy Bones!" Rikki shouted, and they screamed joyfully as they were swallowed up by the crowd.

On a television over Rikki's head, the news reported on a riot that was rapidly spreading across Philadelphia. The state police were called in, and the National Guard was on notice.

A tomahawk smashed into the TV.

In Arlington County, the rest of Team Facemelt watched the same news broadcast from a control room in Langley. On screen, rioters sang "Tonight, for Tomorrow" as they were rounded up and tackled by police. Normally a stoic bunch, the members of the team allowed a round of grins and approving nods—even the deputy director seemed to be pleased with the night's events. The only exception was Brad Mancuso, who sat with his arms crossed, his expression unreadable.

"We are one, we're everywhere!" the crowd sang through the screen.

"Bingo," Boone said.

46

LESTER GOODENOW, better known around Andromeda Records as Big Les, ran through the hallway of his Beverly Hills estate with two bricks of cocaine, spilling white powder onto the marble floor behind him.

They had woken him up by kicking the door open, and when he looked over the railing and saw their sunglasses and bulletproof vests, he knew he was being raided.

Les was fifty-six and had been joyfully distributing cocaine to his friends and business partners since the 1960s. He had long ago forgotten that it was even illegal, thinking of it only as a daily part of his life, a deal greaser, a panty dropper, a benefit of his position of power as executive vice president at one of the largest record companies in the world. Street punks got arrested because of cocaine. Record executives got gold records.

But when he saw the feds swarm in, he quickly remembered that he had enough Schedule II drugs in his house to be charged as a trafficker, which would land him in federal prison for a good long time.

Wearing a silk kimono that hugged his ample belly and nothing else, Les grabbed the two bricks that he kept in his office and ran down the hall to the master bedroom, with news coverage of president-elect Bush's upcoming inauguration blaring on the television in the kitchen and heavy footsteps thudding up the marble staircase toward the balcony on the second floor. Big Les locked the bedroom door behind him and plowed into the bathroom. He hovered over the toilet while he sliced open the plastic wrapper of the first brick with a long pinky fingernail.

The coke, suddenly freed from its compressed packaging, exploded in a cloud of dust that coated the walls and mirror of the bathroom. Very little made it into the toilet.

"Shit!" Big Les screamed. This wasn't good. Behind him, he heard the door to the master bedroom burst open. He held the plastic bag above the toilet and tried to shake out the rest of the contents, then yanked the cover off the back of the john and dropped the other brick in there.

"Hey, Lester," a woman's voice said from behind him. "You know it still counts as possession if it's wet, right?"

Big Les hung his jowly head. *Jesus, they're gonna do me like Doc McGhee,* he was thinking. But he didn't have nearly as much dirt to trade as the hair band manager who went down for smuggling back in '82 and talked his way out of serious jail time. *I wonder who his lawyer was,* thought Big Les, as he turned to get a look at the feds who were going to end his life as he knew it.

Standing in the doorway to his bathroom were a drop-dead gorgeous leggy blonde and a tough-looking Italian guy. They had their arms crossed, and they were smirking.

"I'm Officer Price," the woman said. "This is Officer Mancuso. Come on out of there and get dressed. We have a lot to talk about."

47

THE WORLD TOUR was happening!
    I knew this was the plan, but apparently it took a lot of arm-twisting of Big Les (which I think means blackmail?) to get Andromeda to pay for it. The bad news was that I wasn't supposed to tell anyone I knew about the tour yet, which was par for the course. But in positive news, I was finally welcomed into a CIA defensive training program to prepare for the overseas part of my mission.

Because I couldn't keep flying back and forth to Langley, Brad Mancuso trained me in an empty warehouse in Los Angeles. I would show up in sunglasses and a baseball hat and regular jeans and a T-shirt to avoid being recognized.

The place was a dump, and when we arrived in the morning, we usually had to chase off racoons, or rats, or other musicians. Mancuso was always turning his nose up at the place, but I liked it. It reminded me of how I got started.

"Okay, here it is," Mancuso said on our first day of training while he paced in front of a world map on the wall. "During the American Revolution, there was this bar in New York called the Queen's Head."

"Dope," I said.

"Shut up and listen," Mancuso said without looking at me. "This bar, it's where the revolutionaries met to plan their course of attack. And they got away with it because it was a bar, nobody was watching them there. So that's what this whole wacky, stupid plan is all about. The revolutionaries need to be able to hide in plain sight, so they can organize."

"So, we're, like, revolutionaries?" I asked.

Mancuso snorted. "Not even close. You and your buddies are the goofy jesters in tights and floppy hats, dancing around and playing your instruments. So anyone walking by would think that the place is too ridiculous for anything important to happen inside. You're a distraction."

Mancuso paced some more. "And mark my words," he said. "This whole thing is going to be a big waste of time. But all that is out of my hands, so I'm going to train you for one reason, and one reason alone. Because my boss is making me do it. Understand? Now." He pointed to a big red blob in the upper right-hand corner of the map. "What is this?"

I smiled knowingly. "A map," I said.

Mancuso hung his head. "Jesus Christ," he whispered.

We spent most of our time studying, which was bullshit. I didn't join the CIA to study! But Mancuso insisted. He said that I didn't join the CIA at all, first and foremost; and that I needed to understand the history and traditions of these Eastern Bloc countries, so if the band got ourselves in trouble, I might be able to talk our way out. I said, "That is what the weapons are for," and he said that they weren't giving me any weapons.

This all felt like a bait and switch, and I said so. Mancuso called me a pretty boy and told me that he hated his job now, and then he jabbed two fingers into my shoulder and it felt like somebody had shot me. I dropped to the ground writhing, and Mancuso said that if I was good and paid attention to my lessons, he would teach me how to do that.

So I studied. I learned about Russia, mostly, starting right after World War II when Russia installed communist governments in the Eastern Bloc countries and then we started pointing missiles at each other. I learned about how they kicked our ass at getting people into space, but we kicked their ass at landing on the moon. I asked Mancuso why any of this was important, and he told me to pay attention because it was all important.

I really wanted to learn that shoulder trick, so I kept listening. Mancuso told me about how the Soviets had been at war with

Afghanistan for eight years and it was draining them dry. And how their leader, Gorbachev, *seemed* like he was trying to steer them toward a more open form of government, but most of the KGB and some of the other Eastern Bloc countries like East Germany didn't want to change at all, and all these nationalist and separatist movements inside the countries were fighting against progress and making things worse.

It made me feel sad for all the regular people who were just trying to live their lives, but they couldn't get jobs and their grocery stores were empty because a group of people with a lot of power didn't want to let go of it. It made me excited to go there and give these people a hell of a concert, and maybe help them tip the scales a little bit?

Mancuso explained that the governments in the other Eastern Bloc countries were also pretty shitty. They had these secret police who would actually kill their political opponents, and they controlled what people could say or do on TV and the radio. And they were just dumping all their money into trying to look stronger than us, even though their people were starving. The people of all these countries, like Hungary and Yugoslavia, had been trying to get out from under their dickhead rulers for decades.

More recently, the pressure from people who wanted change was really heating up. Poland held huge strikes at coal mines and shipyards across the country in '88 and were about to hold their first real elections in more than fifty years, just a few weeks after our concert there. Hungary, Yugoslavia, Romania—they were all making moves. Mancuso said that 1989 felt like the year. I asked him if Whyte Python could really make a difference, and he said no, of course not, this was all bullshit, and then he did the shoulder thing to me again.

But then he taught me how to do it.

First Mancuso let me practice on him, and then he brought Boone in without telling him why, and I got to put him down. Then I spent all week practicing on other CIA geeks, pizza delivery guys, and anybody else who wandered into the warehouse while we studied.

One morning I arrived at the warehouse to see that, next to my desk and books, there were wrestling mats on the floor. "You pass a test about the history of the Iron Curtain," Mancuso said, "And I'll teach you a sleeper hold that will knock a man out cold in five seconds."

This is what my mornings were like in the fall of 1988. As far as the public knew, I was working on the next album and partying and dating girls from beer commercials.

To be clear, I actually was doing all those things. But the playboy lifestyle was almost becoming a cover now, something I did to keep everyone off my back while I studied world history and kicking ass.

Metal Bruce Wayne, my dudes.

By the end of winter, I had memorized the street maps around all our Eastern Bloc venues. I could speak at least a hundred words in Russian and German, and a dozen or so in most of the other languages in the region. I had mastered choke holds, pressure points, and knew enough muay Thai and krav maga strikes to defend myself in just about any kind of fight.

Mancuso had not lightened up toward me one bit, though—in fact, the more I absorbed his lessons, the grumpier he seemed to get, like he was rooting against me. I don't know if it was because he just didn't want to be proven wrong when he said this was all a waste of time or what, but the dude really seemed like he *wanted* the whole thing to fall apart.

He did finally drive me out to a shooting range, though, and he showed me how to fire a pistol. But first he made me promise I would never ask to do it again, or ask for a gun, or even try to buy one on my own.

I said, "Fine. I promise, Dad," and Mancuso rolled his eyes and caught himself smiling.

I looked at him sideways and grinned. "I'm winning you over, brah," I said.

Mancuso smiled all the way this time. Then he did the shoulder trick again, took the gun out of my hand, and clubbed me on the temple with it. But right after that—and for the first time ever—he reached out a hand to help me up.

48

⚡

IT HAD BEEN more than a year since Anja used the cigar shop to travel across the rooftops of East Berlin and paint over the CCTV cameras that pointed at the rear entrance of the Palace of the Republic. She believed that it would be safe to do it again. And she had only agreed to take the risk because Peter had devised a plan so diabolical, so powerful, and so hilarious that she felt it was worth it.

The resistance had matured quite a bit over those long months— this time they would have the support of electricians and city waste workers, and there was an inside man who had told them about a new CCTV camera aimed only at the first one. But Anja's equipment was virtually unchanged. A backpack with a can of black spray paint, a cassette tape with a folded map, and a miniature flashlight to signal to the others that her part of the job was done.

She had revisited the shopkeeper at the cigar store a few months earlier, to ensure that he wasn't cross with her. Surely, he had pieced together that her visit to his rooftop had coincided with the defaced flag. He had helped the resistance, and maybe he hadn't really wanted to. But he was delighted when she visited then and seemed to be just as happy now that she returned to ask if she could use his ladder one more time.

Anja arrived a few minutes early, to visit. To her mind, this was an important step before asking for a favor from an innocent bystander. But the truth was, she also liked him. The man was warm and laughed easily, and the tobacco smell of his shop was pleasant. She had not asked his name, because she thought it was better that he not ask for hers; so she addressed him as "Grandfather"—as a callback to the time they first met, when he'd said that Anja reminded him of his granddaughter, but also because there was a nice feeling to the nickname.

While they talked, he noticed the silver pin she was wearing, a Y-shaped electric guitar that transformed into a snake, and asked what it was. Anja's hand rested on it. "His name is Axe," she said. "He's the symbol."

"The symbol?"

"For my favorite band." Anja winked. "And maybe other things."

The old man seemed to understand that she had communicated something to him without saying it, to protect him as much as herself. He changed the subject. Have you heard the song by Bill Haley and the Comets?" he asked. " 'Rock around the Clock'?"

Anja shook her head. The old man didn't appear surprised. "It was a sweet, innocent song," he told her, "but catchy, as popular with children as it was with teenagers. My daughter loved it when she was a child. But then it was banned several decades ago, before you were born." The government did not like the idea of rocking around the clock, as he understood it. This was a dangerous idea. Perhaps too much rocking to them. And rocking around the clock would interfere with curfews.

At the mention curfews, Anja checked her watch and realized that she needed to get going. She had a job to do. She nodded toward the back of his store. "May I?"

The old man swept his arm in a grand gesture to let her pass. Anja stepped past him, and then she stopped. Her fingers found the Axe pin on her jacket. She freed it and placed the snake in the shopkeeper's palm.

He shook his head and tried to hand it back. "I couldn't accept this," he said. "You cherish it."

"I have many," Anja said. "You may see them on the streets, in fact. You've been a friend to me. If you ever need a friend in return, show this."

His fingers closed around Axe, and Anja patted his hand. When she looked in his eyes, there was a new resolve there, a reawakened a sense of purpose. Was it something he had forgotten about, or forcibly buried in order to get by? Anja watched as the old man's chest swelled and he nodded—a salute between compatriots now—and he sent her off to his ladder.

It was easier this time. She had gained so much confidence in these months with the movement, had pulled off more daring feats than this one. The buildings on her path had not changed. That was one reliable thing about the GDR—they didn't like change very much, so they didn't allow it.

Surveying the view, she decided she would take a wider arc this time, to find the camera that had been installed merely to watch another camera. That was first. The camera facing the rear entrance was second, and finally the one on the eastern side. There was no second camera there—or at least that was what the source told Peter, and Peter trusted it. She ran. She leapt. She ran. She leapt. There were no obstacles in her path. She had done this before, and she was a little older and stronger now. So the job was done in less than thirty minutes.

Anja signaled the garbage truck operator as he arrived on the street below. He stopped the truck exactly where he was supposed to, on the same route he took every night. She saw the electrician leave from the passenger side of the cab and duck behind the truck to the junction box. A few seconds later, the spotlight went out.

Now, for the first time, Anja was anxious. A spotlight going out would be noticed. But there didn't seem to be any other way; and besides, there was something about the light going out and then coming back on to reveal something that hadn't been there before. Like a magic trick.

It was Peter's turn now, and Peter moved fast. Anja watched the second hand on her watch tick away as her brother worked in the plaza below. Like clockwork, the spotlight returned in less than a minute.

Anja beamed. Peter's plan—the one that everyone agreed was worth the risk, even though it didn't accomplish anything truly functional—was a success. A new flag glowed under the hard spotlight that shone on the central flagpole behind the Palace of the Republic. Gone were the red, yellow, and black bars of the GDR, and its masculine coat of arms. The flag that waved in its place was simple: white, with a black electric guitar spray-painted in the center that turned into the head of a snake at the bottom.

Anya saluted. "Hey, Axe," she said.

Abracadabra.

49

![lightning bolt ornament]

"AKE IT DOWN," General Becker growled. "*Now.*"

The flag—a tattered white bedsheet with the odd guitar snake in the center, waved gently in the breeze, seemingly at him. Seconds later, it slid down the pole in quick, jagged bursts. Soldiers unclipped the fabric, then stretched it taut and began to perform the standard ceremony for folding a flag. Becker ran across the plaza and slapped it out of their hands.

"What are you doing?" he screamed. "That is not a real flag."

"What should we do with it?" his aide asked.

"Burn it," he said. "And call Los Angeles. I want our agent back here tonight, and if he doesn't catch the perpetrators this time, I'll bury him in a place much worse than California."

"Yes, General."

Back in his office, Becker paced to the humming of the dial tones on the other end of the line. Finally, a voice—slow, Russian accented, sleepy—answered.

"Hello?" Rezident Ivanov said.

"This is General Becker."

"General Becker, hello." Becker could smell the booze through Ivanov's sluggish, careful delivery. It was only six p.m. in Los Angeles, and Ivanov was already drunk. Becker held a hand over the receiver as he cursed at his Soviet counterpart.

This right here was a big part of the problem. His closest ally was living eight time zones away, getting drunk at lunch and soaking up Western propaganda in the California sun. Sometimes Becker worried that the same fate could eventually befall that big, bald maniac

214 · TRAVIS KENNEDY

who reported to him from West Hollywood if he stayed there long enough.

But no, the general doubted this was possible; Ivanov and the spy were cut from different cloth, and they worked for two wildly diverging regimes.

Russia under Gorbachev, he thought. *No discipline.*

"I read your latest briefing," Ivanov said.

"And what do you think?"

"I think your source is exceptionally well placed."

"Yes. We have someone very close. Our confidence level is high."

"What do you make of it?" asked Ivanov.

Becker stood and paced his office, dragging the phone cord behind him. He glanced at his Whyte Python materials—a sprawling collection of papers, photographs, and cassette tapes with recorded phone conversations, among other evidence—that had started as a folder and grown rapidly to a box before taking up near-permanent residence spread across his conference-room desk. "I think Whyte Python may be the single largest threat to our grip on the region."

Ivanov snorted. "No offense, General," he said, "but this sounds dramatic, do you not think? They are a rock and roll band."

"And now I mean no offense," Becker said. "But I must ask. When was the last time you visited your motherland, Rezident?"

"Uh, yes," Ivanov chuckled. "Southern California is pleasant, but make no mistake, General, my place is in *Russia*."

Becker felt a chill. Ivanov was clearly drunk, but this casual disloyalty to his homeland was still shocking.

"Let me inform you, then, of the latest developments," Becker hissed through gritted teeth. "They're singing these songs in the streets. On the buses and trains. In the schools. Read the lyrics. 'No wall can keep us apart tonight?' This is about us! The music is playing in movies and commercials, it's everywhere. They are juggernauts! The number-one song in the world. The number-one album! And just tonight, their followers replaced a flag in front of the Palace of the Republic with the logo of this band. A finger in my eye!"

"I apologize if I made light of the situation," Ivanov said. "You believe the CIA is involved."

Becker stared at the latest report on his desk. "I know the CIA is involved. Keep watching. Our source believes that they'll make a move soon."

50

W E'RE GOING ON a world tour!" Kirby beamed while he delivered the news, and the guys all cheered and jumped up and down on the furniture at Davy's house.

I knew this was coming, of course, but I got into the action just as much as the rest of them. A whole year had already passed since Tawny recruited me into the CIA. And here I was again, sitting on Davy's couch with a plan to trick the guys.

To her credit, Tawny was right—"Tonight, for Tomorrow" was our biggest hit ever. It was a breakthrough song, earning regular rotation on pop radio and a video that basically ran 24/7 on MTV.

We got to enjoy the spoils of that throughout the '88 summer tour, and the CIA mostly left me alone. I would even forget about the whole deal for weeks at a time, focusing mainly on partying and scoring with babes on the road, until Tawny would show up randomly with new talking points or whatever.

I have to admit, despite everything, I was still happy to see her in those first few seconds when she walked in the room. And I still thought about her on the road sometimes, during those long, quiet drives when I was alone with my thoughts and all the good times we had before she told me she was a spy and it was all bullshit. Nostalgia's a bitch, bro. It doesn't just go away because you're mad at somebody; it gets stronger. And I tried to cover that up by going cold.

I will *also* admit: now that I didn't believe in love or trust anybody anymore, I was having a blast! Your buddy Rikki was on the covers of magazines, hooking up with celebrities, and giving ol' Bret Michaels himself a run for his money backstage with the ladies.

I was having such a good time that I almost didn't notice how empty, alone, and pointless it all made me feel whenever I had time to think. So my solution was, no time alone. When we were on the road, that was easy; I couldn't be alone if I tried. When I was home, I kept people around me all the time. I went out a lot, and dated a lot, and drank and took more drugs than I probably should have.

And then there was the stuff that I was supposed to be coy about, to "neither confirm nor deny," as we liked to say in the CIA and in show business. Apparently, it sold more records if I left my relationship status a mystery—like how there was a rumor that I may or may not have gone on a few dates with a certain pop superstar, but it may or may not have just been to make her estranged movie star husband jealous, which she may or may not have explained to me several times over dinner.

And all that cloak-and-dagger relationship stuff made it easier to explain to the band why Tawny wasn't around very much but was still technically my girlfriend.

The guys were doing good, too. Davy got engaged to one of Janet Jackson's backup dancers, but he was the first one to tell us that the wedding was never going to happen. Spencer got a really small part in a Sylvester Stallone movie. Buck bought an Orange Julius store in a mall in Wisconsin, and he worked there whenever he had a break.

Now it was February, and we were in almost the exact same place that we had been a year earlier: Davy's house, sketching out plans for a new album after a few necessary weeks apart.

And of course we had just learned we were going overseas in May. Or at least the other guys learned about it. I had known about the world tour for a long time.

So Kirby dropped the news, and we were high-fiving each other, and Buck was breaking into a spontaneous little lick on his guitar when Kirby introduced the first wrinkle.

"All right!" Davy shouted. "Paris, here we come!"

"Well, not Paris," Kirby said.

"London?" Davy asked.

"Nope."

"Brazil? Rome? Éthpaña?"

"Oh, boy." Kirby took a handkerchief from his blazer pocket and wiped his brow. "I introduced this wrong. Let me start over. Have you boys ever heard of a country called Tajikistan?"

After Davy and Buck had finished pushing Kirby out the front door and slamming it in his face, we settled back into the living room. "Well, he's fired," Davy said. "I don't think we even have to talk about this, right? We're the biggest band in the world. Russia, Romania, Yugoslavia, East Germany? Why does Andromeda think we should do that?"

"Agreed," Buck said.

"I'd rather go on tour across my old man's ball sack," Spencer said.

"Well, hang on," I said.

Everyone turned to me. They looked surprised. "What?" Davy asked.

"Just think about it for a minute," I said. "The people in these countries, they *love* metal, but also, they're *starving*."

More confused looks.

"For music!" I said. *Good save, Secret Agent Thunder.* "They're starving for a band to come put on a show. I bet we'll fill nothing but arenas over there. I bet we'll sell a mountain of merch. Enough to buy you that house in Daytona, Davy. And, Spencer, you can get that Harley with seven wheels that you drew a picture of. And, Buck . . . What do you want, Buck?"

"Stock in Microsoft," Buck said. "Or a bunch of human adrenal glands."

"You can get both, buddy." I patted him twice on the chest. "And the girls over there? Come on! So exotic! And they've never even seen a rock star. Imagine what'll happen when they get their hands on Davy Bones!"

Davy thought about it for what felt like a solid minute. Finally, he got up off the couch and went to the front door. He opened it, and Kirby was sitting on the ground outside. Davy pointed a thumb toward the living room. "Talk," he said.

We were seated on the couch again, with Kirby standing in front of us. "I'm glad you reconsidered, boys," he said. "Because the thing is, we kind of can't say no. This tour just became a big priority for the record label."

"Why?" Davy asked. "I haven't even heard of some of these places."

"Honestly, Davy?" Kirby winced. "I don't know. If I had to guess, it's because we have an undercapitalized market over there and it's dirt cheap to tour. Lowest cost, highest gain."

"Stop using your smart words, warlock!" Spencer shouted.

Kirby regrouped. "We're talking about nothing but massive stadiums, crowds of forty, fifty, eighty thousand. Guaranteed sellouts. A whole market that has never seen anything like you, just sitting there for the taking. We'll double our record sales. It's an enormous opportunity."

What I knew, and I think that even Kirby didn't, was that we would never see a dollar out of most of those countries from record sales. They didn't pay royalties. We would make a pile of cash on merchandise and ticket sales, but the tickets would also be cheaper and the merch would sell at just above cost, because the CIA needed as many people wearing Whyte Python T-shirts in those countries as possible.

We might play for bigger crowds, but we'd be lucky to break even and would surely earn way more by touring for two weeks in the States. But now was not the time to say any of that!

"So, what do we think, guys?" I piled on. "I think Eastern Europe sounds pretty fuckin' choice."

"Good on you, Rikki," Kirby said. "Company man."

"Get out," I said.

It always felt really good to kick Kirby out of the room. He didn't seem to mind, either, this time, because he'd gotten what he needed from us. He headed for the door.

"Kirby, wait," Davy called after him. Kirby stopped. Davy stood and looked at Buck and Spencer and me. Then he smiled. "Do we get our own plane?"

51

I N A SMOKE-FILLED war room somewhere in the Eastern Bloc, intelligence officers from a dozen Soviet-controlled nations sat around a conference table to discuss Whyte Python.

General Becker stood at the head of the table. He studied the room with pride, believing that he had sniffed out a covert United States operation before it took root. And the men in the room represented a show of unity that was uncommon in the Eastern Bloc of late, with Poland on the outs and everybody else just trying to keep the lights on.

Becker rapped a finger on the table, hushing the room. "Good evening, gentlemen," he said in perfect Russian.

Most of the men around the room nodded. The man from Cuba, though, looked confused. "Qué?" he said.

Rezident Ivanov, who was seated next to the Cuban, leaned over and said, "Russian?"

"Oh." He shrugged bashfully. "No." And then, holding his open palms to the sky, he asked, "English?"

Everyone else in the room groaned and rolled their eyes.

Becker took a deep breath and blew it out. "Fine," he said. "English."

"You guys are really supposed to speak Russian," Ivanov said.

This meeting was not getting off to a good start. Becker tried to keep things moving. "Now," he said in English. "Welcome to the first special international intelligence meeting for codename Cobra Dominance. I am Lieutenant General Kurt Becker, with the Ministry for State Security in East Berlin. As is known to you all, the

American rock band Whyte Python has applied to tour in Western Europe and Northern Asia beginning in May 1989."

"I do not know why we care about this," the man from Romania said.

"We care about this," Becker snapped back at him, "because we have reason to believe that the United States is using Whyte Python to run a shadow operation intended to overthrow our governments. We have a reliable source that is very close to the operation."

"Yes," Ivanov said. He stood and walked across the room, joining Becker at the head of the table in a show of solidarity. "We get your briefings every week, General. Your data is convincing. The Soviet Union, too, is concerned with the threat that Whyte Python poses to our dominance in Asia. The band's song "Tonight, for Tomorrow" already appears to promote instability among fans."

"It is just rock and roll," the man from Romania said.

"Buck Sweet fuckin' shreds," the man from Yugoslavia offered in heavily accented English.

"It is not just rock and roll!" Becker roared. He swept papers off the table. "It is an attack! An attack on *our authority*!"

Rezident Ivanov cleared his throat. "General Becker," he said, "on your suggestion, our analysts have reviewed Whyte Python's metrics. There are . . . irregularities."

Becker tried to hide his smile. "Oh, really?" he said, feigning surprise, as if Ivanov had not already told him this information in private. "What irregularities?"

"The band's first album was initially driven by sales concentrated in Washington, D.C.," explained Ivanov. "Those sales were almost exclusively cassettes."

"And what does that mean?" Becker prompted.

"Our theory?" Ivanov said. "Cassettes are easy to transfer. Within weeks, cassettes showed up in our schools."

"Here," Becker growled. He pounded a finger against the table, then he pointed at Ivanov. "And there. And in your country, and in yours." He listed them off as he pointed at the men around the room.

"Correct," Ivanov said. "The new album, same tricks. This is sophisticated coordination."

"Yes, sophisticated. Our source believes that there is a direct connection between the CIA and this band," Becker said.

"Yes," the man from Bulgaria said. "Rikki Thunder. We read in your reports. But what proof do we have?"

"My agent has a source," Becker said. "Very close. I am not at liberty to reveal the identity. And if Whyte Python is what we think they are, then Rikki Thunder is the spark that will light a flaming fire of dissent across our continents."

"So, what do we do?" the man from Hungary asked.

"Perhaps he should be killed," said a man in the rear who had not spoken yet.

The room hung quiet for a moment. "That doesn't seem wise at the moment," Becker said. "But I recommend that we all deny the Whyte Python applications to perform in our countries. Uniform rejection. Keep them outside of our borders. The damage could be catastrophic."

Ivanov steepled his fingers. "I see things differently," he said.

"What?" the man from Yugoslavia hit the shoulder of the man from Romania. "Does Gorbachev think we should hug and kiss the Americans into compliance?"

Everyone laughed. Becker finally held his palms out to calm the room down.

"You are not wrong." Ivanov shrugged. "But the Kremlin has spoken on this already. The rock bands Mötley Crüe, Scorpions, Bon Jovi, Ozzy Osbourne, and others are playing a concert in Moscow later this summer."

"Wait. The Scorpions will be in Moscow?" the man from Yugoslavia asked. "Rezident Ivanov, are there tickets remaining?"

Ivanov ignored him. "Denying Whyte Python could play right into their objectives," he said. "Make Whyte Python martyrs. Send the people into revolt. It is a larger risk than letting the musicians play."

"I disagree," Becker said.

"Concerts are good for loyalty in the people," the man from Czechoslovakia said.

The man from Romania shrugged. "How much damage could they do?"

"Enormous damage!" Becker roared.

"General Becker is correct again," Ivanov said. "Whyte Python demonstrates a significant threat. However, I believe that it is a better strategy to let them play. Metal bands are coming already. If only Whyte Python is denied, the CIA will be alerted that you have spies following the band."

"So Moscow is going to allow them to play?" Becker said.

"Oh, no." Ivanov chuckled. "Whyte Python will not play in Russia. The terms negotiated for the Moscow Music Peace Festival preclude it. Agreements with the bands do not allow any other Western musicians to play in the motherland before the festival's scheduled performances." The Russian returned to his seat and began to thumb through a *People* magazine.

Everyone in the room stared at Ivanov in silence for several seconds.

Becker's face burned plum red. "I just . . ." he started, then stopped himself. "Why did you attend this meeting? Why not tell this to me over the telephone?"

Ivanov shrugged. He didn't lift his eyes from his magazine. Becker stared at the ceiling and blew steam from his nose. Fucking Russians. Just a few years ago, he would have been terrified to even *think* those words. But here was the new normal. The men at this table, Ivanov especially, were looking past the Soviet era—in their eyes, its demise was already etched in stone.

Ivanov's behavior provided an answer to a nagging question that Becker had kept to himself since first contacting the rezidentura office in Los Angeles for this specific project. The rezident was KGB, or had been once. *So why is this man based in California?* Becker wondered. Rezident Ivanov served no purpose to the intelligence community there. Why not Washington, D.C., or at least New York City? The answer was becoming clear: Ivanov had this assignment because he could afford to pay for it. Even career KGB men like Ivanov were giving up on the cause. They were using connections and cash to buy posh assignments from crooked politicians, jumping ship to warm locales and day drinking, with some piece of business secured in their back pocket. Ivanov was reading *People*. He probably thought he was going to work in movies. *Shameful.*

And it wasn't just Russia. Becker's current counterparts were either lazy simps like Ivanov, who was simply waiting to get his ass back to California, or they were opportunistic psychopaths circling the carcass of the Eastern Bloc, anxious to get rich in the chaos. No honor. No courage. Becker picked up a pen from the table and snapped it in half.

"Okay," he said. "Rezident Ivanov has wasted all our time. Where does everyone else stand?"

"We let them play," the man from Romania said.

"Yes," the man from Yugoslavia agreed. One by one, the other members of the group nodded along.

Becker's blood boiled. None of these men had watched a Whyte Python flag wave above their parliamentary buildings. They would, in time. He was sure of it. That vision kept him up at night, and in that moment he committed to redoubling the Stasi's efforts to find the vandals. The fools in the room needed to see what a real fucking patriot looked like.

"Fine," Becker growled. "Whyte Python will play. But do not forget: in every city they visit across our countries, at every moment, no one lets them out of our sights."

52

~~

NJA HUMMED THE riff to "Tonight, for Tomorrow" as she
moved through the alleyway toward her favorite neighborhood. Her eyes naturally scanned the streets for trouble, in
time with her fingers absentmindedly strumming air to the rhythm
of Buck Sweet's epic shred.

Even singing along to the anthem in public was a risk, lately;
hanging the Axe flag may have been a mistake. The *Whyte Album* was
hard to come by all of a sudden—through legal channels, anyway.
The band's music, in any format, seemed to vanish overnight with no
explanation, joining the swollen ranks of Western music deemed too
subversive for East Germany's youth. Somewhere, Whyte Python
tapes surely burned. But that only meant the resistance was working.

Strangely enough, the government never formally declared
Whyte Python to be banned material—the tapes and all else just . . .
went away. And, even stranger, Whyte Python was going to be per-
mitted to perform a live show at the Stadion der Weltjugend in May.
Anja didn't care why. She maintained a policy of not wasting time
attempting to read the minds of leadership at the GDR. The concert,
she knew, would be one of the most memorable nights of her life—
so, better not to question it.

And her mind wasn't on spy craft that night anyway, because she
wasn't going to be jumping onto any rooftops. In fact, now that the
Axe flag had sent the whole East German military complex into a
fit, Anja would probably not risk another visit to a rooftop. There
would be new plans, certainly, new strategies to poke the bear. She
would be keeping an eye out for the next *Whyte Album* cassette for

instructions.

Tonight, Anja was delivering a gift. The old man had been so kind to let her climb up his ladder those times before. She wouldn't need him anymore, but she didn't want to forget him. She had a record to deliver.

Anja hugged *Rock around the Clock* to her chest, zipped inside her jean jacket to shield it from prying eyes. But when she turned the corner onto his street and stepped close enough to see through his storefront window, the album slipped from her hands and landed in the street. The old man was not alone in his shop.

"Oh no," Anja heard herself whisper.

A tall, stern-looking man dressed in a military uniform stood across the desk from the old man. There were four others, all men with large bodies and unyielding stances. They wore black tactical outfits and carried pistols in hip holsters. The military man was hold-ing his fingers a few inches away from the old man's face, pinched together in a strange gesture. Anja didn't know what it meant at first, until she saw the glint of metal in the soldier's grip.

Axe. Her pin. Her fault. Anja knew what she was watching, and she knew she should run away. If he gave her up, she would under-stand. But it also meant that she would need to pull the ripcord on her life as she knew it. She needed as long a head start as she could get. Anja prepared to quietly slip away.

But the old man didn't look like he was giving her up at all. He shook his head while they interrogated him, feigning ignorance or confusion. Acting feeble. She could practically read his lips: *I don't know what that is.* It was convincing.

But it did not fool the military man for a second.

The man in uniform moved toward the door and snapped his fin-gers. The mercenaries grabbed the old man and dragged him along, too.

Anja slipped back into the alley and squeezed between a trash receptacle and the cold brick wall just as the man in uniform stepped outside. His subordinates followed close behind, dragging the old man from his armpits. Her friend was terrified, and Anja had to bite her wrist to keep from shouting. They stopped in front of two parked cars on the street, so close to Anja that she worried they could hear her breathing.

Anja saw fear in the old man's eyes for just a second, before a mercenary pulled a hood over his head. She hiccupped back a scream.

The military man climbed into the back seat of a shiny black limousine, and the car drove away. The mercenaries loaded the old man into the back of their truck.

Hot tears coated her eyes and rolled down her cheeks. She wiped them away lest by some odd chance she might be seen. The tears would give them a reason to suspect that she was affiliated with the innocent old man they were dragging off—to torture, or worse. And she felt enormous shame. Shame for dragging him into this in the first place, and for denying him now, this stranger who had sacrificed so much for her—who was sacrificing for her still.

Anja wanted to risk it all just to call out to him and thank him for his kindness. To tell him he was loved. And she might have done it at that moment, even though she knew the cigar store owner wouldn't want her to. But even if she did call out to him, she wouldn't have known what to say.

He had given so much. He was about to lose more. And Anja didn't even know his name.

53

DEPUTY DIRECTOR ED LONSA sat on a bench in the shadow of a giant mastodon. The beast reared back on its hind legs, striking an aggressive pose, with its massive tusks pointed at the sky.

Lonsa sipped his coffee and cracked his neck. "You don't look so tough," he said to the monster. But the mastodon didn't reply. It didn't react in any way. And the seams evident on the fiberglass body really did kill the illusion when viewed from up close.

The DD didn't think very much of L.A.'s La Brea Tar Pits, an odd natural landmark of liquid asphalt ponds that had preserved fossils tens of thousands of years. In the heat of the day, the caustic fumes from various tar pools mixed with stale piss deposited by local pets and partiers. It reminded him of the sticky floors of the clubs that Whyte Python played in. But the DD's mole had insisted on meeting there—and sometimes you have to let your mole feel like he's calling the shots.

"Quite the beast, isn't it?" a voice said from behind Lonsa. He turned around to find Brad Mancuso standing there, ghostlike—if apparitions wore Lakers hats and massive aviator sunglasses.

Mancuso wasn't a mole, of course. He was Lonsa's direct report, simply doing his job by updating the brass. But Mancuso's Facemelt teammates wouldn't be happy if they learned that he was meeting Lonsa privately every few weeks. For Mancuso, it was direct face time with the higher-up who held the keys to his next assignment. For Lonsa, it served as an opportunity to hear about how the Facemelt rejects were conducting themselves when he wasn't around.

Back in D.C., they met at Langley, where Mancuso would show up in a shirt and tie, with orderly stacks of paper that he would read from and then dutifully shred. Now Mancuso was based in Los Angeles while he trained Rikki Thunder, and he considered everything outside of the Beltway "the field." And when Mancuso was out in the field, he really enjoyed the cloak-and-dagger of it all; hence the "local camouflage," as Mancuso called it. Ironically, neither of them took notice of another person secretly monitoring their conversation from several hundred feet across the park with a well-concealed directional microphone. She had her own local camouflage, and it was better than Mancuso's.

In fairness to Mancuso and Lonsa, there was no reason to survey the other Tar Pits tourists and assess risk. Neither man was on a clandestine mission. All the sillier, Lonsa knew, for Mancuso to get dressed up; but he supposed it didn't hurt to keep the kid in shape. He would be reassigned to a job that mattered eventually, and it benefitted all for Mancuso to keep his skills fresh. The younger officer had even taken to checking out telephoto lenses and phone-tapping equipment from the agency's supply cache in recent months, although Lonsa couldn't imagine what for. Practice, he assumed. Delusional boredom, more likely.

"Sit," Lonsa said.

Mancuso sat. His knee bounced slightly, and the corners of his lips were fighting a smile.

"You all right?" Lonsa asked.

"I'm great," Mancuso said.

"Okay. Let's have it. How are my misfits behaving?" Mancuso's eyebrows dropped behind his glasses and his grin faded. "Present company excluded."

"Yeah," Mancuso said. "Right. So, easy ones first. Stryker is solid. She's doing the work. Seems committed to the mission. I can't tell if she believes in it or not, but that's kind of the point, right?"

Lonsa picked up on Mancuso's question; he was trying to figure out why his teammates were in disciplinary programming. Lonsa had shared more than he was supposed to with Mancuso, but he hadn't gone so far as to tell him why his colleagues had been assigned to Facemelt, and he wasn't going to start now. He waited until Mancuso got the hint and started talking again.

"Price is good," Mancuso went on. "She's doing a nice job managing an asset that still doesn't want anything to do with her. It's not easy. And Boone is status quo—on the right side of sanity for the time being. We've transitioned him to general logistics now that his heavy lifting on lyrics is mostly done, unless you want him getting to work on the next album?"

Lonsa remained silent.

"Fair enough," Mancuso said, and stared out at the asphalt pool in front of them.

"That was a short report," Lonsa said.

"What do you mean, short report?"

"I mean, usually you go on for twenty minutes about how insulting and pointless this is, and how frustrating your teammates are. Where's the goods?"

Mancuso shrugged. "It's all just going smoothly," he said.

"Okay," Lonsa said. "But you left off one person from your report. How are you doing, Brad? More to the point, why are you being weird?"

Mancuso's mouth dropped open. "I'm . . . I'm not being weird," he said, but there was no confidence in it. Lonsa raised his eyebrows.

Mancuso sat back against the bench and took a moment to think before he spoke again. He took a deep breath and then leaned forward.

"Okay," he said. "The thing is, and you know I'd be the last one to admit this, but I think this thing is actually kind of working. The field reports from Eastern Bloc countries show the song is really burrowing into the movement. Kids use the cassette cases we dropped in-country to pass along secret messages. That wasn't even our idea—it's an organic development." Mancuso was talking faster as he reported. He was genuinely excited.

Lonsa felt a cold shiver run up his spine. "That's good," he said, his voice measured and slow.

But this wasn't good. Mancuso was supposed to be the cooler on Project Facemelt—the wet blanket who kept the other team members from getting carried away.

"And I have to tell you, DD." Mancuso shook his head and

smirked. "Rikki Thunder? I think he's a lot cleverer than he lets on. He's conversant in three new languages. And he's level-headed and quick on his feet, and he's a charming kid who wins people over right away."

"Price picked a good one."

"A great one." Mancuso shook his head again and held his hands up, smiling wide. "But don't ever tell Rikki I said that," he said with a guffaw, "or I'll never hear the end of it!"

Christ almighty, Lonsa thought. *What is it about Rikki Thunder?*

The deputy director took off his glasses and scowled. "Oh, it's Rikki now?" he said. "What, are you falling in love with him, too?"

Mancuso got the point immediately, and he dialed down his enthusiasm. "I mean, it's the guy's name," he said. "Anyway, I wanted to let you know that things are going well. The team is staying focused on doing the job. The propaganda saturation is taking hold. And the asset's training is ahead of schedule. I think we'll be in really good shape when we get to Moscow."

"Moscow," Lonsa said. He had been expecting this would come up now that plans for the tour were in motion, but he figured it would come from Price before Mancuso. "What makes you think you're going to Moscow?"

Mancuso tilted his head, confused. "Because that's . . . the mission?"

"No, it's not," Lonsa said. "The mission is to keep the president happy, and stay out of trouble. We have a massive thirty-year operation running in Russia. You should know. You were part of it. You think they're gonna let this ding-dong operation within a hundred miles of Moscow? Run the risk of screwing everything up when we're so close to winning? The CIA isn't going to let Project Facemelt anywhere near Russia."

Mancuso balled up his fist and swallowed a profanity. "How on earth are we supposed to run a mission to end the Cold War without going to Russia?" he muttered.

"The Eastern Bloc isn't just Russia," Lonsa said. "You guys can play around in low-stakes countries all you want. Moscow's off-limits. It's too sensitive. Besides, Whyte Python can't perform there, anyway."

"What?" Mancuso said. "Why not?"

"No visas issued," Lonsa said. "What's the concert that's playing there later in the year, with all those bands?"

"That Peace Festival thing?" Mancuso said. "Ozzy, Mötley Crüe, Scorpions—"

"Yeah, yeah." Lonsa waved Mancuso off before he could finish listing stupid words. "They have an exclusivity clause in their contract. No other bands from Western countries can play in Russia before the show. They want to be first."

Mancuso took off his sunglasses and turned toward his boss. "And how do you know about this?"

Lonsa held his palms to the sky. "Come on. Give the Russian office a little credit here."

"The Russian office," Mancuso said. "Of the Central Intelligence Agency. They did this."

"Correct."

"So, the CIA manipulated the contract for the Moscow Music Peace Festival to keep another CIA operation *out* of the country?"

"Not just any other operation." Lonsa patted Mancuso's leg and got up from the bench. "Project Facemelt. I told you this before. You guys can play the game, but never in prime time."

"DD—"

Lonsa interrupted him. "Remember what's at stake here. For you and me, and for our way of doing business." He pointed at the giant mastodon posing menacingly above them. "Extinction."

54

THE GERMAN DID NOT require much time to pack his things.
Although he had lived in Southern California for several
years, he had barely moved into the little apartment at all. His
clothes and his camera and telescopic lens all fit into one suitcase.

Everything else—his radio, his binoculars, his notebooks full of
useful intelligence on Whyte Python—went into a trash can that he
burned in the parking lot of a Sam Goody record store in the middle
of the night. He had no purpose in Los Angeles anymore.

General Becker had called that night and told him to come home.
The general was the first to admit that the German's deep cover work
in the States had been a pleasant surprise. Very few of his superior
officers expected that he would have so much success transitioning
from a job that mostly required violence to one that mostly required
charm.

Nothing in his file suggested this aptitude.

He was born in 1958 and raised by negligent grandparents in the
slums of East Berlin. By age six, he had developed a reputation as
a neighborhood bully who stole from local shops and homes and
fought like a rabid animal. When he was nine, he was kicked out of
the house after he pushed his grandfather down the front steps. An
especially nasty motorcycle gang took him in. They sent him out to
tip over gravestones in Jewish cemeteries and vandalize the homes of
Afro-German families and suspected homosexuals.

He committed his first armed robbery at thirteen. His first arson
a few months later. Rose in the ranks of his gang. They mugged and
stole, they vandalized and terrorized. But they never faced arrest, due

to their enthusiastic collaboration with the Stasi.

At eighteen, he was conscripted into the National People's Army, where he was trained in supreme discipline while gently nurturing his preexisting ruthless tendencies. At his first opportunity, the German begged for an assignment at the Berlin Wall, in hopes that one day he could shoot a deserter in the back and face no consequences. But he never got the chance. Less than a year into his service, he was recruited by the Stasi—and that was where the real fun began.

The German spent the first half of the eighties climbing the ranks in the Ministry for State Security, where he thrived at interrogating witnesses, intimidating sources, acting as go-between with neo-Nazi gangs, and the occasional black op. He was having a grand old time. By the middle of the decade, General Becker had taken the young man under his wing—and clarified the state of play. If the German aimed to rise in the ranks of the Stasi, he needed to prove that he was more than just a steel fist.

And so, somewhat reluctantly, the German found himself in a whole different training program: charm school. He spent nearly a year in an intensive course on Western intelligence. He was trained on American ideals and trends and popular culture. He was schooled in manipulative psychology. He learned how to smile, even though it hurt his face. And when they decided that he was ready, he was sent to a place he never imagined having to endure . . . Southern California.

His tour in the United States was hell. He spent all his time in the hot sun, surrounded by shiftless hippies and filthy musicians. His days and nights were consumed with the quiet monitoring of idiots. His mole, at least, continued to produce useful data—but extracting that data was a painful experience with this particular asset. He only got two reprieves over those long four years, short missions back to East Berlin on orders from General Becker.

The general had become preoccupied with a gang of vandals who defaced the flags at the Palace of the Republic. Normally, being summoned halfway across the globe for such a task would be humiliating; but the German was happy to do it, because it meant a trip home. And it came with the promise that if he caught the perpetrator, he was allowed to administer brutal justice.

His team spent two weeks traversing rooftops around the city, based on a hunch from General Becker. There were too many directions, too many fire escapes. They would need to interrogate hundreds of people. The German returned to Los Angeles a failure. General Becker was furious. But a year later the gang struck again, and this time they got their man—or *a* man, anyway, which was apparently enough.

Nobody believed the seventy-six-year-old cigar store owner was actually hopping across the rooftops of East Berlin with a can of spray paint in the middle of the night; but he had the snake pin, and he wasn't talking. The German wanted to throw the old man off a boat, but Becker wouldn't allow it—these were not the old days. The old man would have to be returned to his home eventually. But they held him for a while, long enough to make his neighbors believe it was *possible* they had killed him; so when they finally deposited the cigar store owner back in his neighborhood with a sufficiently black-and-blue face, it served as both a warning to his community and—oddly—a demonstration of mercy.

The German, though, was getting an itchy trigger finger. Becker was going to have to let him kill someone eventually. "Patience," Becker counseled his attack dog. "Your moment will come."

But the German had been in Los Angeles for almost half a decade, and his well of patience had long ago run dry.

Mercifully, that tour of duty was coming to an end. His rewards—a promotion, national fame, an *army*—were waiting for him at home in East Germany, once Whyte Python's international tour was over. Two weeks. That was it. The band would land in Germany and travel across the Eastern Bloc, poisoning his homeland and those around it with their nonsensical preoccupations with "partying" and "babes" and "personal autonomy." In this interim period, he would simply follow them, maintaining contact with his mole and awaiting orders from his superiors.

The tour was scheduled to end back in East Germany, and Whyte Python would fly home from there. But the German had not purchased a return ticket. There was no need.

Because General Becker had shared with him a closely guarded secret: a mission that would be his to command in Berlin—a bonus reward for a job well done.

Whyte Python was too dangerous. They had to be stopped, permanently. And so Berlin would be Whyte Python's last concert. The band would not leave East Germany alive.

PART V

The World Tour

55

∿

W<small>E LEFT LOS ANGELES</small> on May 4, 1989.

The tour was going to be two weeks long. We were zigzagging across the Eastern Bloc, beginning and ending in Germany. The plan was to land in West Berlin, make a big publicity deal out of crossing the Berlin Wall into the Eastern Bloc, then fly southeast and ping-pong our way back to where we started. It was way dramatic on purpose, like we were going through the looking glass and then coming back in one piece; but it was also something that Project Facemelt had to cook up at the last minute, since they found out we couldn't go to Moscow.

Our plane would drop us off in West Berlin and then meet us at an airport on the other side of the Wall the next day, where we would fly to our first concert in Romania, then Bulgaria, Yugoslavia, Hungary, Czechoslovakia, Poland, and finally the last concert back in East Berlin. Then we would cross the Wall back to West Berlin and fly home. I guess Tajikistan didn't make the final cut.

The record label had come through for the band with a private jet, which I think the CIA might have borrowed, because they wouldn't let us put our logo on the side. We were also given strict instructions not to trash the plane, or interfere with the pilots while they were trying to fly it. Buck had a lot of questions about what constituted "interfering with the pilots"—enough that the suits got so nervous they almost made him travel separately with the roadies.

Andromeda Records was calling it the Whyrld Peace Tour and promoting us as American dignitaries, spreading our message of joy and hope to the people of the Eastern Bloc through rock 'n' roll. We were doing all this press, and Tawny told us to stop saying "rock the block" and "rock revolution" until the plane landed safely in West Germany; so we mostly just smiled and let them call us heroes on the *Today* show.

On the day that the plane was set to depart from JFK, the label arranged a full-blown carnival at the airport to see us off. Davy insisted on performing James Brown's "Living in America" in a sparkly American-flag suit and top hat, like Apollo Creed did in *Rocky IV*.

Spencer even convinced Sylvester Stallone to show up and pretend to knock Davy out at the end of the song. It was all in good fun. The crowd launched into a big "U.S.A.!" chant as we boarded the plane, and we were on top of the world.

I had to pretend I didn't recognize the pilots as I boarded. I had no idea that Mancuso and Boone knew how to fly a plane! Later I learned that they were both military pilots before the CIA.

I also learned that Stryker started in Army Intelligence. Tawny was recruited right out of grad school. I had to keep all that I was learning about my "colleagues" from my band, and I had gone from feeling bad about lying to the guys to feeling bad about how easy it had become.

We partied pretty hard for the first five hours across the Atlantic, but it was a long-ass flight, and eventually everybody got bored and passed out. I woke up when we were just outside Berlin. Davy was curled up in the aisle next to an empty pint of vodka. He was still wearing his American-flag getup. Buck was spread across a row of seats in his tighty-whities. Spencer was comfortably napping in a little puddle of drool. Eventually I found Kirby sleeping in the bathroom, where he'd hid because of some threats that Davy had made before passing out.

Tawny and Stryker were the only ones on the plane who were awake. They were huddled over a map of Bucharest, planning where to spread leaflet propaganda or blow up a bridge or whatever they did when I wasn't around. Tawny waved me over, using a cup of coffee as bait. I took the cup and sat next to her for a few minutes before we all had to wake up the band so they could buckle up for landing.

"How much has Mancuso told you about East Berlin?" Tawny asked.

"He said it sucks, basically."

"That's true. But what's going to surprise you is how much it will seem like it *doesn't* suck. You'll see clean streets, freshly painted signs, brand-new storefronts."

"Okay."

"But don't be fooled," she said. "They want it to look like they're thriving. But there are people squatting around burning trashcans inside of those empty storefronts. It's all plywood and lighting, like a Hollywood set. It might look pretty, but there's no food."

A huge crowd had turned out to welcome us at the Berlin Tegel Airport; and I mean *huge*. It looked like everyone in West Germany was there. They were screaming and waving flags, and dancing, and drinking in public. "Tonight, for Tomorrow" played on the tinny speakers that announced arrivals and departures. It was a pretty dope party scene. I wished we had someone with a camera there to document it, maybe put it in a future music video; but Tawny said any recordings were going to be property of the United States government.

"I thought these people were supposed to be sad," Spencer whispered to me.

"We're on the cool side of the Wall," I said. "This is West Berlin. I have a feeling things might look a little different on the east side."

A limo waited for us right on the tarmac, and it sped out of the Berlin Tegel and across the city. Along the way we saw smaller groups of fans lining the streets, flashing their Whyte Python shirts and waving West German flags. There was one guy in full lederhosen, drinking beer out of a giant glass boot. We wanted to pick him up and bring him with us, but Tawny said that if he showed up at the Wall without proper clearance the guards on the other side would most likely shoot him. We all laughed, and Tawny said she wasn't joking.

I'll be the first one to admit that the Berlin Wall was pretty fucking intimidating. It was this tall concrete structure, with barbed wire in some places and huge guard towers in the middle, that Buck said looked a lot like the ones they have in prison. No one asked how he knew.

The limo brought us to Checkpoint Charlie, which was apparently the only place that dirty Western animals like ourselves were allowed to cross into East Berlin. A huge crowd was there, too, jollier, partying Germans cheering and dancing around to our tunes.

Crossing the Wall wasn't as dramatic as I thought it would be. I was expecting it to feel like I was entering another dimension or something. But Checkpoint Charlie was a regular gate, like you'd find in a parking garage. There was a whole deal with paperwork and identification, and the guards on the eastern side were not friendly at all; but they let us through, and there was a crowd waiting for us over there that looked a lot like the one we'd left on the other side of the Wall.

They were cheering, too, and for a moment I thought maybe things weren't all that different there after all. But looking a bit closer, these folks did seem a little more desperate about it. Faces looked pale and tired. A lot of people were crying.

"Whoa," Davy whispered. I think maybe he only saw the size of the crowd, and not their individual faces, because he was smiling and laughing and waving. I reminded myself that I had a job to do here. I needed to keep the band's spirits up. I threw an arm around Davy's shoulder and forced a grin.

"Told ya," I said.

Our limo crept through the gate and rolled off toward our hotel, and the crowd closed in behind us. "I'm goin' up," Davy said, and his finger found the button that opened the sunroof. He stood with the top half of his body poking out of the car and held his arms wide.

"Can I get a Whyte Python never dies?" Davy shouted. Faces in the crowd lit up. I could even see that a few of the guards were suppressing grins. You had to admit, Davy really had a skill for this kind of thing. A few people chanted it back at him.

"Aw, we can do better than that!" Davy shouted as the limo crept into the city. "Ready? One, two, three!"

This time, more people chanted, "*Whyte Python never dies,*" along with Davy. Heads started bobbing. A few people high-fived.

Then Davy messed up.

"Now let me hear a U.S.A!" he called out, and this time the crowd stood perfectly still, silent. I watched them closely from my seat in the limo, and I could see eyes in the crowd darting toward the soldiers at the Wall, who were suddenly not smiling anymore.

The street was eerily quiet. Then a man's voice shouted from the crowd, "*Wir sind ein Volk!*" which means "We are one people." Which turned out to be a pretty common way for East Germans to kick off a riot. Chaos erupted. The crowd all started moving at the same time. Some of them were chanting, and others were screaming. A few of them charged toward the Wall, and others followed the limo. But most of them seemed like they were just trying to get the hell out of the spot where Davy Bones had yelled "U.S.A!"

Tawny's eyes became saucers. "Get him in here," she ordered, and Buck and I yanked Davy down through the sunroof just as the bottles started flying. The limo driver stepped on the gas, and we all watched through the rear window as the guards began clubbing protesters with the butts of their rifles.

56

WE WERE STAYING at the Palasthotel in the center of East
Berlin. It was a huge building, relatively new and pretty
fancy inside; but it was also stark and severe, more like
a government building than a hotel. Tawny said that we had to be
careful what we said in the lobby and elevators, because the place was
crawling with East German spooks called "Stasi," and the hotel was
bugged all over the place. She said the Stasi dudes were in the building around the clock, and the government made sure visitors like us
stayed there on purpose so they could keep an eye on us. It was basically your standard international spy intrigue, the shit I was allowed
to know about now that I worked for the CIA.

Tawny told me that she and the team had this whole argument
about whether they should sweep the rooms for spy stuff or not,
because if they found and disabled recording bugs, it would tip off
the Stasi that we were with the CIA. At the end they decided to only
search the important rooms—mine and Facemelt's—and if they
found a bug, they would leave it there and keep our traps shut around
it. Bug or no bug, Tawny told me that any conversations about spy
stuff had to happen in the bathroom with the shower on full blast.

In the evening, a guy called Mr. Becker showed up to welcome
us and escort us to dinner in the hotel's restaurant. Tawny thought
he was the mayor or something—I'm not sure. He was tall and fit,
with short gray hair and grayer eyes. He didn't speak English, and
the band didn't speak German—except for me of course, but I wasn't
allowed to let on. So we just ate in silence and smiled at each other
until he finally left.

The front desk guys were telling Westerners in the lobby not to leave, because a spontaneous riot that started at the Wall had spread, and supposedly the streets weren't safe. So we stayed at the hotel, drinking and bullshitting in the lobby until everyone called it a night and drifted off to their rooms.

I was back in my room, but I wasn't tired. I couldn't believe we were actually doing this thing now, the *mission* that Tawny and Mancuso and the rest of the CIA team never shut up about. It was kind of scary, but it was also hella exciting. I was pacing in my room with that dangerous energy that I get after a concert coursing through my veins, when the door opened.

Tawny came into the room in full goddess mode, with her hair rolling down her back like a river of molten gold and her rockin' bod on display in a clingy, shimmering black dress. I gulped. I had spent the past year trying not to look at her directly, but in that moment, I couldn't look away.

"Hey," I squeaked.

"How you doing so far?" she asked, tossing a garment bag on my bed.

"Uh, yeah. Great."

"Good." She smiled and brushed past me, close enough to hit me with a fresh breeze of her perfume. A roadie came in and put a speaker case on the floor near my bed, then left without saying anything. Tawny dragged the case over to the dresser and opened it, then dropped her purse on the desk chair.

"There's a tux in the bag," she said. "Your size."

"Okay. Why do I need a tux?"

"We're going to a party. A really important one."

I sighed. Parties are obviously awesome, but going to one in East Berlin in the middle of the night—with Tawny—didn't seem like a good idea for me. "Can't you go without me?"

"'Fraid not," Tawny said. "You're the one they invited."

"Are any of the other guys going?"

"I doubt it," she said, in a way that made me wonder if the rest of the band was okay. Tawny moved a tiny black box from the speaker case to her purse. She grabbed me by the collar and pulled me in close, so close that I could feel her hot breath on my neck when she breathed words that were barely a whisper: "This is an audio transmitter."

For a second I forgot why she was getting so close all of a sudden. But Tawny's eyes searched the room while she spoke, and I remembered what she'd said about the team searching my room for bugs earlier. They hadn't found any, but Tawny told me to act like the room was wired, anyway, just in case. Standing close to her now, and against my better judgement, I did not mind one bit.

Then she produced a cigarette case and dropped it into the purse. She mouthed the word "camera." Finally, Tawny took a switchblade from the speaker box, triggered it open and closed a few times to make sure it worked, slipped it into her boot, and winked.

She pulled me in close again. "Now get changed," she breathed in my ear. "You're gonna help me bug the Stasi."

57

WE HAD AN ESCORT, who pointed at himself and said, "Klaus," so I guess his name was Klaus. He didn't say another word after that. He was tall and pale and hunched, with dead eyes. He picked us up at the hotel in a black BMW and tore off, driving fast through the city while Tawny forced small talk with me in the back seat.

I noticed a subtle change in her personality while we were in the car. She sounded more like a California girl than usual, saying things like "She was like this, and I was like, no way, babe," and other stuff about music and partying. I finally realized she was playing a part for Klaus, acting like a groupie who lucked her way onto the tour.

From my lessons with Mancuso, I could tell we were heading north, racing through the city until Berlin just stopped at a dark line of trees. I got a tickling feeling in the back of my head that this whole adventure wasn't safe. Tawny's hand found mine, and she gave my fingers a squeeze that was either supposed to be reassuring or some kind of warning that I didn't understand.

The Beamer dove into the wooded tunnel and along a dark highway for about a half an hour. Eventually, signs of life appeared up ahead, and we arrived in a little country paradise—like we had crossed through a magic portal. We were in a village with big-ass houses, each one with an even bigger-ass garden and a long driveway leading up to it.

"Wandlitz," Tawny whispered. "It's like a different country here." Klaus's eyes shifted toward her in the rearview mirror, and she realized she had made a mistake letting on that she knew the name of the town. "I think?" she corrected.

Klaus weaved the car along a wide, smooth road over rolling fields and past a grove of apple trees to a stone mansion that was all lit up against the black sky. The driveway was the length of a football field, made of tight stone bricks that matched the house and finished in a big circle out front where the other guests had parked.

"Wow," I said. "Whose house is this, the dude who owns Löwenbräu?"

"A government worker," Tawny said. I saw Klaus's shark eyes glance at us in the rearview mirror again, then back on the road. "Ooh," she cooed in character, loud and wide-eyed. "It's such a nice night. Hey, Klaus, we wanna walk up the driveway."

Klaus grumbled, but he stopped the car and waited while we got out. We started the long walk up the stone driveway toward the house, Tawny with an arm hooked around mine and whispering the plan to me.

"The Stasi assigned him to you," she said softly. "Assume he's always listening."

Case in point, Klaus drove right behind us at a crawl instead of just pulling up ahead and parking in the circle. His bumper behind our heels gave me the impression that he might just decide to step on the gas at any moment and flatten us both.

"Remember," Tawny said, "you're the celebrity here. Everyone's eyes are on you. Nobody knows who I am. They won't even notice I'm here."

I stole a glance at her. "I don't think that's possible," I said.

Tawny smirked, and I think she might have blushed. "You know what I mean," she said. "Try to get their attention. They'll all speak English. Tell loud stories, ask them about East Germany, whatever. Just be your charming self and give me enough time to do my thing."

"Okay," I said.

"Are you nervous?"

"No."

Truth be told, though, I was. Mancuso had beaten it into my head that I would never actually get to use any of the spy craft that he trained me in, and my only job was to play the concerts and agree with everything Tawny said. But here we were, before our first stop on the tour, and already I found myself out at midnight, at a mansion in the middle of the East German woods with my unpredictable ex, bugging a Stasi office, with only one little switchblade between the two of us for protection. I rubbed my hands together and blew into them.

"Hey," Tawny said, and she took my hands. We stopped walking, and Klaus stopped driving. Tawny stepped in close to me and put a hand on the back of my neck. Her hands were always so soft and cool. She pulled me in close, so our mouths were only inches apart, and she whispered, "You'll do fine."

Her eyes darted toward the car, and then she kissed me—a short one but a real one, I was sure of it—and I let her do it. "Just another night back on the Strip," she said, and smiled.

Whatever kind of mind trick that was, it worked. I took a deep breath and let it out, and we smiled at each other like we had a secret, the way we used to do a thousand years ago when we'd walk into a party together. Then we continued up the rest of the driveway and walked into the house.

On the inside, it looked like any other party that was way too classy for a punk like me—except everybody was speaking a different language. The room was decorated with heavy gold-and-maroon drapes, and everything looked expensive and old. There was a grand staircase at the back of the big living room that led to a balcony, but it was roped off.

The men wore tuxedos and were huddled together in groups, all red-faced and muttering to one another over glasses of clear alcohol. The women wore gowns and smoked cigarettes on long filters. A small ensemble played the theme song from *Tetris* in the corner.

Mr. Becker—the mayor from dinner—greeted us at the door. "Mr. Thunder," he said. "So glad you could come."

He did speak English! I'd had a feeling this dude had been holding out on us.

"Yes," I said. "Thank you for inviting me."

"And your companion?" he asked, gesturing toward Tawny. He offered a tight smile when I introduced her as Tawny Spice, but she was right: the guy didn't seem to care the least bit about her. To these guys, she was just off-limits arm candy.

"I understand your music is a big success," the guy said.

I nodded. "So far, so good. Do you like it?"

My question caught him off guard, and he laughed for the first time. "I'm afraid I am too busy for such things," he said. "Please. Enjoy the party. Have drinks, food. Many of our guests are excited to meet you."

We shook hands, and I noticed that he did that thing where he tried to roll my wrist over so his hand was on top. Then he vanished into the crowd.

Tawny led me toward the band, where a few other couples were dancing. She put a hand on my shoulder and slid the fingers of her other hand into mine.

"Let's dance," she said, and smiled. "We're going to settle in for a bit."

We moved together closely for three songs, something we hadn't done since I took Tawny to Vince Neil's wedding in '87. We kept the conversation light, mostly about the guys in the band and her "job" at the "rock magazine" that I "definitely read." By the third song, our shoulders had relaxed and our bodies had slowly crept together into each other's grooves, my hand settling into its regular place on the roundness of her hip while the edge of her hairline brushed against my cheek.

It felt so real, so comfortable, so natural, that I was sad when Tawny leaned into my ear and whispered, "Okay, it's time."

I felt the spell break and reminded myself that none of this was real anymore, no matter how good she was at faking it. I nodded and let her give me instructions.

"The men are mostly together, over by the fireplace," she said. "Go do your thing. I'm going to slip upstairs."

"It's roped off," I said. Tawny just gave me a look that said, *Seriously?* And she winked again.

I nodded, and we walked hand in hand across the room. Tawny made a point of saying out loud that she was going to the bathroom, and I closed in on a circle of drunk middle-aged Germans.

They greeted me aggressively, pulling me into their circle and peppering me with questions in broken English about rock 'n' roll, and America, and whether I had ever met Markie Post from *Night Court*.

I did my best to put on a show. I told stories from the road—the dumbest, wildest ones I could think of. I thumped them on the back and laughed with them, even though I mostly didn't understand what they were talking about. I gave Tawny time.

"Mr. Thunder," a voice said from behind me, close enough that it made me jump. Mr. Becker was standing there, holding a drink with a napkin wrapped around the bottom of the glass. "I trust you are enjoying the party?"

"Yes, thank you," I said. "Very much."

He put a hand on my shoulder. "I want to ask you," he said, and then he held a finger to his lips while he thought of his question.

By the time he started talking again, I wasn't listening. I had overheard another conversation in German next to us, a language that my hosts didn't know I could speak if I needed to. Now, I wasn't fluent or anything, but I was pretty sure I understood what was said behind me.

One man said to another, "Where is his woman?"

And the other man said, "Find her."

58

ow, THE WEATHER in California . . ." Mr. Becker said, but his eyes showed absolutely no interest in the conversation. I had a realization, and it sent a chill down my spine: this guy didn't care about the weather in California! He was distracting me while the other guys looked for Tawny.

Tawny who was upstairs, taking pictures of documents and planting a bug in the office.

"It is nice this time of year?" Becker said.

"Huh?" I said. "Oh, the weather. Uh, yeah, all the time, basically." *Stay cool, Rikki.*

"I see." Becker sniffed and looked at the ceiling, and my eyes tracked the two men who had been talking about Tawny a second ago as they began to push their way through the crowd. These two hadn't been part of my little social circle; they were younger, stronger, and sober. Security of some kind.

Sweeping the room.

"I prefer the cold, myself." Becker's hand tightened on my shoulder. "Must be the blood. Like a wolf. Besides, a man grows soft living in ideal conditions."

"Uh-huh." I watched the security guys with my peripheral vision as I carried on a conversation with Becker that neither of us was really paying attention to.

The men swept through the crowd, trying not to draw attention to themselves as they poked their heads into the kitchen and the hallway. Becker glanced away to check on their progress, and I scanned the balcony at the top of the staircase.

Tawny appeared from down a hallway, and we locked eyes. I gave her the tiniest head shake, and she got the message. She ducked back into the hallway just as the mayor caught me redirecting my gaze his way, and he glanced over his shoulder at the balcony. I couldn't risk looking at the same time, so I just kept staring at him with a dumb grin and hoped he hadn't seen her.

The security officers converged at the bottom of the staircase. They were about to slide around the posts that held the velvet rope. If they found her upstairs, they would detain her long enough to find her camera, and then they would sweep the house and find the bug.

And then what? Would they arrest us? Or kill us both? I had to do something. But what? Should I punch Mr. Becker in the face? Start a fire?

An idea came to me. It was a bad one, but it was consistent with my reputation. It was expected of me. It was the one move that I knew I could always count on. The move that just felt right.

Being a total fucking idiot.

I grabbed the drink from Becker's fingers. "Thanks!" I said and downed the whole glass of what turned out to be sambuca—yikes—then I wildly pushed my way back into the middle of my drunken gang and screamed, "Thunderstorm!"

I started banging on a high-top table with my palms, playing an insane drum solo. Heads turned my way. They mostly looked confused, but my new buddies were *into it*. They cheered and clapped and burst into singing a German drinking song while I jammed. Then I intentionally slipped and fell onto the floor.

Then I barfed all over myself. That part was thanks to Becker's sambuca and hadn't been part of my plan, but it definitely helped. Now *everyone* was looking at me, including the two guys at the bottom of the stairs.

I saw a flash of black and gold behind them: Tawny, vaulting off the balcony and landing soundlessly on the stone tiles below, like a cat.

Some of my buddies helped me to my feet, and Tawny swam through the crowd.

"Rikki, honey, are you okay?" she asked. I gave her my dumbest, drunkest look, and I shrugged and smiled.

"Rock 'n' roll U.S.A!" I slurred.

Every single person in the room rolled their eyes.

"I think I should get him home," Tawny said.

"Yes," Mr. Becker said. "I think that would be best."

Tawny led me through the crowd, and they all looked at me with pure disgust.

Outside, Klaus was waiting by the car. He climbed into the driver's seat without opening our door or saying anything.

"Did you get what you need?" I whispered.

"Yes," Tawny whispered back. "That was incredible."

"I can't believe you jumped off the balcony."

"Let's just go," she said.

We started down the steps toward the car, and I looked back over my shoulder at the wild scene that we had just caused. Mr. Becker was standing inside the doorway and staring back at me, like a predator studying prey that had slipped through its fingers.

59

BOY, WAS I glad to get the fuck out of East Germany.

We flew out first thing the next morning, just a few hours after Klaus dropped us off at the hotel. We had spent most of the ride back to the hotel in silence, waiting for a pair of headlights to come screaming up behind us, flashing their lights for Klaus to pull over. But it didn't happen. We got back to the hotel, packed our bags, and left for the airport at sunrise with the front desk guys still warning us about "civil unrest" in the city.

We flew from East Berlin to Bucharest, and I secretly boned up on my Romanian language and maps in the air until my eyes went crossed. Then I slept for six hours at the hotel. The guys had to wake me up by kicking open the door to my room and spraying me with fire extinguishers.

A limousine took us to the Stadionul Steaua. It was a big arena that could hold over thirty thousand people, and they had it jammed tight with Python fans. A row of box trucks lined the back entrance to the stadium, and an army of roadies poured in and out of the building carrying boxes.

Right away I noticed that Andromeda hadn't sent our regular long-haired, burly roadie bros. These new guys had crew cuts, and they were all wearing matching jean jackets and sunglasses.

I nudged Tawny and pointed at the roadies; I mouthed the question, *Spooks?* She held a finger to her lips.

We spilled out of the limo just as our first opener, a Bulgarian band called Cage Match, was handing off to the second opener, a German band called Spyderbyte—I guess the cool *y* trick had made its way over here as well. But the parking lot was still packed with Whyte Python fans hoping to get a look at us.

The crowd immediately swarmed, and a fleet of Romanian security guards appeared out of nowhere to form a human wall. We tried to touch as many outstretched hands as we could on our way to the stadium entrance. Davy led our entourage to the door, where he was greeted by two enormous security guards.

"You are Whyte Python?" one of the beasts asked.

"We are," Kirby shouted from the back. His voice was shaking.

"You guys have an Orange Julius here?" Buck asked.

A second guard eyed Buck, failing to make sense of what he was asking.

"And you are Davy Bones?" the first guard asked Davy. "The one who sings 'Tonight, for Tomorrow'?"

Davy took his sunglasses off and offered his biggest movie-star smile. "That's me, baby," he said.

The guard's scowl melted. "Yes, I like!" he shouted, and threw a giant arm around Davy. "I like this song very much. Welcome to Bucharest, Whyte Python. Have good show."

The guard opened the door. Davy turned to face us, and the mob of bloodthirsty fans. "All right, boys," he said. "Let's give these dirty, starving Reds a show they'll never forget."

And I think we rose to Davy's challenge.

We went straight into the standard set planned for all our Whyrld Peace Tour shows—which was timed down to the minute in order to keep up with a complicated pyro and light show. Unlike the places we played in the United States, this arena was so big and wide-open that we felt a sort of separation from the crowd, but they never stopped swaying and screaming and holding up lighters.

It made me feel good to give them that. For the kids who saw us back home, a Whyte Python concert was a really fun Saturday night; but we came to understand that, for most of the crowd in Bucharest, it would be a once-in-a-lifetime experience.

So we brought it hard. It was May, and cool at night, but we were all in a total lather by the end, with Davy holding a fist in the air and screaming, "Stand up!" into the mic at the top of his lungs as we wrapped the show with "Tonight, for Tomorrow."

I had to admit that it was a little weird not seeing Tawny backstage. Even though I had long ago stopped looking for her, I could always sense her there watching the band, and watching the crowd watch the band. But the last time I'd seen her was at the arena entrance, before she fell back toward the crew trucks. As the guards ushered the band inside, a caught a final look of her hopping into a black van with Stryker.

I didn't see any more of Tawny at all in Romania, which I felt kind of conflicted about. I still didn't totally trust her, and she had put us in serious danger on this trip once already; but that's all kind of hot, right? And I still smiled whenever I thought about her kissing me in front of Klaus's car.

I did, however, get another assignment.

Mancuso pulled me aside in the greenroom after the show, when none of the other guys were around. He and Boone had flown us over, but this was one of the only times I had even seen him since we all left L.A.

"Got a job for you, pretty boy," he said. His voice was stern, but his eyes were playful.

I tried to make my face serious, even though I had just inhaled a shit-ton of nitrous oxide from a tank that Kirby had smuggled into the country, and some Romanian girl was licking honey off her fingers and staring furiously right in my eyes.

"What is it?" I said.

"You're hitting the streets tonight," Mancuso said. "Be seen. Just be your stupid self."

This didn't sound like a typical CIA undercover mission; but it was also possible that I was having trouble understanding my instructions because I was in the process of taking another nitrous hit, and it was making my brain fizzle like Pop Rocks. "Huh?" I said.

"Perfect," Mancuso said.

"No, I don't get it," I said.

Mancuso slapped me across the face and dragged me out of the room, into the empty hallway.

"Straighten up," he said. "There's a riot outside; it's starting already. Just like in East Berlin. You need to cut through those kids in an hour, get them charged up so they *stay* charged up. But be fast. Don't stick around. Then you're going to hit a private party."

He pressed a slip of paper into my hand. "This address. Anyone who managed to get in that room is connected, or their parents are. The regular rules in this country don't apply there. They can actually have fun. This is a simple hearts-and-minds campaign, kid. We want them to love you. Buy drinks, make out with girls, lead singalongs. Win 'em over."

"Okay."

"But don't bring your idiot friends with you. And no matter what"—Mancuso tapped a sharp finger against my chest—"don't. Get. Arrested. Okay?"

"Got it," I said. I felt like now was a good time for a joke. "But wait, don't get arrested or do get arrested?"

Mancuso chuckled and cracked his neck, and then he pressed his fingers into my shoulder, and I yipped like a dog and dropped to one knee. But my head was mostly clear now, so I grabbed his fingers and rolled his wrist over, then hopped to my feet and put the shoulder press right back on him.

"Ow!" Mancuso shouted as his knees collapsed under him. I let him go and helped him to his feet, and I saw that he was smiling wide. "Nice," he said. "Now get out there and get fucked up for your country."

I stood tall, straightened my leather vest, adjusted my sequined choke collar, and saluted. "With liberty and justice for all."

I was a popular man on the streets of Bucharest.

I was Rikki Thunder, fresh off stage from the only Western rock concert to have touched their city in a lifetime, and now I was wandering through the early stages of a riot kicked off in my band's name. A lot of people were, like, hugging me, and tackling me, and shoving their tongues in my mouth, and having me sign things, and grabbing me all over, and stealing my cigarettes, and giving me their cigarettes, and whatever else they could get away with as I weaved through the city streets.

Right around the time somebody threw a couch through a storefront window, and I figured it was time to move on. So I followed the streets that I'd memorized, straight to the address on Mancuso's note. It looked like an abandoned office building, and I wondered— not for the first time—if Brad Mancuso was having me killed.

I knocked on the door, and one of those little windows you see in movies slid open. A pair of beautiful green eyes with heavy red eye shadow appeared on the other side. I was about to panic—if this was anything like the movies, she was going to ask for a password. And I didn't know it.

But apparently "being Rikki Thunder" is enough, because the door flew open and a young brunette grabbed me by both shoulders and yanked me inside. She wore a shredded denim miniskirt and a leather jacket, and she had her hair up in a crimped side-ponytail. She gave me a big wet kiss on each cheek and led me by both hands through a long, unlit hallway to a freight elevator. I could hear the familiar nightclub thump of bass getting louder as we descended to the basement. The door opened up to a serious party. It was a packed house, with Europop blasting from the speakers. The crowd was all hot young Romanians in fancy clothes—people who didn't really look like Whyte Python fans, to be honest. But this was where Mancuso had told me to go, and they seemed happy to see me. The crowd went fucking crazy the second I walked in, and I was practically crowd-surfed to the bar.

I stood up on the bar, and the bartender handed me an electric-green bottle that I figured was one of those fancy Euro liquors that makes you hallucinate. "Stand up for Whyte Python!" I shouted and took a chug—only to discover that it was just vodka, colored green. The crowd cheered again, and I dove off the bar. This time, they really did crowd-surf me around the place before planting me back at the bar, where there was more green vodka waiting for me.

"Hoo boy!" I announced, loud enough for anyone who might be following me to hear. "I'm definitely getting hammered with the locals tonight!"

And I did.

I stayed at the party for two hours, slamming shots and singing and dancing with the Buchies. By the time I steered back toward the hotel,

I was straight-up twisted. I duckwalked along the cobblestone street while the road ahead seemed to rock back and forth like I was on a boat in a storm. I was totally disoriented. The streets looked equally unfamiliar. There were no taxis, almost no cars at all. I stopped to get my bearings, spinning in a slow circle.

I had no idea where to go. The hotel could be in any direction. In the distance I heard a whistle blaring, so I headed toward it. When I turned the corner onto the street, I saw headlights, too close and too fast. And then the car hit me.

60

I<small>T WAS A TAXICAB</small>, and it didn't hit me *too* hard. The guy slammed on the brakes in time, and I had the presence of mind to jump just before the grill took out my knees.

I have been hit by cars plenty of times in the past and will probably be hit by more cars in the future, so I knew this drill. You have a much better shot if you end up on the hood instead of under the tires.

I just skidded across the hood and banged into the windshield until the cab came to a stop, and then I rolled onto the ground. It hurt, but I could tell right away that nothing was broken or anything. The taxi driver got out of his car and helped me to my feet. He looked me up and down, concerned that he had just killed some kind of wild, leather-clad animal.

"*Ești în regulă?*" he asked.

I nodded. "I'm okay," I said back in English.

"You need ride?" the cabbie asked. He nodded to his car.

"Yes," I mumbled. "Please."

I slid into the back seat. "The InterContinental, please," I said, and that really made his eyes bulge. This poor guy probably thought he was gonna drop me off in Bucharest's version of Skid Row, but I had just given him directions to one of the fanciest hotels in town. I could see he was terrified that he'd just hit an eccentric with money, so I held my hands up.

"It's okay," I said. "Not hurt." He relaxed and put the car in gear. The cab pulled away, and we drove closer to the sound of the whistle that I'd just heard. After a minute, I saw what was going on.

A big army van and three jeeps were parked outside a small brick building with no windows. Cops were dragging men out the front and side doors. Most of them were wearing leather vests and chaps and hats, and it kind of looked like a metal concert at first. But then the cabbie huffed in disgust, and I realized what was going on. This was a raid on an underground gay club.

Being gay was illegal there, and these army dudes took that law pretty seriously. Because "raid" was too nice a word. The soldiers were holding down guys and just wailing on them with their batons, kicking them, tossing them up against the van. It was no raid—it was an attack. And it was brutal.

Just as the taxi rolled past the building and I could see the outline of the InterContinental against the night sky, I saw two soldiers dragging a familiar Fraggle shape out of the side door.

Buck.

They had him under the pits, and he was kicking wildly in the air until a third cop came along and hit him in the stomach with his baton.

"Stop," I said, and opened the car door. The car squealed to a stop just as I spilled out onto the street, and then his tires screeched again as he drove away. Mancuso's instructions not to get arrested no matter what were lost on me. I saw my friend getting beaten up for no reason. So I charged.

I ran toward the cop who was hitting Buck in the stomach and judo-chopped him at the back of his neck. He dropped to the ground. Then I drove my palm into the nose of one of the two guys holding Buck up, and he let go. Buck broke free of the other guy and kneed him in the balls. We ran away, and in the whole melee we managed to escape down an alley that came out onto a dark street.

A pair of uniformed militia met us on the other side. One of them had a gun on us.

"What the hell is this?" Buck said.

I gestured my head at Buck. "*Lasa-l sa plece,*" I said. *Let him go.*

"*Nimeni nu merge nicăieri,*" the guy said, and I had enough Romanian to know he was saying that we weren't going anywhere—or something like that.

"*Faci o greseala,*" I hissed. *You're making a mistake.*

"Rikki, do you speak Spanish?" Buck said. "What is this?"

I hung my head and sighed. Studied my enemies. Buck was closer to the gunman, and probably more sober than me.

"Just a couple of Metallica fans," I said.

Buck understood the code. I took a big step to my left, and he took a big step to his right. The gunman swung his piece in my direction, and Buck just grabbed his arm and pushed, and locked a hand on his wrist while he head-butted him. I drove my fists into the other dude's sternum, and he dropped like a rock. The gunman squealed and let go of the gun, which I scooped right up and pointed back at him.

"*Mergi acum,*" I said. *Go now.*

We had pulled the whole thing off in less than three seconds. I'm not sure Mancuso and Boone could've done it better.

This might sound oddly impressive, but the thing is, Buck and I had been in this exact same situation before. It was in Myrtle Beach. Some biker guys cornered us at a bar on our night off between shows and told us that Whyte Python was for "skirts and queers," and that real men only listened to Metallica. We were drunk and maybe a little high, and this hurt our feelings.

The thing is, Buck and I both love Metallica! We tried to communicate that while disagreeing with the negative Whyte Python stuff. But they just wanted a fight, obviously. So they mouthed off some more, and we mouthed off back, and then a gun came out. Something unspoken passed between us, and we took those guys down. I do have to say this: I know why *I'm* a good fighter, but I have no idea why Buck was. I've wondered sometimes if he has also been trained by some covert spy agency. And I know I will never find out.

Anyhoo, I told these two Romanian dipshits to scram, and the gunman helped his buddy up and they limped off.

Once they were a safe distance away, I broke the gun down into its various parts and tossed them in a storm drain, and Buck and I pointed ourselves toward the giant luxury hotel that dominated the skyline ahead. We were both limping and rubbing our heads from our various scrapes, but it was nothing that a handful of aspirin couldn't help.

"So," Buck said, and then there was a long silence between us as we walked. Neither of us quite knew what to say. We had each just learned that the other was keeping a secret from the band; and while

Buck's secret didn't require much explanation, mine sure did.

I opened my mouth to say something—although I wasn't sure just yet what that thing was going to be. But Buck cut me off.

"Good show tonight," he said.

I stuffed my hands in my pockets and grinned. Walked in silence for a few more steps. All that adrenaline from multiple street fights and getting hit by that car had sobered me up, and the cool night air tasted good. "Hell yeah, it was," I said.

And that was it. Buck and I had just agreed, without saying anything, that neither one of us would ever speak about what he'd seen that night—even to each other.

I grinned at Buck and then looked back toward the InterContinental. "A total shredder."

61

I DIDN'T SEE TAWNY until we were seated on the airplane the next afternoon. She and Stryker were the last on, and they both looked just as exhausted as I felt. Against my better judgment, I hoped Tawny would sit next to me. I would've let her sleep on my shoulder. But they collapsed into the seats in front, and didn't budge the whole way to Bulgaria.

Most of the venues we played on the Whyrld Peace Tour were soccer stadiums, and the Vasil Levski National Stadium in Sofia, Bulgaria, was no exception. We gave this crowd the best we had in us, and they gave it right back.

It was already starting to feel like a regular tour—travel into a city, play a big concert, party, skip town the next day. Start over again. The only differences were the bigger crowds, the smaller parties, and the regular post-concert riots.

Once again, Tawny was nowhere to be found after the show.

I was buzzed and lonely when we got back to the hotel. So I went to her room and knocked on the door. I don't know what I was hoping for. I don't think I was looking to hook up, although I'm sure I wouldn't have said no. But I had had fun with her in East Berlin, and I guess I wanted that feeling again.

I figured the odds were low that she would answer it anyway, because she was probably out on the job. I was about to turn around and go back to my own room when the door swung open. Tawny was alone in the room, no makeup, and she looked stressed out.

"Come in," she said, and pulled me into the room.

"Hey," I said. "What's the matter?"

Right away, I wondered if I was in trouble. I had decided not to tell the CIA about my fight with the cops in Bucharest, because there was no way to tell the story without mentioning why I got out of the cab—and how I found Buck.

She wouldn't let me just tell part of the story. She would patiently interrogate the whole thing out of me. Tawny knew how to do that. One time she asked how I got ice cream stains on her car seat, and twenty minutes later I was confessing to shit I'd done in the fourth grade.

If the situation was reversed, I knew Buck would never expose my secret; and I had an extra-unfair advantage, because Buck didn't even really know what my secret was. The CIA might have known about Buck, and they might not; but they certainly weren't going to find out from me.

Tawny's eyes darted around the hotel room like she was seeing it for the first time. She held up a finger and dragged me to the bathroom, turned on the shower and faucet, and leaned in close. She grabbed her purse from the bathroom vanity and took out a red lipstick.

"There's a microfilm in here," she said. "It has the pictures that I took at the Stasi house in Berlin. I need to get across town and drop this off with an East German contact tonight. This is seriously fucking important."

"Okay," I said. "Do you need me to go with you again?"

"No," Tawny said. "Berlin was too risky, us out together. We're done with that. The problem is, I can't go, either. My boss just called. I'm sidelined."

"What does that mean?"

"Last night Stryker and I were on a job," she said. "You don't need to know what it was. But we were tracked by the Securitate. That's like Romania's KGB. They're the ones who repress dissent there. They were on us all night. It got . . . uncomfortable. Fortunately, we made them early, so we diverted from the plan and they didn't see anything."

"Well, that's a good thing," I said.

"It is, and it isn't," she said. "Why were they following us? They have no reason to tail the drummer's girlfriend and the costume designer, unless somebody gives them a reason."

"Who?"

"It's possible that I'm on a list," she said. "I was stationed here before Facemelt, and then there was our adventure in East Berlin. There's chatter."

"Oh shit," I said. My mind went to the city street the night before, Buck and I kicking the shit out of a couple of soldiers in the middle of a raid. *Say something.* "Are they talking about me, too?"

"We don't have any evidence of that," Tawny said. I felt my shoulders loosen. "We get a fresh report each morning. They didn't say anything about you. But, Rikki, I don't think you have to worry about it. If they actually sniff us out, they're going to assume the band is just cover. How did your walkabout go, anyway?"

I decided to start with the truth. "Fine," I said. "I got pretty loaded."

"Did anything weird happen?"

I sniffed. "Just your normal weird shit."

"Good," Tawny rubbed her hands together.

Maybe it really was no big deal. I asked myself, What *really* happened, anyway? I revealed that I speak a little Romanian and got in a scrap, but it was a pair of city cops. Big deal. That shouldn't be all that suspicious. Either way, I felt like I had dodged a serious bullet— and I had protected Buck's secret for now.

"What does that mean for your mission?"

"It means I have to keep a low profile," she said. "Lonsa made the decision a couple of hours ago. We know that they didn't find our bug; we don't think they actually *know* anything about me. They just suspect. So, I have to be a lame fucking tourist, let them follow me, see that I'm behaving. Maybe they'll give up eventually and drop it."

"Is Stryker gonna do it?"

"She's sidelined, too," Tawny said. "Boone and Mancuso have their own job tonight, but Mancuso is gonna call an old contact. We think he's still an ally. He'll run the microfilm across town to the contact I mentioned."

I could see in her eyes that she didn't like it. "You don't like it," I said.

Tawny hesitated. "No," she said. "I don't. The guy has been off our grid for almost two years. We don't even know if he's still a friend of the West or not. It's a risk."

"The roadies?"

"The roadies all have their own jobs to do before they pack your concert shit up and drive it across the border," she said. "They *hate* this mission."

I saw where this was going. "Just give it to me," I said, sighing. "I'll do it."

"What?" Tawny said. "No. Out of the question."

"It's no big deal," I said. "You said we can't be seen together, right? So, fine, I'll take the thing across town. Hand it off. Come back. What's the problem?"

"The problem," Tawny said, "is that you're a massive celebrity, and you're cutting through a riot that *you* just caused to make a clandestine drop of sensitive material."

I honestly didn't know if Tawny was trying to talk me out of it or trying to trick me into talking myself *into* it. Either way, this felt like an important moment. I had committed to Project Facemelt almost two years ago. I felt some ownership over it now.

"I'll put on jeans and a hat," I said. "Nobody will recognize me. It's one of the benefits of wearing a costume most of the time. Somebody's gotta do it. I'll be careful."

Tawny bit her lower lip and shook her head. "I don't like that," she said. "You can't be out there doing this stuff alone."

"I won't be alone," I said. "I'm bringing the one person I know I can trust."

62

SPENCER MET ME in the lobby of the hotel, just like I had instructed.

He had on skintight jeans and a Black Sabbath T-shirt, and a baseball hat with the logo of the Maine Mariners hockey team. I was dressed similarly, in black jeans and a white T-shirt, with my Dodgers hat pulled low.

Considering Buck already had some idea that I was up to something, he might have made more sense to bring along. But he vanished right after the concert. And it was a dangerous game, dragging him in any deeper. Especially somebody as unpredictable as Buck Sweet.

Spencer was a better choice anyway. He wouldn't notice anything weird about the handoff. His only job was to tag along and be friendly. He was visibly drunk and reeked of pot, but that was pretty much normal, and it helped my cover. I could play wasted right alongside him, and it would help to reduce suspicion for anyone who saw us trolling the streets of Sofia together.

And if nothing else, it created a witness.

"Where are we going?" he asked.

"It's a surprise," I said.

Spencer's eyes lit up. He loved surprises. I realized I was going to have to think of somewhere to bring him before the night was over, even if it was just a parking garage where we could smoke weed. But first, I had a job to do.

My instructions were clear. We had to cut through downtown to a city park on the other side of the post-concert riot, where we were meeting a contact who went by the code name Angel. I would sit on a park bench, light a cigarette, take one drag, then drop it with my left hand. Angel would sit on the bench next to me. We would exchange passwords. Then I would put the lipstick on the bench and leave. She would sweep it up on her way out of the park. A pretty classic spy handoff, like they do in the movies.

We moved across Sofia on foot and navigated through the riot scene with a sense of dumbfounded wonder. There had to be hundreds of people marching and chanting and singing "Tonight, for Tomorrow" and cutting holes in flags.

"Keep your hat low," I said to Spencer as we moved in front of a bonfire in the center of a plaza. "These people might love us a little too much."

"They seem cool with Buck," Spencer said. He pointed across the plaza and, sure enough, there was Buck, shaking a trash can over his head and then drop-kicking it. "Hey, Buck," Spencer called out before I could stop him.

"I'm busy," Buck shouted back, without even looking our way. Strangely enough, even though he was violently rioting in the streets of Bulgaria, Buck's eyes were serene. We agreed to leave him alone.

We navigated through a crowd that was gathering around a bonfire to the back of the plaza, where we found the park, just like Tawny had said we would. It was a small green space that was divided by a narrow river, and a footbridge led to the other side. The riot hadn't made its way over there yet; it was mostly dark.

"Hey," I said to Spencer. "I'm gonna take a seat for a second. My legs are tired from all that kicking ass."

"Righteous," Spencer said. He took a flask from his pocket and offered it. I shook my head, and he took a long, gulping pull, then grinned at me. His eyes were half closed. "I'm gonna go watch the bonfire," he said.

He stumbled toward the fire, and his silhouette merged into the faceless mass of rioters against a wall of orange flames.

I sat. Lit the cigarette. Took a drag. Dropped it with my left hand. And then there was a woman sitting on the bench next to me.

She was small and plain, in a brown sweater, with a messy mop of silver hair. She looked at me suspiciously, probably guessing that

I was just some punk from the riot who coincidentally stopped for a smoke break at her handoff spot.

"The moon looks low tonight," I said, reciting the code that Tawny had taught me.

Angel's face relaxed. "But it will always rise," she said.

"Hey." I smiled.

"You don't look like CIA," she said.

"You don't look like a spy, either."

"I am not spy," she said. "I am physicist. We have allowances to travel more than most."

"Cool," I said. I slid the little black lipstick case out of my pocket and let it fall onto the bench. "Nice working with you."

But Angel didn't move. She was looking across the river. "Ach!" she said, and then she muttered something in German.

"What?" I said. "What's wrong?"

Angel trained her eyes on me. "How did they know?" she demanded.

"How did who know what?"

She rolled her eyes and swept the lipstick off the bench, then gestured with her head across the river. I didn't see anything at first.

"I don't see anything," I said, but Angel was already off the bench and moving quickly, back toward the mob. Just before she vanished into the crowd, she swept a hand through her hair, and I saw the silver wig fall away to the ground. The last glimpse I saw of Angel was a bob of short, dark hair, slipping through a gap in the mob.

I looked across the river again. Still nothing. Spencer appeared over my shoulder.

"What are you looking at, bro?" he said.

"Nothing . . ." I said.

But then I spotted movement. A flash of light against metal. And four men, dressed all in black with black ski masks, running along the river toward the bridge.

Fuck.

I stood and grabbed Spencer's shoulder. "Spencer," I whispered. "*Run.*"

63

THANK GOD I had brought Spencer Dooley.

Anybody else would have asked follow-up questions. But when I told Spencer to run, he just smiled and said, "Okay!" And then he tore off running. Unfortunately, he was running right in the direction of the guys in ski masks.

"No!" I whispered. "This way!"

"Okay!" Spencer said again, and he tripped over his own feet trying to change direction. I grabbed him by the shirt between his shoulder blades and pulled him to his feet. Spencer giggled. "Whoa!"

"Shhh," I said. "Come on." We ran back toward the bonfire, and I pushed my way through the mob, dragging Spencer behind me. Back in the park, I heard a voice shout, "*Spri!*" Which I assume meant *halt* or *stop* or something like that.

Spencer was still giggling. "Where are we going?" he asked.

"Back to the hotel," I said. "But we're going the long way." I kept an eye on the park as we weaved through the crowd, and I saw the shapes of the men begin to emerge in the smoke.

I realized that my powder-blue Dodgers hat was like a bright flag on my head, so I took it off and threw it into the fire.

"Kick-ass," Spencer shouted, and threw his hat into the fire, too.

"Whyte Python!" a voice shouted from the mob.

God, these people were quick. Spencer turned toward them and stuck his tongue out. He held up devil horns and let out a screech. The crowd went crazy. I got an idea then that chaos would be on our side, so I held up devil horns, too, and I shouted, "Hey, Bulgaria! Stand up!"

The mob really went nuts then, and the ski-mask guys got completely swallowed up in the churn. "Let's go," I said to Spencer. We ran down a narrow cobblestone street in the direction of our hotel.

But then a strange and unfortunate thing happened. The mob started to run, too.

I'm not sure if they thought it was some kind of game, or an impromptu march, or if they really just wanted to party with us; but now we were being pursued by four guys in ski masks and about three hundred drunken Whyte Python fans, and I didn't know who I was more afraid of.

We ran past a burning trash can, and for a bare second we were invisible behind the thick cloud of smoke pouring out.

"This way." I grabbed Spencer by the shirt again and steered him down an alley. My heart sank when I realized it was a dead end.

There was a dumpster near the back of the alley. I pulled Spencer down to the ground behind it and watched as the mob charged by.

"That was crazy," Spencer said.

I held a finger to my lips. "Shhh," I said.

"Okay," Spencer whispered back.

I listened to the echoes of the riot fade in the distance. Now the streets were silent. We had gotten away with it.

I needed to get our bearings and figure out which direction would take us back to the hotel. I got to my feet and had only taken one step away from the dumpster when shadows fell across the entrance to the alley.

I retreated back to the dumpster, where Spencer had fallen asleep. I peeked around the side of our hiding spot and saw the four men standing in the street, discussing a strategy. They were holding assault rifles and using complicated hand gestures.

If they all came down the alley, we were busted. My first thought was to surrender ourselves and deny everything; we were Whyte Python, after all.

But then I thought about something Angel said, right before she ran away.

How did they know?

It was a good question, and there were only two answers. Either they had followed her to the park, or they followed Spencer and me.

But really, the truth was obvious; when Angel and I parted ways at the park, nobody chased after her. They chased us.

No. They chased me.

Their guys were probably following me in Bucharest, either on a hunch or because of what happened at the party in East Berlin. Then I smacked around a couple of cops and didn't bother to tell anyone on the Facemelt team.

Then I dragged poor Spencer into this, and I might have gotten him killed. What was wrong with me? For the second night in a row, I had endangered one of my friends for this CIA bullshit. *Why didn't I bring Kirby, for fuck's sake?* I thought. *Fuck that guy.*

The men at the end of the alley had a leader. He pointed down the street in the direction that the mob ran. Then he gestured toward the alley across the street from us. Then at our alley.

Keep going. I tried to will them with my mind. *Or split up, at least.*

Thank God they listened. Two of them took off running behind the mob, hedging a bet that we were still up there. One of them crossed the empty plaza and marched down the alley across from us. And the last one came our way, pointing his rifle straight ahead.

I pressed myself against Spencer and the wall, trying to make us both small while footsteps echoed closer and closer toward us.

My hands scrambled around the ground underneath me, looking for any kind of weapon. My left hand landed on something square and hard. It was half of a brick. It would have to do.

Please, God, Spencer, I thought. *Don't snore.*

64

THE MAN WITH the rifle moved slowly. It was dark, and he didn't know for sure whether we were there at all. But he still had every advantage.

I waited as long as I possibly could, until he passed alongside the dumpster. Then I made my move. I squeezed through the space between the dumpster and the wall to the other side and came up behind him.

Just then he spotted Spencer, asleep, lying against the brick wall. He pointed his rifle down at my friend.

I moved quickly, standing behind the guy and swinging the brick around in a wide arc that connected on his left temple. His lights went out, and he dropped onto the ground.

I grabbed his rifle and slid it into the dumpster, then looked over my shoulder to see if the guy across the street had noticed.

I didn't see any movement. But the sleeping mercenary at my feet wouldn't be out for long. We had to move. I shook Spencer awake and got him to his feet. "Let's go, buddy," I said. "Watch your step."

Spencer stepped over the guy on the ground. "Who's that?" he asked.

"I don't know," I said, which I suppose was the truth. I crept to the end of the alley and saw the other guy now, his back to us, near the end of his own alley. There was a metal street sign lying on the ground, a remnant of the riots. I picked it up. "Okay," I said to Spencer. "Get ready to run again. We're going to go behind that statue when I say so."

But now Spencer was groggy and grumpy. "Why are we running

so much?" he whined.

"It's part of the surprise," I said.

"I don't think there's a surprise," Spencer said.

"Now!" I whispered. I hurled the street sign as far down the street as I could, in the direction we had come from. We ran toward a big statue of a guy on a horse and crouched behind it, just as the clang of metal on pavement rang across the street.

The mercenary in the alley ran into the street and then toward our decoy.

"That alley!" I pointed. "Go!"

Spencer ran toward the alley that I had picked out. This one actually opened up on the other side. We sprinted for the narrow tunnel, and I waited for the crack of a rifle that never came.

When Spencer reached the alley, I pushed him to keep going. We came out the other side, onto a city street. I could see the spire of the church that was next to our hotel, a quarter mile away.

I kept running.

Spencer complained from behind me, but he followed. My lungs and legs were burning. I swore I heard a voice shout at us to stop in Bulgarian again, but it might have been Spencer hiccupping.

Finally, we reached the front door of the hotel. The lobby was lit up inside. It felt like we had stepped out of a horror movie and back to safety.

"Hey!" Spencer scowled at me. "We're just back at the hotel!"

I held my arms wide and gasped for breath. "Surprise," I said.

65

THE MEN CROUCHED behind a sedan near the rear entrance to Béke téri Stadion in Budapest, Hungary.

Whyte Python had arrived that morning after playing a concert the night before in Yugoslavia. The show there had resulted in the same long night of protests as the ones in Romania and Bulgaria. The orders were clear: the same thing would not happen here. Whyte Python was not going to play.

The first band, Cage Match, had handed the show over to Spyderbyte. Whyte Python would be backstage now, doing whatever it was that rock bands did to prepare for their show.

Spyderbyte's final song would be "Panic Attack," and then the operators of the control booth would step out for a smoke while the road crew changed up the stage for Whyte Python, and the booth would be empty.

That was when their window would open. It was all timed with military precision—and the men had this whole itinerary down to the second, thanks to a very well-placed asset who knew all the band's movements ahead of time.

One by one, events followed the intelligence provided. Spyderbyte wrapped with "Panic Attack," and the crowd cheered, and the door to the control room opened a few seconds later. Five hairy American technicians stepped out and lit up.

The lead mercenary gave a signal to his compatriots, hunched behind the door with ropes and gags at the ready. The window was open.

Plenty of time.

66

⚡

AMANDA HAD A FEELING that there was trouble a few minutes
before it became obvious to everyone else in the arena.
      She couldn't place her finger on what it was, exactly. But
she had been to so many concerts over the years that her senses recognized a missing element. A hum in the air that was off pitch.

With a concert capacity of just under twelve thousand, the Béke
téri Stadion was smaller than most of the venues they had played on
the tour. Maybe that was why something felt wrong. She had gotten
used to the band playing in caverns. Everything was a little closer in
the Béke téri, a little more tangible.

Maybe that was it. Maybe it just felt different to be able to see the
crowd, to feel the buzz of the speakers.

No. That wasn't it. Amanda left the greenroom and ran to the
stage, where the lights were dimmed. *Lower than usual?* she wondered. The roadies had finished setting up the Whyte Python stage,
and the crowd was showing the early signs of restlessness. But everything appeared to be generally in place.

But it wasn't! Something was off. She could see it, without putting
her finger on it. There was something missing. What was it? Amanda
scanned the lights overhead, following them to the rear of the arena.
And then she realized what it was. It was a tiny light, always up high
and directly across from the stage. The light in the control room. It
was not on.

Like most concerts, the Whyrld Peace Tour had a soundboard set
up in the center of the arena. But unlike most concerts, it was mostly
for show. The majority of the actual performance was controlled in

locked booths where a team of CIA technicians could work without distraction. The official reasoning for this additional precaution given to organizers was pyro; Whyte Python was lugging around enough explosives to blow up a whole city block, and they couldn't risk the controls being disturbed.

The venue operators didn't really care what weird logistics Whyte Python demanded. They would turn over the keys to their control rooms and never ask questions.

But now the booth was empty, and the light wasn't on. The stage lights were dim. The speakers were not humming.

Price knew this was very bad.

She ran through the backstage area, down a hallway that led to a side door and outside of the stadium. She weaved through the buses and trucks to the other side of the building, where another door led to the control room inside.

She found the techs bound and gagged at the bottom of the stairs leading up to the control room. Beaten, but not severely. Just enough to comply. Amanda ran up the stairs to the control room, where the door had been fused shut with a blowtorch.

Whyte Python was supposed to be onstage, but nobody had gone to get them. At Price's command, a small group of CIA roadies force-entered the control room with an improvised battering ram. She knew what she was going to find before she saw it.

The controls were destroyed.

A mad scramble was underway in the control booth.

Had this been a normal short-run tour, they would've been fucked. The concert would be canceled. But fortunately for Whyte Python, the Whyrld Peace Tour was a CIA operation—the agency's mantra being that if you need something, you might as well buy two of them, because it's all coming out of the office-supplies budget in the farm bill or something.

And so, within minutes, identical sound, light, and pyrotechnic boards were unloaded and unboxed, and the road crew worked feverishly to replace every switch and button. Unfortunately, it still took some time to set up.

The Hungarian crowd knew something was up. The lights onstage were still dim, and the stage was set, and nothing was happening. A current of complaints moved through them, beginning with scattered shouts and boos and evolving into jeers and tossed beer cups.

Accustomed to disappointment and betrayal as they were, the fans suspected a trick. Whyte Python wasn't there. They started stomping their feet and chanting, *"Whyte Python, Whyte Python,"* but not in a supportive way. They wanted Whyte Python brought to them, or else.

"This is bad," Price said. "Look at them. They're turning on us."

"We should probably expect more of this from here on out," Stryker said.

"Sabotage?"

"Uh-huh."

"But we have a bigger problem," Price said. "How did they know they would have access to the booth?"

"Looks like they just brought some sledgehammers," Stryker said.

"I mean, how did they access it so fast? We have a leak."

"Oh," Stryker said. "Do you think?"

Amanda had her back to Stryker, and she raised an eyebrow. *What the hell? Of course we have a leak.* Were the machinations of a world tour such a mystery to everyone else? "It's suspicious," she said carefully, not wanting to hurt Stryker's feelings. "They had the timing down to the second."

"Well, let's not jump to conclusions," Stryker said. "One step at a time."

Technicians worked furiously to replace the equipment. In the stadium, a sudden cheer exploded through the stands. Price ran to the window and saw Davy Bones onstage, holding a bullhorn.

What is he doing? Price wondered.

"Hey, everyone," Davy yelled into his bullhorn. "Hang tight. They gotta fix the sound."

The crowd either didn't like that answer or didn't understand it, because they started booing again.

"Hey!" Davy Bones scolded them. "No boos! Everyone, be cool!"

The crowd chose not to be cool.

"He needs to get offstage," Stryker said. "He's making it worse."

"Wait," Price said. "Look."

Down below, small in the distance, Rikki Thunder emerged from behind the curtain. The crowd popped again, but it died down faster this time. Rikki approached Davy Bones and put an arm around his shoulder.

Whispered something in his ear.

Davy shrugged, nodded, and threw an arm around Rikki's shoulders.

"All right," Davy shouted into the bullhorn. It was soft and tinny in the sound booth, but they could understand every word. "We're gonna try something while they get our shit fixed. But I need your help, okay?"

There was some settling in the front rows. Davy held the bullhorn high, and he began to sing. "When I look across the world tonight / I see the pain that's in your eyes / I see our children without hope tonight—"

Immediately, there was recognition among the crowd. Rikki Thunder leaned his head close to Davy's, and Davy held the bullhorn between the two of them.

"I see a warrior meant to rise!" they sang together.

And now the crowd joined in. "'Cause there's a passion in your hearts tonight / I can feel it in the air—"

The Hungarians joined in a slow wave from the front to the back of the stadium. Now they all sang, "And no wall can keep us apart tonight / We are one; we're everywhere—"

Spencer Dooley and Buck Sweet ran onto the stage, Buck catching a bullhorn that a roadie had tossed to him. They huddled around it and joined in. Now everyone in the arena was singing "Tonight, for Tomorrow," a cappella.

"So look me in the eyes right now," they sang, "And let's make that promise real / Because they can't lock up our hearts, our souls / We'll meet their iron with our steel—"

A technician nudged Price. "We're back," he said.

In the arena, the crowd sang, "Yeah, the tears that we cried yesterday / And the blood we draw tonight—"

"Wait," Price said. "Not yet."

"Will mean that all of tomorrow's children / Can sing together in the light!"

"Amanda?" Stryker said.

"Wait," she said.

THE BAND: We are the soul!

THE CROWD: Soul!

THE BAND: We are the heart!

THE CROWD: Heart!

THE BAND: We're ready to roll—

EVERYONE: We're gonna tear it apart!

Price nodded at the technicians in their seats.

"Now," she said.

Dials were turned and switches were flipped, and onstage the lights came on and started to flash, and the speakers buzzed to life, and pyro fired just as everyone screamed, "Stand up!"

The stadium filled with joy. Screams and cries and singing and dancing, all in one instant. Rikki ran to his drums. Roadies tossed guitars to the other three. Davy stepped behind his microphone and his voice boomed through the stadium like the voice of God.

DAVY: Shoulder to shoulder!

THE CROWD: Stand up!

Buck Sweet strummed an improvised riff.

DAVY: Brother to brother!

THE CROWD: Stand up!

Rikki pounded on the drums.

Davy ran to the edge of the stage and leaned over the crowd, touching outstretched hands like Jesus with the lepers.

"Now I see my friends and family / I see my neighbors, standing strong," he sang. "This is our home, our life, our heritage / And in our hearts, this is our song!"

Since the timing was off, anyway, Davy held the note on "song" for ten seconds while Buck's guitar swelled, while Rikki's drums pounded in double-time.

"And when you look me in the eyes tonight / I see my brother, my guiding light / I'll follow you if you lead me now / Let's link our arms, let's sing, let's fight!"

The crowd all screamed *"Let's fight"* in time with Davy. Rikki Thunder appeared on the big screen that hovered about the stage, smiling so hard that his eyes were closed.

"And now we know our cause is just / We link our arms, we swear this creed / That our future will be bright and pure / And free of want, of fear, of need!"

In the sound booth, Amanda Price wiped tears away from her eyes. She pressed her hands against the glass, and she screamed.

"Stand up!"

67

THERE WAS NO riot after the show in Budapest.

We gave them the same concert we gave everyone else, but the whole scene had a different feel. Instead of crashing into each other and flashing us and chugging beers, the crowd spent the rest of the concert with their arms around each other, singing along in harmony, waving flags. Instead of the usual sneers and devil horns, I saw smiles and peace signs.

Typically, at the end of our Whyrld Peace Tour shows, the crowd would spill out into the city streets to spread chaos. But when we left the stadium that night, we found damn near all of them in the parking lot, chanting and singing "Tonight, for Tomorrow."

Their voices hit us like a sonic boom. But it wasn't the aggressive and sort of terrifying brand of band worship that required bodyguards and ropes to keep us safe from our fans.

It was like we were arriving at a surprise party thrown by our five thousand best friends. We were greeted with hugs and high fives, and the energy was so positive it made me feel like I could fly. I could see that the other guys felt the same.

So we stayed for more than two hours. We partied with the crowd, and sang with them, and drank Hungarian wine. At one point, I was sitting in the back of a pickup truck with three teenagers in matching Thunderstorm shirts, chugging beer. Buck plugged into somebody's amp, and we led the crowd in a round of songs by everybody from Guns N' Roses to Joni Mitchell.

The police stayed on the perimeter, watching. But they didn't interfere. I think they understood that the scene was positive here, and breaking it up could turn things sour really fast.

The Budapest crowd was hopeful that change was on the horizon. They talked about opening the border with Austria by the end of the year, and watching the Iron Curtain fall. I had to pretend I didn't know much about it, but it made me feel really proud to know that I was making the music that folks were listening to during all this.

When we finally poured into our limo, we were all grinning and giddy. Davy climbed through the sunroof and led the crowd in a final round of "Tonight, for Tomorrow" as we drove away, and then he filled his mouth with whiskey and blew it out over his head like fireworks. Spencer fell asleep instantly. Buck and I sat on the back bench, and I saw that I had a rare opportunity to have a little one-on-one with him.

Spencer and I talked all the time, and despite the occasional blowup, Davy and I had really gotten to know each other while we were writing songs. But Buck was usually in his own world, doing his own thing. There was something I had wanted to say to him since Bucharest, and I didn't know when we'd get another chance—alone, with our spirits high like that.

"Hey, Buck," I said. He looked at me, and it was refreshing to see his eyes were bloodshot but mostly focused, since nobody in the parking lot had any hard drugs.

"Look, man," I said. "I just want you to know, like, it's cool."

Buck raised an eyebrow. "What's cool?"

Dammit. I cracked my neck. This topic was, like, not familiar territory for me, 'cause, you know, I'm such a legendary poon hound. But I soldiered on. "Like," I said, "backstage, or whatever. If you wanna hook up with whoever you wanna hook up with, you know?" I nudged his shoulder and smiled. "Go for it."

Buck's smile faded, and his brow furrowed.

"Oh, I can go for it?" he said, with surprising sarcasm. "Thanks, Your Highness."

Ah, fuck, I thought. "Dude, sorry—that came out wrong." I was really flailing. I felt the sweat start to form on my forehead.

"I get it—you didn't mean anything," Buck said. "Just, I don't need permission."

Jesus. I felt like an asshole. Did I really think he was waiting for my fuckin' clearance?

"Dude, I should've said something years ago," I said. "Whatever, I got your back. I mean not in a sex way, but you know."

Buck chuckled and nodded.

"I mean, we *know*, you know? Spencer is cool. Davy is cool."

I hoped—and mostly believed—that was true. Davy and Spencer and I hadn't said a word about this to each other. You just didn't talk about it.

He looked out the window. "It's complicated," Buck said. "Being on the road."

I thought about Tawny, and I nodded. "Jesus, dude, you can say that again."

Buck's eyes went back out the window. "Thanks, Thunder," he said. "That was only marginally offensive." I could see that he appreciated my fumbling gesture, but I also knew I was sort of violating an unspoken agreement between us from Bucharest. I felt like I owed him the chance to even the score.

"Bro," I said. "Is there anything you want to ask me about?"

If Buck had asked in that moment what secretive shit I had going on, I would have given him an honest answer. Or at least something close enough.

Buck turned back to look at me, and his eyes locked with mine.

He shook his head. "Nope," he said.

And that was the end of it.

The adrenaline wore off on the ride back to the hotel. We were red-eyed and groggy as we stumbled into the lobby, where we exchanged high fives and hugs and went our separate ways to bed.

I steered down the hallway toward my room, and leaned against the door while I dug the key out of my pocket. I unlocked the door, then nudged my way into the room.

Flicked on the lights.

And then I jumped.

There was somebody else in the room.

68

TAWNY WAS SITTING on the bed, her back against the headrest, her bare legs crossed.

"Jesus, Tawny," I said. "You scared the shit out of me. How did you get in here?"

She swung her legs off the bed and stood. She was wearing a lacy pink bra and matching thong, the pair that she knew was my favorite.

"I'm in the CIA," she said. Her voice was deep and throaty, and she didn't seem to care if the room was bugged. She started to move toward me in long, slow steps, her hips swaying back and forth in perfect rhythm.

"Oh," I heard myself say. "Right."

Her eyes burned into mine as she floated across the room like a hungry lioness, breathing so deeply and rapidly that her chest heaved up and down. The room key fell out of my hand.

This. Was. Happening.

We collided in the middle of the room, a mess of tongues and hands and limbs wrapping themselves around each other. She tore off my clothes and I tore off what was left of hers. I grabbed the backs of her thighs and lifted her up, and she wrapped her legs around me and pulled me in. And then we fucked like it was a competition, across every inch of the hotel room.

After a while we slowed down, and then it became the long, burning pleasure of scratching an itch that had been tormenting both of us for months.

It was different than before. Tawny and I had slept together countless times, so in some ways it was familiar and comfortable; but it was also the first time I'd done it with the real person underneath the undercover officer. And she let herself go in ways that I had never realized she was holding back.

We had finally tired each other out when the sun came up. We lay on top of the bed, sweaty and spent and smiling at each other. I tried to just enjoy the moment for as long as I could before the inevitable questions started to nag at my brain.

What were we doing? Was this stupid? Was it dangerous? Did I actually think we could be together after everything that had happened? *Could* we be together?

Finally, Tawny broke the silence. "I think we have a mole," she said with a sigh into my ear.

"Seriously?" I sat up and looked around the hotel room. "I mean, the place is kind of skeevy but—"

She pulled me close again. "No, I mean on Facemelt," she whispered. "I think someone is playing both sides. The way they sabotaged the show last night, they had to have inside information. I am really not supposed to tell you this, but in my heart I know it's not you."

"What are you gonna do?"

"I don't know," she said. "I just have to watch, for now. The thing is, there aren't a lot of people who it could be. So I need to be sure."

"Tell me if I can help."

"I will," she said, and nudged me back onto the pillow and rested her head on my shoulder. "Just don't say anything for now, all right?"

"Okay."

We were quiet for a while. "Where did you get that idea?" she finally asked. "To make the crowd sing?"

"Oh. Spencer's birthday, remember? Davy got the crowd to sing to him. Nothing brings strangers together faster than singing the same song."

Tawny's face snapped alert. She sat up. "You guys should start every show that way."

"I don't know," I said. "It was a special thing because it was different, you know? It was real."

She got off the bed. "But *they* don't know that," she said. "The crowd. You have three more stops. I think we should stage a technical delay at all of them, and then bring Davy out with the bullhorn, and do the sing-along." Tawny rushed back at me and straddled me, pulling my ear close to her lips again. "You saw what happened last night," she said, although I was having a difficult time paying attention all of a sudden. "That crowd would have followed you guys into war. If we can do this in Czechoslovakia, in Poland? In fucking East Germany? You cracked the code! This is it!"

She climbed off me and paced naked in front of the bed, her eyes darting while she did the math, and my heart sank. "Right," I said. "This is all just work for you."

She turned to look at me, confused at first.

And then her face fell. In that moment, we both understood just how big the gap was between us, and that we would never be able to close it.

"Oh, Rikki," she said. "I can't help it."

"I know."

And I did know. Last night was real, but so was her passion for what we were all doing here in Eastern Europe. It's what she was meant to do, and I couldn't be pissed about it.

But to me, the sing-along was a spontaneous moment that pulled people together. To her, it was a chess move. We saw the world differently. She was never going to see things through my eyes, and I had to be honest about the fact that I didn't *want* to see them through hers.

No hard feelings. She hadn't tricked me into bed. She just needed it, as bad as I did, and we showed each other everything. And at the end of it, we both saw the truth.

"You know," I said, "that was the last time."

"Yeah," she said. Suddenly she realized she was naked. She scooped her clothes off the floor and got dressed. "I should go."

"Okay," I said. "But, Tawny? We're not gonna start every show with the sing-along."

"I know," she said. "It was a bad idea." She moved to the door and peeked through the peephole before turning the handle.

"Hey," I called after her. She stopped and looked back at me. "You're really good at your job."

Tawny smiled. Her eyes sparkled, but it was because they were coated with tears.

"Thanks," she said. And then she left.

69

O FFICERS DARRELL BOONE and Amanda Price leaned against
a rented black van in the parking lot outside the Great
Strahov Stadium in Prague, passing a cigarette back and
forth while Whyte Python played the historic arena's first-ever rock
concert.

The Great Strahov opened in the 1920s, and it was the largest
stadium ever built. Whyte Python had sold almost one hundred
thousand tickets. From inside, Davy Bones's voice blended with the
muffled bass and guitars, and lights and lasers flashed into the sky
overhead while pyrotechnic smoke wafted above the risers.

"You're extra quiet today," Boone said.

Amanda had been exceptionally quiet since leaving Rikki's room
that morning. She shouldn't have slept with him. She hadn't been
thinking about gaining closure on their relationship—or whatever it
was—when she broke into his room, stripped off her clothes, and lay
in wait for him to show up.

She was only thinking about taking what she wanted. She knew
before Rikki said so that it couldn't last, but she felt sad about it
nonetheless. She'd thought maybe it could have lasted until the end
of the tour.

The band had just transitioned from "Never-Ending Party" into
"Tonight, for Tomorrow." An ear-splitting cheer rose with the first
few chords, and Boone crossed his arms and smiled.

"I feel like this is the most important thing I've ever done with my
life," he said.

Amanda was taken aback by her colleague's misty-eyed sincerity.

But she understood. "We could really help change a lot of lives over here," she said.

"Huh?" Boone looked at her sideways. "Oh, right. The revolutions. Yeah, that'll be great. But I mean *this*." He gestured to the stadium. "This *song*! It just, really hits you in the stones, doesn't it?"

"I guess so."

"Listen to that crowd." Boone shook his head. "They can't get enough of the song that *I wrote*."

"You helped Rikki write it, yeah."

Boone ignored her. "I mean. *Wow*. Ol' Darrell Boone wrote a number-one hit." He slapped his hands together. "Can you believe it?"

"It's a really good song, Darrell."

"And, hey"—Boone pointed at Amanda—"you can't fool me, Price. You love this life, too. I get why you held out on telling Thunder the truth for so long."

"What?" Amanda said. "No. I was managing the asset. I've explained this a hundred times. And look: it all worked out perfectly."

Boone rolled his eyes. "Uh-huh. Worked out perfectly for everyone, right?"

"Boone—"

"What I'm saying is, I get it. I know you aren't in love with him like everybody thinks. Do you have complicated feelings for him? Sure, and don't let anyone tell you you're the first officer that's ever happened to. But, Price, you did fall in love with *somebody* on this mission."

"What are you talking about? Who?"

Boone leaned against the van next to her and smiled. "You, my friend, are in love with Tawny Spice. And who wouldn't be?" He winked. "Don't worry. I won't tell. We metalheads need to stick together."

Amanda considered arguing, but then she thought about what Boone said. She had become so defensive whenever somebody accused her of slowing down the mission because she was in love with Rikki.

But Boone was saying something different. He was saying that she slowed down the mission because she loved being a different person.

Was he right?

Tawny Spice lived in Los Angeles and worked at a music magazine. She dated a drummer and slept in on the weekends.

She wasn't the navy brat who grew up on air bases across Europe, never staying anywhere long enough to make real friends or connections.

She wasn't the girl who had distant parents and a bully for an older brother, who would give her rug burns and titty twisters, and pin her down and pull on her ears until they burned.

She wasn't the one who finally settled in Nevada for her last years of high school, where all the girls hated her because she was new and didn't fit in, and all the boys just wanted to screw her.

Tawny Spice definitely wasn't the girl who got slapped around in an empty parking lot by a senior because she refused to put out.

And she wasn't the girl who trained in kickboxing for her entire junior year, then followed that boy home two days before his graduation and beat the shit out of him in his own garage.

Tawny Spice wasn't the girl who was arrested for the assault and almost went to prison over it, got expelled, earned her GED, enrolled in a small college in New England, managed to get into the graduate psych program, and was recruited into the Central Intelligence Agency by her professor, a retired spook.

Tawny Spice didn't sleep with one eye open, brace herself against exposure, keep track of aliases, manipulate assets, and drag dickheads out to the woods to break their arms.

Tawny Spice's life was sweet and simple. She grew up in a suburban house with nice parents in Oregon, and now she had a good job, and she had Rikki Thunder, and she listened to good music, and she knew what it felt like to have fun for no reason.

Being Tawny Spice was pretty great.

Amanda took a deep breath of cool spring air into her nostrils and rested her head back against the van. Her eyes drifted to the arena, to the lights and sounds inside. And it dawned on her that it was almost over.

Within days, the Whyrld Peace Tour would end. Within weeks, Poland would hold an election that could turn power over to the Solidarity party and peacefully transition the country out from communist rule.

The dominoes would keep falling from there. The Eastern Bloc would collapse from the inside out, and Project Facemelt would probably be shut down. She had been holding out hope that this was the new model: that she would keep working with Whyte Python to secure a stable, democratic East, and then maybe they would move on to spread peace and rock in another dark corner of the world.

But she suspected that wasn't likely. They were the right band in the right place, at the right time, and they had done their job.

The CIA wouldn't need Whyte Python or Rikki Thunder anymore. He would sign an NDA, and probably be paid something for his trouble, and the band would sink or swim on their own in the 1990s.

Tawny Spice would disappear, and Amanda Price would move on to a new mission somewhere else. She had two concerts left. Four days. And that would be it.

Meanwhile, she was almost certain someone in her orbit was leaking to the other side. Protocol would be to report that suspicion to her direct report; she would need to call Lonsa in the morning. They would have to search bank records, maybe even dig through the trashcans of, what, dozens of people? The record label, some CIA lackey? No. It had to be someone closer than that. Someone who knew Rikki was going out on a mission in Sofia. Someone on the tour . . .

"Earth to Amanda." Stryker's voice knocked her out of her daze.

Amanda turned around to see Stryker poking out the van's back door.

"Sorry," Amanda said. "What did you say?"

"You need to hear this," Stryker said.

Amanda got into the van and took a seat on the bench in front of the spinning tapes and lights that made up their traveling surveillance office. Catherine Stryker handed her a pair of headphones.

"We just picked this up," Stryker said. She rewound a tape while Amanda put the headphones on, and then Amanda heard two voices chattering in Czech, a language that she was not totally familiar with. The voices went back and forth, one high and intense, the other low and flat.

"I don't speak Czech—" she started to say.

Stryker cut her off. "You don't have to. You'll get the gist. The high-pitched voice is ŠtB," Stryker said, referring to the Czech secret police. "The deep voice is Stasi."

Amanda recognized a word here and there; "contraband" and "surveillance," and nobody needed to translate "CIA." Then her eyes went wide when the deep voice spoke two words that anyone on earth would recognize in the spring of 1989: "Rikki Thunder."

70

W E PLAYED Czechoslovakia and Poland, both huge shows in front of rabid crowds.

Nobody asked me to conduct any more dangerous night missions in either city; in fact, I noticed that Team Facemelt was mostly sticking close to the band, too. We had barely seen them throughout the tour, but now it seemed like Tawny and Stryker were never out of our sight—although Tawny and I didn't talk very much. Even Mancuso and Boone turned up backstage in Chorzów, giving instructions to roadies and scanning the crowd through binoculars.

We only had East Germany left to play before heading home. I wondered if their work was done. Or maybe they just realized that they had been touring with the biggest band in the world for two weeks and hadn't caught a single show.

I had just brushed my teeth and was headed out of my hotel room to meet the guys outside the lobby, where a limo would take us to the airport. But just before I turned the handle, there was a knock. I knew it was Tawny right away; sometimes you get to know somebody so well that you can recognize their knuckles on the other side of a door.

I opened it, and she was holding her hands together in the hallway. She was bouncing back and forth on the balls of her feet, looking anxious.

"Hey," I said.

"Hey," she said. "Can I come in?"

This kind of formality was the new normal between us, since Hungary. Tawny had never asked for permission to come into my room before. Usually, she just strolled in and started bossing me around. But now she waited for me to say it was okay, which was definitely making both of us uncomfortable.

I nodded and stepped aside, and she darted past me into the bathroom, then turned on the shower.

I closed the door behind us and stuffed my hands in my pockets. "So, what's up?" I asked.

"Everything's okay," she said, like everything was not okay. "But we're gonna have to make some changes in Berlin. For safety."

I raised an eyebrow. "Okay," I said. "What kind of changes?"

"We're still going to do the city tour, the school visits, and all the rest of the stuff we have planned for the day after the show," she said. "And of course, we go back through Checkpoint Charlie like we came in. But otherwise, no excursions. The band needs to stay together and travel with the team from the airport to the hotel, to the venue, then back to the hotel tonight. You guys can't split up. You can't go out for dinner."

"Jeez," I said. "Where is this coming from?"

Tawny paced in front of the shower. "That's not all," she said. "We're going to establish a safe house in the city. The Palasthotel is basically a Stasi outpost. If we think it's not safe to go back there, we'll go into hiding."

I felt my breath hitch in my throat. Nobody had ever mentioned that we might have to go into hiding before.

"Tawny, are we in danger?" I whispered.

"No," she said, but it sounded like she was asking herself a question. "I don't think so. But I'm going to tell you where the safe house is, and I need you to memorize the map between the arena and there in case you guys get stranded somewhere."

This all sounded insane. "Why would I need to do that?" I asked.

"Because right now, you need to assume that anyone you run into in Berlin is working for the Stasi. Many of them will be. You shouldn't get in a taxi."

"Tawny, why is this happening?"

"We picked up some chatter," she said. "In Prague. They know the band is involved in clandestine activities."

"But you figured they would be suspicious about that before we even got here," I said.

"Right," Tawny said. "But now they have a lot of details. They referenced specific objectives at other stops in the tour. And they talked about you."

"Me?" I said. My whole body broke out in goose bumps. I was pretty used to people talking about me by then, and I had been kind of bracing myself for this moment since Romania, but the idea of foreign spooks singling me out gave me chills. "What did they say?"

Tawny stopped pacing and looked directly at me. "A lot," she said. "They seemed to know all about you and Spencer's excursion in Sofia. They found our bug in Wandlitz." Her eyebrows furrowed. "And there was something about a fight at an underground gay bar in Bucharest, but I think that was bad information."

I shrugged.

"Anyway, they talked about your habits, and your patterns." She hesitated. "And they were really interested in your favorite drinks."

"Why?" I asked.

Tawny took a deep breath. "Presumably, that's in case they want to tamper with your food."

"Oh," I said. "Wait. Tamper how?"

She rolled her eyes. "Not in a nice way," she said. "Think about it."

"Like *poison* me?"

"We're not going to let that happen. We'll keep a chain of command on everything you eat and drink. Boone is securing weed right now."

I crossed my arms. "Is all this really necessary?"

"Honestly?" she said. "I don't know. But Mancuso is the field expert here, and he's spooked. He said he's seen this kind of chatter, and it's usually before something bad happens."

"Okay." I shivered. "Well, at least it's the last stop, right? The guys will be pissed, but what are you gonna do?"

Tawny winced. "That's the other thing. You're gonna have to sell all this to the band. You have to convince them to stick together, and you have to tell them the address to the safe house, and to not share it with anyone at all. And you can't tell them why."

My arms dropped to my sides. "Nuh-uh," I said. "No way. How

the hell am I supposed to do that?"

"I don't know," Tawny said. "But I know you'll figure it out."

"For God's sake, Tawny," I said. "I'm not in the CIA. I don't know how to mind fuck people like you guys. Can't someone else do this?"

"Who?" she asked. "Kirby? Catherine, who they think is a costume designer? It definitely can't be *me*. Davy bites my head off every time I make a suggestion. You're the only one they'll listen to."

"Come on," I said. "What about someone from Andromeda?"

She leaned in close. "Rikki, I don't know if we can trust anyone from Andromeda with the address to the safe house. I've spent the past forty-eight hours going over lists. Who's had access to stop schedules, who might know these things or be able to find out. I'm looking at every roadie sideways. These people know *too much*. Somebody is leaking, and it's a pretty short list of who it could be. Nobody knows the safe house exists, outside of Facemelt. You have to do it."

"Oh, right," I said. " 'Hey, guys, let's all hold hands for the next twenty-four hours and never leave each other's sight and not party. And also, by the way, I set up this safe house in case the East German government tries to kill us.' I'm sure that will go over great."

Tawny stepped toward me, and she clasped her hands to stop herself from touching my chest.

"You've done everything right for a year and a half," she said. "You got them to record the song, to wear the costumes, to come on this tour in the first place. And then the party in Berlin? The handoff in Sofia? The goddamn *sing-along* in Hungary? You're a natural, and you can do this, too. I knew you had it in you all this time. It's why I picked you. It's why I put you in the band."

Hang on.

"What do you mean, you put me in the band?" I said. "Barry broke his arms in a motorcycle accident. They had tryouts, and I won."

Tawny looked at the floor for a few solid seconds.

"Tawny?" I said. "Right?"

She looked up at me and smirked in a sad, small way. Then she shrugged her shoulders.

Oh, dude. For the third time, I got chills. I felt dizzy. I didn't want to hear this. But I had to. "Did you . . . break Barry's arms?"

"Of course I did," she said. "Come on. You never figured that out?"

I probably should have. But I had been in Whyte Python for a while by the time Tawny told me about the whole CIA deal. By then I had practically forgotten how I ended up in the band. I only remembered earning it, and that meant a lot to me.

"That's fucking twisted," I said. "You didn't have to break his arms. Barry has tarantulas to take care of!"

"This is big kid's work," she said. "We aren't holding a town hall meeting here."

"So, even when you came clean about all this, you left out some important parts, huh?" I said. "What else?"

"What do you mean?"

"I mean, what else did you do? To get me into Whyte Python. Tell me. I want to know."

"Okay," she said. And then she looked at the ceiling, like she was trying to remember. "Let's see. I threatened Kirby. But just a little! And we food-poisoned a few other drummers that morning just in case, so nobody else could try out."

I leaned against the door and slid down to the floor.

"And then I guess Spencer's friend Kevin sent somebody over just before you?" she said. "Which we weren't expecting, and everyone freaked out for a couple of minutes. But it turned out the guy didn't know how to play the drums? So we got lucky there—"

"Stop," I said. "Just stop, will you? I knew you were playing me. Telling me you loved me and all that bullshit. But the one thing I thought I did on my own. Getting in this band. Being good enough. That was all bullshit, too?"

"No!" Tawny said. "You earned it. I knew they would pick you, because you're a great drummer. You belong here. They just had to *see* you, and they wouldn't have bothered if they could bring in somebody they already knew."

"Okay," I said. "Fine. Thank you for doing everything important in my life for me. Are you happy? But I think I've repaid the favor by now, since the Stasi is planning to have me killed and all. I'm not getting murdered for this. I'm done."

"Rikki—"

"Nope," I said. "I'm buying my own ticket when we get to the airport, and I'm going home. Cancel the concert. I'm not risking my life for you. I'm out."

Tawny stood over me. "It's too late for that," she said. She sounded kind of sad about it.

"What does that mean?"

"It means you've gone too far into this. You participated in an active covert mission to foment regime change in half a dozen countries. You are on watch lists. We can't just let you go walking around with that information."

"I thought this concert was the end of it."

"We don't know that for sure," she said. "We have to wait and see what happens here. If the Wall comes down, yeah, probably, we're done. But until then, this is an active mission. And if you walk out tonight, in the city where we need to make an impact the most? If you end the mission *before Ed Lonsa says so*? How do you think my bosses will feel about that? I can't protect you against the consequences."

"So, what, are you gonna, like, kill me if I quit? After everything I've done for you?"

"No." Tawny rolled her eyes. "But we'd probably have to keep you under wraps for a while. Long enough that Whyte Python would have to replace you."

My stomach rolled. "Replace me? Like the way you replaced Barry?"

"I don't want any of this, either."

I stood up and held my arms wide. "This is bullshit."

"Rikki, please."

But I was done listening. I left the room and slammed the door behind me.

71

ᛝ

"ALL RIGHT, so here's the thing, guys," I started. "I was hoping we could do some stuff a little different in Berlin."

We were in the limo, riding from the hotel to the airport. Boone was driving instead of a local guy, but nobody else noticed. It was a morning flight after a concert, so everyone was hungover and grumpy.

"Huh?" Davy tipped his sunglasses down. "Why are you talking like you're giving a speech?"

"I'm just saying," I said. "This is the last stop of our tour. I think we should, like, get a big dinner catered at the hotel and just enjoy each other's company, you know? Davy's going to Spain from here, we're not gonna see each other for a while, and we just had this big, amazing experience. Let's just live in it as a band for the night, okay? Dinner's on me. And after the show, I just wanna hang with you guys for one night."

"This is weird," Davy said. "What, are you dying or something?"

"No," I said.

"Are you quitting the band?"

"Hell no," I said. "Never."

"That all sounds good to me," Spencer said. Buck shrugged.

"Yeah, fine," Davy said.

"Cool," I said. "Thanks, guys." I took a deep breath and hesitated. The easy part was done. Now it was about to get weird.

"Hey," I said. "Did you guys know that Spencer and I got chased in Sofia? It was actually kind of freaky."

Spencer chimed in. "I threw my hat in the fire.".

"Spencer threw his hat in the fire!" I said.

"Chased by who?" Davy asked.

"The riot. After the show."

"Oh, those guys were all right," Buck said. "Good rioters. Solid arsonists. Nothing to worry about there."

"No," I said. "These guys were different. They were really mad at us. And they were yelling shit like 'We actually hate Whyte Python' and 'U.S.A. sucks.'"

"They were?" Spencer looked confused.

"Yup."

"Crazy," Davy said, like he didn't really care about how crazy it was.

The airport appeared on the horizon. I realized I should have held this conversation for the plane, but I had a feeling they were all going to fall asleep the minute the wheels went up; and besides, it was too late now. I had to get down to it.

"Anyway," I said, "there are people in East Germany like that, maybe a lot more of them, who might not like that we're there."

"What are you talking about?" Davy said. "People don't want us there? We sold the place out in a day! These people *love* us."

My eyes darted at Tawny. She was sitting next to me, doing her best to keep our hips from touching each other. She just stared out the window.

"I'm just saying," I said. "I read the newspapers. The government here is pretty strict. Just because we sell out the show doesn't mean every person in the city loves us."

"Okay, got it," Davy said. He put his shades back on and leaned against the headrest. "You're a real ray of sunshine this morning, Thunder."

I ignored that. "I was thinking," I said. "It might be a good idea for us to have, like an offsite place set up that nobody knows about. I asked Tawny to make some calls and set it up."

"What do you mean, 'an offsite place?'" Davy asked.

"Shouldn't I be doing that kind of thing?" Kirby asked.

"Stop the car," I said to Boone. He pulled over. I pushed the door open. "Get out."

"What?" Kirby said. "But, Rikki—"

"You can see the airport from here." I pointed at the air traffic control tower in the far distance. "Just walk in that direction. Jesus! What an asshole." Everybody waited until Kirby got out of the car, and Boone started driving again.

"He's got a point," Davy said. "Your girl's overstepping her bounds again."

"Don't start this," I said.

"So, is it, like, a party house?" Buck asked.

"Not really," I said. "More like an unmarked office building with good sightlines."

"Why do we need that?" Spencer asked.

Buck smiled and snapped his fingers. "Obviously!" he said. "For crimes!"

I wasn't sure if Buck remembered our misadventure in Bucharest and was trying to help me out, or if he didn't connect the dots at all and was just hoping to commit crimes. I think I've thoroughly documented Buck's drug problem by now. Either way, I didn't want to promise a crime spree that I wasn't going to be able to deliver on.

"No," I said. "Just, like, it's a safe place in case things get weird."

"Why would things get weird, Rikki?" Spencer asked innocently.

"Yeah, why would things get weird, Rikki?" Davy asked accusingly.

"I'm just saying, like, we don't know anything about these countries. I'm gonna tell you the address of the safe house in case we get separated or in trouble. But you can't share it with anybody."

"So, you're in control of the safe house," Davy said.

"Me and Tawny."

"You and Tawny. And you took it upon yourself to do this, without even talking to us."

"Kind of."

"You and Tawny are making a lot of decisions on this trip," Davy said. "You seem pretty tight with the designer and the pilots, too. What are you up to, Thunder?"

"I can't . . ." I started, then I sighed. "Nothing."

"Sure," Davy said. "We definitely believe you. Seems pretty normal to me. How about you guys?"

"This is weird, Rikki," Spencer said.

"Davy, bro, this isn't a big deal," I said. "I'm just feeling weird about this stop, and it'll make me feel better, okay? I'm being a pussy. Just say you'll play along, and after tonight you'll get a nice long break from me. Okay, bro? Can we not be dicks to each other, and will you just promise you'll listen when I tell you the address?"

"Whatever," Davy said. "Fine."

That was the best I was going to get out of him, so I stopped there. I told them the address. They promised to memorize it. Honestly, I wasn't sure they were paying attention. I made them each repeat it back to me.

We arrived at the airport, and Boone drove us straight through a set of cones onto the tarmac, where our plane was gassed up and ready to go. The guys filed out of the limo and straight onto the plane. Tawny and I were the last ones in the car.

"Good job," she said.

"Just get out," I said. I was pissed as shit, but also startled by how hard that came out.

Tawny's face crumpled, but she didn't argue. She got out of the car and headed for the stair car. Once I saw her boarding the plane, I tapped Boone on the shoulder.

"Hey," I said. "Let's go get Kirby."

Boone nodded and turned the car around. We headed back in the direction that we'd come from and found Kirby about a mile back, being chased by a stray dog. I opened the door, and he fell inside.

"Thank you," he huffed. "Thank you, Rikki. Good golly, that was scary."

"Sorry, Kirby. I went too far."

"Hey," he said. "At least you had him stop the car first. Remember the time Davy pushed me out of that train?"

He was right; Davy did once push him out of a moving train. But in Davy's defense, it was extremely funny watching Kirby roll down an embankment and into a stream. I'm sure it didn't help his opinion of me that I laughed pretty hard when he reminded me of it just then.

But I also realized something: Kirby didn't want this job. The label stuck him on us, and they wouldn't let him leave, even though we treated him like shit and put him in harm's way.

This guy was a kid once, who wanted to work in music—just like me. That is a hard-ass ladder to climb. You gotta work around the clock, be the bad cop all the time, and master a bunch of random skills that you can't take with you to any other job. By the time you realize you spent your whole life fighting to get a job where people treat you like garbage, you're basically trapped in it. So Kirby and I were kind of in the same situation, but at least everyone was nice to me. I decided it was time to start treating Kirby Smoot like a human being, even if the other guys didn't.

I was the last one to get on the plane. Nobody looked happy, and I didn't want to talk to anyone. I walked past Tawny without looking at her. Then I did the same to Davy. I took a seat at the back of the jet and rested my head against the cool glass window.

And then the plane was rolling, and we were wheels up on our way to the final stop of the Whyrld Peace Tour.

72

GENERAL BECKER PACED in front of the conference table at the latest meeting of Operation Cobra Dominance.

The mood in the room was dour. Several of the seats were empty, as members had read the writing on the wall in their home nations and given up trying to stop Whyte Python's systematic destruction of apparatuses that had taken years and the Eastern Bloc's best minds to construct.

"Well, I tried to warn you guys," Becker said, shaking his head. The other men around the table groaned.

"I warned you last year." Becker counted on his fingers. "I warned you six months ago. I definitely warned you two weeks ago, after I stared directly into the enemy's eyes and saw cities burning."

"The party. We know," the man from Romania said. "You met Rikki Thunder. You told us."

"I didn't just meet him!" Becker snarled. He clenched his fists and shook them at the ceiling. "I baited him into the lion's den. The man walked into a house full of Stasi agents and loyalists, and he planted a bug under all our noses! I looked in Rikki Thunder's eyes, and I saw immeasurable depth and cunning. He is a diabolical menace. And I warned you all, and still you did nothing!"

The man from Czechoslovakia raised his hand. "Didn't he puke on himself?" he asked.

"This is not a constructive way to start meeting," the man from Romania said.

Becker silenced the room with a stare. "How did we let this happen?" he demanded. "Why didn't you sabotage their equipment?

Injure them? Frame them for crimes?"

The other men in the room looked at one another, each waiting for someone else to speak up.

"We sabotaged their equipment," the man from Hungary offered.

"Yes," Becker said. "I heard about that. And what happened afterward?"

The man from Hungary hung his head. "They united the nation in song," he muttered.

"They united the nation in song," Becker repeated. "Good job."

"It is not our fault," the man from Hungary shouted. "They are too wily!"

"You should have destroyed their pretty faces!" Becker punched the table.

The man from Yugoslavia cleared his throat. "Yes. The thing is, we do not really have necessary resources."

"Our dynamite got wet," the man from Bulgaria said.

"We have resources," the man from North Korea said.

"No you don't," the man from Romania said.

"This reminds me." The man from Yugoslavia stood and paced in front of the table. He laced his fingers together in front of his waist and looked to the ceiling, as if he were about to deliver an important speech. "I was hoping," he said, "someone could give me a ride home from this meeting."

"Enough!" Becker roared. "It's happening just as we predicted! Look around you! This room is half empty! Who's next? You, Czechoslovakia? You, Russia? Rikki Thunder planted a bug at a Stasi gathering in Wandlitz! He carried classified materials across Sofia and handed them off to a spy! Our great nations are fighting the Cold War against Whyte fucking Python! And we're *losing*!"

Ivanov stood. "I'll concede that we underestimated their power."

"We underestimate no longer," Becker said. "This ends tonight."

PART VI

The Last Concert

PART VI

The Last Concert

73

D ESPITE THE WAY we left things in Poland, we were all ready
to be good sports at the airport in East Berlin.

There was yet another mob of adoring fans waiting for
us; and maybe it was because it was the last show, or maybe it was
because Germans just really love Whyte Python, but these folks
seemed to be the wildest yet. The mood was much lighter here than
it had been back at the Berlin Wall, when we crossed over. The East
Germans were packed at least fifty feet deep on both sides of the narrow alley that the Schönefeld Airport staff had set up for us, and they
were chanting and stomping their feet.

We weaved through them, taking our time. Posing for pictures.
Signing autographs. Hands grabbed at us, pulling our clothes and
hair, and the fans cried and screamed and threw roses at our feet. I
imagine that this must be what Jesus felt like. But of course, wherever
Jesus went, he could make unlimited booze for his fans, so maybe
Whyte Python wasn't quite at his level.

Anyway, I was on edge as we swam through the mob, seeing as
Tawny had just told me that people here might try to kill me.

Mancuso had briefed me on the East German Stasi back at home,
and how they were probably more powerful and ruthless than the
KGB. The Stasi sent spies all over the world, including the United
States. They sponsored terrorist organizations in West Germany
and funded neo-Nazi groups in other countries, who did their dirty
work of desecrating Jewish cemeteries, blackmailing politicians, and
spreading disinformation across the globe.

Basically, in addition to being an intelligence agency, the Stasi were a bunch of dicks, so these East Germans were going to be a tough nut to crack. They had mastered intelligence gathering and using spies in the field to crush dissent. And they were the last ones to get the memo that the war over the Eastern Bloc was mostly over.

I found myself eyeing every hand that reached out and grabbed at me, waiting for one of them to be holding a gun or a combat knife. I was trying to keep my anxiety hidden from the crowd, but I'm sure my smile looked a lot more like a wince.

"Rikki Thunder!" a young voice called from the crowd. "Rikki Thunder!" I saw heads moving, bodies being shoved and parted. A tall head full of black hair weaved through them, nudging its way to the front, and a gangly teenager burst through the front row just ahead of me.

He lunged across the barrier. Security guards began to move toward him from both sides, but he had a beeline on me now. This was it. He reached for me and wrapped his arms around my shoulders. I braced for the stabbing.

But it didn't come. The kid was just hugging me, and he was sobbing.

"Thank you," he said softly. "Thank you, Rikki Thunder. Thank you, Whyte Python."

In a matter of seconds, I shifted from terrified to confused to understanding. I patted him on the back.

"You're welcome," I said. Meanwhile, some of our "roadies" pushed through the band and grabbed him by the shoulders. But I had realized that this was one of those "friendly attacks" from a genuine fan, and I waved them off.

I gently released the boy's grip and held him at arm's length. He was smiling, though his cheeks were stained with tears. He wore a homemade Thunderstorm T-shirt. He wore that shirt like it was the most important piece of clothing he had ever owned.

"I come to see Whyte Python, and I pray for a unified Germany," he said. " 'Tonight, for Tomorrow' gives me strength."

And finally, I saw it.

Tawny had explained this to me plenty of times, and, in concept, I understood that our music was inspiring people living in shitty circumstances in all these countries. I understood that they sang

"Tonight, for Tomorrow" while they marched, but also that they passed notes organizing protests hidden in their Whyte Python cassette cases, and that they wore our shirts so they could recognize allies if they got in a jam. And I thought all that was pretty cool.

But when I looked into that kid's eyes and saw his hope and fear and belief, I finally understood the power of what we were doing. Whyte Python was important to these people, but not because of our music; and not because of me or Spencer or Buck or Davy. We were only important because we connected them to one another. We didn't give them strength—we showed them their own strength.

I remembered Mancuso telling me about the Queen's Head bar in New York, how it gave the revolutionaries a place to organize. He was right about one thing: we weren't the revolutionaries. But he was wrong about something, too. We weren't the jesters dancing out in front of the bar, either. And we definitely weren't heroic symbols of the future, or their fearless new leaders, like Tawny always said.

We were the Queen's Head. We were the bar. Or the record store, or the band room, or the space under the bleachers in corn country where misfits could take shelter together from bullies and realize they aren't alone. We gave them a place to gather while they organized themselves. That was our job. We were Whyte fucking Python, dammit, and I'd never been so proud of anything in my life.

I dug into my duffel bag and found a band T-shirt. "Hey," I said. "Enjoy the show, man." I stuffed the shirt in his hands and pulled him in tight for another hug. "Don't give up," I whispered in his ear. "On revolution. We're on your side."

And then I let him go, and the roadies nudged him back behind the line. "We will never forget!" he called out to me as he vanished into the crowd.

"Yeah," I said, mostly to myself. "Me either."

We had stopped moving, and the rest of the guys took notice. Davy and I locked eyes, and I could see him recognize something in my face. His expression softened, and then he flashed his real smile at me, and he dug into his own duffel. He brought out a handful of Whyte Python tees and tossed them into the crowd.

Spencer and Buck did the same. Then Davy took off his scarf and tossed it into the crowd, and then his sunglasses.

I let out a rooster crow and tossed my wristbands and shades. When those things were gone, I took off my leather jacket and handed it to a little girl.

Buck was shirtless now. Spencer took off his sneakers and gave them away and just stood there on the tarmac in his white gym socks.

We kept right on giving away everything we could put our hands on, shedding our rock star images and the remnants of the Whyrld Peace Tour until we melted into the East German crowd as if we were a part of them instead of on some imaginary pedestal above them.

When we had nothing left to give away, I pushed through the crowd to Davy and wrapped an arm around his shoulders. He hugged me back. Spencer and Buck closed in, and the crowd surrounded us.

"Who are we?" Davy yelled.

"Whyte Python!" we yelled back.

"And why are we here?"

"To tear the roof off!"

"Why else?"

"To get laid!"

"Why else?"

And then I screamed, "For revolution!" And the crowd erupted, a thousand people bouncing and screaming and pumping fists in the air.

Davy threw his arms above his head. "Whyte Python never dies!" he shouted.

"Whyte Python never dies!" everyone in all of East Germany seemed to shout back.

74

⚡

THEY SET UP our band dinner in a conference room at the Palasthotel. It was just the guys in Whyte Python—Project Facemelt
stayed out of the room. I asked the band how they felt about
letting Kirby eat with us, but that idea earned a pretty quick vote of
three-to-one against.

The CIA brought in a special chef and his own team of line
cooks, after making sure none of them wanted to kill me. They had a
supply-chain record of every bite of food and every drop of alcohol,
and Boone and Mancuso supervised everything from food prep to
washing the dishes. It was delicious. It was a preshow meal, all small
plates loaded with carbs and protein. We drank light beers and vodka
while we picked at our feast.

Everybody was pretty quiet at first, marinating in our own
thoughts. It was a little awkward.

Technically I had accomplished Tawny's goal of keeping the band
together and away from the general public, but I had also really meant
it when I said that I wanted us to hang out and enjoy one another's
company. For the first time in three years, we didn't have an agenda
to go home to. Davy had struck up a friendship with Madonna, and
she'd advised us to hold off on recording another album because *The
Whyte Album* was still releasing singles that hung around the top of
the charts for months. "Just let it ride," she'd said, and we were more
than happy to do that.

We had no argument there from the CIA. They didn't seem to
care about the next album at all. Back when this whole thing started,
Tawny had promised that at a certain point, we would be done with

Project Facemelt. The band would be on top of the world, and nobody would be pulling our strings anymore. I could stop leading a double life and just enjoy being rich and famous.

Of course, I had stopped believing that line of bullshit—it felt like I was going to be stuck in this shit CIA job forever. But the closer we got to the end of the tour, the more it felt like we were hitting the end of the road with the CIA, too. I mean, if the Eastern Bloc really did collapse, what else was there for us to do?

Before we left for the Whyrld Peace Tour, we agreed not to schedule road shows for the summer. We needed a break from touring, and from each other. So we weren't recording another album; and we weren't going on tour back in the States, either. We would play in Berlin, and then the next morning Davy was taking his own flight to Spain for a "mega-siesta." The rest of us would go our separate ways until October, when we were supposed to finish the year with a few major shows in the southern states.

So this was it. And I hoped that at this dinner we could just hang for a couple of hours and joke around like we used to in the early touring days, but I also wasn't going to force the issue. Despite the nice moment at the airport, things were still tense between the rest of the guys and me, and I could sense that Davy was just waiting for me to open my mouth so he could start criticizing my motives again.

Spencer tried to break the silence. "Hey," he said. "Isn't Napoleon from here?"

"France," Buck said.

Spencer nodded and looked back down at his dinner.

Then Buck leaned across the table and cleared his throat. "But do you know where he kept his armies?"

"Where?" Spencer asked.

Buck grinned. "Up his sleevies."

Silence.

Then Davy laughed so hard, he spit out his food.

From that point on, dinner was fantastic.

We joked around about the tour, and made fun of one another, and tried to top one another's stories. We went through half a bottle of schnapps toasting to things, like the chef, and the good people at Budweiser, and pythons, and Heather Locklear.

Davy actually toasted me for being "the missing piece that made Whyte Python a band," and I felt my body release about a thousand pounds of tension that it had been holding for most of the tour. Davy can be a suspicious asshole, for sure; but when I tried to look at the situation through his eyes, I could see why he would have such a hard time with all this.

I deserved suspicion. His radar was especially sensitive, and it wasn't wrong.

I was glad to see that we were cool—for now, at least. We split up after dinner, just long enough to run to our rooms and grab anything we might need before the car took us over to the stadium.

I was feeling good, all things considered. I felt like we were going to go into the break on a good note after all; and if I could get the CIA off my ass once we got back in the States, then we could finally reach a place where Davy felt secure as the leader of the band and I could just play the drums.

My mood soured when I stepped off the elevator and found Tawny waiting outside my room. I didn't say anything. I just stepped past her and unlocked the door, let myself into the room, and turned back to look at her. I raised an eyebrow but didn't say anything.

"Can I come in?"

I leaned on the door frame, blocking the entrance. "What do you need?" I asked.

She crossed her arms and her eyes flared. "Goddamn it, Rikki," she whispered. "Can I *talk* to you?"

Tawny's glare reminded me that we couldn't say anything in the hallways of this hotel. My shoulders slumped as I stood aside and let her into the room.

Once the shower was on full blast, Tawny leaned close and whispered, "We need you to do something different tonight."

"Okay."

"There are revolutionaries coming to the show," she whispered. "They'll be dressed as groupies. We're going to get them backstage passes. We need you to hand off some materials to them."

"I thought nobody was getting a backstage pass."

"Yeah, that makes things a little complicated. We're going to have to let a group in. All girls, some of them with the revolution, some of them just random fans. We'll do our best to clear their backgrounds, and obviously they'll get a thorough pat-down. You'll get instructions before showtime on how to engage with your contact."

"Fine."

"Great," Tawny said. "Thank you." She started to leave, but then she hesitated and turned around to face me. "You need to know that there's a risk—more than before. These women are known to intelligence officers here. If you're seen giving them contraband, it would implicate you directly in espionage."

"How is that any different than Bulgaria?"

"It's different because they're onto us now," she said. "In Bulgaria they suspected, but they didn't know. And they didn't know who Angel was, either, so we had some confidence that we could get away with an easy handoff."

"And you were wrong about that."

"We were." She nodded. "That's why I wanted to be up-front about the elevated risk here."

"Tell me the truth," I said. "Am I done after this? 'Cause the tour is over. And you said it worked."

Tawny shrugged, and I had to meet my ear to her lips to hear what she said next. "I'll tell you the truth," she said breathily. "I don't know. We'll have to see how things go over here. If the Curtain falls, we might need some help with messaging around rebuilding these countries in a way that works best for everyone."

Her hot breath on my ear distracted me, but what she was saying did not. This was exactly what I was afraid of. Project Facemelt had worked too well. They were never going to let us go.

"I want it to be over," I said.

"I know," she said. "I'm just being honest. I don't know what they're going to do. It's over my head. Mancuso's going to walk you through the handoff, okay?"

"Well, it's not exactly like I can say no, is it?"

Tawny's eyes dropped to the floor. "Rikki," she said, "can we talk?"

"Yeah, sure," I said, and turned and walked out of the bathroom, and then out of the hotel room entirely, slamming the door with Tawny still standing on the other side.

75

A MAN WITH a big belly and a bushy beard knocked on the door of an unmarked office building just a few miles east of the Stadion der Weltjugend in the Mitte borough of East Berlin.

A younger man opened the door. No words were exchanged. The older man handed the young man a sheaf of papers, and then he ambled off.

The young man flipped through the papers, nodding as he read the message they contained. On the third sheet, he stopped. This was it.

He stepped into the hall and closed the door, then took the stairs to the second floor of the building, passing guards posted on each stair landing and in front of each door of the newly set up facility near the Stadion der Weltjugend. All hands were preparing for the Whyte Python performance, making security especially tight inside. The young man passed numerous posted colleagues, earning their clearance one by one, until he reached a locked office door.

He knocked. General Kurt Becker opened the door.

"You need to see this," the young Stasi officer said. Becker welcomed him into the office. He yanked the papers from the officer's hand. "Page three," the younger man said. "Look at the VIP list."

Becker flipped through the pages until he landed on a sheet of paper with the Whyte Python logo on top. It was a short list of approved guests who would be allowed backstage during their concert at the Stadion der Weltjugend that night.

Becker nodded. He grinned and handed the papers back to his

officer. "Bring him in," he said.

The young officer left the room without saying another word. He stepped gingerly down the hall to another office and rapped his knuckles on the door, then took several steps back.

The door swung open, and a tall, mustachioed man with a razor-bald head stood fuming on the other side.

"What?" he demanded. The tall man's eyes were bloodshot, and veins bulged in his temples and down his neck.

"G-General Becker," the young man stammered. "He would like to see you now." He stepped aside and pressed his back against the wall as his fellow statesman, a full head taller, pushed past him and entered Becker's office without a knock. The bald man remained in the doorway, shoulders heaving. He said nothing.

Becker actually slid backward in his chair, a subconscious show of deference to the massive attack dog that had heeled in his doorway.

"Are you ready?" Becker asked.

"Yes," the man said.

"Good," General Becker said. He tossed the sheets of intelligence across his desk, keeping his hands safe on his side, as if he were feeding a shark. He smiled.

"The time has come. Eliminate Rikki Thunder."

76

W E WENT INTO the greenroom loose and happy, cracking
open a bottle of Jägermeister just as Spyderbyte took the
stage.

I had decided to put thoughts about Project Facemelt out of my mind for the time being. I mean, I knew I had a job to do before the show started, and it carried some risk—but I had been in scarier situations plenty of times over the past few weeks. Once I handed off the package to my contact, I could play the concert, get a decent night's sleep, and coast through the next day's public events before heading home.

The guys were pleasantly surprised by the small group of people with backstage passes. They were all women, they all spoke some English, and they all looked like European models.

Davy sat on the couch with a babe on each side, and they hung on his every word while he talked about life as a celebrity in California.

Spencer was hanging out with a girl in the corner, and it looked like she was teaching him some new dance moves. Buck and I played *Ice Hockey* on a Nintendo and drank whiskey while the groupies picked sides and cheered us on. The few locals that Tawny had managed to round up were fascinated by the gaming system and the Jack Daniels, because apparently neither was allowed there.

I wasn't sure who my contacts were. All I knew was that there were two of them, and at a certain point I would signal them.

I tried not to think about it, instead just focusing on the right combination of strong, average, and fast hockey players that it would take to defeat Buck. Every time one of us scored, the other had to take a shot. The score was tied at four, and we were teetering on the edge of getting shit-faced.

Fortunately, Spyderbite went into their last song before either Buck or I had the chance to score another goal. It was time. I tucked a cigarette between my lips and sparked a Zippo a few times but never lit it. That was the signal.

Right on cue, two women sat on the couch, one on either side of me. The one to my right was a redhead, and she never looked my way. The blonde on my left, though, locked eyes with me right away. I was surprised by the sight of her; Mancuso had said this spy was high up in the resistance, but I could see that, under the heavy purple eye shadow and blush and hair spray, she was really young. Maybe still in high school. Her eyes were hard, though. They looked like they had seen some shit. And they looked pissed.

"You are Rikki Thunder," she said.

"I am."

"Why do they call you this?"

"Because I bang on those drums like a thunderstorm, babe."

"I am Anja." She gestured at my lighter. "You should save your fuel."

"There's always more fuel if you have a big enough spark."

"What the hell are you guys talking about?" Buck said.

But I didn't need to say anything else. Anja and I had just successfully introduced ourselves to each other, through code. And we had given each other the all clear to complete the handoff. I took the cigarette from my lips and tucked it between hers.

Nobody else in the room would have been able to see the microscopic writing on the inside of the paper. Whatever was stuffed inside this thing, it wasn't tobacco. And when Anja got somewhere safe and unwrapped it, she would have whatever it was she needed.

"Have a good show," Anja said.

"Hey, Davy," I said. "Are we ready to chant?"

Davy spit whiskey in the air and waved his hands dramatically, clearing the room of everyone but the band. Anja and her friend blended in with the rest of the crowd, and they were gone. My job was done. All I had to do was get word to Team Facemelt that the handoff was complete, and my CIA responsibilities in the Eastern bloc were over.

"Huddle up!" Davy shouted. We met in a circle in the middle of the room and put our hands in the center, and Davy led the standard pre-show chant.

We confirmed that we were Whyte Python, that we were there to blow the roof off and get laid, and that Whyte Python never dies.

Then we banged heads together, and high-fived, and broke some bottles on the floor. Buck flipped the coffee table over. Spencer barfed. Davy kicked the door open.

"Let's go!" he shouted.

"Yeah!" I yelled, and then I made a big performance of patting myself down. "Oh shit," I said.

"What? What's wrong?" Davy asked.

"Nothing. Just my lucky shark-tooth necklace. I left it in that office down the hall when I used the phone earlier."

"Well, go fuckin' get it!" Davy said. "We got a house to shred!" And then he ran off down the hall, toward the stage. Buck and Spencer followed.

I stepped into the hallway just in time to see Buck vanish behind a black curtain to the holding space directly behind the stage. And then I turned the other way and walked down the dark hallway to an office at the end of the hall.

I took an extra look back down the hallway to make sure I was still alone and then stepped inside and closed the door behind me. It was a little room with a desk and a phone and a couple of steel chairs. There were soccer posters on the wall in frames. I dug into my pocket and took out my shark-tooth necklace and put it on.

Then I stood at the desk and picked up the phone. I dialed the number I'd memorized, waited for a series of beeps, then dialed a whole different number. A toneless switchboard operator answered.

"Moon Valley Travel Agency, how can I direct your call?"

"I need to speak to Mr. Robinson," I said.

"What is the call regarding?"

"The Edgewater account," I said.

"Connecting."

"Moon Valley," Mancuso said on the other side of the line.

"It's done."

"Roger. Any problems?"

But before I could answer him, there was a bang behind me. The door to the office had been kicked in.

There was a massive guy with a shaved head and a mustache standing in the doorway. He was at least six feet eight and jacked like Drago from *Rocky IV*. He looked kind of like one of those carnival strongmen, except his eyes were all bloodshot and he was holding an eight-inch-long combat knife. His face was red and twitchy, and he seemed very upset with me.

The guy stepped into the room and shut the door. Then he smiled like an alligator would smile, and he growled, "Fuck you, Rikki Thunder . . . Prepare to die."

77

I HAVE TO SAY up front that I appreciated how he went out of his way to threaten me in my native language, even though I was a visitor in his country. But "Prepare to die"? Not today, Hans Gruber!

I put my hands up in a clinch pose, like Mancuso had taught me to do if the shit ever went down. But Mancuso's advice for defending yourself against a knife was "You don't want to mess with a knife." So that wasn't terribly helpful or reassuring. And now I couldn't run, because the assassin moved in front of the door, and he came at me swinging his knife around.

I backed up as he swung within range. He just barely missed my throat and then just missed it again. This guy was not fooling around.

I was lucky that he was too mad to slow down a little, or I'd be dead. He swung one more time, and I could feel the breeze from the blade pass in front of my nose. I took another step back and bumped into the desk.

He had me pinned.

So I just kept the momentum going. I rolled backward over the desk and onto the floor, and I heard a thud over my head, which was the guy stabbing the desk right where I'd been a second ago.

And then I spotted it—a little metal trash can. It wasn't the same as a knife, but it was something. I knew I needed to move fast, so I grabbed the trash can and leapt to my feet, and I swung the thing just as he pried his knife out of the desk. My trash can connected with his hand.

"*Aiiieee!*" he yelled, as the knife flew across the room and bounced off the wall.

I swung the trash can backhand-style at his head, but now *I* missed, and Gruber grabbed my arm and twisted my wrist like a pro.

I turned my body with his momentum to keep him from breaking my wrist, dropped the trash can, and made a wedge with my other hand. I chopped the back of his neck and he let go of my hand, and then I swung my flat palm around and smacked him on the ear.

"*Scheisse!*" he screamed, and dropped to one knee.

I scurried around the room, putting myself between Gruber and his knife. I went into a defensive pose and started moving backward toward the blade, which was lying on the floor.

I saw the fear in his eyes as he realized two things at the same time.

One: I was a better fighter than he expected.

And two: I was about to get his knife.

He couldn't allow that, so he sprang to his feet and charged.

I scrambled backward and swept my hand on the floor behind me, hoping I'd get lucky and find the knife. No dice.

Gruber tackled me at the waist, and we both fell to the floor. I felt the knife lying flat under my back. He was on top of me, and he punched me in the ribs four times with his enormous hands.

I felt all the breath leave my lungs and wondered if the crack I'd heard was the sound of my ribs breaking. He got on his knees and straddled me, his hand immediately reaching for the knife under my back.

I planted a hand on his arm and then drove my forehead up into his nose. There was a loud, wet thwack as the cartilage splattered against bone, and a burst of blood. His hands went to his face.

I still couldn't really breathe, but I managed to bring my fists together and drive them into his sternum. Now he fell off me completely.

I got to my knees and sucked in a deep breath, then swept my hands across the floor for his knife. It wasn't there.

I didn't even bother to look at him. I knew he must have it. I hobbled behind the desk just as Gruber got to his feet. Blood was pouring out of his nostrils into his mustache and his mouth and down his chin, but he had the knife in an icepick grip and was coming at me again.

I grabbed the metal phone by its base and waited. He was too angry to be strategic now, and he was panicking because he could probably barely see me through the tears in his eyes. But that didn't mean he was any less dangerous.

Hans Gruber charged again, slicing air back and forth, and when he reached his end of the desk he leapt across it, blade out.

I stepped to the side, just in time, and brought the heavy phone base around. It was a big, ugly gray thing, and it must have weighed ten pounds. I connected against his ear again, which really fucking hurts.

He dropped the knife on the floor. I didn't bother going for it. Instead, I climbed on his back and wrapped the phone cord around his throat.

But even with all my weight on him, Gruber stood up like I was nothing at all. He tossed me off his back and started moving toward the knife again. I kicked at the back of his knee, and he dropped to the floor, then got up and hopped to the nearest wall. Just as I was about to attack, he took a thick-framed poster off the wall and shattered it over my head.

Everything went white for a second, then black. I dropped to the floor like a sack of potatoes, and then big hands flipped me over onto my back I felt a knee press against my stomach and thick hands around my neck. Squeezing tight, then tighter.

I had no air. He was strangling me. I opened my eyes and could barely see him through the saline blur. My vision was darkening.

I was about to die.

Then something crashed against his head, and his hands let go, and he fell off me. I saw a flash of blond hair and realized that Tawny had come to save me.

I rolled over onto my knees again and gasped for air. My windpipe sounded like grinding metal, and I was worried that he had broken something in there and I was going to die anyway. But I guess it was only because of the panic, because after a few seconds my airway opened back up and I was able to breathe. I wiped my eyes clean in time to see Hans Gruber push himself up to a crawl on shaky arms, just like me, his bald head bleeding. There was a broken glass vase on the floor next to him. He got to his feet and stumbled toward the desk.

For the knife.

He had it in a heartbeat and then turned toward his bigger risk in the moment—Tawny, still standing in the entrance like a deer frozen in the headlights. *Why wasn't she moving?*

But when my eyes focused, I realized it wasn't Tawny at all. It was Anja, the spy. She stood in the doorway, looking even younger now in this giant's shadow than she had before. Her jaw quivered, and her eyes looked equally pissed off and scared. I could tell she knew for sure that this guy would kill her if they fought, but she wanted to try anyway. Anja knew him from somewhere. That was clear. And she fucking hated him. Hans Gruber turned the knife over his wrist into an ice-pick grip again, and he lurched toward her.

Anja pulled her arms tight in front of her body and froze—not running, not doing anything to defend herself. She wasn't a ninja, like me. She wasn't trained for this. She had attacked him to save my life, without knowing what to do next. It was the bravest thing I had ever seen anyone do; and now she would be dead in a few seconds.

So I got to my feet and stumbled into the guy from behind, before he could reach her, and did the only thing I could think of: I jammed two fingers into the pressure point on his shoulder. It was the first trick that Mancuso had taught me, and I could do it blind if I had to. His arm collapsed, and he dropped to one knee, his whole body retreating from the sudden pain.

I landed on top of him and locked him in my sleeper hold. This guy was big and strong, and he fought back harder than all the dudes I'd practiced on in West Hollywood. But a throat's a throat, and if you put pressure on it in the right place, it stops the flow of blood to the brain, and you pass out—no matter how big you are.

Eventually I felt his movements get lazy and weak. And then he was out. He dropped onto the floor with me on his back. He still had the knife in his hand.

I climbed off the dude and looked at Anja. "You saved my ass," I gasped. "That was really brave."

Her chest was heaving and her arms shook, but she stared down at Hans Gruber with pure disgust. "Is he dead?"

He was very much not dead. I slipped the blade from his grip.

"Nope," I said. "He's gonna wake up in a minute or so."

"We should kill him, then."

Damn. I looked at her again. She was just a kid, basically. The things she must have seen, to hate this man like that. But it was a good point. If the situation was reversed, this motherfucker would slit both of our throats in a heartbeat. It was why he was there. He had just tried to kill me. If we gave him the chance, he would keep trying.

There wasn't room in this town for the both of us.

But the situation wasn't reversed. I wasn't going to kill some dude in his sleep, even if he would have done it to me. I tucked the knife into my belt. "You have a mission to finish," I said to Anja. She was still glaring at Hans. I rested a hand on her shoulder, and her eyes finally met mine. "Don't let this asshole slow you down. Go. I'll take care of him."

She nodded a silent thank-you, and I saw relief in her eyes. I had this kid pegged. She was hurt, and scared, and angry as hell—but she wasn't a killer, any more than me.

"Josef Wiedemann," she said.

I raised an eyebrow. "What?"

"He sold cigars, in my neighborhood, or he used to. He is a good man. This monster took him away and beat him. They closed his business, left him with nothing. All because he protected me. I didn't even know his name, didn't learn it until after they took him and it was too late." She gestured at the assassin on the floor. "And his name should be remembered, long after this animal is forgotten." She kicked Hans Gruber's foot. "Say his name to me, Rikki Thunder," Anja said. "And promise you'll remember it."

"Josef Wiedemann."

Satisfied, she headed for the door. "Whyte Python never dies," she said over her shoulder.

"*Wir sind ein Volk,*" I said back. And then Anja was gone.

I limped over to the desk and picked up the receiver. "Uh, yeah," I said. "One problem."

78

And we're all caught up! In case you don't remember, this is
where our story started.

I limp onstage, bleeding and paranoid. My eyesight is way
out whack, and I'm probably concussed pretty badly. I reject Buck's
offer to lick the blood off my face and get that massive cheer from the
audience that wipes the pain away. I start to play.

We finish "Till the Bell Rings" and start into "Detention." I can
see the eyes of my bandmates darting my way occasionally, trying to
figure out what the hell happened to me and if I might die onstage.
I'm actually feeling okay, aside from the headache, and the pain in
my ribs, and the fear.

Davy locks eyes with me. *You okay?* he mouths.

I nod. He raises an eyebrow, like he doesn't believe me. I realize
that I should probably get a drink of water and have somebody look
me over, so I gesture over my shoulder to the backstage area. Davy
nods.

Buck is observing all this. Now Davy gives him a nod, and he steps
toward the front of the stage.

"Shred it, Buck!" Davy shouts, and Buck launches into a complicated guitar solo.

We've broken from our choreography, and I can just imagine
the guys in the booth panicking. But they're pros, and before long
a spotlight finds Buck. The rest of the stage dims. Spencer keeps
the bass beat while Buck's guitar wails and whines. I get up from my
drum set and sneak backstage.

I grab a cold beer from a bucket and slip into the hallway. The door to the office is open, and I can see a familiar sight—the back of Tawny's head. I limp toward her.

"Oh my God, Rikki," she gasps. Her hands reach out to touch my face, and she hugs me. I feel a sharp pain in my side.

"Ooh, easy," I say. "I took a few shots to the ribs."

"Catherine," Tawny says, "he's hurt."

Stryker steps into the doorway. "Come in," she says. They lead me into the office. Mancuso and Boone are there. Stryker points a penlight in my eyes and ears, inspects the cut on my head and the bruise on my torso.

"The head wound is clotting. That's good," she says. "You should probably get stitches, but you don't have to go straight to the hospital. It looks like your ribs are bruised, but I don't think anything's broken. You got away all right."

"Gnarly," I say, and take a long pull from my beer.

"Although, Rikki, you probably have a concussion," Stryker says. "You shouldn't drink alcohol." But I am too busy drinking alcohol to listen to her.

"Did you get him?" I ask. "The guy?"

Mancuso crosses his arms. "There was nobody here," he says.

"*What?*" I say. "When did you guys get here?"

"Sixty seconds after you called us."

"No," I say. "There's no way he got away that fast. I hog-tied him with the phone cord after I hung up with you guys."

"Then he isn't here alone," Stryker says. "What did he look like?"

"He was really tall," I say. "Shaved head. Mustache. I broke his nose. Look, you gotta find Anja. She might be in danger if he's out there looking for her."

"Let's go," Stryker says to Boone. She taps a finger to her ear. "Get to the exits," she says to someone on the other end. "Suspect is tall, bald, mustache. His nose is broken. Assume armed. Boone and I are en route."

Stryker slaps the beer out of my hand, onto the floor, and then she opens the door and leaves, with Boone at her heels. With the door open, I can hear Buck, still shredding onstage. It sounds like he's playing the theme song to *The A-Team*.

"Do we stop the concert?" I ask. "'Cause otherwise I gotta get back out there."

"No," Tawny says. "You're safest onstage; they know better. The last thing they want is to make you a martyr in front of the crowd. Go play. It'll buy us time to find this asshole."

"Then what?"

"Then we go into hiding until we have clearance to get out of Dodge," Mancuso says. "We'll get new tail numbers on the jet. But that will take a few hours."

"New tail numbers?" I say. "Why would we need that?"

Mancuso and Tawny look at each other, then back at me.

"Like, because they would *shoot us out of the sky*?" I shout.

"Every precaution," Mancuso says.

"Brad, wait," Tawny says.

"Once we get the new numbers," Mancuso says, "we sneak the band to the airport, and we're wheels up the second everybody is on board."

"We still have work to do," Tawny says. "We're touring two schools tomorrow. And the peace rally, at the Academy of Arts. Do you know how hard it was to get permission for that?" She paces the room, wringing her hands. "I'll give it to you: it's too dangerous to go back through Checkpoint Charlie. But if we bail on everything now, they'll make us. We'll be done."

Mancuso looks at her like she's the one with a head injury. "We're made already," he says slowly. "Project Facemelt is over."

"Easy, now," Tawny says. "We don't know anything. It might have just been a crazy fan."

"Price, it's over."

Tawny shakes her head. "It's just *one more day*, Brad! Then we can keep the option, at least."

"No."

"Stryker already put out a BOLO to the roadies," Tawny keeps arguing. "The guy can't be far. If we catch him, we can find out how much he knows. Rikki—"

"I don't know, Tawny," I say.

Mancuso slaps his palms against the desk. "Her name isn't Tawny!" he shouts, then growls more quietly: "Her name is Amanda Price. She's an officer with the CIA—but she seems to have forgotten that.

Time to start acting like it, Price."

Tawny steps into Mancuso's personal space. "I am acting like it," she says. "We can save Facemelt. If we quit now, the program is over. Come on, guys, let's just wait—"

"What the hell are you talking about?" Mancuso says. "I told you, Facemelt is over already. This is the last nail in the coffin. We won."

"No, it's . . ." Tawny says quietly. Her face falls. Despite everything, her heartbroken sigh hits me hard.

Maybe it's the concussion, but I don't entirely understand what's going on here. She's so sad, even though her mission is a success. We won. Why bother with a couple of school tours tomorrow? Doesn't she want to go home?

Her eyes flit up at me, just for a second. Then they fall back to the floor.

And I get it.

It dawns on me that Tawny and I have more in common than I thought. I keep forgetting that her name is really Amanda Price, which has always felt like a prank she was pulling on me. But I don't go by my real name, either. Rikki Thunder is a name I gave myself, the alter ego I created so I could live like the person I felt like I was inside. I always assumed Tawny—Amanda—just created her fake name for work. But maybe it's more than that?

There have been too many times over the years when I've seen this joy in her eyes, something so real and pure that I don't think even the best spies could fake it. I fell in love with that joy at the Qyksand house, and saw it at concerts all the time, and definitely when we slept together in Budapest. So could there be more to "Tawny" than a job? I've only been thinking about her double life as a big con, a cold trick that she played on me.

But she's human. Maybe she found something precious in that new person, got used to living in that skin, and she just realized that she's about to vanish forever. How scary is that? How sad?

I feel my voice soften, and I search for her eyes with mine. I want her to see that I understand: if I'm alive tomorrow, I still get to be Rikki Thunder. But she has to be someone else. Tawny Spice will be gone.

I see her shoulders pull in close to her body. For the first time in

334 · TRAVIS KENNEDY

the years that I've known her, she looks . . . fragile.

"Hey," I say. "We had a good run, right?"

She doesn't say anything.

"Rikki, get out there," Mancuso says. "Finish the show. We'll have an exfiltration plan in place by the end of the encore."

I can hear Buck's solo in the distance, steering pretty far away from anything resembling music now. Mancuso is right—no matter what happens, I need to get back onstage.

I glance back and forth between them one last time. Tawny finally lifts her eyes to meet mine. "Rikki," she says. "Tear the roof off this motherfucker."

79

B UCK HAS CLIMBED the scaffolding above the stage.
He is at least twenty feet up now, digging pretty deep into his guitar solo. Bless his heart. He's doing this for me, stalling the whole concert so I could stagger offstage mid song for reasons that he will probably never ask about.

I creep onto the stage and take my seat. Buck is gyrating wildly and, lit by a single spotlight against the black scaffolding, he looks like he's flying. We all watch him in awe for a few moments.

I give some light taps to the high-hat to let everybody know I'm back. Davy glances at me and nods. I start with the kick drum. Buck steers his solo into something resembling a rhythm.

Now Spencer comes in with a consistent bass beat.

Davy joins in on rhythm guitar. "Buck Sweet, ladies and gentlemen!" he shrieks into the mic, and Berlin roars.

I drill down on the drums like a machine gun. Buck swings the guitar by its strap around his shoulders and leaps toward a cable. He catches it, and it snaps, and he begins to swing down toward the stage like Tarzan.

Then the cable snaps on the other side, too, and Buck plummets to the stage from twelve feet up and lands in a heap.

He doesn't move.

We keep playing.

Buck slowly reanimates as the crowd cheers him on. He gets to his feet, and one of his arms is hanging limp at his side.

Spencer strolls over, grabs Buck's wrist, and pops his shoulder back into place. Davy holds the microphone in front of Buck's mouth while he lets out a primal scream, and then he jams back in.

Buck Sweet, ladies and gentlemen.

We pick back up with our planned set. Like always, I direct all my pain and anxiety down my arms and out through the drumsticks, and by the end of the show I'm feeling just about as euphoric as I normally do. It was a pretty good concert, despite all the serious injuries and attempted murder.

It's only after the final explosions go off and we gather onstage, arms around each other's shoulders, waving goodnight to East Germany and the Whyrld Peace Tour, that Spencer bumps into my ribs and it feels like I'm being stabbed. I whimper, and Davy throws a suspicious look my way. Reality crashes back in.

It dawns on me that I haven't seen Tawny or Mancuso or Stryker or Boone since they pushed me back onstage two hours ago. I hope they're still alive. I'm in the lead as we climb down the steps at the rear of the stage and into the hallway.

My eyes scan the path ahead for friends or enemies. I only see Kirby, who is honestly not important enough to be either.

"Good show, gentlemen," he cheers.

"Thunder!" Davy roars from behind.

Right, I remember. *These guys are gonna need some answers.*

I turn and face them. "Davy," I say. "I'm sorry, bro."

"Don't bro me, bro!" Davy points at my bloody head. "You've got some explaining to do."

"You're right," I say. Just then, Tawny and Mancuso arrive. They both look pale and tired. They open their mouths to talk at the same time, but I hold a hand up to tell them, *Wait.*

"Anja?" I ask.

"Checked in," Tawny says. "With her people. She's okay."

"Phew."

"Excuse me," Davy says. "Attention over here, please? You practically beg us to go on this tour. You bring all these people along we don't know, you keep vanishing on us, and you tell us about some secret house that you have set up. You think we don't notice? Come on, Rikki. We all know what's going on here. Just say it."

The other guys nod. *Oh shit*, I think, *did they actually figure it out?* Maybe I haven't been giving them enough credit. "Okay," I say. I take a deep breath.

"You are trying to take over this band," Davy spurts.

"What?" I say. "No. No, Davy, that's not it, bro."

"Well, what is it, then?"

"All right, I'm gonna tell you guys everything."

"Rikki . . ." Tawny warns.

"No!" I make eye contact with each of the guys, one at a time. "They deserve to know, and you guys can deal with it. Guys, these people work for the government. Tawny's in the CIA. They're using our tour as cover to help out with the revolutions over here."

Nobody says anything for a moment. Eventually, Buck snorts.

"I thought she worked for a magazine," Kirby says.

"I thought she was a stripper," Spencer says.

"The CIA?" Davy asks. "Um . . . Holy fuck. Is this true, Tawny?"

Tawny stalls for a moment, exchanging a look with Mancuso. He shrugs. Tawny nods. "It's all over anyway," she says.

"So, let me get this straight," Davy paces the hall, looking back and forth between Tawny and me. "For, what, years now, you two have been manipulating our band, and putting us in danger every night on this tour over some kind of Cold War power struggle?"

"Yeah, man," I say. "I guess so."

"And you're not making a power play for creative control?"

"No," I say. It feels so good to tell the truth about all this. "Not at all."

Davy scratches his chin. "Well, that's actually a huge relief," he says. "But this CIA thing might be worse. I don't know! I'm gonna have to think about it. But I do think I'm pissed at you, brah!"

"I understand."

"This is awesome," Spencer says.

"No, it's not," Mancuso says. "Now listen. We have an exfiltration plan. There's a limo waiting out the back door that will bring you guys to the safe house."

"Okay," I say.

"The driver is one of our guys, and even he doesn't know where he's supposed to take you," Mancuso says. "The only ones who know the safe house location are you guys and Team Facemelt. Give him the address, and keep an eye on the streets. Right?"

"Right," I say.

"We'll meet you there," Tawny says. "We'll be providing cover."

"Cover for what?" Davy asks.

"Uh, yeah," I say. "A guy tried to kill me before the show tonight."

Davy and Buck both scream, "*What?*"

A second later, Spencer screams, "*What?*"

"Hopefully the cover is just an extra precaution," Mancuso says. "But we aren't taking any chances. Go."

80

ROADIES HAVE CORDONED off an area behind the stadium with the tour trucks, so nobody can see us leave the building and run into the open door of an idling limousine.

The driver is an older guy with a livery cap, but he speaks perfect, accentless English when he asks where we're headed.

I give him the address, and I try to recall the route that Tawny made me memorize backward and forward just in case. I am probably concussed, which we hadn't planned on; but I think I can remember how to get there if we run into any trouble.

"Come on, Rikki," Spencer says. "This is a joke, right? You're taking us to some cool underground party."

"No, buddy," I say. "Guys, I wish that was true. But we're in serious danger here. This mission was never supposed to touch the band, but something went wrong. Our cover got blown somehow. Now the bad guys know what we're doing, and they're pissed."

Davy's eyes light up. "This is so metal," he says.

"Dude, these East Germans don't screw around," I say. "And they do *not* want us going back to the U.S. and making them look like idiots "

We coast past the crowd of raging East Berliners as they pour out of the stadium. Buck has found a bottle of Wild Turkey in the car, and he begins to pour glasses for everyone. I hear a mechanical purr overhead, and when I look up, I see that the sunroof is opening.

"What the hell?" I shout. "Who's opening the sunroof?"

"I'm goin' up," Davy announces. "Whiskey me, bro." Buck tosses the bottle to Davy.

"No, dude!" I say. "Are you fucking crazy?"

Davy leans toward me. I can see fear and guilt in his eyes. "Rikki," he says somberly. "It. Is. A. Limo." He gazes up at the sunroof. "I have no choice."

81

⚡

PERCHED BEHIND SPOTLIGHTS on top of the Stadion der Weltjugend, Officers Brad Mancuso and Amanda Price watch through high-powered scopes attached to rifles as the band piles into their limo and the car rolls toward the exit. Officer Darrell Boone scans the crowd with binoculars. Price lets out a small sigh of relief.

"All clear," Boone says.

"Wait," Mancuso says. "They're opening the goddamn sunroof!"

All three sets of eyes drift to the limo, where the sunroof is, indeed, opening. Davy Bones emerges, holding a bottle of Wild Turkey, as the vehicle rolls toward the thousands of fans pouring out of the stadium.

The crowd takes notice and charges toward the car, which is the exact opposite of the effect that Team Facemelt had been hoping for.

"What the fuck is he doing?" Mancuso hisses as Davy raises his arms in the air, spraying booze out of his mouth and over his head, while the limo speeds toward the exit and the crowd chases after it.

Boone drops his binoculars and watches the scene unfold with awe. "He's partying," he whispers.

Price rolls her eyes.

"Jesus, Mary, and Joseph," Mancuso says.

"*Whyte Python never dies!*" Davy Bones shouts from below.

"So brave," Boone says.

"If Rikki can't get them to take this seriously, they all might die tonight," Mancuso says.

82

I KEEP THE PARTITION down between me and the driver, so we can communicate as the limo navigates the streets of East Berlin.

The guys are enjoying this way too much and drinking pretty fast. Only Kirby looks afraid. Every once in a while he tries to get the others to settle down and take our situation more seriously, but I finally tell him that it's definitely not helping.

Our safe house is a single-story office building in a quiet industrial neighborhood. My eyes scan the rooftops and windows of the surrounding buildings.

"Okay," I say. "It's right up here." I can see the building just up ahead, its front porch lit by a single light bulb. And I notice right away that even though I've pointed out where to park, the driver isn't slowing down.

"Dude," I say. "Did you hear me? It's right there."

The driver grips the wheel and stays on the gas. We drive past the safe house without slowing down, and fear grips my body.

We are being kidnapped.

"Fuck," I mutter, and I reach across the back row. I grab the half-empty bottle of whiskey from Buck, and I'm about to turn around to brain the driver before he can raise the partition and drive us straight into the clutches of the Stasi. But the driver speaks up first.

"Sit down—we have a tail!" he barks at me. I look in his rearview mirror and see a pair of headlights a few blocks behind us. "It's a black wagon. We picked them up a couple of miles ago, but I wasn't sure until now." He takes a right at the next intersection and guns the engine, letting the tail of the limo sway slightly before it rights itself.

The car behind us speeds up just as we vanish between two tall, gray buildings.

"Okay, listen," the driver says. "I'm gonna take us for a little ride. We're going to lose these guys just long enough for you all to ditch the car, and then I'm going to let them catch up to me again so I can lead them out of here."

"Bitchin'," Buck says. He points at the whiskey and snaps his fingers. I roll my eyes and hand the bottle back over.

We weave through the neighborhood, the car making wild turns and then driving at high speed between stops. He's clearly a pro. The guys who are following us drop back a little each time.

"We might not have time to totally stop," the driver warns us. "Once I find a good spot for you guys to hide, I'll get us down to five or ten miles an hour. Open the doors, tuck your arms against your head, and roll out. When you hit the ground, keep rolling. You'll be okay. Good?"

"When you say 'hit the ground'—" Kirby starts.

"Shut up, Kirby," Davy says as he rests his hand on the door handle.

"Here it comes," the driver says. I can see rows of tall manufacturing facilities ahead, built on both sides of the road. The driver points to a corner. If he turns left, he'll drive us across a little bridge over a culvert. "Once I straighten the car out in front of the bridge, everyone ditches. Then get underneath it. Got it?"

"Got it," I say. The boys look thrilled about this. Kirby looks terrified. I know already that I'm going to have to push him out of the car.

"Open the doors," the driver says. He steps on the gas again. The headlights behind us vanish. He cuts the wheel, and the tires screech as we take a hard left turn and cruise toward the bridge.

"Now!" the driver shouts. Davy pushes open his door and dives out, with Spencer right on his heels.

Buck does the same on the other side, and before I can get to Kirby to push him, Buck grabs his collar and yanks him out.

I'm last out the door, and I dive to the ground and roll, feeling the hard asphalt against my aching ribs. My head throbs. I see stars. Up ahead, the limo tears away. Behind me, yellow headlights paint the buildings along the road we just pulled off of.

I feel a hand grab the back of my vest and yank. It's Buck, pulling me to my feet.

Buck, Kirby, and I run to one side of the road and slide down under the bridge. Davy and Spencer do the same thing on the other side. I look back at the road just in time to see the tail car turn onto the street, and its headlights sweep across the bridge. I duck, and close my eyes, and pray that I didn't hide too late.

The car rumbles across the bridge overhead and follows the limo out of the neighborhood. I hold up a hand to the boys, telling them to wait, while I watch the taillights disappear around a corner.

"Now," I whisper. "Follow me."

The guys fall in line, and the backslapping starts. They still think this is fun. Spencer and Davy stand back-to-back like Charlie's Angels. Buck sips on the whiskey serenely, and when I thank him for pulling me out of the road, he shrugs like it was no big deal.

I shake my head, waiting for my double vision to fully correct, and then I look for a road sign. We navigate along the road with as much stealth as a bunch of guys in leather chaps and studded jackets with massive hair-sprayed manes are capable of, back toward the safe house.

When I find it, I call the guys in for a huddle.

"Okay, guys," I say. "We're gonna be all right. When we get inside, we're just gonna hunker down and wait for Tawny and the others to come in. I'm really sorry about this. I wish I didn't put you guys in this situation. But I wouldn't want to be in it with anyone else."

"All good, Rikki," Buck says.

"Yeah, this is fun," Spencer says.

"I can't stress enough that it's not," I say. Then I turn toward the safe house and climb the front steps. The guys are a few steps behind me.

I grab the doorknob and turn it, and as I'm pushing the door open, I get a tingling sensation that something is wrong.

I swing the door open and see six East German soldiers sitting on chairs inside. They're all startled and scramble to their feet. The one closest to me lifts a shotgun and points it at my face.

"Oh shit," I have time to say before slamming the door shut

and jumping to the side, just as a hole the size of my head explodes through the top of the door.

"What the fuck!" Davy screams, plugging his ears.

"It's not a party! It's not a party!" Spencer is shouting and running in little circles.

Buck throws his head back and laughs demonically.

I leap down the stairs. "Scatter!" I shout at the band. And then we run.

83

ONE LAST TIME, let's peek in on the soundtrack inside of Rikki
Thunder's mind!

"RUN FOR YOUR LIFE"
Music and lyrics by R. Thunder

You're in the devil's grip
You're on an acid trip
You know you're playin' with a
    loaded gun
You're dancin' in the fire
You're hangin' from a wire
You got no choice, boy, you
    gotta run!

Before the axe comes down
You gotta get outta town
You know you're skimming on
    the edge of a knife
You gotta shake and jive
You gotta stay alive
You gotta drop it all and run
    for your life!

(*Chorus:*)
Run for your life!
Run for your life!

Ruuuuuun for your life!
(You gotta . . . you gotta . . .)
Run for your life!
Run for your life!
Ruuuuuun for your life!

You're starin' down a train
You're circling the drain
You're out of options and
    you're full of regrets
You fell for all of their lines
About a thousand times
And now the devil's callin' in
    his bets!

This ain't no game or dream
They're gonna make you
    scream
You know you're skimming on
    the edge of a knife
You gotta dodge the fire

It's comin' down to the wire
You gotta drop it all and run
   for your life!

(*Chorus*)

(*Face-melting guitar solo*)

(*Chorus*)

We're all gonna die!

84

W<small>E CUT DOWN</small> a dark, narrow street, running as fast as we can.

Behind us we hear voices shouting in German, echoing off the vacant buildings. At our first opportunity to turn, we cut down an alley. There is a soft pop from behind us, followed by a loud ping as a bullet ricochets off a street sign back at the road.

The alley ends at a tall fence. We scale it two at a time, all of us huffing and wheezing from a life of partying and smoking and laughing at exercise.

When we get onto the other side of the gate and run through to the alley's exit, we find that we're on a private industrial campus that appears to be out of business. Tall buildings and smokestacks encircle a little concrete plaza littered with industrial waste. The entire park is ringed with a tall iron gate. It's an excellent place to hide, but a hard place to escape.

Voices close in on the other side of our alley. We have to move.

"This way," I whisper, and we tear across the plaza and turn to our right, toward a gap between a massive brick factory and a long, narrow two-story administrative building.

Davy slows down, grabs Kirby by the shoulders, and throws him to the ground. "Take him!" he shouts over his shoulder at the Germans.

"Davy!" Kirby yells as I help him to his feet, and we keep running.

We vanish into the passageway, ducking below pipes and trash chutes that run between the two buildings. The bad guys pop their heads into the open plaza, and they agree to split up in different directions to comb the place.

We creep toward the rear of the narrow alley that we're hiding in. It ends at a steel door into the factory, with the lock broken off.

There is a fire escape dangling overhead that leads to a window on the top floor of the office building. In this live-action version of a Choose Your Own Adventure novel, we have two choices: through the door and inside the big building, or up the ladder and inside the smaller one.

Everyone looks at me for instructions, as if I've done this before. I guess technically I have, but nobody ever gave me alley training or anything.

I forget that we're crouching because there are pipes and shit overhead, and I stand up fully to think. My head touches a pipe, and the heat singes my hair.

"*Aaaah!*" I wail. I touch the pipe. It's hot. Something is still operating in this place.

The bad guys are making a quick circle in both directions of the plaza. They will be on top of us any minute. We have to choose a path. The bigger building makes sense—there must be more places to hide in there.

"I got an idea," Buck says. "We're going in the office building. Go up the fire escape, and in the window. We'll find a way out the other side."

Nobody argues. We line up and climb the fire escape to the second floor, where the window is unlocked. Down below, Buck leans his shoulder into the door that leads into the bigger factory building and pushes until it groans open.

The squealing metal might as well be a jet taking off. We hear scrambling across the plaza as the East German Army runs toward the alley.

Buck backtracks toward the same pipe I'd burned my hair on a moment earlier. He jumps into the air and kicks the pipe, over and over, and it bursts just before the bad guys arrive.

Hot steam sprays into the alley, masking everything that is going on behind it like a smoke bomb.

Buck scrambles up the fire escape and into the office building where we're hiding, and we run through a small clerical room and down the hall, all the way to the other side.

The Germans must have taken the bait after fighting through the steam and finding an open door to the factory, because it looks like they've vanished into it, and we don't hear them enter our building. Buck tricked them into going the other way.

Buck Sweet, ladies and gentlemen!

At the far end of the administrative building, we pile into the stairwell and run down to the first floor.

"Look for a door that goes out back," I call out to the guys. "It might take us out of this whole compound."

We spread out across the building looking for an exit. Kirby finally finds it, in the back of a kitchen. The door is locked, but given that everything in this place is rusted and warped, we give it a few kicks, and—abracadabra!—it pops open.

Now we are outside, and beyond the fence. Amazingly, we've escaped the manufacturing site altogether. A long, dark road stretches ahead, lined with concrete buildings and rusted cars, many with no tires.

"Keep going," I say. "We don't have much time."

We run. We're all exhausted and terrified, but we keep our legs moving. We make it a few hundred yards down this strange, long road before headlights sweep across us and cast skinny shadows twelve feet high on the industrial-gray stone walls. Lit from behind by the spotlight, our massive hair is distorted against our skinny bodies, and we look like silhouettes of palm trees flailing in a hurricane.

There is a vehicle behind us, barreling down.

"I got an idea," Spencer shouts, which everyone responds to with some skepticism. "Gimme the whiskey," he shouts at Buck. Buck gives him the bottle. "Now keep running," Spencer demands.

He yanks a silk scarf from around his neck and pours Wild Turkey on it.

A van appears down the street, gaining fast. Right behind it, a small car. The road is narrow, and there's nowhere for us to hide.

"Spencer, come on!" Davy shouts.

"Wait!" Spencer yells. Then he runs to the closest car and stuffs the scarf into the gas tank. He takes a lighter from his pocket and lights the scarf. And then he runs as hard as he can.

Behind Spencer, the car explodes just before the van reaches it.

Tires squeal, and the van breaks hard to the left. It hits the corner of the sidewalk at thirty miles an hour and flips over, crashing roof first into a building.

Spencer Dooley, ladies and gentlemen!

"Spencer, you're a genius!" I shout. "Guys! Scarves!"

We all scramble to pull scarves off, and Spencer douses them with what's left of the whiskey. We spread out across the road and stuff gas tanks as a second car closes in and slows down to navigate past the crashed van and the exploded car. We light our scarves and run.

I like to imagine a sick guitar solo playing as we run in slow motion, backlit by the explosions that begin to fire behind us. Some of our exploding cars set off chain reactions as other cheap junkers with leaky oil pans and gas tanks catch flame and blow.

Our attackers either are stuck on the road or have exploded— either way, we have some space to escape now. We pause just long enough to exchange an epic five-way high five, and then we keep on running.

85

⚡

WE RUN UNTIL we're in a commercial neighborhood with some traffic. I choose a small business park, just a single story of small businesses in a straight line, because it looks easy to hide in and hard to sneak up on. I use the empty bottle of Wild Turkey to smash open a window, and we creep inside.

We're in a little office, with a reception desk and two smaller offices in the back.

"No lights," I say. "Everyone, stay low to the floor."

We crawl to one of the rear offices, where we can keep an eye out the window, and we all collapse onto the floor. We're silent for several minutes while we catch our breath. When the wheezing finally stops and everyone has a minute to think, Davy breaks the silence.

"Thunder," he says. "What the fuck have you gotten us into?"

"Dude, I'm so sorry," I say. "None of this was supposed to happen."

"So, what are we going to do now?" Kirby asks, and it's such an important question that nobody tells him to shut up.

"I'm gonna call in the cavalry," I say. I take the phone from the desk and pull it down to the floor. I check for a dial tone and find one. I dial.

The same switchboard operator answers. "Moon Valley Travel Agency, how can I direct your call?"

"I need to speak to Mr. Robinson," I say.

"What is the call regarding?"

"The Edgewater account," I say.

"Connecting," the voice says, and then silence. There's a staticky sound, followed by a few clicks. And then I hear Tawny.

"Moon Valley," she says. There's a hopeful edge to her voice.

"It's me," I say.

I hear her blow out a deep breath. "Rikki, thank God," she says. "What happened?"

"We got sabotaged," I say. "There were guys waiting for us at the safe house."

"Dammit," Tawny mutters. She lowers her voice. "That confirms it. We have a mole. Where are you guys?"

"We're safe," I say. "For now. We're hiding out. Did you figure out who it is?"

"Just listen," she says. "Don't say anything, okay? Somebody very close is feeding information to the Stasi."

"What's going on, bro?" Davy asks. I shake my head and hold up a finger.

"Hold on," Tawny says. I hear a door close. "It's just me and Mancuso now. We're running through a list of everyone who could know the things that have leaked. The control room in Hungary, the band's schedule, the handoff in Sofia, the safe room. The problem is, it's a really short list."

"Rikki?" Spencer asks.

"Don't tell them what's going on," Tawny says. "Not yet."

"Why not?" I ask.

"Because they're all on the short list," she says.

I roll my eyes. These guys didn't even know we were working with the CIA three hours ago. *Fuck this*, I decide. *They deserve to know.*

"Somebody is leaking to the Germans or whatever, you guys," I announce to the room.

"Rikki!" Tawny shouts.

"We all just got shot at, chased across the city, and almost run over," I say to Tawny. "They're not in on it. They just found out about it. And they deserve to know what's happening. So, who's your leak? Because it's not Whyte Python."

"Oh!" Davy says. "Well, it's Kirby, obviously."

Everyone turns to look at Kirby. He holds up his hands, and his eyes dart back and forth.

"It's not a bad theory, Rikki," Tawny whispers into the receiver. "He didn't know we're CIA, but he must have known somebody was pulling strings at the label." Buck crawls across the floor toward Kirby with murder in his eyes.

"He had access to all the information you guys had," Tawny says. "And honestly, who can blame him? You all treat him like shit."

"Dude," I said. "The CIA thinks it's him, too."

"No!" Kirby shouts.

I can't believe it. Kirby! Now that I think about it, this explains his hushed phone calls, and insisting on riding the bus just to collect information, even when he's being abused constantly. I assumed he was just tattling to Andromeda—but no. He has been floating around right under our noses, spying on us all this time, and feeding our shit to the enemy. I regret being nice to him that one time. Davy grabs Kirby's collar. Buck grabs his legs.

"Wait!" Kirby shrieks. "Wait, wait, wait! It can't be me!" Spencer covers Kirby's mouth with his hands.

"Find out what he knows," Tawny says.

"Hang on," I say. "Let him talk."

"He's licking my hand," Spencer says.

"Let him go," I say. "You're going to keep your voice down," I say to Kirby. "Or we're going to kick your ass. Understand?" He nods. I hold up the receiver so Tawny can hear. Spencer takes his hand away.

"Think about it," Kirby says, his voice shaking. "How could it be me? I didn't know where the safe house was. I never know anything. You kick me out of the room before you make any decisions. I don't even know Buck's real name!"

"Is that true?" I hear Tawny's tinny voice through the handset. I hold it to my ear. "Did he know where the safe house is?"

I try to remember. I had told them the address once, and I assumed nobody was paying attention. It was a sore spot, and we were getting along so well afterward, and they agreed to stick together, so I never mentioned it again. That was in the limo in Poland.

I had kicked Kirby out of the limo.

"Did I kick him out of the limo before or after I told everyone about the safe house?" I ask the room.

Blank stares look back at me, except for Kirby. "Before!" he shouts.

"Shhh," everyone whispers.

"I think he's right, Rikki," Tawny says. "I think it was before.

And besides, he couldn't have known about your handoff mission in Sofia . . . It's not him."

"It's not Kirby, you guys," I say. "He's not important enough to be the leak.

"And that means Whyte Python is in the clear," I say to Tawny. "Because it wasn't me, and it wasn't Kirby, and the other guys didn't know anything. So you've got some explaining to do, Tawny."

"What?" she says. "Why?"

"Because you have a snitch on your team."

86

THAT'S IMPOSSIBLE," Amanda Price says. "We can't have a leak. Almost nobody in the CIA has access to all the information. Pieces, sure, but not all of it. The only ones who knew the address of the safe house were the band and Team Facemelt."

"Okay," Rikki Thunder says over the phone. It is not an agreeable "okay." It is an "okay" that sounds like an accusation.

"No," she says. "Not possible. Everyone on Facemelt is a career officer with unquestionable loyalty." But Amanda Price has suspected that isn't true for some time now.

She hasn't wanted to admit it, but since the sabotage in the sound booth back in Hungary, she has been watching her team through skeptical eyes. An agency leak made more sense than a band leak. And her bullshit meter went sky-high when Stryker dismissed the idea of a mole out of hand.

In fact, Amanda's mentor on Team Facemelt was also the most likely suspect. She had spent the most time with Amanda, working on logistics in the States and then carrying out operations together on tour. She knew the most about the operation from the inside out. Amanda could hear Stryker's voice echoing in her head, in that bar in Portland, complaining about the purpose of the mission. About what would happen to the Eastern Bloc if they reprogrammed the whole region to look like Whyte Python.

Then there was Boone. This seemed impossible; the man had the longest service record out of all of them, even Lonsa, and he had become so obsessed with the mission that he was talking about retiring early and starting a band. He bled Project Facemelt.

But this was also Boone's MO. Everyone knew that. He was kind of a legend—the guy who gets way too deep into his mission.

Christ, Amanda thinks, suddenly picturing Boone as a withdrawn and power-hungry Kurtz in a war-torn Congo. Or what if he had become a double agent? If he was turned, he would sink so far into character that nobody would ever see it. Darrell Boone could be the best double agent to ever live. Unlikely, but—

"I don't know what to tell you," Rikki says, cutting off her frantic thinking. "It didn't come from us, so it had to come from your team. So you gotta think. Who would want this mission to fail?"

But that's the thing. Stryker said it herself: it's better than leaving things the way they are. She wanted Project Facemelt to succeed. *She's a true believer*, Amanda thinks. *It can't be her.*

"Nobody . . ." Price says, but her voice fades. It's all so much simpler than she was making it. It's not Stryker. It's definitely not Boone.

And then her eyes settle on Senior Officer Brad Mancuso.

"What?" Mancuso says.

"Oh my God." Amanda's eyes harden.

It's him.

Mancuso tilts his head slowly. "Price, what is it?"

He tanked the mission because he doesn't agree with it. He considers himself to be the only Eastern Bloc expert.

"Nothing," she says. She remembers him scribbling notes in the board room that he didn't want anyone to see. Hovering outside the door, listening in. "Just, Rikki doesn't think the band could have a leak."

Mancuso crosses his arms. She sees a vein throbbing in his neck. "Yeah, of course he doesn't."

Be cool, she thinks. *Don't let on.*

"Brad," she says carefully.

He saw the agency shifting away from his brand of fieldwork. So he sabotaged us. He didn't think we'd figure it out.

But Mancuso is good at reading people. He probably knows exactly what Amanda is thinking. *If he knows I'm onto him, he could kill me right now. Frame me for it. It would be easy.*

Is he onto her? Is she right? It could make the difference between whether they're about to fight to the death or not. He looks over his shoulder at the closed door behind him and takes a step toward Amanda. *Fuck.*

"Price," he says carefully, "think about what you're about to say. You're on the edge of accusing a superior of treason."

"I'm not accusing anyone of anything." *Your budget was vanishing,* she thinks. *You were going extinct. You wanted to press the reset button.*

Mancuso takes another step closer. Amanda puts up her hands, like she's prepared to push him off.

"I think you are," Mancuso says, his voice low and controlled. "I can see it in your eyes. Careful, now, Amanda. I've been working on breaking up the Eastern Bloc since you were in kindergarten."

"I'm not saying anything." She tries to keep her voice calm, too, but she can hear it wavering just a little. She knows Mancuso hears that, too. He's trained to. "But at this point we should probably pull in the DD."

"No," Mancuso snaps back. He hangs his head and sighs. "Look—you're right. There are aspects of this mission that I haven't been honest with you about."

⚡

87

I THINK TAWNY has forgotten I'm still on the phone. I hear this argument building between her and Mancuso, and I feel betrayed yet again.

I know Mancuso hated this job and resented me for being in the middle of it. But I did everything he told me to do. I studied his boring history lessons, memorized languages and maps, and practiced choke holds and hip tosses and pressure-point attacks and slap fights until my whole body was sore and bruised. And I had bailed the CIA out, like, twenty times on the Whyrld Peace Tour.

"It's gotta be him," I say into the phone. "'Cause it's like you said. *Nobody* knew about the safe house except for the band and you guys."

"And my friend Kevin," Spencer chimes in.

I turn to face Spencer. "What did you say?"

"Wait," Tawny says through the receiver. "What did he say?"

"Kevin." Spencer smiles. "You know, my best friend. We talk about everything."

I feel the receiver slip out of my hand and drop onto the floor. All the weird shit that we've heard about Kevin comes to me in a series of flashbacks.

Spencer telling us that Kevin wanted to design the band's outfits.

Tawny telling me that Kevin sent someone over to try out for drums.

Buck asking why none of us have ever met Kevin.

And now that I think about it, there were some other red flags that we'd been tuning out and I haven't even bothered to mention to you guys, because they didn't seem important. Like Spencer telling us he didn't know where Kevin lived, and that Kevin spoke a bunch of languages, and that Kevin bought him a radio that was always making weird sounds, even when it was unplugged, and that Kevin was always saying that the Russians "really have it figured out." Honestly, when he said those things, it all just made Kevin sound too bizarre to be a real person.

Shit.

"Spencer," I say. "Did you tell Kevin the address for the safe house?"

Spencer doesn't even hesitate. "Yeah," he says. "He was *super* interested in that!"

"Find out the number he called," I hear Tawny say through the receiver on the floor.

"Okay, dude," I say. "What phone number did you call him at?"

Spencer looks confused. "I didn't have to call him," he says. "He's here."

"Uh-oh," Davy says.

I grab the receiver from the floor and shove it toward Spencer, who is still smiling innocently. "Spencer," I say. "Would you tell Tawny everything about Kevin? Right now?"

But before Spencer can take the phone from my hand, the door bursts open. Men in Stasi uniforms pour in, one after another, filling the room. They lift their guns and point them at us.

Hammers click back. We can do nothing but put our hands in front of our faces and wait for the firing squad to begin.

"*Nein!*" a voice calls from the back. There is commotion in the crowd of soldiers as someone pushes his way to the front.

It's the giant carnival strongman who I fought in the office back at the stadium, the one I thought of as Hans Gruber. His nose is taped, and he has two black eyes.

"Hey, there he is," Spencer says. "Kevin!" He stops to think, and then his eyes light up. "Wait, dude, are you here to save us?"

I sigh. "He's here to kill us."

Kevin holds up a hand to halt the men.

He leans in toward me, close enough that I can see the bloodshot veins in his eyes. "No, Rikki Thunder," he grumbles in English. "Our orders have changed. We take you alive."

I lift the receiver. *"We're in an office park a mile away from the safe house,"* I manage to shout before a rifle butt crashes into my face. The world goes black.

88

I NOTICE THE pain first.

I'm waking up with a screaming headache. My ribs are sore, and my legs are burning. I'm lying in the fetal position on a concrete floor. I open my eyes.

I'm inside a jail cell. Davy, Buck, and Spencer are in here with me, all awake and sitting with their backs against the wall. I push off the floor, feeling a sharp pain in my side when I turn onto my butt and sit.

"Where are we?" I ask.

"Jail somewhere," Davy says. "They put hoods on us. It was a long ride."

"How long was I out?"

"A couple of hours," Davy says.

I probably had a concussion already, and Kevin just gave me another one. I'm lucky to be alive, for however much longer. "Where are we?" I ask again.

"I think we're in the woods," Buck says. "I heard an owl when they brought us in."

"They didn't knock you guys out?"

"Nope." Davy actually smiles a little. "That was just for you."

I can't believe this is happening. As much as the Facemelt team had warned me that this was serious, that I had to be careful, that these people would not go easy on me because I'm a celebrity, it never completely sank in until now.

We're in a little windowless cell, lit by a dim greenish bulb on the ceiling. The room is split in two by old-school bars, with us on one side and a guard sitting at a desk on the other side. He has his back to us, and he's watching a little black-and-white TV. There's a toilet in the middle of the cell, but nothing else. No benches or water. No phone on the wall.

It's more like a cage in a basement than a cell in a real jail, which is terrifying. Buck said he heard an owl; we're probably in the middle of the woods, in a basement where nobody will ever find us.

"I guess I deserved it," I say, and I see no sympathy from my friends. "Hey, you guys. Again, I'm so, so sorry I got you in this. I was just trying to help people."

"Enough fucking apologizing, Thunder," Davy says to the ceiling. "Just cut the bullshit. You were helping yourself."

"No, dude," I say. "The revolutions—"

"Right!" Davy cuts me off. "The revolutions! They lined up nice with you quitting your little garage band the first chance you got, didn't they? They lined up nice with you getting rich and famous. You say you're our friend, but you knew all this crap was dangerous, and you never told us. Some friend."

Now I was getting pissed, too. "Don't go there, Davy," I say. "You've put the band in danger before, too. You stole the tour bus in Boston and left us in a parking lot so you could play street hockey with Kip Winger. Everyone in this band has done stupid shit."

"I brought that white python that almost killed me on the plane and didn't tell you guys," Buck says.

"Fine," Davy says. "Proves my point. You strut around here like you're better than us. Just admit it, Rikki. You're as selfish as every other guy in this room."

"Fine," I say. "I'm a dick. I admit it."

Spencer's head hangs. "This is all my fault," he says to the floor.

"No," I say, putting a hand on his shoulder. "No, it's not. I got us in this situation. I brought us on the tour. They sent Kevin after you to get to me. Don't blame yourself. Blame me."

Spencer looks up at me, confused. "But I met Kevin before you joined the band," he says.

"You did?"

"Yeah," Spencer says. "Like, a year before."

"Huh," I say. *That's strange.*

"You never told us Kevin is a scary, hulking German dude," Davy says.

"That's because you guys never ask any questions about him!" Spencer spits back. "Anyway, it turns out he's not much of a friend, so joke's on Spencer, right?"

Nobody says anything to that. The joke kind of is on Spencer, after all. In the silence, I realize we had gone straight into fighting so fast that I didn't notice someone was missing.

"Wait," I say. "Where's Kirby?"

"Oh, right," Davy says. "Well, the thing about Kirby is, he wouldn't shut up. He kept saying he wasn't in the band, and he hates us, and he didn't really care about the Cold War, either, and he would tell them whatever they wanted to hear if they would just let him go."

"Yeah, so we got pissed and tried to pin the whole thing on him," Buck says.

"Right," Davy says. "Then he really starts freaking out, and the German guys had heard enough from him, so . . ."

"Oh no," I whisper.

"Huh?" Davy says. "Oh, dude, they didn't kill him. Even though we told them they probably should, or else he was never gonna shut up. But I guess it wasn't worth burying the body or whatever, because they just opened the door and told him to leave."

"Oh, thank God," I say. If Kirby is running free out there, we have a chance. "He got away. Maybe he'll make it to a phone."

"Yeah, he got away into the Black Forest, like Hansel and Gretel," Buck says. "When they opened the door, I heard wolves howling."

"He tried to come back in," Spencer says.

"Yeah, I wouldn't exactly count on Kirby to save the day," Davy says. "Just be glad he's finally gone."

I have nothing to say to that. I guess I am glad he's gone. I lean toward Davy and gesture over my shoulder toward the guard, then whisper, "What did you tell them?"

Davy shrugs. "Nothing," he whispers back. "They didn't ask us anything."

Relief washes over me. They're pretty sure about me, but they don't suspect the band. And so long as nobody says the letters *C*, *I*, or *A*, we might get out of this alive.

THE WHYTE PYTHON WORLD TOUR · 365

"Nothing from Tawny?" I ask.

"No sign," Davy says.

I lean back against the concrete wall and close my eyes. "I'm sure she's working on getting us out of here," I say. "Sit tight, guys. Face-melt will take care of this."

89

THE MEMBERS OF Project Facemelt gather around an expensive PictureTel video conference screen networked into their undisclosed location in West Germany. Amanda and Boone hover over maps of Berlin and the surrounding area while Stryker and Mancuso make phone calls to resistance contacts, trying to determine where the Stasi might be holding the band.

Deputy Director Lonsa appears on screen, and right away he scowls at the pile of maps and documents on the table in front of Team Facemelt.

"What is all that?" he asks.

"We think they're at Waldsiedlung," Price says, referencing the forest camp that serves as a housing settlement for leaders of the German Democratic Republic. Located in the woods outside of East Berlin, it is remote and guarded.

"Who is at Waldsiedlung?" Lonsa asks. "Do you mean Whyte Python?"

Amanda wrinkles her nose. "Of course I mean Whyte Python," she says. "The West Germans have provisionally agreed to lend us an operations chopper, but first they need a formal request to come from the secretary of defense or higher. Might as well go straight to the White House, because you'll need to ask the president for a SEAL team to help with exfiltration. We don't have much time."

"Hang on, hang on." Lonsa holds his hands in the air. "Navy SEALs? Have you lost your mind, Price?"

Amanda stops flipping through maps and looks around the room. Mancuso and Stryker hang up their phones. Amanda notices pained expressions on their faces. They understand something that she doesn't. She tries to make eye contact with Boone, but he keeps his eyes down on the table. He snaps a pencil in half and shakes his head.

"We can't just leave them . . ." she says.

"This was a covert CIA operation," Lonsa says. "We can't tip our hand about Project Facemelt with a raid, for Christ's sake. If we sent a team of SEALs in there guns blazing, we're creating an international crisis. Rikki Thunder understood the risks. We're not gonna start a hot war over Whyte Python twenty minutes before the Cold War ends."

"Well, what do we do, then?" Price asks.

"We wait," Lonsa says. "Especially if Thunder is talking. If the Stasi claims that they have a CIA operative, we have to deny Rikki Thunder's involvement as hard as possible. Eventually they'll decide he's full of it, and they'll probably just cut the band loose. Otherwise, if the Wall actually falls, they'll be looking for every bit of collateral they can scrape together to negotiate. Whyte Python might be a pretty valuable commodity sometime next year."

"Yeah, if they don't kill them," Boone says.

"Don't be dramatic, Boone," Lonsa says. "They'll hold them. Probably interrogate them. It might not be comfortable for these boys, but Thunder only knows so much, and he can't prove any of it. We all agreed to the policy here. We deny any connection to Whyte Python. And we sure as hell don't storm the gates to pull them out."

"DD—" Price said.

Lonsa holds up a hand to silence her, and even through the screen it sends a chill through her body. "What if they retaliate?" he says. "And besides, we'd have to admit the whole thing, and that would be a humiliating black mark on the entire apparatus."

"So we leave them rotting in a jail cell," Price says. "To get tortured until Rikki gives up our names, all the details of our operation."

"And then we deny," Lonsa says. "And Thunder looks crazy, and they show him the door. It's better for the band, Price. If we ask them to send the band back, we're admitting that we had them in the first place. They'll tear those guys apart one toenail at a time for information."

"But—"

"Look," Lonsa interrupts. "Whyte Python is the most famous band in the world. They can't vanish for long. They'll get charged with some bullshit. They'll sit in a cell for a while. Whoever's holding them will get tired of them eventually and let them go."

"Or they'll stage a plane crash," Mancuso says. "It's a clean way to kill them off. They went the way of the Big Bopper."

"Really, Brad?" Lonsa says.

Mancuso shrugs. "I'm just saying, I know how these guys operate."

Lonsa takes a deep breath and stands. He paces the room. Everyone waits for him to speak.

"All right, gang," he says. "I don't like it, either. But if that's what happens, we all agreed that four glam rockers are acceptable collateral damage for a mission of this scale. This is the way we do things. Anyway, you're wheels up to the states in an hour. And get those expense forms in to me by the end of the week. Accounting is up my ass sideways on this one. We went way over our jean jacket budget."

"DD—" Mancuso says.

"Jesus Christ, Brad!" Lonsa actually raps his knuckles against the screen. "You're getting what you want! I put in for it this morning, a plum assignment in Moscow. Your own office, probably! You're all getting letters of commendation. You'll be back in the real rotation tomorrow!"

Amanda Price levels her gaze on Brad Mancuso. With all that has happened, she forgot about something he said in Berlin just before the Stasi captured Whyte Python. *What were the words, exactly?* she thinks. *"There are aspects of this mission that I haven't been honest with you about."*

"What's he talking about, Brad?" Amanda says.

"Shit," Lonsa says.

"What does that mean, DD?" Price turns to her boss. "Back in the *real* rotation?"

Lonsa blows out steam. He holds his palms to the ceiling. "Do I really have to explain it?"

Everyone sits quietly for several seconds. Mancuso crosses his arms and looks down at the table. His face is red.

"Wait," Amanda says. "Is this some kind of side project? Is this disciplinary?"

"He's not supposed to say," Mancuso says.

Stryker crosses her arms. "What's my offense?" she asks, matter-of-fact.

Lonsa shrugs. "Classified."

"I figured it was the toilets, right?" Stryker slaps the table. "Well, that's a load of—"

"You knew?" Amanda cuts her off, swiveling to face down her mentor. "And you never said anything?"

Lonsa scowls. "What part about being in the CIA don't you get?"

"Amanda—" Stryker says. Her voice is gentle, in a way that only makes Amanda angrier. She cuts Stryker off again, turning on Boone instead.

"How about you, Darrell? Did you know?"

Boone shrugs. "I mean, I guess I figured," he says. "I've spent most of my career on discipline. Doesn't mean I don't work hard."

"At least Boone and I haven't been tattling the whole time," Stryker says, her glare focused on Mancuso now.

"Easy now," Lonsa warns. "Mancuso was reporting to me on my orders."

Amanda looks at Mancuso. His ears are the color of a fire engine. "He was doing what?"

"How did you figure it out?" Mancuso says under his breath, his eyes still on the table.

"Oh, come on, Brad," Stryker says. "Taking your little notes all the time, listening in on our conversations. I heard every word between you two at the La Brea Tar Pits."

"You were following me?"

"Give me some credit," she says. "I've suspected we had a leak for more than a year. I thought you were the mole."

Mancuso finally looks up. "I thought *you* were the mole."

Amanda faces Stryker. "Why the hell didn't you say anything in the sound booth when I told you my suspicions?"

"I was conducting an investigation," Stryker says. "And by then, I thought it might be you."

Mancuso shrugs. "So did I."

Lonsa presses his forehead against the screen. "Oh my God," he mumbles.

"So this is all a big joke," Amanda says. "To punish us for reasons we aren't allowed to know about. And now Rikki and the band are gonna get tortured or killed."

"It's not a joke," Mancuso says. "It's a real mission."

"Don't." Amanda points across the table at him. "I expected better from you."

Lonsa takes his glasses off and drops them in his lap, then rubs his palms down his cheeks. "Price," he says. "This project has cost us millions of dollars over half a decade. Does that sound like a joke to you? We gave it a try. It worked better than we expected. That's a credit to you and your team. As I said, you can all walk away from here with plum assignments."

Now Lonsa's expression darkens to something cold and stern, and his electrified voice lowers. He points at the screen. "Or not. So you'd better think really hard about where you want to get assigned next, before you say another word. You have limitless talent and zero respect for authority. Those two qualities don't get along. You're young. You still have time to get in line, kiddo. But not much."

Amanda stands in the middle of the room, speechless. They all are. Finally, Boone takes a deep breath. "You guys liked my song, though, right?" he says softly.

Lonsa sighs. "I don't know, Boone. I'm more of a Steely Dan guy."

90

I'M PRESSED AGAINST the bars of our cell, snapping my fingers at the guard sitting behind the desk.

We have been here for around three days now. This is my best guess, based on the guards changing shifts. They've given us stale bread and water, but we have not seen the sun, and the light bulb overhead never turns off. Nobody has spoken to us, including the guards. They just sit at the desk with their backs to us and watch TV.

"Hey, man, you like money?" I call out to the guard. I haven't seen this one before, so I figure it's worth a try to bribe him. "How much is ten grand in American cash worth in Germany? All yours, my man. Just let me make one phone call. I'll give you twenty if you open the door and let us walk out."

The guard doesn't react. None of them have. I actually don't know if these guys speak English.

"Where are your buddies, Rikki?" Davy calls over my shoulder. He has not taken off his sunglasses in two days. "'Cause it's been a while," he taunts. "I thought they were gonna have our back."

"I don't know," I say.

Davy shakes his head and tucks his hands under his armpits. "I can't believe you fell for their bullshit, man. What, did they tell you you'd be a hero? Put you on the dollar bill or something?"

"Go easy on him," Spencer says. "I got tricked, too."

"The difference is, he was in on it," Davy says, pointing at me. "He wanted to be the Greatest American Hero."

Buck says nothing. He has been sitting in a meditative state with his legs crossed and sweat rolling down his cheeks from his forehead since sometime yesterday. Once in a while he trembles for a few seconds and then stops. In the time that we've been here, he has grown a full beard. I'm not sure if he's awake.

Spencer thinks we're witnessing his unique form of withdrawal. I don't know anything about that. But I do know Davy is wrong. I wasn't trying to be a hero at all.

"No," I say. My headache has finally cleared, and the aches and pains across my body are starting to dull, too. I didn't have the energy to get into it earlier; I just kept apologizing and hoping we could avoid talking about this shit. But now I'm feeling better and losing my patience with Davy's pestering.

"The truth, man?" I say. "They said they would make us the number one band in the world if I helped them. And they did. They bought thousands of copies when *All Squeeze* dropped. They pushed us up the hill. So I lied to you guys in order to make you superstars. And if we get out of this alive, I know it means I'm out of the band. But I did it for us."

"What?" Buck opens an eye and scowls at me.

"Out of the band?" Spencer says.

"Dude," Davy says. "We're not gonna throw you out of the band."

I slump against the wall, down to the floor between Buck and Spencer. "You're not?"

"Rikki, bro, I lie to you guys all the time," Davy says. "We're just busting your beans."

Buck pats me on the back. "If we tossed a guy out every time he almost got us killed, we wouldn't have a band left," he says.

"Well, yeah," Davy says. "We might be a bunch of fucked-up rock stars, but we are a family. And you're in it, Thunder. Like it or not."

"Family?" I say. That word makes me choke up a little. I've never technically had one of those.

The guard mutters from the desk, "This is like bad episode of *Growing Pains*."

"That's right, bro, you're fuckin' stuck with us," Davy says to me. "Well, just don't go breaking both of your arms, though!"

Everyone in the cell laughs.

"Uh, yeah," I say. "About Barry."

"What about him?" Buck says.

"So, I just found this out the other day." I sigh. "Barry didn't break his arms on his motorcycle. Tawny broke 'em on purpose, to get me in the band."

There is a long silence in the cell. The guys all stare at me in shock.

Finally, Davy snorts. And laughs. "Are you serious?"

"I mean, that's what she told me."

Davy is smiling. Spencer's mouth falls open. Buck straight-up giggles. That's the one that breaks us. We're all laughing now.

"Why didn't you tell us that earlier?" Davy says. "I would've been way nicer to her!"

"Remember when Barry lost his drums?" Spencer says. "How do you lose drums?"

"This Barry guy sounds like loser," the guard says.

"Man," Buck says as he wipes a tear from his eye. "That guy can't catch a break."

"Well, he can't catch anything now," Davy says. Now we're all laughing hysterically. Spencer is rolling on the floor, holding his stomach. We've forgotten about our situation for a few wonderful moments. But one at a time, the smiles fade.

"So how long have you known?" Davy asks. "About Tawny?"

"A while," I say. "They helped write 'Tonight, for Tomorrow.'"

"Uh, dude, I wrote 'Tonight, for Tomorrow,'" Davy says.

"No, man," I say. "I helped Boone write it. We brought it to you guys, remember?"

Spencer's face scrunches. "The pilot wrote 'Tonight, for Tomorrow'?" he says.

"No, you're wrong, Rikki," Davy says. "I wrote it. Check the liner notes, bro. You're remembering it wrong."

I can't tell from his expression whether he really believes this or just needs to, but I give it to him anyway. "All right, Davy," I say. "Maybe you're right."

I get to my feet and go back to the bars. "Hey, bro?" I say to the guard. "We know you speak English. Is anybody going to talk to us or what?"

At that moment, the door opens. Kevin strolls in, flanked by four armed men. They are all wearing black tactical uniforms and face masks.

Kevin smiles. "Hello, Rikki."

I back away from the bars to the wall. Buck, Spencer, and Davy stand on either side of me.

"I think we're gonna get tortured," Buck says, and I can't help but notice that he seems a little excited about it.

"They can't torture us," Davy says. "It's against the law. They did a treaty or something, right?"

The jail guard swivels in his chair so he's facing the TV, and he turns the volume all the way up.

"Oh, that's not good," Davy says.

"We know you work for CIA," Kevin says. He cracks his knuckles and then his neck. "Only question is, what do you know? And how hard will we have to work to find out?"

"But, Kevin, why?" Spencer asks.

"Simple." Kevin shrugs. "We were doing same thing. Our plan was to infiltrate Whyte Python and use the band to spread pro-government propaganda."

"Through Spencer?" Davy says.

"Yes," Kevin says.

"Spencer *Dooley?*" Davy says.

"Then drummer gets hurt," Kevin goes on. "Good for us, yes! I send in agent to join the band, but he is all I can find on short notice, and he is not good drummer. You all rejected him. But we were still sitting in parking lot when Thunder showed up. Naturally we follow him, and we see that he is already being followed by someone else."

Davy scrunches his face. "So, like . . ." he says, and takes a long pause before he starts again. "Is the whole global Cold War being fought exclusively within Whyte Python now?"

"Sort of," Kevin concedes.

"Well, I feel left out," Buck says.

"Right?" Davy says.

"Enough," Kevin barks. He nods to one of his cronies, and the man takes the key off the desk and moves toward the cell. He unlocks the gate. I put one foot in front of the other and shift my weight backward, stretch my fingers and clench my fists open and closed.

"How about just you come in?" I say to Kevin. "I kicked your ass once. Maybe this time all our friends can watch."

Kevin snorts. "You don't have the little girl to help you this time."

"A little girl beat him up, too?" Buck says.

That pushes Kevin over the edge. He enters the cell, with his cronies behind him. Kevin stays at the back while his goons move in and tie our hands together behind our backs with cords, at gunpoint, one by one. Then Kevin steps forward. Smiles at me. Punches me in the jaw.

My legs buckle and I drop to the floor, landing hard on my knees. My ears are ringing, and I'm seeing double. I barely have time to get my bearings before the kick lands on my ribs, right in the spot that he had bruised the last time we met. I scream and gasp for air.

"Hey," Spencer shouts. "Not cool, Kevin!"

"Shut up," Kevin shouts back. "I only want to hear from you, Rikki Thunder. Who are you working for? Tell me about your mission objectives." He kicks me again.

I pull myself into a ball and groan. "I work for . . . Ozzy Osbourne . . ." I say between coughs, "on a mission from hell."

"Liar!" Kevin screams, and he grabs a handful of my hair and pulls my head back.

"Hey!" Davy shouts, and he starts to move toward Kevin. The other Stasi guys pin the rest of my band against the wall.

"Talk, Rikki Thunder!" Kevin shouts in my ear. "Tell me your mission! Give me names!"

He pushes my face down onto the concrete floor and kneels on my back. Now he's just pulling my hair like we're a couple of kids fighting on the playground, but it fucking hurts.

I try to go to another place in my mind. My eyes dart around the room. They land on the TV.

The guard is watching the news. I don't understand what the reporter is saying, but on screen I see a team of volunteers setting up voting stations in Poland. Some of them are wearing our shirts.

The guard changes the channel. I see border guards taking apart that fence between Austria and Hungary. There are people wearing Python merch, cheering and collecting scrap metal.

He changes the channel again. Someone has taken down the Russian flag and replaced it with a homemade one. It looks like a white bedsheet, with our mascot, Axe, spray-painted in the middle.

Rock 'n' roll.

Despite the beating, I smile. And I give him a name.

"Josef Wiedemann," I whisper.

"What's that?" Kevin growls. "How do you know that name?" It's strange. Saying the name that Anja told me to remember after we kicked Kevin's ass together doesn't just make him angry. He sounds . . . afraid? "Tell me, Rikki Thunder!" He pulls my head back again, hard enough to make me scream.

Buck has seen enough. He drives a knee into his guard and escapes his grip. He runs across the cell and crashes into Kevin. They both fall to the floor. Buck sinks his teeth into Kevin's ear.

Kevin screams as Buck spits out a chunk of cartilage. The goons pull Buck off Kevin and hit him in the stomach and face with the butts of their rifles. Buck spits blood and drops to the floor, and the men keep hitting him.

Now Davy and Spencer jump into the fray, crashing into the Germans with reckless abandon. They're quickly subdued, though, and they each take punches and kicks for their trouble.

"*Scheisse!*" Kevin screeches, and he holds his hand to his ear. It's the same ear that I hit a few times in our fight, and now the top of it is missing. Blood seeps through his fingers. Kevin hovers over Buck.

"I'll kill you for that," he growls. Then he looks at me and smiles. "But not yet. We are just getting started."

One of the goons hands Kevin a handkerchief. He holds it to his ear, and when he pulls it back, he sees that it's soaked with blood—and the blood keeps coming. Buck's teeth must've nicked a vein behind his ear, because Kevin has himself a grade A gusher. He grunts.

"*Krankenhaus,*" he growls at his goons. That was definitely one of the German words Mancuso made me memorize. It means hospital.

The Stasi men leave the cell. Kevin points a finger at me. "We will be back," he says. "And next time, not so nice."

91

▰

S EVERAL HOURS have passed.
We sit in silence, waiting for Kevin to come back and torture us again.

"Hey, guys," Buck says.

We turn to look at him. He looks like shit after the beatings, but his eyes are clear, and he's not sweating anymore. He must be through the worst of his withdrawal. "Since we're all being honest with each other . . ." he starts, but then he doesn't say anything else. His eyes search for whatever it is he wants to say next.

Spencer puts a hand on Buck's shoulder. "Hey, man," he says. "Relax. We know, and we're cool. You don't have to, like, hide it or whatever."

Buck nods. Smiles. Blows out steam. "Okay," he says. Then he arches an eyebrow. "But wait, which thing do you know about?"

Davy groans and swipes at the air in front of his face. "Buck, dude, press release," he says. "Everyone already knows you're a homo. Whatever, dude."

After the talk Buck and I had in the limo back in Budapest, I think "whatever, dude" sounds like kind of a dick thing to say, even though it's not how Davy means it. But Buck is perfectly capable of telling his buddy to shut the fuck up, so I shut the fuck up myself.

Buck, meanwhile, just looks relieved. "No, not that," he says. "I mean, yeah, sure, I hadn't really thought of myself that way, but okay. That's not what I wanted to say, though."

"So, is it that you take too many drugs?" Spencer asks.

Buck looks confused, and I don't know if it's because he didn't realize we were all worried about him, or because he didn't even realize he had a problem until that moment.

"No," he says, and just lets that hang.

Anticipation spreads across the cell now as it dawns on the rest of us that we're about to learn something new about Buck. Even the guard turns down his TV. But just before Buck comes clean with whatever his big secret is, the door opens.

Two men in black tactical gear and masks enter the room. Our hands are still tied behind our backs. We all scramble to the back wall of our cell and sit with our shoulders pressed against one another.

The goons hover over the desk and exchange words with the guard in German. I recognize some of it, and none of what I hear is good. Words like "dispose" and "hide" and "silence."

The guard hands over the key to the cell, and then he turns the TV up again. One goon unlocks the door while the other one trains an assault rifle at me. With the door open, the first goon draws his rifle and holds it on Buck.

"Out," the first goon says in thick, German-accented English.

"Where are we going?" I ask.

The goons laugh. So does the guard at the desk, even though he has his back to us and is pretending not to listen.

"Last stop on tour," the chatty goon says.

92

THIRD GUY in tactical gear enters the room carrying bur-
lap bags. He stuffs the bags over the guys' heads and pulls
a drawstring around their necks one at a time. When they
get to Buck, he tries to bite the bagman's hand, but now everybody
knows that Buck is a biter, and he pulls the hand away in time. They
save me for last, then nudge us out of the cell.

"Walk," the first goon says. We are marched out of the jail into a
cold spring night.

Buck was right—we can hear nothing but the faint sounds of wild-
life and a breeze passing through the leaves overhead. I wonder how
far they're going to make us walk into the woods before they execute
us. Will they make us dig our own grave?

Remember a few years ago, when I thought the worst thing that
could happen to me would be losing some flyers?

We haven't walked far before the voice shouts at us to stop. My
whole body tenses up. Nobody is speaking. I wait for the shot.

Then two hands hit my back and push. I fall forward and land on
a cold metal surface. Another pair of hands grabs me from under my
armpits.

"Stand," the voice says. I climb onto my knees, and then my feet,
and then my captor pushes me down onto a bench. "Sit," he says.

One by one, the other guys are pushed and dragged into this small
space and forced to sit.

Then the sound of car doors closing, and an engine groaning to
life. The bench rumbles.

We're in the back of a van. It starts to drive away, and I crash into whoever's next to me.

We both almost fall off the bench, but we hold on. The van picks up speed.

And we ride for a very long time. I'm not sure how much time has passed before Spencer thinks to speak, but it has been at least half an hour.

"Where do you think they're bringing us?" he asks.

"A hole in the ground, probably," Davy says.

Quiet, for a while. Then Buck speaks, softly. "I have to stop doing this," he says. And maybe I'm just going crazy, but it kind of sounds like Buck has an Australian accent all of a sudden.

"Doing what, Buck?" Davy asks, but Buck doesn't answer. He wasn't talking to us.

I'm afraid to even say it out loud, but I think the bags over our heads might actually be a good sign. Why would they bother covering up what we can see if they're just going to kill us any minute?

It's hope. I don't know what to do with it just yet. I could give it to the guys, give them a last few hours believing things might turn out okay. Or would it only be cruel to give them hope, just before the axe comes down?

I decide to split the difference. "I don't plan on going out like this," I say.

"How'd you draw it up, Thunder?" Davy asks.

I think about that. "I guess I just figured I would drown in a hot tub."

"Toilet for me," Davy says.

"I always assumed I would drown in a shark tank," Spencer says.

"Orange Julius machine," Buck says.

Then silence again. And I pick up on a new sound. It's a kind of high-pitched humming.

"Do you guys hear that?" Spencer asks.

"Shhh," I say. We listen again. It's coming from down around our feet. And when I figure out what it is, my heart sinks.

It's a human voice. It sounds like somebody who has their mouth gagged so they can't talk.

Somebody else is in the van, lying on the floor. The whole band is accounted for, so that only leaves one person. And I immediately understand why they gagged him.

Kirby. They must have found him in the woods. *Dammit*. I had hoped he would get away. He would have been able to tell our story. And besides, Kirby didn't deserve this any more than the guys in the band.

"There's somebody else in here," I say. "I think it's Kirby, you guys. Hey, Kirby," I say, tapping him gently with my foot. "You were a good manager."

He stops babbling. The entire van is silent for a few seconds. Then Davy groans.

"All right," he says. "Rikki's right. You did a good job, Smoot."

"His last name is *Smoot*?" Buck says.

"Good job, Kirby," Spencer says.

"Ah, fuck this," Davy says. I hear him struggle to his feet. "Hey, guys. Who are we?"

Nobody responds at first, but then I realize what he's doing. I stand up, too.

The van is moving, and I'm constantly adjusting my weight on the balls of my feet to stay vertical. But I'm not going to sit back down. "Whyte Python," I say.

"What?" Davy commands.

Buck and Spencer scramble to their feet. "Whyte Python!" we all say.

"And why are we here?" Davy asks.

"To blow the roof off!" we chant together.

"Why else?" Davy says, his voice rising.

"To get laid!"

"Why else?" Davy is screaming now, and we all scream back at him:

"There is nothing else!"

"Whyte!"

"Python!"

"Whyte!"

"Python!"

"Whyte!"

"Python!"

"Let's go!" Davy cries. We all crash into each other, and then we turn in different directions and crash into the walls of the van, rocking it back and forth.

The driver steps on the brakes, and we collide at the front of the van as it drops in speed.

Then, all together, we charge toward the back. Each one of us trips over Kirby on the floor, and we hear him grunt each time, and we collide with the two doors in the back.

They pop open, and we're airborne.

The van has slowed to a crawl, thank God. We hit the ground and roll, all of us in different directions, each sustaining more injuries.

Our hands are tied and our heads are covered, but when we roll to a stop, none of us takes the time to think about it. We all scramble to our feet, and run in different directions, crashing into each other again as we try to escape.

Rifles rack in the silent air, and the voice shouts at us. "Stop!"

We stop.

"You don't want to ride?" the goon says. "Fine. Walk."

93

WE ARE ON a dirt road. We march in a line, still blindfolded by hoods, and tied together around the waists with some kind of cord. The van rolls at a creep behind us.

Wherever we are, these dudes are clearly not too worried about a bunch of guys in leather and spandex with hoods over their heads being marched down the road at gunpoint. We never hear anything, aside from our own footsteps and the rumble of the van's engine, its tires rolling over packed dirt.

My mouth is dry; I'm probably dehydrated. I'm injured in a dozen places, and my body is so damn tired. Once in a while I trip over my own feet, and I hear the other guys do it, too.

Our captors just bark, "Keep going." There is no point to this torture. Either they're gonna kill us or they're not.

I've had a lot of time to think on this walk, and it dawns on me that I might have some leverage. "Hey, man," I call out. "Just let them go, all right? Take off their hoods and cut their hands free, and let these guys go. I'll go with you. I'll tell you everything I know."

There's no point in holding back anymore. The CIA hasn't come to save us. If we're on our own, I'm going to do whatever I can to get my bros out of trouble, even if it's too late for me.

I'll tell them about Ed Lonsa, Project Facemelt, Amanda Price, Brad Mancuso, Cathy Stryker. I might not mention Darrell Boone, if I can get away with it. That dude is cool.

But nobody says anything. If I didn't hear their footsteps following mine in shaggy lockstep, I could convince myself that I'm alone in the wilderness.

"Hello?" I say. "I'm ready to talk. Just let them go. They don't know anything."

"Is too late for that," the head goon says. "Stop here."

I feel a firm tug on the cord, and I stop walking. We all do.

"On knees," the goon says.

"No, it's not too late!" I shout. "My handlers, the whole mission. I'll tell you. Guys, get Barry back. Go home, go on tour, forget about me. You don't deserve this."

"Rikki," Davy says. He sounds resigned. Tired. He sounds like he's given up. "You can stop."

"On knees," the goon orders again. A hand pushes my shoulder, and I drop to my knees.

"No!" I shout again. "You're right, Davy, this is all my fault. I'm a selfish asshole. I left my friends in Qyksand behind. Then you guys let me in and I betrayed you, too. I just wanted to keep playing, no matter what."

Now I'm just rambling. If these are my final words, I want something good to come out.

"But you know what?" I say. "It's not just about the music. It's about doing right by your family."

"Hey, Rikki," Davy says. "I love you, bro. It's okay."

Tears fill my eyes. I wish Davy would blame me, or beg for them to let him go and do whatever they want to me. In the moment when I need him to be selfish, he's doing the opposite. It makes me furious that we're in this situation at all, because of a war that's basically over.

"And also, the guys you work for are dicks!" I shout. "And the government here is fucked now, so you can kill me all you want, but you're too late to stop the revolutions. You're done, and you know it. And I'm glad I was a part of that. So go ahead. Torture me or kill me, man. But let my band go."

"Technically, it's my band," Davy says.

"It's okay, Rikki," Spencer says.

"Whyte Python never dies," Buck says. "We'll shred together in hell."

"*Shut up*," the goon shouts at us. He pokes me with his rifle. "Stand up."

"We just got on our knees," Buck whines.

"Stand up!" the voice demands. "Shoulder to shoulder."

We all stand. I feel a skinny shoulder press against my arm on one side, and another skinny shoulder on the other.

"Stand up," the goon says again, but now he's singing it. "Brother to brother . . ."

What the fuck? Is this asshole singing "Tonight, for Tomorrow"?

The hood is yanked off my head. I am facing our lead captor. He removes his own balaclava.

He is Brad Mancuso. The thug next to him takes off his mask. It's Darrell Boone.

And they cannot stop laughing.

94

⚡

"WHAT THE—" I start to say. I'm too confused to be relieved or angry. Boone yanks the hoods off Davy and Spencer and Buck, and they all look even more confused than me. But Boone is absolutely cackling. "You should see your faces!" he says.

We're standing on a long, straight dirt road in the woods. There is nothing in either direction but road and forest, as far as the eye can see. A white van idles behind us, its headlights illuminating our little circle.

"You guys say 'I love you' a lot," Mancuso says. He unsheathes a black combat knife from his utility belt.

"Oh no!" Spencer yells. "The pilots are gonna kill us!"

"They're saving us, buddy," I say to Spencer. Then I question whether that's even true. I'm still not entirely sure what's happening. It's been an emotional few hours, and I'm nursing several recent brain injuries. I raise an eyebrow to Mancuso. "Right?" I ask.

The van's engine shuts down, and Catherine Stryker gets out of the driver's seat. She waves her hand in the air, and lights pop on in the distance. There is a small hill to our right, and at the top is a clearing. The lights are coming from the inside of a helicopter.

A figure slides out of the rear. I can't see clearly from this distance, through the trees and my blurry vision. But I'd know that strut anywhere.

Tawny.

"That answer your question, rock star?" Mancuso asks.

"Not necessarily."

"We're saving you, asshole," Mancuso says, but he smiles at me. He moves behind us and cuts the cord binding our waists. Then he cuts our hands loose.

We hug each other, and high-five, and Spencer does some karate kicks that are pretty impressive. I feel so much relief that I start to cry. It's not just that I'm going to survive after all. I didn't get the boys killed.

I punch Boone on the shoulder.

"What the hell, dude," I yell at him. "We thought you were gonna kill us!"

"Yeah," Boone rubs the back of his neck. "Sorry if we were kind'a rough on you back there. They were holding you guys in a compound out in the woods. They thought we were on their side. We had to put on a good show, dragging you out of there and tossing you in the van like that."

"Okay," I say, "but what about making us march down the road and get on our knees, though?"

Mancuso grins bashfully. "That was just for fun," he says.

I have some issues with this, but then I remember that one member of the band is still bound and gagged in the van and I should take care of that first.

"Oh, wait," I shout. "Kirby!"

I run to the back of the van and see that he's still lying on his side with a bag over his head.

"Help me get him out of here," I call out to the band. The guys join me at the back of the van.

"Hey, hold up," Mancuso calls after us.

I grab Kirby by the ankles and yank him out of the van. He is shockingly heavy. But nobody else tries to catch him as I pull him through the doors, so he just crashes to the ground.

"Oh shit," I say, reaching for the bag over his head. "Sorry, Kirby."

"That's not—" Mancuso starts to say as I yank the hood off. "Kirby."

He's right. It's not Kirby. "Holy shit," I say. "It's Kevin!"

Sure enough, our least favorite assassin is lying on the ground with his hands tied behind his back and a ball gag in his mouth.

In addition to the two black eyes that I gave him back at the stadium and his chewed-up ear, Kevin's cheek is swollen, and he has a big lump on his head. He immediately begins to squirm and scream.

"What happened to him?" I ask.

"Price beat the shit out of him," Mancuso says.

I look toward the helicopter just as Tawny emerges from the woods, grinning.

"He's how we found you," Boone says. "We crossed the border into East Germany last night. A few hours ago, Mancuso got a tip from an asset, a doctor at the local hospital. He said a Stasi assassin turned up with half of his ear bitten off. We figured that sounded like you guys. The doc took his time sewing him up while we got into position to follow him back to camp."

"Shit, dude," I say. I hold up a hand for a high five.

"'Shit, dude' is right!" Boone says, and he obliges. "Then we jumped him just before his car got back to the gate, and Price knocked him around while the rest of us subdued his team. We took their uniforms and car, and we drove onto the compound with dickhead here in the front seat, smiling and waving while Stryker had a gun pointed at his spine the whole time."

"What are we gonna do with him?" Spencer asks.

"In order to not completely disobey the rules, we agreed to a few things," Tawny says. "No shooting, and no trace that we were ever here."

We all look at Kevin again. "I could finish eating him," Buck offers, and we all laugh because we're not sure if he's serious or not.

Kevin is writhing around on the ground. His face is fire-engine red, and he's grunting German swears at us from behind his ball gag. I reach down and carefully pull the gag out.

"What do you think?" I ask him. "What should we do with you?"

"You should go fuck yourself, Rikki Thunder," Kevin hisses at me. "*Auferstanden aus Ruinen!*"

"What?" Davy says.

"It's the East German national anthem," Mancuso says, rolling his eyes. "It means 'risen from ruins.'"

"Leave me alive and I'll hunt you down!" Kevin spits at me. "Kill me, and I'll haunt you forever!" And then the crazy fuck starts laughing!

We all look at each other. I can see in their eyes that the rest of the band is thinking the same thing I am: *How fucking metal is this guy!* I feel a grudging respect for Kevin then, but I also can't get past all those times he tried to kill me. Everyone waits for me to decide what to do next. Even Team Facemelt.

This feels like a big moment. I have defeated Kevin, my mortal enemy. There's a black ops chopper firing up in the distance, ready to whisk the biggest band in the world out of East Germany. I need to walk away from this moment on top. I need to deliver the ultimate killer line, like something Arnold Schwarzenegger or Sylvester Stallone would say to the bad guy at the end of a movie.

The perfect line comes to me. I lean forward. I lock eyes with Kevin. And then I deliver.

"Whatever, dude," I say.

"Good one," Mancuso says. He stuffs the gag back in Kevin's mouth and starts to cut through the woods toward the field, where the idling helicopter is waiting on top of the hill. "Now hurry up— we gotta get off the ground *yesterday*."

Everybody follows him except for Stryker, who gets back behind the wheel of the van. But before I step into the woods to hike up to the field, Tawny grabs my arm and holds me back.

"Hey," she says.

"Tawny," I say, "we gotta get on the chopper."

"I'm not getting on the chopper." She nods toward the van just as Stryker turns the engine over. "We're gonna go find Kirby. But call me Amanda, okay? I want to do this honestly."

It dawns on me now that we're saying goodbye. I take a deep breath. Try to slow it down. "Okay," I say, and force a smile. "You know, I thought you left us here."

"Technically, we did," Amanda says. "The CIA, anyway. We're on vacation."

I look at the helicopter. Boone is handing out helmets to the guys while Mancuso straps himself into the cockpit. The blades begin to spin.

"Aren't you gonna get in trouble for this?" I ask.

"Yup," Amanda says.

"That's really punk rock of you."

"Punk is for crybabies and British people," Amanda says. We stand there and smile at each other while the wind from the chopper blades picks up, blowing our hair back. If we were still in love, this is the point where electric guitars would shred out a sweet power ballad while Amanda and I have a crazy make-out session.

But we're not.

Whatever we are—whatever we were—this is how it ends. And I think we're both okay with that.

"Boone said something that I haven't been able to forget," she says. "He said I held off for so long telling you about me because I was enjoying this life. I was enjoying being a normal person, and I was enjoying being with you. And he was right. It was real for me, too. And just wanted you to know that."

I gulp. I'm not sure what to say to that, so I leave it hanging. "This is it, huh?"

She nods.

"Where are you going?"

"Aw, Rikki," she says. "You know I can't tell you that."

"Right," I say. "So, will I ever see you again?"

Amanda thinks about that. "Hey, who knows?" She smiles. "The world may come calling for your special set of skills again someday."

I smile back. "Well," I say, "until then."

"Until then. Goodbye, Rikki Thunder."

"Goodbye, Tawny Spice."

"Price," Stryker calls from the van. "Wrap it up!"

She moves in for a hug and I take it. Then she turns to the van and walks away from me.

"Hey," I call after her. "Don't be a stranger!"

Amanda stops at the passenger-side door of the van and looks over her shoulder, back at me. "Being a stranger's my job, babe," she calls back. She winks. And then she's gone.

I run through the woods and then across the field and climb aboard the chopper. I accept my helmet from Boone and take a seat. We fiddle with seatbelts, and then Boone slaps the roof, and we take to the sky.

95

Two Months Later

I SEE RON SWEEPING the sidewalk in front of the entrance to the grocery store where he started picking up shifts at the end of our run together. His hair only hangs to his shoulders now, and it's parted in the middle and combed behind his ears, above his white collared shirt and apron. His skin has cleared up, and he's filled out a little. He looks good—grown-up and healthy. And he even looks kind of happy.

I approach him slowly, and he doesn't notice me at first. He's whistling "Straight Up" by Paula Abdul. "Ron?" I say.

He stops sweeping and looks at me. His eyes light up immediately, and then they shift from surprise to joy to pained to neutral, all within two seconds.

"Rikki," he says. "Hey, man. How's it going?" Ron extends a hand to me, and we shake.

This is strange. I don't think Ron and I have ever shaken each other's hand in our lives.

"It's good." *That's the best I can do? Jesus!* The silence is immediate and deafening.

"Cool. So, I heard you guys were in Germany or some shit?"

"Yeah. All over that area for a couple of weeks."

"Cool," Ron says again, nodding his head. We're both looking at the ground.

"So . . . are you guys still playing?" I ask. "Qyksand?"

Ron chuckles. "No. We made a go of it for a little while, but the gigs dried up. Just too many bands, I guess."

"Yeah."

"But hey," Ron says, "you gotta grow up sometime, right?"

"I guess so."

"And, dude, I made shift manager last week!" We finally make eye contact again. He's smiling, proud. I'm proud for him.

"No shit," I say. "That's awesome, bro. Congrats."

"Thanks."

"So you're, like, gonna be a businessman."

"Yeah, titan of industry or whatever." Ron's eyes light up again. "Oh, and you're not gonna *believe* this."

I feel myself smiling. Ron's energy has always been infectious. "What?"

"Sully? He's gonna be a *dad*."

"What?" We both laugh now. "Poor kid!"

"That's what I said!" Ron says. We're settling into an old groove now, just a couple of kids in the band room joking around. It feels nice. "So, how was the world tour, anyway?"

"It was all right. A little weird."

"Yeah." Ron looks at his feet. "You and Tawny still . . ."

"Naw."

"Sorry, bro," Ron says. "Hey, you mind if I go after her?"

Now it's my turn to chuckle. "Go for it. But hey, listen. We're laying down the next album after New Year's. Going experimental on this one. Buck's learning how to play the lute."

"Yeah?" Ron says. "Tight."

It's true: the next Whyte Python album will be a departure from the norm. We're on the doorstep of the nineties, and it feels like the right time to mix up our format—once we get a new manager, that is.

Relax. Kirby's fine. Amanda and Stryker found him twenty feet up a tree outside that camp where they were holding us. They sent him home and put an NDA in front of him, and he said he would only sign it if they promised he would never have to spend another day as the manager for Whyte Python.

So Kirby Smoot finally stood up for himself, and good for him. And it's a good thing, too—we definitely would have gotten him killed eventually. Andromeda reassigned him to mentor a young solo musician, just starting out. I don't know anything about the dude, but I'm sure it will be a much smoother gig than babysitting us four maniacs. I have a good feeling that Kirby will find peace and stability in his career with this DMX guy.

"So anyway, we could use some extra sound," I tell Ron. "You guys wanna do fill-ins?"

I expected him to jump at the invitation, but Ron's eyebrows scrunch down as he thinks. And then he looks over my shoulder. "I don't think so," he says. "I mean, I'll ask the guys, sure; but, dude, we're done. We haven't played a note in years. We were a garage band, you know?"

I don't nod, or shake my head, or look away. I just let him talk.

"I've thought a lot about how it ended," Ron says. "When you left. And I think I just didn't want to admit that you were carrying us, and you deserved better."

"Ron, no."

"It's cool," Ron says. "Look at you now! You're in the biggest band in the world. You were right to leave."

"I was wrong to be an asshole about it."

"Yeah, you were," Ron says. "But so was I."

Now it's silent again. I don't know what to say next. Fortunately, Ron does.

"So we're not gonna play fill-ins. But we are having a barbecue at Marty's place on Sunday. And if you want to come, I know the guys would love to see you."

"Yeah!" My whole body feels like it is filling with helium. "I'd like that a lot." Which is an understatement. I don't want to be anywhere else on Sunday.

"All right, bro," Ron says. "I gotta get back inside. But come by later, I'll give you the address, all right?" He holds up a hand. I grab it and we pull each other in for a quick hug.

"Definitely."

Ron steps back inside the grocery store, and I put my hands in my pockets and keep moving. There's somebody else I have to talk to.

The CIA made us sign a bunch of stuff when we got back to the States, but otherwise I hadn't heard a word from them—until about a week ago. A postcard showed up in my mailbox with a picture of the Washington, D.C., skyline. All it said on the back was "Rikki: Call your plumber," and there was a phone number. It was Amanda Price's handwriting; she had tracked down Ben Pratt.

Now I'm home in my apartment, and the postcard with his number is next to the phone on an end table in the living room—untouched for more than a week. I've walked over with the full intention of making a call to Ben Pratt, but for some reason I can't seem to pick up the receiver. Why am I so nervous about dialing that number?

It's no big mystery. The guy casts a big shadow. How do you properly thank someone for giving you the most important gift of your life, anyway? For helping you figure out who you're supposed to be? Will he still be the soft-spoken guy I remember? Will he still be kind? Will he be proud of me? Will he be disappointed in me? Will he even *remember* me?

And do I really want to know?

Look, life is full of mysteries. Like, I wonder what big secret Buck was about to tell us before Kevin showed up in the jail cell. But honestly, I don't care. It's better that way, leaving some things to mystery. Maybe I should add "a conversation with Ben Pratt" to the list of things better left unexplored. Preserve the memory, exactly as it is now.

Or maybe I'm just being a chicken.

I step away from the phone and over to the record cabinet, where I skip past the cassette towers and growing shelves of CDs and dig out my old records. I find *Live at Leeds*, blow off the dust, and slide the record out of its sleeve. I tilt the black disc toward the light so I can catch a glimpse of the thin grooves that carve each song into recorded history.

There's something about it, a record. It's like a little sculpture, scratched carefully onto vinyl instead of printed on cassette tape or translated into a series of numbers committed to the memory of a CD. The grooves feel more permanent. It's not just some disposable thing, a means to get the music from the store to your ears. A vinyl record is like a monument to a song, an album, a concert. *A moment.*

People can forever appreciate it, can run their fingertips over the slim depressions, feel the music itself, and let it chisel its own impression into their lives. I wonder if, years from now, people in the Eastern Bloc will run their fingers over the grooves of their *Whyte*

Album records and remember this moment in time—and maybe for a second they'll feel it all again, the uncertainty and hope.

I load the album onto the little pink record player and get it spinning. The needle needs replacing, and the toy player's power source is slowly dying. The sound is muted and scratchy on my brand-new speakers, and it's not quite playing at full speed, but that's okay.

I grab a cold beer from the fridge and sit in my blond leather La-Z-Boy recliner, pointed at the floor-to-ceiling windows that overlook the Hollywood Hills. I guess I haven't actually spent that much time here. Now, gazing out at the sun-kissed palette of greens and yellows and blues, I have one of those moments where I see my life as little Richard Henderson would. I imagine that lonely little kid looking out this window, and I can almost hear him asking me if this is real. If I can believe that we're actually here.

Ben Pratt's number is still next to the phone, staring back at me like a dare.

I close my eyes and rap my fingers against the table like drumsticks, knocking out the beat to "Young Man Blues" along with Keith Moon as the music crackles from an old record on a cheap kid's toy through five-thousand-dollar speakers. The song ends. My hands aren't shaking.

I pick up the receiver and dial.

The story you just read is a product of my imagination. I set out to create a heightened and satirical version of real events and places that dominated the global conversation during the late eighties, and so I threaded in fictionalized versions of people and places to ground the world of Whyte Python in that really unique time and place.

The book is populated with plenty of characters who are inspired by the public personas of real-life people. Those characters and their role in the story were wholly imagined and intended to be a tribute to people who were—and still are—larger than life.

ACKNOWLEDGMENTS

I always read these. It's like watching the credits at the end of the movie. If you had a good time, you should show gratitude to all of the people who helped make it happen. I had a *great* time. I hope you did, too!

First: I cannot express how grateful I am for my patient, loyal, and endlessly talented agent, Yfat Reiss Gendell—who cares about this book just as much as I do and has put so much of her own heart and soul into making it what it is. Yfat, I couldn't have done it with anyone else. Huge thanks to the team who supports her at YRG Partners, especially rights director Ashley M. Napier and finance director Lisa Tilman.

Enormous thanks to my editor, Jason Kaufman, who has been Whyte Python's constant champion at Doubleday. His guidance and thoughtful notes improved the book immensely, and his sky-high enthusiasm has been infectious for me and for his team. Jason is ably supported by Lily Dondoshansky, who is a pleasure to work with.

I'm grateful to Doubleday's publisher, Bill Thomas, who has been so supportive of the book from day one; Kathleen Cook and Mimi Lipson, for their incredibly thorough copyediting and fact-checking; Oliver Munday, for designing that amazing book jacket; publicist Julie Ertl; production manager Hilary DiLoreto; managing editor Vimi Santokhi; and text designer Marisa Nakasone.

Huge thanks to Elena Stokes and Tanya Farrell, and their whole team at Wunderkind PR. I'm also grateful to Phil Cohen at Paramount, who supported the book early and often; and to Bradley Garrett and his team at Garrett Legal, for supporting me in the film rights adaptation process.

Enormous thanks to my UK rights agent, Caspian Dennis, whose early enthusiasm and hard work on Whyte Python's behalf launched the band's early march toward world domination.

This book is very obviously a work of fiction, but I studied a lot of real-life source material to develop it. If you enjoyed the life and times of Whyte Python, I highly recommend the following: the books *The Dirt: Confessions of the World's Most Notorious Rock Band* by Mötley Crüe with Neil Strauss, *Slash* by Slash with Anthony Bozza, *Nothin' But a Good Time* by Tom Beaujour and Richard Bienstock, and *Life* by Keith Richards and James Fox; the film *The Decline of Western Civilization, Part II: The Metal Years*, directed by Penelope Spheeris; and the podcast series *Wind of Change* by Patrick Radden Keefe. Thanks to the website setlist.fm for details on all the real tours and concerts that intersect with the band's journeys.

I've been fortunate to have a life surrounded by so many supportive and encouraging people. My dad, Bob Kennedy, passed away in 2019. He was the only person I knew who was as obsessed with reading as I am. He took me to the Portland Public Library within a week of our family moving to Maine in 1986, because he knew that a local library card would make me feel like I was home; and I know that he's watching over my shoulder now, celebrating where it all led.

My mom, Marcia Kennedy, is my longest-serving editor, motivator, agent, and publicist. She helped me figure out story submissions pre-Internet, starting at age nine (a sample of the rejection letter from *Highlights* magazine: "We don't usually publish stories with this much blood"), and patiently edited my first attempt at crime fiction, age twelve (sample note: "I'm not sure the police chief would keep a six-pack of beer in his office 'to help him think.' Maybe a healthy snack instead?"). She's still an early reader of all my work, and she has notes!

Huge thanks to my wife, Liv, and my brother, Casey Kennedy, who provide really thoughtful edits to everything I write as my most constant and reliable first readers. It's a better story thanks to both of you. And to my brother, Adam Kennedy, whose hype-work is second to none in every room we've walked into together for the past two years. The sales team at Penguin Random House have stiff competition.

Last—and most—to the three people who support, encourage, inspire (and tolerate) me every single day: my wife, Liv, and our kids, Ella and Cole. I couldn't do any of this without you, and I wouldn't want to try. I love you all—here we go!

A NOTE ABOUT THE AUTHOR

TRAVIS KENNEDY is the grand prize winner of Screencraft's 2021 Cinematic Book Contest for "Sharks in the Valley," to be published as *Welcome to Redemption*. His work has been recognized in the *Best American Mystery Stories* anthology (Houghton Mifflin Harcourt, 2019). He has been featured in *Ellery Queen Mystery Magazine*, McSweeney's Internet Tendency, and multiple editions of the *Best New England Crime Stories* anthology, among other publications. He lives in Scarborough, Maine, with his wife and their two children.